Sign up for our newsletter to hear
about new and upcoming releases.

www.ylva-publishing.com

Other Books by L.T. Smith

DRIVING ME MAD

Ylva

L.T. Smith

Acknowledgements

Firstly, I would like to *more* than "acknowledge" the hard work and dedication of Astrid Ohletz and her wonderful other half, Daniela. Without their guidance and understanding, I doubt I would be in the position to write the opening section to *Driving Me Mad* in the first place. Therefore, I would like to give a huge thank you to both of these women for giving my writing a platform, a home for my stories, and a place to showcase the ideas that swarm around in my head, looking for an escape. Ladies—you are lifesavers.

Day Petersen. How many times can I tell you that you are amazing? You have, as usual, gone above and beyond the editing role. Gentle guidance, thoughtful suggestions, and an eagle eye have enabled this story to become the tale I have always wanted to tell. As usual, I've learned so much from you, and I appreciate how you strive to make me think more deeply about the words I use and how I shuffle these collections of letters into some semblance of organisation to create something that I'm proud to put my name to.

Never judge a book by a cover, they say. I just hope my story lives up to the wonderful casing designed by Amanda Chron. Dark, moody, brooding, and a little bit creepy—just how I like it. Thank you, Amanda, for making *DMM* stand out. Big thumbs up. (Just like to add, my thumbs are of a normal size—the expression about **big** thumbs was an…erm…expression?)

Last, but by no means least, I would like to thank you, the reader. Without your ongoing support, I wouldn't keep writing. What would be the point of pulling out hair, crying about "not being good enough", striving to find that exact word, living the lives of all my characters, and believing the story to be real without knowing you will feel part of the end result? Yes, I write for me. But I also write with the hope that someone, somewhere, will like it, too.

I know you were expecting me to finish at the end of the last paragraph, but I have to add just a tad more. If you are familiar with my writing from other novels, I would like to give you the heads-up here. *Driving Me Mad* is a little different to the others. There may be parts you will find distressing, and for this I apologise. But it is not done lightly. The story needed a little bit of rough to go with the smooth. I just hope you enjoy the overall effect.

Thank you. And happy reading.

Linda T Smith

Dedication

Dedicated to the loved ones we have lost. They are never really gone—just waiting until the right time to come back into our lives.

Part 1

"Be with me always—take any form—drive me mad! Only do not leave me in this abyss, where I cannot find you! Oh, God! It is unutterable! I cannot live without my life! I cannot live without my soul!"

Emily Bronte

Part 1

Chapter One

I'd been driving for over four and a half hours. Four and a half bloody hours. It wouldn't have been so bad if I hadn't already been awake and on the go for nearly twelve hours before I'd plonked my backside in the car, but I had. The convention I attended that day had overrun its time, and I'd been stuck with a mishmash of sales reps from all over the UK, some of whom would bore a train spotter. Believe me, I was surprised I didn't catnap standing up.

Like a fool, I thought I was good to go when the final speeches were over, thought I was alert enough to get to the hotel where I was staying for the night without any mishaps. I couldn't have been more wrong. I think I must've had some kind of mild brain trauma, considering I'd been afflicted with shite all day. It was sort of a sales rep version of concussion, wherein the violent shake to the head was me trying to keep awake.

Like a fool, I thought I would beat my rivals to the next venue, which was to take place the following day, one hundred and ten miles away. By getting to the hotel just on the outskirts of Morley in the Peak District that same evening, I would be refreshed the next morning. I'd only have to stroll down the stairs, eat breakfast, and take a pew right at the front.

Unfortunately, I didn't allow for tiredness, shite directions, or a crap signal for my mobile. I found myself in the arse end of nowhere. The journey to the hotel should have taken me just shy of two hours, but I'd been driving for over four and a half naffing hours, and I had no clue where I was.

Trees, trees, and more trees continuously lined the sides of the narrow road along which I was driving. The trees were overgrown and half hanging over the road, limiting my view of the route ahead. These trees would not have looked out of place in *The Wizard of Oz* or some teen *Cabin in the Woods* slash horror flick. The full beam of my headlights barely made an impression on the darkness, and I couldn't make any sense of my bearings.

"Turn left."

The disembodied voice that sounded from beside me made me grip the steering wheel a little too hard, forcing a slight, sharp swerve to my left.

"Fucking Susan," I ground out between gritted teeth.

Susan was not a ghost, not a phantom hitchhiker suddenly appearing in my car, reminding lost travellers of the terrors that claimed people along this stretch of tarmac. Susan was the name given to the useless piece of shit Sat Nav sitting on the passenger seat.

"Speak now, yeah? Now there isn't a left turn."

My hand fumbled for the device I had tossed on the seat earlier. The cool plastic of the casing slipped into my grasp. Eyes still riveted on the road, I felt around the oblong casing and pressed the off switch. With even that tiny decrease of light, my car's interior dipped into deeper darkness.

It was too quiet, both inside and outside the car. I'd killed the radio miles back, because all I seemed to be picking up was the tune of interference. Although music today does mainly sound like it is "off key", it doesn't usually sound as if it is white noise with distorted voices drifting in sporadically. Not the most reassuring sound when driving on my own at just turned midnight at the end of October. Not reassuring at all.

I glanced down and checked my petrol. I was just under half a tank. That made me feel a little better about my dilemma. Not much better, but a little, and at that stage, a little was better than nothing.

My eyes were aching. It was at least partly due to me being tired, but staring intently into darkness half lit by crappy headlights didn't help the growing headache that was inching up my forehead like a mini mountain climber using small sky hooks to dig into my skull. I also needed to pee. My bladder was bulging, and if I ever reached civilisation, I was definite that it was going to be a case of getting my car seat valeted, especially if that buggered up Sat Nav had the nerve to speak again.

A fleeting hope of finding a public toilet skittered into my head. Why I honestly thought there would be a public toilet out in the middle of nowhere is beyond me. The powers of the local council hadn't even thought it necessary to put up road signs, never mind a toilet to help the stranded.

Another half hour went by. My belly was as bulging as that of an eight months pregnant woman by this stage, and I was feeling the pinch of it every time I shifted my feet on the pedals. I was still in the middle of Deliverance country, and I knew I wasn't going to see the bright lights of Civilisation any time soon.

That settled it. It was pee time. Pee time behind a bush, behind a tree. Hell, pee time in the middle of the fucking road. It wasn't as if I was going to be spotlighted by headlights as I was flashing my arse to passing cars. Not surprisingly, I hadn't seen another soul for the past two hours. Normal people were in bed by now.

Of course that didn't mean serial killers weren't out and about.

A nervous laugh escaped with difficulty through my tightly clamped lips. "I'll set Susan on them." A snigger came next. "If she decides to work."

Decision made, I pulled over to the side of the road. If I thought it had been quiet before, this beat it tenfold.

I turned my engine off and opened my car door. The ping pinging started, alerting me I'd left my lights on. Too right. My car could ping ping as much as it wanted to, but there was no way I was getting out into complete darkness. I was also going to leave my car door open so the interior light would aid my call of nature.

Stretching, I looked about. Nothing. No one. There was just the dark, with a glint of light from the car. A memory of peeing at the side of the road with my mother popped into my mind, and I opened the back door too, making a little cubicle between car doors.

"Nice trick, Mum."

I was not too sure why I was hiding myself from prying eyes that weren't there; I also wondered why I was talking to myself. I doubted anyone would be out there, and even if they were, the lights from inside my car would illuminate me to a voyeur anyway, making the "cubicle" idea redundant.

For the first time, another thought hit me. What if there actually was someone watching me? What if that person wanted to do a little more than watch?

Back to the thoughts about a serial killer, or rapist, or person with a pee fetish. And there I was, knickers around my ankles, silently inviting them to come and get some.

I wish I could say I decided I could hold on until I found a lovely, clean, white, and sterile place, safe from death or sexual assault, but I had passed that point. It was a case of taking my chances with my life or my bladder.

Squatting, I slipped my underwear down to the point where it was just beyond being peed on. It would have been a damned sight easier if I'd been wearing a skirt, but alas, I was in trousers. It would also have been a damned sight easier if I hadn't been such a twat and decided to beat the rush to the next venue, but that, too, was a matter for retrospection, although being a twat still stood.

Amazing, isn't it? When you're bursting to go, it won't come immediately. It aches, it cries, it deliberates before trickling out slowly, and all the while I was on watch for an attacker. Every whisper of the wind, every movement of the leaves, I involuntarily clenched and stopped the flow. My ears seemed to grow into points, and I perched like a German Shepherd on guard duty in the tiny hub between my car doors.

Finished. Finally. And I'd forgotten to bring some tissues from my glove compartment. Joy. It was October. End of October. Nearly one in the morning on a bloody cold end of October, at that. I doubted I would "air dry" in this environment. I was more likely to freeze my fou fou instead of drying her.

I stood and began to pull up my underwear and trousers. A noise from my left alerted me to something moving in the foliage. Like my fou, I froze.

There it was again—a crunching, a snapping of twigs, like someone moving towards me. My hands hovered over my zipper as if I had a concealed weapon beneath it. The rustling stopped, then started again.

As if on cue, the interior light went off, and I made a noise I could never have imagined would come from me. I couldn't even tell anyone, onomatopoeically, how it sounded. It was just a sound of fear, if fear could be summed up in wheezing and choking, with an additional indescribable noise thrown into the mix.

The noises from the darkness came again, and I staggered backwards, totally ignoring the recently made puddle. This wasn't the time to worry about standing in my own urine. I was more concerned about lying in a pool of my own blood to care if I had pee on my shoes.

"Who's there?"

My voice reflected how I felt—shitted up. Why I'd decided to confront my nocturnal assailant was beyond me. If there even was a nocturnal assailant to confront. Imagination can be a powerful thing, especially in the wrong hands, or head, or whatever. My imagination was usually limited to my work, but apparently, as I had only just found out, also images of death and destruction. Pity I couldn't amalgamate all three into my daily life. I would have been the top of my imaginative field and the CEO of my own little fucked up company instead of travelling in the middle of the night to get the best seat, so I could get the latest and best information about how to sell shit.

I realised my thoughts were rambling. I tended to ramble when I was scared. Since the fear was still with me, I knew that I would probably continue to ramble for several more miles.

I knew that imagination could mess with a person so that they believed things were knocking about when they were not. I wasn't going to risk finding out if the noises I had heard were just in my head. Bravery was not my forte. I was more of a "run and hide" kind of girl.

It wasn't until after I slammed the driver's side door, put on my seatbelt, and started my engine that I realised I'd left the back door open. I was tempted to just drive off and hope the damned thing would shut on its own, but knowing my luck, whoever was in the woods would grab the door, get in, put a knife to my throat, and growl, "Drive."

Leaning over the seat, I struggled to grab the edge of the door. I didn't want to climb out into the darkness again, but it looked as if I was going to have to.

"Fuck it!"

One hand moved to undo my seatbelt whilst the other grabbed the handle on my door, but I stopped before opening either. It wasn't because I was undecided; it was because the back door did something I wanted it to do, though not in the way I wanted it to, if you know what I mean. It slammed.

The squeal of my tyres surely left a mark on the road, and I didn't want to think about the marks that had just as surely appeared in my underwear. I never knew I could drive without holding on to the steering wheel, but considering one hand was on the door handle and the other was on the gear stick as the car started forward, I must have. And there was certainly not the recommended safety progression from mirror, to signal, to manoeuvre.

Almost as if I was joyriding, my heart was racing wildly. It was driving faster than I was, and I was clocking up the speed in my haste to get away from whatever had slammed the door shut. It wasn't until I was a couple of minutes down the road—and it did not hurt so much for me to breathe—that I had another thought: What if the door slammed shut *after* someone had climbed inside the car with me?

The blood in my veins seemed to freeze. A tingling of apprehension rippled over my skin, making the hairs stand to attention. I wanted to look in my rear view mirror and check out the back seat, but I just couldn't summon the nerve. What if I did look, and someone was looking back at me? What if I saw the glint of a blade or the prominent curve of vampiric teeth? Jesus. This wasn't *Twilight*.

A little voice piped up inside my mind, "But you could so easily be on the front page of a national newspaper by tomorrow."

Weirdly, I took a detour in my head at that point and wondered what photo they would use of me on the front page.

What the...?

I had to make a decision, and quickly. I didn't have the nerve to look, and I couldn't really risk not looking. But I had to do something. Had to... Had to do what? Deliberate? Do nothing? Act stupid instead of acting quickly?

SLAM!

My feet jammed on the brake and clutch, and my body snapped forward. Thankfully I didn't hit anything with my sudden stop, either in the road or my body hitting the steering wheel, so the air bag didn't deploy. I wanted to see if the person, if there was a person in the back, would slam into my seat, or come flying through to the front. I doubted the would-be killer/rapist/attacker/hitchhiker would have thought to put on a seatbelt, but then I wasn't au fait with the etiquette of frightening the shit out of someone by climbing through an open door into a backseat.

As soon as my heart slid back down my throat to its proper position, I was out of the car and standing about four feet away. The back seat looked innocently empty, but I was still not sure. I slowly moved towards the exposed vehicle, my door open, the lights blazing eerily into the darkness. I tipped my head from side to side, trying to gauge the "emptiness" of the rear seat.

The breath I'd been holding began to seep out and mix with the cool night air. White puffs floated in front of me, and I felt overwhelming relief to still be breathing at all.

I climbed back into the car and placed my hands on the steering wheel. Not surprisingly, they were shaking. I was cold, scared, lost, and tired. I was imagining things. I was becoming desperate and hysterical. These were not a very promising foundation for careful driving at night in a place where everything looked the same. For all I knew, I'd been driving in circles for hours.

Tears brimmed in my eyes, and I could feel the rumblings of a full-fledged breakdown inching through my body. A sob broke free, and I angrily swiped my hand across my eyes. I was not going to lose the plot. I was going to keep on driving until I found a sign of life, or even a road sign that would direct me to life.

Suddenly I saw something, something that looked almost familiar. Well, it was familiar, but something I hadn't seen for the last two and a half hours. It was light, and it was coming from a house. Out in the middle of nowhere, I was approaching a house. It might shelter a person, or people, or a family with a dog and a cat and a phone and directions. I no longer cared that the person living at the house might be out to get me. By this time I was willing to take my chances. I wouldn't care if the dwelling was the Bates Motel and Norman offered me a shower, I was going to knock on the door and ask for help. Of course I would take my wheel brace with me, hidden inside my jacket. That was a given.

Instead of feeling scared, a bubble of excitement rushed through me. It wasn't from anticipating the duel to the death between me and a could-be attacker, wielding our weapons for changing tyres. What had me excited was just the thought of getting back to light and life. I slipped the car into gear and moved forward, towards the yellow glow a few hundred yards up the road.

Gravel crunching under my tyres as I pulled into the driveway of the house gave me a bit of reassurance. It was the outside light I had seen, but the lights downstairs were also on. At least I wouldn't have to wake someone up to ask for help, unless they had fallen asleep with the lights on. If that was the case, they should be happy I was about to save them from a huge electricity bill at the end of the quarter, and so should welcome me with open arms instead of a shotgun. Yep. That was my fucked up reasoning to help me keep calm.

Alas, it wasn't working. As soon as I stepped out of my car, I felt someone watching me. I still had to get my wheel brace from the boot of my car, but that idea was losing some of its lustre. Bending over into the blackness of the boot to rummage around for it would leave me open and exposed to anyone who was watching. I'd seen *Silence of the Lambs*. I was well aware that an attacker could thwack a woman on the back of the head, shove her into the back of a van, and drive off to claim her skin as his trophy.

My overactive imagination was back full force. I didn't have a van; I had a Mazda 3.

Decision made, I grabbed my keys and my handbag, sucked in a breath and slammed the door, then made a run for the welcoming light on the porch. I didn't look about to see if there was a doorbell. My fist went straight to the wood and hammered hard. I couldn't seem to stand in one place, couldn't seem to just wait innocently for the person in the house to open the door. I was too busy checking my perimeters, looking for someone sneaking up on me.

Hands grabbed my shoulders and pulled. The scream I had been saving for that very moment seemed to lodge in my throat and refuse to budge. I had to get it out before the person assaulting me covered my mouth and silenced me forever.

I was turned roughly, and the same hands that had grabbed me now slipped around my shoulders and pulled me more fully into a body. Warmth blanketed me, along with a distinct sense of protection.

How could I feel protected when I was being manhandled by a stranger? A stranger with breasts and a strong grip. A stranger who was shaking just as hard as I was.

I knew that if I was to save my life, I should kick, punch, bite, and scratch this person, but I couldn't seem to make myself move away from the cocoon that surrounded me. The stranger's hands slipped down my back in reassuring strokes, then one lifted to the back of my head and pulled me more securely against the softness of her chest.

"I knew you would come. I knew it!" The female voice above me was fraught with evident agony. "God, I've looked everywhere for you! Everywhere."

Me? Looked everywhere for me? And what did she mean by she knew I would come? I'd never been in this area before. I think I would have remembered if—

A soft kiss on the top of my head stopped my thoughts. The woman gently kissed my hair again before nuzzling my cheek.

This wasn't right, not right at all. But strangely, it *felt* right. It felt right to be held in the arms of a stranger at gone one in the morning, in a place I didn't know. In her arms, I felt safe, like whoever had been watching me from the woods couldn't hurt me now that she was holding me close.

My eyes fluttered closed and I nestled into the contact, inhaling a scent that seemed familiar. I didn't care that I didn't know her, didn't even know what she looked like. All that mattered was that she keep holding me.

"Come on, Ellen. Let's get you inside."

Who was Ellen?

"You're shivering."

The woman drew away slightly to lead me inside the house. Still on the porch, I looked around. Maybe Ellen was the person I had thought was watching me. But I couldn't see anyone there other than me and the unidentified woman.

"What's up, Ellen?"

Her soft voice sounded concerned, as if it was directed to someone who was acting strangely.

The light dawned. Did the woman think *I* was Ellen? Considering there was a light right outside the door, I didn't think it was dark enough for her to have mistaken me for someone else.

I twisted slightly and she released me from her grasp. Taking a step back, I turned and faced the woman. The light behind her cast a shadow over her face. "Who's Ellen?" I asked.

She took a small step forward, then faltered. Her head cocked to the side, and she appeared to absorb every aspect of me. Given the tilt of her head, I could see the outline of a firm jaw, a jaw that was moving as if it was chewing words, but no sound came out.

"I'm Rebecca." She seemed to stiffen when she heard my name, so I thought I would elaborate. "Rebecca Gibson."

She stepped backwards, as if she was trying to back into the house. Not without me she wasn't. I took a step forwards. "Sorry. I...well...I'm lost and..."

"Rebecca?"

"Gibson. Yes."

For each step she took backwards, I took one forwards. Soon we were both standing in her hallway. Beautiful, dark brown eyes looked into mine, quizzical brown eyes framed by long lashes. They showed confusion, as if what they were seeing wasn't real. My own eyes drifted down a straight, defined nose and settled on full red lips, parted slightly as if they were readying themselves to allow words to come forth.

"I'm sorry to impose on you at such a late hour, but..."

Her shoulders slumped before straightening again. "Not a problem. *Rebecca.*"

Why did she feel the need to separate my name from her statement?

"Come inside. You must be freezing." Her voice had lost its initial softness, and there was a distinct edge to it now, almost business like.

She moved past me and grabbed the door handle. Before she closed the door, she stared out into the darkness again, then sighed as she clicked the door into place and attached the chain.

"Come in here by the fire." She walked past me and disappeared into a room to the right. I shrugged and followed her.

There was an open fireplace in the room, the flames long gone but the embers glowing fiercely. The furniture was in keeping with the age of the house, classically rustic and well worn. My hostess was standing beside the armchair closest to the fire, and she gestured for me to sit. As I moved past her, my arm brushed hers. A spark seemed to ignite between us, and she jerked away with a gasp.

As I sat, she hurried from the room, and I found myself alone again. The ticking of a clock seemed to be the only noise I could hear, and my eyes searched it out. One thirty-four. Shit. No wonder she was pissed at me. It certainly wasn't etiquette to knock on someone's door at such a late hour, especially since it was apparent she had been expecting someone else.

The memory of how it had felt to be held in her arms flitted into my mind. I couldn't shake the feeling of belonging there, however strange that might sound. It wasn't just the feel of her, the protection I felt, or even the smell of her. It was so much more than that. But whatever it was, I couldn't say.

My eyes flicked back to the clock. One thirty-nine. Where had she gone? I looked around the room—a leather sofa with throws draped over it, a coffee table littered with magazines. Might as well occupy my time doing something other than noting the décor. If I didn't, I would probably start rooting through the drawers of her sideboard. I reached out and pulled one towards me.

Picture Post magazine, October 31, 1953. I couldn't believe I was looking at a magazine that was sixty years old. It didn't appear to be that old, although the picture on the front was not exactly worthy of *Hello* magazine. It was far too dated for that. London smog? Nurses? 4D or 4 pennies—the price, that was— before decimalisation.

"I thought you might need a cup of tea."

The sound of the woman's voice made me start, and the magazine flew from my hands and onto the floor.

"Sorry. Didn't mean to make you jump."

An awkward moment, that. I had been nosing around her collectable magazines and got caught, then tossed it into the air and ruffled the buggering thing up.

Shooting out of the chair, I went to snatch it up, but due to my haste, I felt a page tear slightly. Fuck. And fuck again.

Carefully—a little late for that—I lifted the magazine and offered it to her as if it was a sacrifice.

The woman just stared at me, a tray laden with teacups, sugar, and a teapot and milk jug balanced in her hands.

"I...well... God, I'm sorry."

A laugh warmed her cool façade. "Don't worry. I've already read it."

Considering it was a vintage piece, I opened my mouth to apologise again, but she shook her head. "Just throw it to the side, will you? I need to set this down."

I didn't toss it. I placed it neatly on the floor underneath the table. A couple of minutes passed as she was finalising the tea. After she'd poured, and I had accepted milk but no sugar, she settled into the seat opposite mine.

"So, Rebecca, you were saying you're lost," she prompted.

I sipped my tea, wincing at the heat of it before placing my cup and saucer onto the table. Before I could answer her, she spoke again.

"Annabel Howell."

"Excuse me?"

"My name. I thought it was past time I introduced myself." Annabel leaned back into the armchair and raised her cup to her lips, but she didn't drink. She just stared at me over the rim, as if she was assessing me.

I was being scrutinised. It wouldn't have been so bad if her eyes weren't so intense, weren't so beautiful, but I felt as if I was under a microscope and she could see every single one of my shortcomings. A blush crept up my neck and spread over my face. I never blushed. Being a sales rep demanded that skill. So why was I blushing now?

"Erm." Good call, Rebecca—three letters and a little intonation. Could work on the pace, though. "Yes. I... Well, I'm lost." Jesus. Why did I repeat the only thing apart from my name that she already knew?

As if she was aware I was a moron, a smile flitted over Annabel's face before she sipped her tea. The thought of her smirking at my unease raised my hackles. I was tired and pissed off, and my headache was still clinging to the inside of my skull. The blush receded.

"I was travelling up from Cambridge to Morley and took a wrong turn somewhere along the line." Annabel tilted her head as if indicating I should continue. "I'm supposed to be at Breadsall Priory for a convention in the morning."

"Breadsall Priory? Do you know the Haslams?"

"Haslams?"

"The owners."

Why on earth would I know the owners of the bloody Marriott? I laughed. She glared. I laughed again. "Not really, no. Although I have contemplated adding them to Facebook."

Her face scrunched as if in thought, and I believed she would laugh with me. But no. She just looked pissed off.

"You're not too far from the Priory. About ten miles." She leaned forward and placed her cup on the table, her eyes fixed on mine. "But I wouldn't advise driving at night. Not here."

It seemed as if Annabel wanted to scare me, and I was fully expecting tales of goblins and will-o'-the-wisps. I felt like laughing again, but thought better of it.

"The trees block the view of the road in parts, so it's wisest to travel in the day."

Maybe she was just being practical.

Annabel kept looking at me, staring into my face. I was beginning to feel uncomfortable, and yet not, if you know what I mean. Soft eyes scrutinised my features. They dwelled on each aspect of my face for what seemed an interminable amount of time. All the while she was looking at me, I couldn't help but be amazed by her natural beauty—the finely chiselled jaw, the high cheekbones, the way the glow from the fire seemed to dance over her skin and enhance each line and muscle. I felt as if I knew her, had known her, but I couldn't say from where.

"I feel as if we've already met." It wasn't me who spoke; it was her. "Have you been to Kirk Langley before?"

Her voice was soft, lilting, almost addictively so. There seemed to be an aura around her that was not caused by the fire. The moisture in my mouth evaporated, and I swallowed a couple of times before remembering I had a cup of tea. A quick sip, a wince at the heat of it, and I felt able to answer.

"I don't even know where I am, never mind having been here before."

Her eyes were riveted on my mouth, and I licked my lips in reflex. She did the same. Then it seemed to occur to her what she had done. Her face froze, her eyes widened slightly in acknowledgement, and then she slowly leaned back in her chair.

Back to the sound of the ticking clock. The atmosphere was charged with something indefinable, but also expectant. There were so many questions I wanted to ask her, but for some reason I didn't feel as if I could. I wanted to ask who Ellen was and why Annabel had thought I was her, but that would have seemed as if I was prying into her private life.

"Who's Ellen?" What the fuck? Couldn't I take my own advice of it being something that a person didn't bring up?

Annabel's eyes met mine, and I saw a flicker of pain surface before being buried once again.

"She's my friend." Her voice was calm, but also guarded.

I couldn't think of a single time I had ever greeted my friends the way Annabel had greeted me at the door, though she'd thought I was someone else at the time. Come to think of it, I didn't think I had ever greeted any of my girlfriends with such fervour. If they went AWOL, they usually stayed AWOL. I didn't know whether they were coming back, probably because I didn't care if they did. I certainly didn't "look everywhere" for them, like Annabel had looked for Ellen.

It was obvious that Ellen was more than Annabel's friend, but I wasn't going to push it. Annabel's relationship with the other woman was none of my business. After several moments of uncomfortable silence, I stood to leave. I had definitely outstayed my welcome. "I think I'd better take my chances at getting to the hotel."

Annabel shot to her feet, her hands reaching out to me. "No! No. Stay. I insist."

The sheer panic on her face made my heart clench. Didn't she want to stay there alone? Nah. That couldn't be it.

"It really isn't safe for you to go at this time of night."

"But..."

She quickly moved around the table and grabbed my arm, and I could feel the heat of her, smell her scent. It was intoxicating.

Looking up, I met her eyes. I had thought they were beautiful before, but I was wrong. Up close, her eyes enthralled me. Brown, so very brown, and deep and soulful and all-consuming. I believed I could see my future within their depths.

"I insist."

Two tiny words that were tender, inviting, magical. I couldn't answer her, just nodded my agreement, my heart pounding in my chest.

Annabel released a breath, and the softness of it touched my skin and sent sparks through me. She was still holding my arm, as if she believed I would disappear if she released it.

"You can sleep in my bed."

Huh? Even to me that sounded a little bit forward.

"I'll sleep down here."

Her hand continued to rest on my arm. I looked at it, and then looked back into her eyes. They held a question, and I answered without it being asked.

"Thank you, but..." She squinted as she waited for me to continue. "If I do stay, I'll sleep down here." Annabel looked as if she was going to decline, but I beat her to it. "Now it is my turn to insist."

She pursed her lips and tilted her head to one side, as if she was assessing me again, then a sigh slipped through her lips, followed by a single nod of her head.

Her hand left my arm, and I missed the heat of it immediately, desperately missed the contact of her skin on the sleeve of my sweater. Annabel took a step back, her eyes glancing away from mine before returning to devour me again. In my peripheral vision, I saw her hand stretch towards me, then drop to her side. Her eyes closed so deliberately, it seemed as if they did so in slow motion. She kept them closed for a long moment before opening them. Annabel inhaled deeply, held it, and then exhaled in one long breath.

All the while, I was transfixed.

"I'll get you some blankets."

And she was gone, and I was left wondering what on earth had just happened.

I heard her on the stairs, thuds against wooden slats. I listened to her quick footsteps across what must have been a bare wooden landing. And all the time I just stood there, just bloody stood there as if my feet were nailed to the floor.

What had just happened? What had been going through her mind as she touched my arm, held my gaze, closed her eyes and held the image of something only she could see inside? We had never met before, but it seemed to me that I had known her before, known her as something more than a woman who had been kind enough to offer me shelter. By the way she was acting, I had a feeling she felt the same way.

"Here you go." Annabel was back, arms full of blankets and pillows. "It'll get colder in here when the fire is banked." She placed the stack onto the sofa, her back to me.

I didn't comment, just watched her shoulders working as they arranged the linens over the place where I was to sleep.

Annabel interrupted her task to peer over at me. "Or I could put more logs on, if you'd like."

I forced a smile and shook my head. "I'll be fine. Honestly." Her brow furrowed slightly and her mouth opened to speak, so I tried to reassure her. "I get quite hot in bed."

Fuck. And fuck. Not because of my inability to phrase things better, but the blush was coming back full force.

A crooked smile lit her face. "Really?"

This was a clear opportunity for me to flirt shamelessly, but I just couldn't. I didn't want to flirt with Annabel. Didn't want to cheapen how I felt about her by coming back with corny one liners and moving my eyebrows suggestively, like they do in trashy novels. I didn't even stop to question what, exactly, I did feel for her. I just turned away and started to stack the tea things back onto the tray.

A couple of minutes later, I was carrying the tray into the kitchen. The odd thing about that was, I didn't know where the kitchen was, and yet I knew where it was. The room was rustic, as I expected it to be. There was no sign of the usual things one would expect to find in a kitchen. No, that wasn't quite right. It did hold the usual, but then again, it didn't.

I wasn't making any sense, and I knew it. The Aga cooker seemed dated, as did the steel kettle that sat on top of the stove. There was no microwave, no toaster, no coffee maker, just a huge wooden table with four chairs, cupboards, a cooker, a rectangle pot sink and drainer, and a cream coloured fridge. Copper pans hung from a rack over the cooker, and I could see my distorted face in their shiny surface.

Plonking the tray on the drainer, I stood back and stared at the small window above the sink. It was dark outside, obviously, and I could see my reflection in the glass. My face seemed to be cast in shadow, but I could see the definition of my nose, mouth, and eyes. My expression was intense, like I was trying to work out the meaning of life. I don't know why, because the only thing I was concerned about was why I suddenly had the sensation of feeling something more than gratitude toward my hostess.

Something wasn't right, didn't add up. In the window pane, my face looked distorted, like it had when I'd looked at the side of the copper pans. It wasn't like when a person checks his or her reflection in the back of a spoon, not like that at all.

I leaned closer, and the image in the window moved closer too. Squinting, I tried to decipher what the image was. Maybe it was because the window was double glazed that it appeared I was wearing one face over another. But the glass didn't seem as if it was double—

The image blinked. I didn't blink, the image did. I swear. It must've been fatigue; I'd been up for over seventeen hours. No wonder I was imagining things. I scrunched my eyes and shook my head and looked again. Now everything looked as it should. I was just—

Tap

I pulled back from the glass.

TAP TAP

Something was tapping on the window pane from outside. Initially I thought it was a branch, until the noise came a third time.

TAP TAP

I realised it wasn't a branch. Branches don't have knuckles.

My scream was loud and long. It reverberated off the walls, bounced off the copper pans, and hit me like a punch. Scrambling backwards, I rammed into the table, which made me scream again.

The tapping became insistent, and I looked at the window and saw myself still waiting there. That was impossible. I couldn't be reflected in the glass; I was halfway across the room.

Annabel came rushing into the kitchen. "What's...?"

I couldn't speak, couldn't do anything but grab hold of her and clutch her to me. I was shaking, the sobs intermittent between words that scrambled for coherence. Annabel placed her arms around me and pulled me close, her hands rubbing my back in long, soothing strokes.

I couldn't believe how wonderful it felt to be in her arms, how reassuring it was to be held in such safety. She was making shushing noises to calm me and, strangely, it was working. At least it was working enough for me to splutter out a little of what I had seen.

Her body stiffened, her hands freezing in mid stroke, as did the look on her face. She slipped away from me and moved towards the window. Strong hands rested on either side of the frame as she peered into the glass, her shoulders rigid.

The tapping had stopped. When I cast my mind back, I realised that it had stopped as soon as Annabel had entered the kitchen. "I'm so sorry," I said. "I must've imagined it."

Annabel didn't turn or acknowledge me, just kept staring out into the inky blackness.

Slowly, I moved towards her, my hand reaching out to touch her back. The stiffness I felt seemed to evaporate on contact, but there was a slight trembling in her.

"What did you see, exactly?" Her voice was cold, distant.

"Nothing, I guess. It was—" She turned abruptly, and my hand fell dejectedly to my side.

Brown eyes bored into mine. "No. You did." She took a step forward. "What was it?"

I held out my hands palms up, and shrugged. Her expression didn't change. She just stared into me.

I felt like a fool. I was tired, that was all. There wasn't anyone outside tapping on the glass like Catherine fucking Earnshaw. It was a case of playing Bloody Mary, like I had when I was a kid. Stare at the glass and say Bloody Mary three times, and you'd see...

As I recalled it, though, the game had never said anything about hearing a tapping sound, nor had it mentioned BM's knuckles.

"It was just my reflection. It seemed odd, though."

Annabel stepped forward. "Odd?"

"It was just your double glazing."

"Double what?"

"Glazing. Your window glass."

Annabel shook her head and glanced back at the window. I could see the outline of her in the glass and part of my face peering around her. Her eyes looked at me from her reflection in the pane, and I knew she was expecting me to say more. What could I say? That I saw my doppelganger at the window and it had tapped on the glass? Fuck that.

"Honestly, Annabel, I just freaked myself out." I stepped back and started to turn away from her. She grabbed my wrist. "I'm just tired, that's all."

It seemed as if time held its breath and waited along with me. At last the stiffness of her touch gentled, and she released me, along with a sigh.

"I suppose you'd better get to bed then."

I nodded.

Annabel walked past me and out of the room. With a last glance at the window, I followed her. There was no way I wanted to be in the kitchen on my own.

Chapter Two

Within ten minutes, I was alone in the living room and sprawled on the sofa. Woollen blankets covered me, their heat seeping into my skin. Annabel had offered me something to wear, but I refused. I had a suitcase in the car, but there was no way I was going to go back outside and root around to find my pjs, not after what I thought I had seen. I was too much of a chicken shit to step outside until daylight arrived. Sleeping in my underwear and sweater would suffice, as my hostess had put another log on the fire to warm the room for a while longer.

I could hear her getting ready for bed, walking around directly above me. The sounds were like a comforter, a sense of safety after everything that had transpired that evening. It wasn't long before I felt the pull of sleep, and my eyelids submitted to the respite of rest.

My dreams were definitely fucked up. The first one had me standing at the side of a road that was obscured by bushes. It was dark and cold. I tried to keep warm, but warmth escaped me. In addition to the cold, I felt fear, fear of something, but I couldn't quite grasp what. Pain shot through my chest as if I had been running and had finally stopped from utter exhaustion. The reasoning part of my brain questioned why I was still cold when I should have been sweating. Maybe the fear coursing through me took dominance over the weather conditions.

A noise came out of the blackness, and my heart lurched into my throat. I felt as if I was a hunted animal that believed it had escaped the hunter, only to find that was not the case. I wanted to run, to hide, to find safety of any sort, but I couldn't. In my dream I knew where I was, knew I was close to reaching a safe haven. The vivid lights of a car came into view and pulled over at the side of the road. It was not just any random car. No. It was my car, distinctly *my* car. I watched in rapt fascination as a person climbed out. Me. *I* climbed out of the car.

I gripped the trunk of the tree and tried to steady myself. This was too fucked up even for a dream. How could I be twenty feet away, watching myself get out of my car? Was this a somnambulant out of body experience?

My breathing was becoming shallow, and I believed if I couldn't control it I would pass out. I tried to take a deep breath, but panic made it impossible. I tried again, and again, and again. My other self was opening the back door to the car to make what I knew was going to be a cubicle. I knew exactly what was about to happen. I should do. I'd experienced it.

The memory of how scared I actually *had* been when I'd lived that moment compounded how I was feeling now. I wanted to contact my other self and put "my" mind at rest, but I couldn't speak. I just needed to get into the car and escape. Stumbling forward, I bumped into a tree and the bark grazed my arm. I could feel the pain of it, believed that if I woke at that precise moment I would see the mark of it on my skin. My other self was getting up, pulling up her trousers, and readying herself to leave, when "I" stopped before zipping up "my" fly.

Another stumbling step forward, another attempt to shout out there was nothing to worry about, but the words still wouldn't come. Twigs snapped underfoot and leaves scattered away as I staggered toward the road, a single halting step at a time. The interior car lights dimmed, and I could sense the panic from the other me. A noise squeaked from my panicked other self as I moved forward again.

"Who's there?"

I wanted to shout back, "You," but what good would that do? I already knew I was scared. To be accurate, both of us were.

Instead of calling out, I decided it would be better to reach the car before it sped away, although I didn't have any idea how "I" would cope with seeing myself come stumbling out of the darkness.

Just as I reached the edge of the forest, the engine roared to life and I knew I had mere seconds to get there before it was too late. The back door was still open, and I reached out to grab it. All thoughts of revealing myself to the driver evaporated. What was the point? I was freaked out enough for the both of us.

The door had barely closed when the car drew away at lightning speed, tyres squealing. I just stood there in the middle of the road, staring at the disappearing car. Just bloody stood there, remembering how frightened I'd been as I'd sped away from that spot in my car.

And yet, I felt even more frightened standing in the middle of the road in the dead of night, knowing there was someone still out to get me.

A noise alerted me that I was not alone. It was time to run.

Jolting awake, I shot up, grabbed the covers, and pulled them up around me as if they had the ability to protect me from whatever was coming for me. Sweat slicked my body. I didn't want to push away the blankets lest I be seen. I know. Fucked up.

My heart was racing. The dream had been so real that it took me a moment to realise I wasn't standing in the middle of the road at all. I was, in fact, hunched up on Annabel's sofa. The fireplace was still giving off heat, but the flames had long since died down.

I didn't know how long I had been asleep, but I knew it wasn't yet time to get up. I didn't know what to do. It wouldn't be right to get up and look around Annabel's house. That would be no way to reward a hostess. I figured I wouldn't be able to sleep again that night; I was too scared to close my eyes. So I lay there, and lay there, and continued to lay there.

Minutes seem like hours when you're waiting for morning to come. My eyes were burning, and my joints were seizing up from being cramped up on the sofa. Sleep beat me in the end.

In this dream, I wasn't standing in the woods. This time I was outside a window looking into the bright light of a kitchen, Annabel's kitchen.

I saw "myself" enter, carrying a tray. The shock of it immobilised me. "I" came to the glass and stared out. I could see the greenness of "my" eyes, the loose tendrils of my hair falling forward as "I" leaned forward. It was so different seeing myself that way. It was not like looking into a mirror at all. The movements were all fucked up, out of synch.

I had to get away, had to leave before I scared the living shit out of myself—both myself and "myself."

I did say my dreams were fucked up.

I turned away, but my jacket clipped the window, making a tapping sound. I saw the person inside straighten, cock her head, listen. It was too late to slip away unnoticed.

From behind me I heard the distinct sound of footsteps on gravel. He was here. I didn't know who "he" was, but I knew for certain that he had found me. I also knew it would not be a pleasant thing when he caught me.

Fuck it. I had to get the attention of the people inside the house, had to try to get them to come outside. I tapped on the glass. Tapped and tapped and banged and banged. But all that seemed to do was frighten the other me, make "me" rush backwards, make "me" scream out.

I saw Annabel enter, saw the woman I loved enter the room and race to the other "me." I lifted my hand to get her attention, but I was grabbed from behind. My body fell backwards and was pulled in against a hard chest.

"Ya thought she'd 'elp ya, eh?"

It was *his* voice, just as dark, just as cruel, just as wickedly spiteful as he had always been. This time it wouldn't be a just beating, not just a fall. No. This time he would take everything, including my life.

'Fuck!' I shot up again and saw that the room was filling with the first touches of dawn. The fire was completely out, and there was a chill in the room. My heart was drumming a staccato rhythm in my ears.

"You okay?"

Just the sound of her voice drifting into the room eased the residual fear from my dreams. A sob, then another, then another, until they blended together into a cacophony of weeping. Strong hands slipped around my shoulders and pulled me close, the softness of her chest a contrast to the hardness of the man in my dream. I didn't care that it seemed I was always an emotional wreck when she was near; all that mattered was that I felt safe. Annabel made me feel as if that man could never hurt me.

She held me until the tears abated, and then a while longer. Her voice was gentle, the words incoherent, but being in her arms and hearing her voice was so comforting that the sluggish drag of exhaustion overrode my need to cry. My fear had subsided, assuaged by the sensation of being close to Annabel. I remembered a wisp of my dream. When I saw Annabel in the kitchen, I had the sense that I was seeing the woman I loved.

Loved? I had only just met her, so how on earth could I love her? Attraction, admittedly, but love?

Annabel leaned back slightly, her eyes glistening. "How are you feeling?"

So soft, so enticing. I shifted forward, our faces impossibly close without touching. Her hand cupped my jaw, and the thumb stroked my skin. My eyelids fluttered as an out of control urge raced through me to close the gap between us and take those beautiful lips with mine. I didn't get the chance.

Annabel's kiss was initially a brushing, a tasting, a chaste connection between one person and another. Then her lips became firmer, more demanding, more delectable. Her hand moved from my jaw and cupped the back of my head, pressing us closer, connecting us more deeply.

I knew these lips, the texture and the taste. I knew just how they would claim my own, which I believed in my core they had done a thousand times before.

I leaned backwards and pulled her down onto the sofa with me. The warmth of her body seeped through the blankets and connected with my own heat.

A tentative tongue trailed against my lips, a tongue that was begging for access. I couldn't refuse her. I never could refuse her. At that moment, it didn't even occur to me to wonder about that thought.

The sensation was overwhelming. A moan climbed up my throat and surrounded her tongue as if it was the welcome committee. Annabel moved over me, her body pressing more firmly into mine, her breathing raspier, needy.

I slipped my arms around her and pulled her nearer. I needed to feel the solidness of her, to know I wasn't dreaming. This was real. This was happening. I was back with her.

Back with her?

My eyes shot open and I looked at the woman who was kissing me. Her eyes stayed closed, her mouth and tongue still searching mine.

Back with her?

My brain hurt. It remembered her, but it didn't. Remembered the feel of her lips, the smell of her, the brownness of her eyes, but it didn't. It was almost as if there were someone else's memories working in synch with mine and totally confusing the situation.

Annabel stopped in mid-kiss. Her mouth was warm against mine, but immobile. Her eyes opened and looked straight into me—not just into my eyes, but into me. When she pulled back, I felt the loss immediately.

"Ellen?"

Ellen? Had she thought she was kissing Ellen? The Ellen she believed I was last night?

"I'm Rebecca."

My voice sounded as if it belonged to someone else. The assertion was quiet yet firm. I didn't want to be kissed by someone, however much I was attracted to them, if they believed they were with someone else.

Her face contorted as her mouth moved around the feeling of my name. A flash of pain flitted across her face and she stumbled backwards and fell to the floor.

I watched in fascination as she scooted backwards, as if I would hurt her if she turned away from me. Her eyes filled with panic, then hurt, then what I could only identify as grief.

Then she was up and gone, and I was left dumbfounded on the sofa, alone.

Chapter Three

I didn't stay for breakfast. There was no way I wanted every time I looked at my hostess to remind me about what had happened. And I certainly didn't need to experience the repeated emotional slap for not being who she wanted.

When we parted at the front door, Annabel was very quiet. Her face was pale, those beautiful eyes dull. As I began to back away, she reached out to me but I just stuck out my hand to shake hers. There was no denying the sensation that raced from her to me, and from me to her. No denying the irresistible pull of connection or the sudden surety that I definitely knew her.

Her face brightened, and her mouth opened as if she wanted to speak.

"Thank you, Annabel." I held up the directions she had written down in small, neat handwriting. "It was lovely meeting you."

Her mouth closed, and so did her expression. She gave a brief nod of acknowledgement.

Then, without a backwards glance, I was on my way to Breadsall Priory and a day of more shit.

The drive to the Priory bore no resemblance whatsoever to the interminable trek of the previous evening. Roads I had thought to be deserted actually were lined with houses and shops. Why hadn't I seen them the night before? Perhaps they were closed then, so there had been no lights on to catch my attention. Or perhaps it was sheer panic that had made me pass them by without notice.

I signed in at the hotel and offered my apologies for not arriving the night before. I didn't go into detail, as I doubted the man on Reception actually gave two shits about my life story. The room was being paid for by my company, so it didn't matter either way to them whether or not I used it.

Then it was up to my room, toting my own bag instead of having to make small talk with the bellboy. Showered and changed, I was in the meeting hall, seated at the back. I didn't want to be an eager beaver today. Far from it. I wanted to wallow in self-pity and forget everything that had happened the night before.

Today was the final convention stop for me for a while. I had booked an overnight stay at the Priory for that evening as well, but I decided to go home instead. But then the scenes from the previous evening kept popping into my head throughout the day, and I eventually decided to stay the night and drive back to Norwich as soon as the sun was up the following morning. At least I would have little chance of getting lost in full daylight.

It was more of the same old faces, same old shit, and same old me. Actually, I had always loved my job and so I suffered through the obligatory conventions, but now they seemed just a waste of my time. I found myself mentally drifting off, thinking about what had happened that morning.

I usually used meetings as an opportunity to network, but not today. Today I isolated myself from the other reps, shut myself off from the rest of the world.

Bedtime was earlier than usual. I was mentally and physically exhausted. No surprise really, considering I must've had no more than three hours sleep the night before. I opted for a bath instead of a shower, and soaked myself until my skin pruned.

When I opened my case and pulled out my pjs, I thought again about the previous night. Pulling off the side of the road and feeling as if I was being watched; the feelings of fear, of being hunted; meeting Annabel and her believing I was someone else.

I stopped, my pjs hanging loosely in my hand. Everything that had happened after that seemed out of place, as if I'd entered a world that I did and didn't belong in, like I was stepping into the shoes of someone else and the shoes fit perfectly.

Fuck that. I wasn't Cinderella. I must've been even more tired than I'd thought the night before. How else could I explain the face at the kitchen window?

Then I remembered the dreams, the feeling of being on the outside of my life and looking in. I snorted derisively as I acknowledged how true that was. It seemed I'd always felt that way—on the outside of my own fucking life and looking at it as if seeing it under a microscope.

That didn't change the fact that my dreams were even more fucked up than my real life, although I did recognise that was usually what happened in dreams.

For the first time in a long time, I felt the pangs of loneliness. I didn't get lonely; I kept busy. Kept on the move and didn't allow people to invade my private life. Even visiting my family was a chore, something to be endured at Christmas and on birthdays. I was happy being on my own, happy not having anyone to answer to. So why was I suddenly feeling as if my life might not be quite enough?

This introspection was too deep, too intimate. I was tired, that was all. I needed a good night's sleep, and I would be good to go. A night of restful sleep would take care of these feelings of loneliness, of not belonging and not fitting in.

I slipped into my pjs and then under the covers. Sleep was waiting for me almost immediately. So were the dreams.

The scene was different, so very different from the night before. I was inside Annabel's house, sprawled on the sofa. Soft music was playing in another part of the house, and the sound of it was calming. A fire blazed in the hearth. Candles scattered around the room added to the ambience. It was relaxing, peaceful. I felt completely at home.

In my dream, I closed my eyes and allowed the serenity to completely envelop me. The warmth, the music, the perception of safety was wonderful.

Someone came into the room, but I didn't feel alarmed. In fact, I didn't even open my eyes. Fingers danced over my face, tracing from eyebrows to mouth and back again. They focused on my lips, following the curve of the lazy smile the stroking had conjured.

"You are so very beautiful."

The words seemed to seep into my skin and warm me to the core. Fingers were replaced by soft kisses, kisses that I returned. I knew those lips—the texture and the taste of them, and how they would claim my own. I also knew without a shadow of a doubt that I had kissed those lips a thousand times before.

Even before I opened my eyes to drown in pools of chocolate, I knew it was my Annabel. Just the feel of her lips, the smell of her skin—it was all her, the love of my life. This was the woman who had made me feel alive from the moment I met her nearly four years ago. It was a pity I'd met her younger brother just before that. Her brother was my husband.

This wasn't the time to remember his cruelty, wasn't the time to recollect his fists, his biting words, his hatred for anything that didn't fit into his bigoted view of life. This was time for me to be with Annabel, and I wanted to make the most of it.

My eyes opened and I absorbed her beauty. My breathing stopped whilst I examined every feature of her face. One eyebrow raised in question made her expression sexy. I trailed my fingers down the side of her face, and she turned and kissed them.

"Is Bella asleep?" My voice was husky.

Annabel made a mewling noise before answering. "Yes. Like a lamb. She always has liked the bed in the spare room being especially her size."

More kisses along my fingers, until she slipped one inside her mouth and sucked. I gasped at the sensation of her mouth and tongue. Heat raced to my core, and I shifted closer to her. "Did...did you read to her?"

"Ahuh. *Madeline's Rescue* is going down well." Her lips curled into a smile before she pulled away and looked lovingly into my eyes. "She wants me to tell you she wants a dog."

"Really? My three-year-old daughter said she wants a dog, eh?"

Her eyes widened in feigned innocence. "Yep. One like Genevieve."

I laughed. "You mean *you* want a dog like Genevieve."

Annabel scrunched up her nose before grinning widely and nodding.

"Thought so." I cupped my hand behind her head and pulled her to me. I wanted to feel those lips and that tongue again. Before I could kiss her, she pulled back and looked straight into me.

"You will, won't you?"

I didn't have to question what she meant. I knew she wasn't talking about a dog. Annabel was asking if we were still leaving Kirk Langley the following evening, as we'd planned. It was a monumental step for both of us. I would be leaving my husband and taking our only child away from him; Annabel would be leaving her home.

Freddie would never accept our leaving together, never let the shame of it die. No one left Freddie Howell, no one, especially not his wife. He would hunt us down like animals.

Until now Annabel and I had kept our love a secret, but it would all come out when she left with me. People would not understand that two women could be in love and want to spend their lives together. Freddie would definitely not be happy that someone else now possessed his property, even if it was his own sister. I knew I was committing adultery, but that sin paled in comparison to the abuse Freddie had heaped on me over the years.

I sat up and met her gaze. "Nothing will keep me from you. Nothing."

The force of her kiss pushed me back onto the sofa. My fingers threaded through her hair and gripped. Just having Annabel with me made all right with my world. Everything we had suffered would be worth it.

She moved over me, her body making contact with the full length of mine. The kiss was intense, and desire sparked throughout my body.

My hands slipped around the front of Annabel's shirt and began to release the buttons. The heat of her skin against my fingers made me hunger for more. I pushed her shirt over her shoulders and shifted my lips to her bared flesh. Annabel's head tipped to the side, exposing her throat. I kissed my way up to it, taking the opportunity to taste her.

Annabel leaned back and sat up. She grabbed the tail of her shirt and pulled it free from her body in one swift movement; she wasn't wearing a bra. The light of the fire danced over toned muscles and caressed the soft swell of her breasts.

My hand explored the dips and curves of her. Brown eyes met mine, almost black with their desire. I opened the button on her slacks and then slowly moved the zipper down. Slipping my hands back up, I grabbed the waistband and moved the pants downwards.

She placed her hands on top of mine and stopped me. "I want to see you, feel you." The words seemed to be dragged from her throat, as if each was difficult to say.

I lifted my arms so she could unwrap me like a gift. Annabel lifted my jumper and pulled it over my head, then leaned forward and unclasped my bra, freeing my breasts.

"Jesus, Ellen."

The shock in her voice made me freeze for an instant before my eyes followed her gaze. Bruises purpled my ribcage, dark and angry blotches that marred what should have been pale soft skin. Anger choked her, and tears filled her eyes with the effort of pushing it down. Tentative fingers traced the outline of each one, and although they were tender, I suppressed the wince.

Her eyes shifted from my skin and captured my gaze. "When?" She spluttered just the one word.

I shook my head. I didn't want to ruin our time together by discussing how my husband had used me as a punch bag to vent his frustration over something that had gone wrong for him at work.

Annabel didn't give up. "When, Ellen?"

The pain in her eyes made me cave in. "Tuesday."

She pushed away from me, and I felt the loss of her.

"Tuesday?" she spat. "Tuesday! It's Friday today. Friday!"

Her anger boiled over, but it was not aimed at me. I knew part of the reason she was angry was because I hadn't told her about Freddie hitting me, but what was the point? Women were battered by their husbands all the time. It was a cold, hard fact that men could do as they wanted. It wasn't right, but it was still done. Annabel and I were leaving the next evening to start life afresh somewhere else. I knew if I'd told her, she would have confronted him. We were so close to escaping this life that I didn't want Annabel giving her brother any indication that she was in love with his wife. He was bound to realise that was the only reason Annabel would try to defend me.

"Annie." I used the nickname I had for her. No one else called her Annie. No one else was allowed to. "Please, don't." I could see she was trying to let go of her anger, but so far it wasn't working.

I stood up and moved over to her. My hands slipped around her waist and pulled her close. She was slightly taller than me, and I had to tilt my head back to look into her eyes. "Baby, we are close, so close. Let it go." I could feel the rage vibrating through her, so I kissed her chin once, then again. Slowly, the emotion drained from her, and she slumped against me.

"I'm sorry, so sorry." Tears were streaming down her face, so I brushed them away. "I just...just..."

More tears. I was making shushing noises and stroking her face and hair. I felt her body stiffen, and I knew what was coming next.

"I'm not like him, am I? You know—with my anger?"

I smiled at her and shook my head. Annabel Howell was the gentlest woman I had ever met. The thought of anyone being hurt made her hurt right along with them, and it came out as anger. It was a mystery how she could be related to that bastard Freddie Howell. They looked alike, but that was where the similarity ended.

I took her hands in mine and gently led her to the sofa and sat her down, then guided her back until she was lying down. Before I joined her, I slipped out of the rest of my clothes and stood before her naked. Her eyes drank me in almost reverently, like I was a divine creation sent to earth for her. No one else had ever looked at me that way, had ever made me feel so loved with just a look.

I leaned over, my mouth close to hers. She lifted her head, expecting me to kiss her, but I pulled back. "Your turn to get naked," I murmured.

The shiver that passed through her was visible even in the half light.

I kissed along heated skin, glorying in the involuntary flexing of taut muscle. Gripping the top of her trousers, I pulled them down and then moved up to take off her panties. One hand on each foot soon got rid of her thick socks, and she lay before me completely undressed. Annabel was a vision, a balm to my soul. Each time I looked at her, my heart understood why it kept beating each day.

She reached forward and tentatively touched my bruises, but instead of getting angry again, she sighed and drew me closer until my body covered hers. "I love you so much, Ellen, so very much."

Her words found their way into my soul. "I love you, too." And God, I did.

Mouth met mouth, lips and tongues and teeth. Hands explored secret places, longing for no one but each other. I nudged her legs apart and settled between strong thighs. It felt so right to be with her, no matter what society forbade.

Annabel lifted her hips, seeking firmer contact, and I happily obliged her. Heat pooled at my core and I wanted to share it with her, share my essence with her, mix our essences until we two became one.

I kissed her skin, tasted her, revelled in her. A rhythm built between us, the tempo increasing with each thrust of our bodies moving in practiced synchrony. At that moment, it was all that mattered—the two of us reaffirming our love, our connection.

I kissed her and pressed harder against her. I wanted to climb inside, love her from the inside out, live forever within the woman who had stolen my heart almost from the moment I met her.

Annabel's fingers were digging into my back, and I gasped into her mouth. Her thighs moved higher around my waist and opened her secret sanctum more fully against me. I could feel she was wet, and I wanted more contact. With her, I always wanted more.

I gripped one leg and then pushed the other thigh down to the sofa. I positioned myself over her thigh and slicked my need across her skin. When she groaned, I nuzzled her ear and whispered, "I want to make love to you." The soft moan that slipped from her mouth almost made me cum right then. I took it as a yes.

I slid against her again and again, full strokes, my thigh pressing against her heat. My mouth moved to her breast, and I licked around the pert nipple before capturing it between my lips. The sensation of holding such perfection was divine.

Annabel's hands gripped my backside and drew me closer, and my nub rubbed along the glorious length of her thigh. Desire flooded me, and I released her nipple and returned to her mouth. My lips met hers ferociously, and I am definite I heard myself growl as I pulled away to kiss her neck again. I could feel her heart hammering against my mouth, hear her ragged breathing, the scent of her need radiating in the air.

Her hands were in my hair, wrapping around the tendrils and tugging slightly. My hips were gyrating on her thigh, and the shocks of pleasure rippling through me made me pant, made me groan, made me need her even more.

Slipping my hand between us, I felt wetness, heat. Slick folds parted and permitted me entry to her most secret place, a place reserved for only me. I slowly circled her opening. Annabel rocked forward in an attempt to force my fingers inside, but I drew back.

"Please!" The word was a gasp.

I lifted my head and looked into beautiful eyes that were hooded, expectant. The rhythm between us never faltered.

She whispered, "I love you."

A wonderful ache began in my heart. I loved this woman so bloody much.

I entered her slowly, gently, watching her eyes flicker at the sensation of being filled by two fingers. I held them still, giving her time to become accustomed to the feeling, but Annabel was impatient for more. Her hips moved backwards and forwards, creating a tempo I was happy to follow.

My own orgasm was simmering and would careen out of control if not held back, but I wanted to share my release with Annabel's. Seeing her lying there open and vulnerable made it difficult to hold back, but I tried.

Her hips moved more quickly as my fingers took her. I reached deep inside her, pulled back, delved deeply again. Sweat coated our skin, and the movement of our bodies each against the other was smooth. My wetness was dripping onto her thigh, and the sensation of rubbing against her was delicious torture.

Faster, deeper, harder. I couldn't get enough of Annabel, would never tire of hearing the delightful sounds of pleasure coming from her. I could feel her walls tightening around my fingers and knew her release was imminent.

Our breasts rubbed together, heightening the bliss of the moment. So soft, so feminine, so perfectly and magically us. Annabel tensed, clenched around my fingers, and held her breath. I curved my fingers inside her and felt for the spot I knew would tip her over the edge.

We had shared our bodies before, shared our love, but this time seemed to hold something more. It was as if at the moment of climax, something inside my head recorded the image of her, the absolute perfection that was Annabel Howell. Her head was thrown back, her mouth open, eyes closed. Breasts lifted and pressed into me, as did her fingers. I rubbed the spot again, pressing and caressing until another orgasm ripped through her.

Blinding white light shook me as I orgasmed. I wanted to tell her I loved her, but words were impossible. There were just the primitive sounds of two souls reuniting.

I fell forward, my body covering hers. Strong arms wrapped around me and held me close, soft kisses pressing into my hair, and a feeling of contentment flooded through me. This was what I wanted for the rest of my life—to be with her, to be held by her, feeling safe and loved and wanted.

This time tomorrow, our "forever" would begin, Annabel, Bella, and me starting over. The three of us together at last.

And then Freddie could never hurt us ever again. How perfect that would be.

With a start, I sat up in bed. The room was dark and at first I wondered where I was, since the last thing I remembered was being on a sofa. And where was Annabel?

Stumbling from the bed, I nearly fell to the floor but caught myself at the side of the bed and plonked back onto the mattress. It felt strange, the room I mean. I should have known where I was, but everything seemed foggy. I was still wondering where Annabel had gone, but I didn't call for her. I guess I knew it hadn't really happened. That wasn't the best feeling in the world, but that was the length and breadth of it.

Focusing my attention, I peered around and tried to make out the shapes in the darkness. I was in a hotel room. *My* hotel room to be precise. To be honest, the feeling that came with the realisation was an ache that clawed up from inside me and travelled up my throat. I knew it had only been a dream, but apparently my heart couldn't accept the disappointment of it quite yet. Stupid, I know. I had never before allowed the vestiges of sleep to overrule my practical side, and I wasn't about to start now.

I clicked on the bedside lamp and felt even worse. So much for my determination to be practical. Seeing the room bathed in a subtle orange glow banished all hopes of actually being in my fantasy world. It was just me on my own again, like usual.

I tried to swallow down the nausea. I couldn't understand why I was feeling sick in the first place. It wasn't as if my dream had been so horrific that I should want to dump the meagre contents of my stomach over it. The dream had been pleasant, very pleasant. Too pleasant, actually. And that thought helped me understand why I wanted to vomit.

Racing to the bathroom, I barely got bent over the toilet before I let loose. Heave after heave after heave, and then the dry kind, the hurting kind. My legs gave out on me and I hit the cold hard tile, the chill a reminder that this was my real world after all.

I sat there for what seemed like an age, but was only about fifteen minutes. Tears were streaming down my face, and I put it down to my feeling ill. Even at that stage, I was trying to fool myself.

The smell of putrid stomach contents was making my gut roil, and I knew I had to soak underneath the hot jets of the shower and allow them to work their magic. Maybe they would wash away the sadness that was swamping me from the inside out. I could only hope.

Readying myself for my shower, I removed my sleeping top. Something in the mirror caught my attention, something underneath my breasts.

I walked over to the mirror, lifted my arm, and leaned closer. Deep, dark purple bruises peppered the ribs below my breasts, bruises I hadn't noticed earlier when I'd been soaking in the bath. Could I have hit myself as I slumped next to the toilet? And if that was the case, why hadn't I felt it?

Gently pressing the bruises, I winced. They were fresh enough to still cause pain, but that didn't add up. I would have felt it if I'd hit myself on the toilet seat. And even if I had hurt myself, the bruises wouldn't be all over me. It was almost as if I'd been beaten.

"Fuck!" Battered. "Fucking hell!" Battered as if I had been on the receiving end of someone's fists. I knew I would have remembered that.

Weirdly enough, I did, but not in the way I should have remembered it.

My hands were shaking as I traced the outline of the dark mass. Were they the same as the bruises I had seen in my dream? No. That would be *too* fucked up, even given everything that had happened in the last twenty-four hours. People didn't have dreams about being bruised and then wake up with bruises, not on this scale they didn't. It wasn't as if I'd banged my hand on the bedside table.

Turning the cold tap on full, I cupped handfuls of water and splashed my face. Part of me believed I must still be in some kind of sleep/wake limbo. But when I looked back into the mirror, the bruises were still there.

It was then that I felt it—something behind me, something waiting to be acknowledged. I knew I should be scared, should almost be shitting myself, but I wasn't. It was as if, on some subconscious level, I was expecting it.

"I'm so sorry. So sorry."

The voice drifted into me, as if it bypassed my ears and went through my skin, through my pores. And it was a voice full of pain and torment.

I spun around and looked for her, for Annabel. She was the one who spoke. I knew it was her. I could sense her presence, feel her near me. But apart from me, the bathroom was empty.

That was not even the most worrying thing about the whole situation. The thing that worried me the most was the disappointment I felt when I realised I was on my own. How fucked up was that? To be disappointed when the woman from my dream wasn't manifesting in my hotel bathroom?

And why was I disappointed that I hadn't seen a ghost in my bathroom? Simple. If Annabel Howell *had* been standing behind me, I might not have started to believe I was losing my mind.

Chapter Four

I washed up, but I waited until the next morning to shower. There was no way I was going to strip off completely and climb into the shower, not with what had transpired in the early hours. I'd seen *Psycho*, watched Janet Leigh's character be slashed to death by a madman. I wasn't going to be the next victim of Norman Bates. Stuff that. Marion Crane I am not.

It was difficult to shower whilst avoiding looking at myself. I tried to avoid acknowledging the presence of the bruises, but by doing so, I just highlighted their existence. To be honest, it was the quickest shower I had ever taken. I wasn't too sure I'd rinsed all of the shampoo out of my hair, but I didn't care. I was happy that I was still breathing. Breathing quickly, but breathing all the same.

Breakfast was a croissant and a coffee. I couldn't stomach anything else. Just the smell of the fried breakfast being served made my stomach churn, and I had the distinct impression I would do an encore of my bathroom yodelling if I didn't get out of the restaurant.

All I wanted to do was go home and forget everything that had happened. Go home, kick off my shoes, and enjoy the rest of my weekend, terror free.

So, why didn't I turn off the A38 instead of joining the A61? I had to join the A52, but this route would take me in the completely opposite direction of Norwich. This way was taking me back to Kirk Langley.

I acknowledged my misdirection, but I couldn't seem to stop myself. Unlike the previous evening, I knew exactly where I was going and how to get there. I didn't need a Sat Nav; something else was guiding me. Instinct. I felt a definite pull to the house that had seemingly changed everything in my life since the moment I stepped foot over the threshold. I wanted to put it down to my being a woman, a woman who needed to clarify events in the light of day to put them to rest. But that would have made me a big fat liar.

To be honest, I just wanted to see Annabel again, to make sure she did exist. If she was there, at least only part of my mind would be going mad. The jury was still out on the other part.

All the way to Annabel's house, something was building inside me. It wasn't butterflies, unless butterflies came wearing hobnailed boots. It was a sick feeling, a foreshadowing that when I arrived at Kirk Langley, I wouldn't be happy with what I found. I narrowed the feeling down to either fear or a sense of impending doom. How fucking dramatic was that? Fear, I could understand, but "impending doom?" Jesus. I knew at that point that I was a twat, a twat who just couldn't let things go. More's the pity.

The car seemed to swallow up the miles, and yet it appeared to take longer to get there than the previous day's journey to the hotel. Expectation is a wonderful thing, isn't it? No. Actually, it was terrifying. All the way, I kept arguing with myself. Why was I doing this? Why couldn't I just let things go? But I kept on driving.

I nearly drove past Annabel's house, nearly carried on and missed it completely. Not because I wasn't paying attention. That wasn't it. It was the appearance of the house; it was different. Colder. Emptier.

As I pulled into the driveway, I saw a car parked near the front door, the boot open and bags piled inside. It looked as if I had just caught Annabel as she was setting off on a trip.

My mind flashed to what she had said in my dream last night, her talking about the journey she was to take with the dream "me."

"No. That was a dream, Becky," I ground out through clenched teeth.

I pulled the handbrake on and then just sat in the car for a few moments. My heart was racing and my hand trembled as I reached for the door handle. I stopped, took a deep breath, said a little prayer, and then exited the car.

I couldn't see anyone, but I could hear talking. It was a man and woman. Laughter drifted from the open doorway, and I hesitated before moving onto the porch and stepping inside the house. I was amazed that I hadn't noticed how battered the door was, how in need of a touch of paint it had been the previous morning. It was probably because I had been so anxious to get away after kissing my hostess. A person doesn't usually hang about to check the paint job when she is dying of disappointment and embarrassment. At least not this woman.

"Hello!" My voice echoed down the hallway, and I heard the people stop moving about. "Sorry to disturb you." Was I? I didn't exactly know. But I did know I needed to get this over and done with, and fuck off into my own life again.

Footsteps sounded on the floorboards upstairs, and I thought about having heard the same movement when Annabel had scurried upstairs to get me some blankets. Jean-clad legs appeared at the top of the stairs, and a voice drifted down to me.

"Can I help you?"

Was that Annabel? It sounded like her, but not. A booted foot descended a stair and stopped.

"Hello? Are you still there?"

It was her. It had to be.

"Annabel?"

The second foot stopped momentarily in mid-air before landing on the next step and stopping again.

"Sorry to disturb you again, but..." The feet moved down the stairs more quickly, and the words I was going to say jammed in my throat.

My eyes followed the trajectory of her body as it appeared, and I found myself taking in a thick cream coloured sweater covering her torso, then a slender neck, a firm jaw, red lips, and a fine straight nose. I closed my eyes, anticipating looking into her eyes again.

Beautiful, dark brown eyes looked into mine, quizzical brown eyes framed by long lashes. They showed confusion.

I stepped back, stumbled slightly, and tried to steady myself on the doorframe. The woman before me wasn't Annabel, but she was Annabel. I knew it was fucked up, but it *was* and it *wasn't* her. I couldn't think of any other way of describing it.

A hand rested on my arm, and an electric jolt of connection flowed through me. Even the sensation of being touched by her was the same, but it wasn't. I know I'm not making any sense, but it didn't make any sense to me either.

"Are you okay?" Her voice was gentle, calming. "You've gone all white."

I felt white, too. Deathly white. White enough to piss over and black out. Instead of doing that, I nodded. "I'm fine."

She tilted her head and looked at me, assessing. "Well, you certainly don't look it. Come in and sit down."

The woman, who I by now realised definitely wasn't Annabel, cupped my elbow and led me down the hallway to the living room. It was exactly the same as I remembered it, although it was also distinctly different. There was the open fireplace, the flames long gone and the space filled with ash. The furniture was still classically rustic, but even more worn than I remembered. My hostess was standing next to the armchair closest to the fireplace, gesturing for me to sit. It was déjà vu, with a twist.

As if on auto pilot, I moved past her, my arm brushing against hers. A spark of recognition slithered into my head, but this time the woman didn't jerk away, didn't gasp.

"Would you like some water?"

Her expression showed concern, as if she thought I was on the verge of keeling over and snuffing it in her house. I wasn't entirely sure that I wasn't going to do just that.

I nodded again, and she was gone and I was left on my own. This time there was no ticking of a clock marking the passing of time. Though the clock was still there, it was not working. As I had on my previous visit, I started to look around the room. The leather sofa was still there, but the throws were absent. The coffee table was pushed to one side and was sans magazines. The changes in the room were clear now, as I put the differences down to everything having aged. A stopped clock, missing throws, no magazines, but there was more. The décor, for a start. When I was there two nights before, I hadn't noticed how in need of updating everything had been. I couldn't even put it down to the lighting, as I had been there in the morning too.

"Here you go."

The sound of her voice so close to me made me start. A glass of water was being offered, and I slipped my fingers around the cool glass. I felt the urge to pour the contents over my head to see if anything I was seeing or feeling would change, but decided I had probably freaked out the woman enough already.

I took a sip. The coldness refreshed my throat, but nothing more. The woman stepped back and sat in the armchair opposite mine, her face still showing confusion.

"I feel as if we've met already."

It wasn't me who spoke; it was her. As it had been with Annabel.

"Have you been to Kirk Langley before?" Her voice was soft, and so much like Annabel's it was unnerving.

At that point I wanted to say that we had met, kind of, two nights ago, and I had slept on her sofa. But I knew she would think I was an idiot. Probably because I was beginning to think that very thing myself.

"No. I don't think so." I don't think so? What the fuck?

The woman stared at me as if she wanted to say the same thing as the words in my mental monologue, especially the "what the fuck?" part.

"Clare Davies."

What? But aloud, I said, "Excuse me?"

"My name. I thought it was about time I introduced myself."

She leaned forward in her armchair, her hands dangling between her legs. On first impression, a person might be forgiven for thinking she was relaxed, but she wasn't. Not by a long shot. Clare's eyes flickered over my face before settling on my eyes as if she was searching for something. Then I realised I hadn't introduced myself.

"Sorry." I let out a shaky laugh. "Rebecca Gibson."

A smile graced her lips, and her face lit up. My heart skipped a beat, as if it had been squeezed by an unseen hand, and then resumed its staccato rhythm.

"Well, *Rebecca...*"

Jesus. She even said that the same.

Clare reached over, her hand extended in greeting. "Nice to meet you."

As soon as my fingers touched hers, the feeling of connection was back. Her eyes widened and she looked at me in wonder, like she couldn't process what was going on. Neither of us withdrew immediately. It seemed to me that the longer we held on, the clearer everything would become. Alas, that was not the case.

It was me who broke the contact first, but I could still feel the tingle, the sensation of her skin on mine.

Clare slumped back, her eyes looking furtively from her hand to my face. When she shook her head, I knew she was trying to get rid of the feelings that must've been coursing through her.

"Erm...well, erm."

I just sat there and waited for her to pull herself together.

At last she said, "You mentioned Annabel when you arrived."

I stiffened, but still waited in silence.

Clare noticed the change in my demeanour, and her eyes narrowed. "Did you know her well?"

Images of the dream I'd had the night before sprang into my head. If making love with someone on a sofa wasn't "knowing" her, I didn't know what was. However, I was asleep at the time, so maybe it didn't count.

"Kind of." Kind of? What "kind of" statement was that?

Clare's expression changed again, the suspicion dissipating. "Sorry. You mustn't know then." A dark eyebrow rose in question.

"Know?"

"My great aunt died in September."

"Great aunt?" I have to admit, my intonation was off. The pitch was a little too high.

"Sorry. If I'd known about you, I'd have invited you to the funeral."

"Great aunt?" Although the pitch and volume were unquestionably better, the repetition was redundant. There was no way we were talking about the same woman. The woman I'd met was younger than the woman seated in front of me, by at least ten years. Annabel was about twenty-five, give or take a couple of years. "Are we talking about the same Annabel? Annabel Howell?"

Clare nodded. "Yes. My great aunt." She sighed. "She did really well living here all on her own until she was eighty-five but—"

"Eighty-five!" Pitch and tone were all over the fucking shop now, but come on! Eighty-five?

I think I unnerved my hostess, as she held her hands out in front of her as if to ward off my voice.

"Clare!"

That wasn't me. I was too busy shouting "eighty-five" as if I was at a darts match.

"Who ya talkin' to?" The male voice came from above us.

Instead of getting up and going upstairs to explain that she was talking to an idiot, Clare looked towards the ceiling and bellowed, "It's all right, Granddad. It's just a friend of Aunt Annie's!" Clare smiled apologetically at me.

"Yer aunt din't have no friends!" came the reply.

Footsteps moved above us, slow, laboured footsteps that allowed us to track the journey of Clare's granddad as he made his way to the top of the stairs. Deliberate steps hit the stairs, and I could see Clare was becoming agitated.

"Excuse me, Rebecca. He finds coming downstairs difficult these days."

Once again, I was left on my own as Clare went to help. I heard her race up the stairs, then speak in low tones to the gentleman. Then came his, "Speak up, lass. Ya know 'm deaf," followed by a shushing noise. So that's probably why I was so surprised when I turned back to the empty armchair, and saw Clare sitting in the recently vacated seat?

That, and because it wasn't Clare.

I knew this not because she was dressed differently, not because her hair was a shade lighter than Clare's, not because the dark brown eyes bored into me. No. It was because I could still hear Clare helping her granddad down the stairs.

I wanted to scream, to run, to be all dramatic and swoon in a dead faint. But I didn't. I just fucking stared right back, like it was the most natural thing in the world to be seated in front of a dead woman who was looking straight at me.

It was Annabel. Not eighty-five; twenty-five at a push. Seated in front of me, her mouth moving, her eyes filled with agony. Her hand reached out as if to touch me, but stopped mere inches away. I could feel the coldness seeping from her into me. And along with the chill, I could feel her utter heartbreak, her torment, her loss. I knew she was asking me to do something, find someone, solve something. What, I didn't know, but I knew it as surely as I knew my name.

A word slipped from her mouth and seeped into me. Just like in the bathroom of the hotel, my ears were redundant.

"Clare."

One word, but I felt it everywhere, almost as if it filled up my head.

Clare and her granddad were in the hallway, coming closer, their voices jovial. Annabel's eyes widened, and her brown hair fell forward as if in slow motion when she tipped her head in a gesture that told me to look behind me. I turned my head to look.

Clare was smiling at me as she walked up the hallway, holding the old man's elbow as she had with mine. The old man was staring at his feet, probably making sure he didn't trip over anything. Why wasn't she looking shocked? From where she was, she must've been able to see the woman seated right in front of me.

A noise from behind me made me whip my head back around. It wasn't as if I thought the ghost of Annabel would hurt me in any way. To be honest, I was probably more worried that she would disappear before anyone else witnessed her apparition. If she was still there, I would be less likely to believe that I might be going mad.

But maybe I was going mad. Maybe my imagination, dormant for anything other than work purposes until this trip, had decided it was time to kick in and add excitement to my drab, solitary life.

The chair was empty. As it should have been. Empty. Just how I was feeling.

"Here you go, Granddad. I told you there was a lovely young lady here."

Clare's voice was so full of love that I knew I had to turn and act as if everything was normal. My eyes met hers immediately, her face alight with the most wonderful smile. She was so breathtakingly beautiful that the smile I wanted to give her in return faltered a little before falling into place.

Clare's eyes narrowed, as if she was reading me, before she turned her attention to the man holding on to her arm. My eyes followed hers, and I waited for the old man to meet my gaze.

His head slowly raised, and his attention initially went to his granddaughter. His smile was genuine, loving. I felt an ache in my chest when I saw the connection, as I had never really known either of my grandfathers and I'd always wished I had.

When his face turned to me, I changed my mind. Not in the first few seconds, no. It took a little longer than that. His mouth was still in a smile as he turned to me, the echo of his affection for Clare still lingering in the curve of his lips. But the smile slipped off his mouth like it had been wiped away with a rag.

"*Ellen?*" The word croaked through his lips.

Unlike the last time I'd heard that name, this time the voice was not full of concern and love. No, not at all. This time the name was an accusation. His eyes widened and his jaw dropped in shock. He lurched towards me, his hands balling into fists, and my hands flew to my body where the bruises had been.

"Granddad, no!" Clare pulled him back, her horror at the events unfolding clearly written on her face. "This is Rebecca, Rebecca Gibson."

The old man's face churned into a grimace of hatred before he seemed to regain some semblance of control. Colour drained from him as if he'd been bled, and then he stumbled forward.

Without thought, I shot forward and helped to catch him before he fell. He was dead weight, true, but that wasn't the only thing I experienced as I touched him. Images of running, of hate, fear, anger, and guilt flashed through my mind, and I nearly let go of him. Dark brown eyes looked up into mine, and I saw in him all his evil personified—Freddie Howell.

"Get him to the chair." Clare's voice was strained, probably with the exertion of supporting a man a lot bigger than she was.

I wanted to let him fall, let him slump defenceless to the ground and then pummel him senseless. I wanted to see him suffer, afraid for his life. I wanted him to experience the feeling of being beaten, both physically and emotionally, just like his wife had.

I closed my eyes and tried to shut down my emotions. This was too fucking weird even for me, and I'd experienced some weird assed shit in the last two days.

By the time we got him into the chair, he seemed to come around a bit. He waved Clare off. "Leave me be. I'm okay. It's just bein' in the 'ouse after all the years of bein' away."

I think I knew deep down why he hadn't been in the house, but it was not something a stranger would just happen to know, so I kept any comment to myself.

Even though I had no concrete proof, I believed Freddie Howell had killed his wife. If that was the case, why on earth was he walking about playing the doting grandfather? Maybe he had paid for his crime, but even then, would he still be accepted into the family fold as if nothing had happened? I doubted it.

"I think I should go." My voice was strained, weak. I knew it was the right thing to do. Clare had enough to deal with without the added burden of entertaining a stranger. It wasn't as if I wanted to make small talk with the old bastard.

"No. Please. Sorry about all this."

Clare's voice sounded panicked, and I thought she might be worried about being left on her own with a sickly man. But that impression seemed to change as she looked straight at me. It was disappointment, not panic, that coloured her voice.

With that understanding, I didn't want to leave her. Not because I thought Freddie would hurt her, no. He was incapable of climbing the stairs on his own, so I doubted he would tackle Clare down to the ground and choke the life out of her.

Choke the life out of her? Where had that thought come from? Was that the way he ended Ellen's life?

A sigh broke through my musing, and it wasn't from me.

"I'll walk you out."

Shit. Trust me to be reflective at a crucial point. I had taken too long to respond to her invitation to stay, and now it was too late to change my mind.

"Will you be okay for a minute, Granddad?"

The old fucker grunted, and I wanted to slap him. I didn't care that he was over eighty.

"I'll just be outside," Clare assured him.

Less than a minute later, we were standing next to the open boot of Clare's car. Although Clare at first kept looking back to see that everything was okay with her granddad, it wasn't long before she started to speak.

"I think you shocked him." Too fucking right I did. "I thought I knew you from somewhere, but then I realised it wasn't you." A small laugh hit the air like music. "You look like my grandmother, his wife."

Just a minute. Clare knew her grandmother? Then I was wrong. He hadn't kil—

"Not that I ever met her. She ran off years ago." Clare leaned forward conspiratorially. "He's never forgiven her for leaving him to bring up my mother on his own."

"She ran off?" My tone was intended to convey disbelief, because I doubted her grandmother had run off. However, Clare seemed to interpret my question the wrong way.

"Yep. Broke his heart. Never remarried." She sighed wistfully. "He loved her so much, you see."

No. I didn't. What Freddie Howell felt for his wife was not love, it was ownership. But I nodded and tsked in the right places.

"He always keeps a picture of her with him, especially now that he is at the home." Clare sighed again, as if she couldn't get over his enduring love. I wanted to gag at the thought. "The photo was taken when they were courting, somewhere near the Roaches in Derbyshire." She reached out as if to touch my arm, but stopped. "You look so like she does in that picture." Clare studied me as if trying to compare the photograph with the living, breathing woman standing in front of her. "Honestly, it's uncanny."

I pursed my lips and then forced them into a smile. She smiled back, and the air between us fell silent for a minute. Brown eyes were looking deeply into mine, and I wondered if she was still comparing me to her grandmother. Part of me was hoping that she was looking at me so intently for a different reason. Actually, it was more than just a part of me that hoped; it was more like all of me.

"He fell out with his sister, too. Aunt Annabel."

I jumped slightly at the sudden sound of Clare's voice, but I didn't think she noticed.

"They hadn't spoken for years." I bet they hadn't. "I only got to know her when I was old enough to make my own decisions, although I had visited her with my mum on occasion." Clare leaned back and looked me straight in the face, a smile appearing like magic. "Sorry." A small laugh punctuated her apology. "I doubt you want to hear my life story."

"I would love to." For once in my life, the tone came out exactly as I wanted it to, with just a hint of flirtation. I'd fully expected to sound polite, which she then would have noticed and closed off.

But Clare acknowledged it for what it was—an open invitation to a chance for us to meet again. I had no idea how that would happen, as I lived in Norwich and she lived in Kirk Langley, or thereabouts.

Clare tilted her head, and a soft smile played over her lips. I had to look up to watch her, as she was slightly taller than I was. "I would love that too."

Fuck. That voice. It seeped into me, not through the ears, but *into* me, deeply *into* me.

"Clare!"

The old twat was calling for her, and she glanced over her shoulder in his direction.

"Can we get going?"

"In a minute, Granddad!" she called back, her eyes once again on mine. "Where were we?"

Another smile. God. My poor heart. Then I saw her stiffen.

"What am I thinking? I don't live here." I figured that. The house looked like it should be demolished. "I live in Norfolk."

What the fuck? "Norfolk?"

The disappointment stood starkly on her face. "I'm leaving here this afternoon. Shit!" She took a step forward, but stopped. "I suppose I could stay another day if...if you'd like to get dinner or something?"

I smiled at her and she nodded, her face brightening.

"Where in Norfolk?"

Confusion flitted over her face and momentarily dulled the brightness of her eyes. "Wells. Wells–next–the–Sea."

"Great fish and chips at French's on the Quay."

More confusion slipped over her features. "You've been?" A snort of laughter. "Of course you have, if you know French's." Then she was back to looking serious again. "Just a minute, are you from here?"

I shook my head and smiled at her.

"So, are you going to tell me, or are you going to leave me hanging?"

"Norwich." I had to laugh at the "No way!" she almost shouted.

A figure seemed to hover in the doorway just behind her, and initially I thought it was Granddad Wife Killer. But unless he had been dipped into the Fountain of Youth and also had a sex change, it wasn't him. Annabel was leaning on the doorframe, her body relaxed, her expression open and contented. I wanted to wave to her, to beckon her out to experience the moment, but even I knew that was pushing my sanity. Not really a moment to introduce a dream lover to, hopefully, a future one. Especially since one was dead and haunting me, and the other one didn't know I was prone to seeing her dead great aunt as she had been sixty years ago.

Annabel seemed to be watching Clare and me, approving of us talking, getting to know each other. It was good to see. I remembered the softly spoken "Clare" when she had appeared in the living room, and it all was beginning to make sense. Even though Annabel's spirit wanted me to know what Freddie had done, for some reason she also wanted me to take care of Clare.

Then I caught a glimpse of him behind Annabel, staggering down the hall towards us, his face full of anger and hatred. He couldn't half shift, considering he was in his eighties. I knew he wanted me to leave, wanted Clare's attention away from me. He wanted to ruin another couple's chance at happiness, but he wasn't going to do it this time. No way.

Just as he reached the doorway, I leaned forward and grabbed Clare's arm. I needed her to look at me and ignore the old fart who wanted to stop what we had before it started. But it wasn't me who stopped him; it was the front door slamming shut in his face. I could see the handle twisting maniacally before it stopped dead.

Clare's head shot around, her expression anxious. "The—"

"Wind, yes. It slammed the door shut." I smiled at her and squeezed her arm lightly. Her eyes drifted to the contact, and I noted the small smile that danced in her eyes and became something I could only class as sublime.

I wasn't going to tell her that her great aunt had slammed the door on the old git. Why would I? Not only would it make me look like a *Ghost Whisperer* wannabe, but she would probably go and check to see if he was okay, after she told me to, "Fucking get away from me, you demented woman!"

"So, where were we?" I was smooth, uncharacteristically so.

Clare seemed to think for a moment before nodding. "I think..."

She turned away, and my hand slipped from her arm. Shit. She was going to check on him after all. Hark at me and my ultimate smoothness.

But she didn't move towards the house to go see how he was. I was surprised at that, considering he'd recently had some kind of "episode" and he was clocking on in years. She moved to the boot of the car and began to rummage through the bags. While she was rummaging, I was trying to think of something else to say, something memorable, something that would be quoted in years to come as the epitome of smoothness. Alas, the brain just whirred around and did fuck all. Well, except for conjuring blank screens and noises of cogs turning.

"I was just..." Her voice was muffled, and although I heard her, I stepped closer. "...looking..." Another step, and I was right behind her. "...for this."

She turned to face me, her smile radiant, at first, until she realised how close I was. She screamed and dropped the item in her hand. It crunched on the gravel, and I looked at the book at my feet, its pages splayed and vulnerable.

We both bent down to retrieve it at the same time and slammed our heads together. The clunk of two skulls meeting should have made us cry out, but instead we laughed, albeit nervously. Then thunk, we did it again. I believe I actually felt my brain shift inside my head after the second thwack, and the image I got was one of a grape floating around in a pickle jar.

I stood still and gestured at the book, indicating that she should be the one to retrieve it. It would give me time to rub the sore spot on my head, which stung like a bitch. But I was waiting with a ready smile when she stood up with the book in her grasp.

"That's an old one." I nodded my head at the notebook in her hand. "W H Smith's, I believe. One of the original ones from Bridge House, Lambeth."

She stared at me as if I was talking gibberish. To any lay person, I would have been. But stationery was my thing. I was a stationery rep, after all. Not the paper clip variety, more the upper end of the market—notebooks, diaries, writing sets—all the good stuff, the expensive stuff.

Clare turned the book over and checked the back. "Erm... Yes?"

I grinned at her and waggled my hand for her to pass it over, which she did, although she did hold onto it and tug as I tried to take it. I lifted an eyebrow and gave her my best "Give it up" look. She laughed as she released it into my care.

I liked that. The teasing, I mean. It seemed natural, like we had done the same thing a thousand times. I wasn't used to feeling so connected to another person, male or female. I was a bit of a Billy-No-Mates, really.

With that epiphany, I felt the blush climb up my throat, and I focused my attention on the book, hoping she wouldn't notice how vulnerable and exposed I was feeling.

The notebook was a beauty. I know that sounds as if I was a total fucking nerd, but it was. My hands travelled over the binding as if I was caressing a lover. This book's owner had taken care of it; there was no doubt about that. There was no adornment on the front; it was just soft brown leather. I turned it over and looked at the back to check the markings of the stationery house. When I finally lifted my gaze to meet Clare's, she was watching me intently.

"May I?" I gestured as if to open it, and she nodded.

Inside was a name written in small neat writing: *Annabel Howell*. I had known it would be there. I'd felt her mark even before I opened the cover. The date underneath the name announced *December 1949*. On the inside of the cover, opposite her name, was written: *To you, from me. x E x*. I also knew the E stood for Ellen. I'm not a prophet, or seer, it just made sense.

"It belonged to my great aunt."

I nodded, but continued to turn the pages, pages that were full of words, full of memories of a time long gone. As I looked at the flowing script, I had an image of the words being lovingly placed on each page.

Clare laughed nervously, and I looked up and gave her a questioning look.

"Sorry," she said. "I feel bad now."

I tilted my head and looked at her. "Bad? Why?"

She laughed again. "I actually just fetched the book to rip a page out to give you my mobile number."

My eyes widened in shock, and not because she was going to give me her number. I wasn't that retarded. "Sacrilege!"

Clare looked embarrassed, and I smiled to let her know I was teasing. It was her turn to blush.

"I'm joking, Clare. It's your book. You can rip out as many pages as you want." I offered it back to her, and she deliberated before taking it.

"I couldn't do it now. I'd feel like I was destroying a piece of history."

"One tick." I turned and ran back to my car, leaving her standing there. Less than a minute later, I was back, holding out a business card. "You can write your mobile number on the back of that." She opened her mouth to speak, but I was prepared. Lifting my hand, I waggled another card. "And you can take this one to keep."

A grin split her face, and she tried to pull the card from my hand. However, I copied her previous stunt and held on to it, tugging it back before finally releasing it. Lame, I know. But Clare thought it was amusing, so who gave a shit if I was a moron? I didn't.

"There you go." She handed the card back to me with a wink.

I gasped as I read the words on the small card. It wasn't because she had written her name, mobile, landline, and email address in such a short space of time. It was that Clare had the exact same handwriting as her great aunt.

I lifted my eyes quickly and saw Clare grimacing, as if she was expecting me to say something about the amount of information she'd given me. She must've thought that was why I gasped. It would have been so easy to just explain the reason for my response, but I felt silly. Why would it be important for me to point that out?

"You write like your great aunt." What the fuckity fuck?

Those perfect lips parted, then moved, then closed.

"I just thought..."

"Funnily enough, everyone says I look like her, too."

Damned right she did. And then I wondered if her lips were as soft as Annabel's.

Yeah. As soft as any eighty-five year old woman's lips. I was thankful that thought stayed inside my head. I tried to repress the image of what I had dreamed about—not the actual dream, but the *changed* dream, where Annabel was in her eighties. No good.

A knocking came from behind us, Freddie knocking on the door. Man. It had taken him a while to think of that one.

A look of sheer dismay appeared on Clare's face. "*Shit*! Oh, excuse me."

Was she apologising for saying shit? I would be saying sorry every five minutes if that was the case.

"I..." She looked torn—like she wanted to keep talking to me, but knew she was needed elsewhere. "I'll... Can I?" She cast a thumb over her shoulder, indicating she had to leave.

"Sure, sure, you get going." I started to back away, but she moved towards me, a hint of panic on her face.

"Can you, will you, erm..."

A smile crept onto my face. "Go to him, Clare. I'll wait in my car, and we can make some arrangements, okay?"

I'd been waiting for nearly fifteen minutes for her to come back out of the house, but I wasn't worried. At least it indicated that he hadn't been lying dead on the floor when she got back inside, nor was he likely clasping his chest in agony. To be honest, I didn't quite know if I was pro or con in regards to that last thought.

I kept looking furtively at the house. I didn't want to seem too eager when Clare reappeared, and just sitting in the driver's seat of my Mazda would probably give her the impression that I was desperate. I needed to find something to occupy myself so she might think I was catching up on work, not just hanging around like a sad loser.

I turned around and stretched to retrieve my handbag from where I had thrown it on the back seat when I'd rummaged around for the business cards. The little fucker was an inch shy of being captured, so I continued to do myself an injury by jamming my body through the gap between the front seats. It would have been so much easier to get out of the car and open the back door, but now it had become a mission.

Just as the tips of my fingers touched the strap, I froze. It wasn't because I had pulled a muscle. No. I was getting the distinct impression that I was being watched.

I looked towards the house, half expecting Clare to be grinning at me through the side window of my car, but no one was there. Frowning, I refocused on my target, my middle finger inching under the strap and slowly pulling the handle towards me. Then I felt it again, eyes watching me. Another glance to my left showed the area was still empty, with not even the ghostly figure of Annabel.

I waited a moment, the memories of the first time I had thought I was being watched slipping into my mind. The circumstances had been different, granted. For starters, now it was broad daylight, and I wasn't peeing at the side of the road. That didn't keep the hairs on my arms and at the back of my neck from standing to attention, as if they could somehow stop what was happening.

"Find me."

The voice, an unidentified female voice, came from beside me. It was soft, yet insistent. Even though it had only said two words, each one penetrated to deep inside my core. The blood seemed to stop flowing in my veins, making the sensation even more terrifying. I sensed a patch of coldness pressing against my right side, and I closed my eyes to ready myself for what was about to come.

Releasing the handle of my purse, I slid my body back through the gap between the two front seats, my eyes still firmly shut. I felt a hand touch the small of my back and guide me, but I didn't fear it. This wasn't an ill-intentioned hand, not by a long shot.

The cushion of the driver's seat felt reassuring, but I waited a couple more seconds before opening my eyes. I knew someone was staring at me from the passenger seat. Knew she was waiting for me to grow some balls and turn to meet her gaze.

I swallowed, then swallowed again. My whole body seemed to vibrate, and it wasn't from excitement. To be honest, I wasn't even sure it was from fear, as I knew she wasn't there to hurt me. Somehow I knew she never had, and never would.

Slowly, I turned. Green eyes were expectant, inquisitive, and so very much like my own that it was like looking into a mirror. It was me, but it wasn't me. Shoulder length blonde hair framed her face, her long fringe tucked behind one ear. A half smile played along her lips as she looked me over. She was probably thinking the same thing about me—that we looked alike, I mean.

"Ellen?" I knew I sounded like I'd lost the plot when I said it, but what else could I do?

She nodded, her eyes flicking shut rapidly, slowly. That didn't make sense to me, but that's how it appeared.

What does a person say to a ghost? I know mediums wail out, "Is there anybody there?" when they are trying to make contact, but what came next? "How's the weather where you are?" or "What's it like being dead?"

I went with stating the obvious. "You're dead." Not the best way to start a conversation, I knew that. But I was feeling the pressure.

Ellen smiled at me. Even she knew I was a twat, and we'd only just met. I usually can fool people for a little longer than that, but there was no fooling those green eyes.

"Did he kill you?"

The smile completely faded and was replaced by fear. Her hand raised, and she pointed at the house.

Why didn't she answer me? She had spoken when I wasn't looking at her, so why not now?

I turned to where she was pointing and saw Clare outside with her granddad. She was helping him down the steps, her focus not on him but on me. She looked concerned, as if she knew there was something happening inside my car but couldn't make out what it was.

Could she see Ellen? Was she wondering why there were two of "me" inside the car? Or was she just thinking about why I was still waiting.

"You belong with her."

Ellen's voice broke through my mental confusion, and I jumped. I turned back to her, but there was nothing there. The empty seat looked innocently vacant, as if no one had been there. Whiteness caught my eye, and I spotted a small card sitting on the seat, waiting to be discovered. I tentatively reached out to pick it up, even though I knew it was my own business card, the one I'd given to Clare. There was something different, though, something added: *To you, from me. x E x.*

"Fuck." The word slipped from my lips in disbelief. How had that happened? Ghosts didn't write messages did they? I thought when people talked about a ghost writer, it meant something completely different, not fucking ghosts *actually* writing!

Tap.

The noise at the window was my undoing. "FUCK!" I grimaced as I saw Clare's expression change to shock. "Sorry... I..." Was I apologising for swearing, as she had? No. I was apologising for frightening the crap out of her.

Clare mimed the action of rolling down the window, and I complied immediately.

"Everything okay?" She leaned forward, her head poking inside the car, and the scent of her shampoo drifted in and engulfed my senses. "I saw you talking to someone..."

She saw me talking to Ellen! Thank fuck for that! My relief was short lived.

"And I didn't want to disturb you while you were on the phone."

Phone? What phone? Shit. Exactly. She thought I was talking to someone because she could see me engaged in something that looked like a conversation, although it had been rather truncated.

Was now the right time to tell her that I had been seeing her bloody relatives for the last two days, had even made dream love with one of them?

"You look a little pale. You okay?"

Not really, no. I'd just been sitting next to a woman who had been dead for sixty years and could've been my twin. I think that could have been a factor in my pallor. Actually, I was surprised I was still lucid.

"Clare! Come on."

Freddie Howell was shouting from her car, and I could feel my hackles rise.

"I've got to get back!" he added.

"I'll be there in be a minute, Granddad." She looked at me apologetically. "Sorry, Rebecca. He wants to get back to the home. Too many memories for him here."

I bet there were, and none of them good.

"I was thinking..." Her eyes shifted nervously around the inside of my car before briefly landing on my hands.

A smile crept over her face, and I realised she had noticed the business card I was holding. "You were thinking?" I prodded.

Sparkling brown eyes looked into mine, and I was transfixed. It was as if I could see right inside her.

"I'll be heading out as soon as I've got Granddad settled." Her voice was gloriously addictive, soft and rich and full.

"And?" My tone lowered suggestively.

"How about we meet for lunch?" She paused and I waited for her to continue, which she did. "There's a lovely pub on Adam's Road, not far from here."

Another pause, and her eyes seemed to be prompting me for an answer. I was too occupied with staring at her to comprehend the message.

"Erm... The Blue Bell Inn?"

God. She was beautiful. So perfectly beautiful.

"Or maybe not?" she added hesitantly.

It sort of drifted into my subconscious as she was pulling her head out of my window. Reaching out, I grabbed her and pulled her back until her face was mere inches from mine. "I'd love to."

Being so close to her, within kissing distance, I wanted to bridge the small gap between us. Take the initiative and brush my lips over hers. Luxuriate in the softness I knew would be waiting for me.

I licked my lips in anticipation, and she did the same. Claire's eyes flitted to my mouth and then back to my eyes. I could see she wanted to kiss me too. I couldn't miss it, just like she couldn't miss the fact I wanted to kiss her. Considering neither of us had actually said we were gay, it was a huge assumption, but one I was sure of.

Her face moved closer to mine, and her eyes fluttered shut. I knew it was coming, and that the sensation would be magical, what I had been waiting for my whole life.

"Clare!"

The old bastard!

Clare's eyes shot open and she rapidly pulled back, cracking her head on the top of the doorframe in her hasty retreat. "Shit. Sorry."

I hoped she was apologising for swearing and not for nearly kissing me. That was one thing I hoped she would never be sorry for.

"I've got to go. About one?" She waited for my nod, then smiled. "See you there."

She walked backwards, her eyes fixed on mine. I couldn't seem to tear my eyes away from her, either, even after she'd gotten into her car.

Minutes later, she was driving past me. I held up my Sat Nav to show her I was finding directions for The Blue Bell Inn, and she gave me a thumbs up before mouthing, "One."

I nodded and held up a single digit.

Freddie glared at me, his eyes full of hatred, and I fully expected him to stick his middle finger up as the car passed, but he was using all of his energy to try and intimidate me. It might have worked when he was twenty, but I had a feeling I would be fine now that he was in his eighties.

I snorted. I couldn't believe I was thinking about an old man like that. Not even in my wildest dreams had I ever thought about hurting another human being, never mind someone who could barely walk unassisted.

"Turn left."

The disembodied voice from my lap made me jump, and I dropped the useless piece of shit that was my Sat Nav.

"I've got to turn around first, Susan." I tried to act cool, but my hand was shaking as I stuck the oblong device onto my windscreen. Considering all I had experienced of late, I was surprised I was unnerved by a mere piece of electronics.

The engine roared to life, and I pressed the accelerator to give it another kick. I slammed the gear into reverse, my attention fully engaged on the action of backing up. There were a few bushes knocking about, and I didn't want to drive into them.

As I was looking back, Annabel's house seemed lost, so old and deserted that I felt a pang of sadness wash through me. I knew deep down that she had waited all her life in the hopes that Ellen would come back. It was never to be. How sad was that? How desperately heart breaking?

But...I'd met Clare. A grin split my face as I moved the car forwards. I needed to reverse again, as the area I'd parked in was not as big as I'd first thought. Instead of moving back, I put my handbrake on. I still had two and a half hours before I had to meet Clare, so I wasn't in a hurry. I decided to sit and try to make sense of what had happened, past and present.

Had Freddie found out about the affair between Ellen and Annabel? If so, why just kill Ellen? Why didn't he do anything to Annabel? I tipped my head in thought. It could have been because by killing Ellen, he would also effectively be killing his sister.

Fuck. I knew things like that did happen in the world. People did evil and wicked things to other people for many different reasons, too many reasons to list. But to kill someone because she loved someone else? What had happened to acceptance, understanding? Even letting the person they professed to love be happy without them?

I'm not saying it wouldn't hurt to know he wasn't her one and only; the agony of being second best would cut deep. But murder? Yes, I understand that things can get out of control, that sometimes things are said and done that we wish we could take back. But to take a life? To see the light fade from the eyes of someone he said he loved? No. I couldn't understand that, and I didn't think I ever would. Granted, I had never been in that situation, never had someone I loved with my all tell me that I wasn't good enough, so who was I to judge?

There was one thing I knew for sure, and that was that I would never hurt Clare. Clare? Why was I linking the thought of someone being my all to a woman I had known for an hour at most?

A sigh released some of the pressure I hadn't noticed building in my chest. I would be lying if I said I wasn't attracted to Clare Davies, really attracted to her. But... *my all*? I think I was jumping the gun a bit with that thought, although there was a little voice trying to disagree with me coming from somewhere inside me.

It was time for me to leave. Better to be early to meet Clare. With my travel history, better yet would be to get to The Blue Bell without getting lost.

I slipped the car into reverse, released the handbrake, and moved backwards. My mind was elsewhere. My thoughts were all over the place. I found this out the hard way.

I didn't look ahead of me as I put the car into first gear and began to move forward. Why would I? I was on the driveway on my own. It wasn't as if I was on the road, was it?

There he was—tall, dark, and in front of my car. His dark brown eyes widened as I lurched towards him, my feet slamming onto the brake and the clutch at the same time. The car skidded and pitched forward just enough to thud into him. Hands splayed over my car bonnet and he fell forward, his face contorted with surprise and pain. I lifted my hands from the steering wheel, for what reason, I don't know. I think I screamed, but I'm not sure.

He slipped from the front of my car, and I saw him collapse in front of my bumper, heard the distinct crunch of a body hitting gravel.

No! I couldn't have killed him, not at that speed. It should've barely affected him, not made him slump to the ground.

I covered my mouth to hold back the sobs. I felt the blood drain from my face as I tried to decide what to do. I hadn't even moved into second gear. The practical side of my mind insisted that someone was trying to get me out of the car, someone who wanted to hurt or rob me or both. That's what it had to be.

But his face. That face didn't make me think of a trickster, a robber, a thief. It had been the face of someone who had hurt me and who had been hurt by me.

Turning the engine off, I unclipped my seatbelt and tried to peer out of my windows. I couldn't see anything, not even a splayed arm peeping out. He must've fallen slap bang in front of my car. I considered reversing to take in the scene, but that could hurt him even more, as I didn't know exactly where he was.

As I reached for the door handle, an image of the man's face appeared again. Dark brown eyes filled with pain, or surprise. Or *was* it pain and surprise I saw? I wasn't so sure now. It could've been something else, something a little more in keeping with what had happened. Anger, maybe. I would have been angry too, if some stupid bitch had mowed me over on a driveway.

But back to the eyes. I knew them, fucking knew them.

No. No no no. It wasn't Freddie Howell. It couldn't be Freddie Howell. I'd just seen him being driven away in the passenger seat of Clare's car. Ghosts were dead people, weren't they?

Decision made, I opened the car door and stepped out, my foot crunching on the gravel. I edged my way around to the front of the vehicle, my stomach clenching in rhythm with my heartbeat.

I didn't know quite how to feel when the ground in front of the car was empty—no slumped man, nothing but weeds and gravel. It had appeared so real, felt so real. I could visualise the moment clearly—his expression, the impact of a body hitting the bonnet, the sound of weight hitting the ground. But though I could relive it, that didn't necessarily mean it had actually happened, did it?

I propped my backside on the hood of the car. Was I going mad? I looked about me, taking in my surroundings. It was quiet, deserted. It didn't look as if anyone had been there for years. My attention focused on the ground in front of me as I stared at the spot where I believed there should have been a man, a man named Freddie Howell.

I cast my mind back two nights to when I had been driving down the deserted roads, completely lost. Finding this place had been like coming upon an oasis. But ever since then, my world had been tipped upside down. Dreams of running, of fear, of trying to escape; dreams of being loved, being wanted; waking to find bruises; hearing voices; seeing fucking dead people everywhere I looked.

I scraped my fingertips down my face, as if the movement would wake me up from this life. That's when it hit me. Did Clare actually exist! Or was she part of this screwed up world I found myself in?

Jumping from the bonnet, I then rushed to the door and leaned over the seat. There was nothing there—no card, no handwriting, no email or phone numbers. I leaned back out to suck in some much needed air.

Fuck. And fuck. And what the fuck?

I leaned back inside the car and rummaged down the side of the seat, but found nothing. Tears filled my eyes, and I knew I was on the verge of losing it. "It has to be here. It has to be." A sob broke free. So much had happened, so bloody much, but I couldn't bear to think that I had imagined Clare Davies.

I stopped my search and slumped down onto the ground. My tears fell unchecked. I didn't care who saw me. If someone else was here, he or she would probably be in my screwed up imagination.

I must've cried for solid ten minutes, quite a short amount of time considering I had just realised I had lost the plot. Sniffling, I wiped my face with my hands, rubbing my cheeks to motivate the blood to move around my body.

It was time to go home, to get back in the car and drive back to Norwich. A shaky laugh slipped from my mouth. "No wonder you lived in Wells." It was probably because my imagination couldn't think of anywhere else to locate my dream woman.

I'd been working a lot of hours. I'd been here, there, and everywhere in a short span of time, but it was part and parcel of the job. I knew I'd not been sleeping or eating well, that I'd been closing myself off from friends and family by saying I was too busy to see them. Had that all finally resulted in this?

When I stood, I felt slightly lightheaded, so I steadied myself against the side of my car. I took a couple of deep breaths, and just before I got inside, my mobile sounded, the ring stark and shrill in the desolate setting.

Galvanized, I opened the back door, grabbed my handbag, and rummaged through the junk inside. Thankfully, I got to my phone before the caller hung up.

"Rebecca?"

The voice seemed echoey, as if I was on speaker phone. Instead of speaking, I grunted.

"Sorry to call, but I didn't know what else to do."

I heard the sound of a turn indicator and knew the person calling was driving.

"It's okay," she said to someone other than me, or so I assumed. "We're nearly there."

"Excuse me, who is this?" I knew the voice, but I didn't have a clue what she was talking about.

"It's Clare."

As in, my imaginary Clare?

"Granddad has had a turn, and I'm taking him to the hospital."

Hospital?

"I doubt I'll be able to make it by one."

Granddad has had a turn? A turn?

"Rebecca, are you still there?"

"Yes. Erm...yes."

"Can we say later?"

I felt some of the heaviness lift from me. Maybe I wasn't losing the plot after all. I grimaced as I thought about all that had happened. Or maybe I was still losing the plot, and it had become more digitally advanced.

"Rebecca? Can you still hear me?"

"Yes. Yes. We can meet later. Or..." I had to find out once and for all if I was imagining this. "I could meet you at the hospital instead." The line went quiet for a moment. Expecting a knock back, I gritted my teeth.

"Have you got a pen?" A grin split my face. "And a piece of paper?"

"Sure. Wait up." Digging through my pockets for a pen, instead I found a card. A business card. The same business card I had searched the interior of my car for and then broke down in tears because I thought I was going mad. I kissed the card and slipped it back into my pocket. "Just tell me the address. I've a good memory."

Although a slightly fucked up one, by all lights.

Chapter Five

Nearly an hour later, I was parking in the car park at the Royal Derby Hospital. I could have been there sooner if the bloody Sat Nav hadn't sent me the wrong way, nearly into the centre of town.

As I approached the entrance, I saw a familiar person standing outside. She was even more beautiful than I remembered, although a little pale. I felt my heart kick start all over again, and it wasn't just because Clare was flesh and blood.

"Hey, Clare. How is he?" I didn't give a flying fuck about Freddie Howell, but that's not what one says to the man's granddaughter, is it?

Her face brightened when she heard my voice. "I thought I'd lost him at one point, but he's fine now." Her tears were threatening to spill over, and I placed my arm around her and pulled her close to me. Clare clutched at me and pulled me closer still, a sob slipping from her.

"Come on, he's a tough one. He'll be okay." I was amazed that the words didn't scald my tongue on their way out.

Clare lifted her head and looked into my eyes. The sheen of tears made hers even more striking than usual, and I leaned forward as if I was being pulled.

This was not the time to kiss her. Not just because I didn't know her that well, but it would have been taking advantage of the situation—her feeling fragile and vulnerable after what had happened to her granddad. However, a small part of me thought that if I did kiss her, maybe I could verify that this meeting was actually taking place and wasn't just another chapter in my mental breakdown.

No. That wasn't the done thing, was it—to kiss someone in part to check your sanity?

Soft lips met mine, and my mind went blank. The only thing that mattered was the feel of her mouth. We were only gently kissing, but I could feel the connection to her in every fibre of my being. If this was what it was like to be going mad, I would willingly lose my mind for her, lose my all for her.

Clare drew back, the redness of her lips stark against the paleness of her skin. "Sorry, I—"

"Shush." I placed my finger over her mouth, forestalling any apology for what had just happened between us. I smiled up at her, shyness in my admission, "I wanted it too."

The pallor of her face blossomed into a beautiful blush, and my heart skipped a beat. How on earth had I ever believed she was a figment of my imagination? There was no way I could dream this.

"Good."

The word was spoken softly, but its intention seeped deep within me.

She stood straighter, seemed to collect herself. "I've got to get back to check on Granddad in an hour, but maybe we could grab some lunch?"

I grinned widely. "I'd love to."

Clare slipped her arm through mine and turned me towards the entrance. After a couple of steps, she stopped and looked down at me. "And over lunch, you can tell me how you knew my great aunt."

Fuck.

I mumbled a reply, but I couldn't say exactly what it was.

I'd been driving for over four and a half hours. Four and a half bloody hours. It wouldn't have been so bad if I hadn't have left a beautiful woman standing in a hospital car park waving me off, but I had. The journey should have taken me all of three and a half hours, but traffic was bad, though for once, I didn't get lost.

I didn't want to leave Clare, didn't want to say goodbye so soon after finding her, but she insisted. Freddie had to stay in hospital overnight for observation, and she wasn't going to leave until he got the all clear. Trust him to put the brakes on what could be a budding romance.

Funnily enough, that was the reason why he'd ended up in the hospital in the first place.

"Do you know what Granddad said about you?"

Clare's voice held a hint of humour, but I had a feeling I wouldn't be seeing the funny side of any comment Freddie Wife Killer might have made. "Hmm. Something along the lines of me being a bit of a catch?"

Clare laughed. "Not quite. He doesn't even know I'm gay."

My eyebrows raised in surprise and I noted that Clare blushed slightly.

"It has nothing to do with anyone else who I sleep with."

"If you say so."

Clare's head spun around, her mouth half open and ready to retort, but thankfully she recognised I was only pulling her leg.

"Yes, I do say so. My love life is my business."

I wanted to add that I was hoping to make it mine, too, but decided to keep my gob shut for a change.

"What he said was more along the lines of you looking like a shifty character and me being wary of you leading me astray."

I clamped my lips together with such force that the clack of my teeth was audible. Cheeky bastard.

Clare leaned closer, her hand touching my arm. "It has nothing to do with you. I told him in no uncertain terms that my life has nothing at all to do with him."

I was beginning to see that Clare liked to keep her life at a distance from her granddad's, and given my growing knowledge of Freddie Howell, I didn't blame her one whit.

"What did he say to that?" Just saying that sentence hurt, as I had to hold back what I wanted to say, which included him being a lying, murdering bastard who was a hundred times more dangerous than a shifty character. Even if I was one. Which I wasn't.

Clare's face scrunched, as if she was trying to work something out. "I'm not too sure what he meant."

"By?"

"Well, he went quiet and then spluttered something like 'done it once,' then promptly passed out again." Clare turned to me, the frown disappearing behind a wonderful smile. "But let's not worry about that, yes?"

Though Clare had no idea of what he meant, I certainly did, but I nodded anyway.

Obviously he wanted to stop us from starting. He hadn't been able to stop the relationship his wife had with his sister, but he had taken care of them as soon as he did find out about it. That was assuming that he knew about the affair between Annabel and Ellen, which I believed he did.

Welcome to Norwich. A Fine City. The sign lit up like a beacon, but instead of feeling happy that I was just about home, for some fucked up reason I wanted to cry.

Fifteen minutes later I was pulling into my driveway. The house looked cold and dark and totally uninviting. Nothing new there.

I got out of the car and stretched, and the muscles groaned back into place. I needed a hot bath and an early night, in that order. Tomorrow would come soon enough, and I still had notes from my meetings to copy.

Immediately after I finished my bath, I was in bed. The last few nights I had gone without much sleep, and I was shattered.

I don't know how long I had been asleep before the dreams began. Too many images, too many sounds and emotions—too much of everything. Everything mishmashed together and made no sense whatsoever. I wanted to get things in order, to tell those sounds and images to get in line and wait their turn, but it didn't happen. The dreams turned more frantic.

I could feel hands around my throat, strong hands, capable hands. They were applying pressure, taking pressure away, applying it again. In my dream I was becoming weaker, losing the fight, drifting away from life into something dark and unwelcoming.

"Ellen!"

The voice was female. Female, not male.

"Look at me, Ellen!"

I tried to open my eyes, tried to look at the person who had her hands around my throat.

So very brown and beautiful and deep and dark, her eyes looked into mine, quizzical brown eyes framed by long lashes. They showed confusion, as if what they were seeing wasn't real. My own eyes fluttered closed, the effort of keeping them open too much for me.

"Please. Don't. Look at me." The voice was frantic, almost as if it wasn't quite sane.

I wanted to tell her to let me go, let me sleep, let me drift away, but I couldn't. The pressure on my windpipe was killing me. I could feel her tugging, pulling, sobbing, but I couldn't help her.

Coated in sweat, I sat up in bed, my hands clawing at my throat, a choking cough spluttering from within. It was like I was taking my first breath after being under water. My heart was hammering in my chest, and I wondered if I was having a heart attack.

"Shit!" I rasped. I was shaking, and my body ached as if I'd been beaten.

I struggled out of bed and staggered to the bathroom, my balance all over the show. I was like a pinball, bouncing off the furniture.

I clicked the switch, and bright light illuminated the room around me as I stumbled to the mirror over the sink. A dark mark circled my neck, almost as if a cord or a rope had been tied around it. I tentatively touched my throat, and the pain that comes with a recent injury shot through me.

Images and noises from my dream flooded into my head, and sickness washed over me.

Annabel had been there. I'd seen her, heard her. Annabel had been the one who had her hands around my throat. I felt again those hands applying pressure, then releasing it before increasing the pressure again. The sensation of losing the fight to live, the weakening of my body, the wanting to give in and let the blackness take me seemed real, even now that I was awake. And there was Annabel's voice demanding that I look at her in a voice that seemed not quite sane.

Had Annabel killed Ellen? No. She loved Ellen. I knew that. She wanted to be with her, move away and live with her, start fresh with her and Bella.

The memory of my dream making love to Annabel popped into my head. "I'm not like him am I? You know, with my anger?" The words echoed in my mind, took on new implications.

No. Annabel wasn't like her brother. She loved Ellen. She would do anything for Ellen. Ellen knew this, she'd said so. She'd told me in a dream that even though Annabel and Freddie might look alike, that's where the similarity ended.

As in the aftermath of the dream I'd had in the hotel, I slumped to the floor. It was too much. My brain was hurting, and so was my heart.

My own thoughts from the previous day came back to haunt me. Why would anyone want to hurt another because someone didn't feel the same way they did? But Ellen did feel the same as Annabel. I knew that. I also knew that emotions could get out of control, that sometimes things were said and done in anger that we all wished we could take back.

Had Ellen died because she'd decided to stay with her husband after all? Had she decided that a life of shame living with another woman in the Fifties was not worth it?

No. Ellen wanted so much to be with Annabel, she would have coped with the stares and disapproval of society, wouldn't she?

The coldness of the floor was beginning to chill me, either that or the chill was from the thoughts I was having. I wanted to put it all down to a bad dream, but I couldn't shake it off.

Pulling myself to my feet by grabbing hold of the sink, I turned one last time to look into the mirror. The mark seemed angry, dark and threatening. I leaned closer, looked harder. Faint lines of whiteness were visible among the purple and red splotches, and I lifted my head so the bathroom light could better illuminate them.

I reined in my imagination and tried to concentrate. I had felt hands on my throat. Hands. Fingers and hands. There were no finger marks on my neck, just the signs of a rope or cord. I hadn't linked it to the other sensation in my dream, maybe because the thought of being strangled had become my sole focus when my life was being sucked out of me.

Annabel had been frantic, her voice pleading, her expression confused and slightly insane, true. But the pressure had been intermittent, almost as if she was untying something. Her desperate, *"Please. Don't. Look at me"* could've been because she had been trying to resuscitate Ellen not kill her.

My eyes widened. Fuck. And double and treble that fuck. Had Annabel found Ellen and tried to save her, but then Ellen had died anyway?

Questions swamped me. Questions about why Ellen would have been bound by a rope in the first place. Had she done it herself? Did Freddie try to hang her? Had Annabel used a rope and then became sane enough to see what she was doing was wrong?

No. Annabel had tried to save Ellen. I could feel it.

There were a couple of other things to consider. Where was Ellen's body? And if Annabel was involved, why was she still waiting for Ellen to turn up? The latter could have been denial, the inability to accept losing the one she loved. Or, perhaps Annabel Howell had been haunted by Ellen's spirit.

I had joked earlier about not being Catherine Earnshaw tapping on the glass in the kitchen window, but what if that tapping had happened to Annabel as well as me? If it could happen once, I was sure it could happen again. Though that did seem rather farfetched.

My head was hurting. I couldn't think straight. My brain was conjuring images of lost souls wandering in the night looking for their true love, a true love that either killed them or tried to save them.

It was bedtime. I imagined that sleep would not come, and that I would stew over things until I could make some sense of what had happened, and that might never come.

As I sat on my bed, I noticed something white on my bedside table. It was the business card that had Clare's information. I hadn't put it there. I'd put it safely in the small inside pocket in my handbag. I wasn't worried; it didn't freak me out. I'd come to expect things like that to happen to me. I mean, waking up from a dream in which a dead woman was trying to strangle you made a small card appearing next to your bed pale in comparison.

I picked up the card and read the contact numbers and email. Why this? Why now? I wondered. I tapped the card against my palm and tried to think it through.

The company logo caught my attention—*Jonson's Stationery.* So? Why would I be focused on that?

I read through my name and contact numbers, trying to make the connection. What would stationery have to do with anything? I scrunched up my face and tried to make myself think harder. Not an easy feat. Bam. Like a bolt of lightning, it came to me.

Stationery. I did stationery; that was my bag. I was a boring fucker who knew all about stationery. So much so, I had commented on the notebook Clare had been holding—Annabel's book, the one with the small, neat handwriting and Ellen's dedication to her. The notebook with pages and pages filled with thoughts, ideas, events.

A grin split my face, and I leaned back onto the pillows. I knew what I had to do, why I'd become embroiled in everything. It wasn't just because I looked like Ellen. It wasn't even so that I would meet Clare Davies. I don't think it was even because someone, somewhere was testing my sanity. The key was connecting the things I'd dreamed about with the contents of *that* book. I was the link, the pivotal person who was to find out what had happened, and maybe even find the remains of Ellen Howell. No wonder Freddie hated me and thought I was a bad news.

It was time to get to sleep. I was no longer worried about what I would dream about, I actually welcomed it. It would add to the store of knowledge I had already gained.

Tomorrow I would call Clare and make arrangements for us to meet. I would ask her to bring the book, and tell her that I had something to share with her, as well. I hadn't yet told her how I knew her great aunt. I'd waffled on about shite for an hour. Maybe if I told her first what I knew, she wouldn't think I was a crackpot. Initially she might think I was mad, but I hoped she'd get past that. I grinned stupidly. "Or maybe not."

I snuggled further under the covers. I had to get some rest; tomorrow was going to be a busy day. A woman needs her rest, especially when she has a murder to solve.

When I closed my eyes, I saw brown orbs dancing on the inside of my eyelids. Soft, gorgeous brown eyes. The eyes of Clare Davies.

A sigh of contentment slipped through my lips. My last conscious thought was, *I hope I dream about her.*

And I did. How wonderfully magical is that?

Part 2

"Heaven did not seem to be my home; and I broke my heart with weeping to come back to earth; and the angels were so angry that they flung me out into the middle of the heath on the top of Wuthering Heights; where I woke sobbing for joy."

Emily Bronte

Chapter Six

I called Claire on the Sunday, but she seemed harried. She said she didn't know when she'd be home, but she would call me. Me being me, I thought it was a knock back, a nice way of telling me either to back off or fuck off. I made the cringing face as I clicked off the phone and wanted to curl up and die of embarrassment.

It wasn't just about me and my attraction to Clare, it was about Ellen and Annabel and so much more. To be perfectly honest, it was all those things. I wanted to get to know Clare, and not just as a friend. I wasn't an idiot. Well, I was, but that was by-the-by. I presumed that my attraction to her must be a lot stronger than hers to me. Yes, she kissed me outside the hospital, but I was hoping for something more deeply rooted than a quick kiss. Bottom line was, I felt an inexplicable connection with her; I wasn't sure that Clare felt the same.

Weirdly enough, nothing supernatural had happened since the night I'd gotten back from the convention circuit. The troubling dreams were absent and, in an odd way, I missed them. Not the choking one, obviously, but I missed the connection to Annabel and Ellen. I realised that even though I had desired Annabel in my dream, it was not me who was feeling that. Yes, I'd woken with the sensation of hands around my throat and a rope mark around my neck, but it wasn't me who had actually lived that experience.

I knew that was well and truly fucked up. If bruises and an inability to breathe didn't equate to being the "chosen one," I didn't know what did.

Aw, bugger it.

Clare emailed me on Wednesday. As it turned out, Freddie was kept in hospital for three days. Then she hadn't wanted to leave him when he was discharged, so she stayed with him in the home.

You can imagine the epithets tumbling from my mouth when I read that snippet. I bet he was in his element. Bastard. Old bastard at that.

The great news was that she also wrote that she would love to meet up on Saturday, if I was free. It had just barely hit my inbox when I read it, clicked reply, and tried not to sound like a lovesick fool, or, worse still, a stalker. I don't think I've ever replied to an email as quickly in my life. When I checked my mail a few moments later, it gave me a wonderful feeling to find she had replied with the same enthusiasm. I pressed Refresh over and over and over again, so many times that I think Hotmail was relieved when I just sat and stared, dreamy eyed, at the words.

Saturday came around too bloody slowly. I really wished I had arranged to meet her earlier than one o'clock, but a person doesn't usually have lunch at nine in the morning, do they? Maybe if I hadn't got out of bed at the crack of dawn, it might have been a little easier on my nerves.

I arrived in Wells just before twelve and wandered around the small seaside town for a while. It was bloody freezing. And when I say freezing, I mean it was raining like a bitch and the wind from the seafront was cold enough to freeze the tits off a witch. I tried to brave it, but I couldn't. I lasted all of twenty minutes before returning to sit in my car, soaked through and bedraggled. Apart from the bits that were slapped flat onto my head by the pounding rain, my hair stuck out in all directions. I thanked the Lord I hadn't decided to put a little makeup on, as it would now be smeared all over my face and I would have looked like an extra from the *Rocky Horror Picture Show*.

A look in my rear view mirror confirmed that I definitely looked like a drowned rat. I turned on my engine and whipped up the heater. I had to try to dry off, even a little bit, and getting warm wouldn't hurt either.

The car park was only half full, an oddity for Wells, as it was an exceptionally popular place to visit, especially on a Saturday. Once again, I was like Billy-No-Mates as I sat and watched everybody rushing about trying to dodge the rain, whilst I periodically checked the time on my watch, car clock, mobile, iPad, and the town clock. I even started drumming out, "One elephant, two elephants, three," rechecking all my devices and time gadgets every time I got to ten elephants. Sad, but very, very true.

It was about ten to one when something caught my attention and made me lose count. Just in the doorway to the public toilets stood a figure that I initially thought was using it as a place to shelter. I could see a shoulder, then dark hair above the indistinct face that was peeking from the doorway of the Ladies loos. I was amazed to see the shoulder was covered only in a jumper, no jacket. Granted, some people did tend to leave off the coat until there were six inches of snow on the ground, but it just seemed odd. Odd enough that I turned off my engine and stepped out of the car to tentatively make my way over to the doorway.

I was about five feet away when a hand emerged from the doorway and beckoned me forward. I froze, and not just because I was freezing and pissed wet through, either. Why would someone be summoning me into a bloody public convenience, of all places? Had the person seen me looking over and now wanted to do "unmentionables" with me in one of the cubicles? Did that actually happen between women?

That thought was quickly replaced by, "If it *is* a woman." Just because the figure had long hair, a slender, feminine hand,

and was hanging about near the Ladies loos didn't mean it was a female. Charles Manson had long hair, but I think I would have heard about him breaking out of Corcoran State Prison, catching a flight to Blighty, hitching a lift to Wells, and finding a public toilet to wait in until I turned up, dishevelled, wet, and very suspicious.

I laughed nervously. I was being daft. Again. It might have been a—

"*Rebecca.*"

...a person who knew my name. In Wells. In the car park toilets. Thankfully, I'd heard nary a hint of a male American accent.

It could have also been a woman who had hissed the word, as if she was talking to an idiot. She must've known me then, because I was, and am, an idiot. But why would she be trying to get me inside the toilets? Was it because it was raining?

Was it Clare? She had dark hair. I shook my head. I was supposed to be meeting Clare outside French's, not in the car park.

I knew I could be quite dense at times, but I couldn't quite figure out why the woman, or man, would be acting all cloak and daggerish if he or she knew me.

Stepping forward, I peered at the doorway to try to see who it was. The figure moved backwards, deeper into the shadows. That was the moment I should have turned and fled, but no. I had to act like the victims in nearly every horror film I had ever seen in my life—I ignored the warning sounding in my brain. I stepped forward. Stopped. Started again.

I couldn't see clearly, as the rain was running into my eyes. I should've stopped, should've decided that I really didn't need to know who was loitering with intent, but I was a woman after all.

Inside the toilets, it was darker than it should've been for not quite one in the afternoon. It was raining, and the sun was a stranger in Wells that day, but it was still darker than I'd expected. I couldn't see anyone, male or female, just inside the short hallway near the entrance, but instead of deterring me, that made me even more curious. I took a step forward. A soft scraping noise stopped me in my tracks, but despite the fact that I am not the bravest woman in the world, I decided to proceed.

There were three cubicles. The doors on the two closest to me stood wide open, but the door to the one at the end was partially closed. The sound of my footsteps echoed off the porcelain and tile as I cautiously walked to the end stall. Even as I reached out a hand, I knew I should turn and walk away. My fingers seemed tight, as if they were seizing up, so I flexed and wiggled them to get the blood flowing all the way to the fingertips. My hands were trembling; so was the rest of me. It wasn't until my hand was flat on the door that the shaking stopped, in that one hand at any rate. The churning I felt in my stomach was alive and kicking, and my knees were not the steadiest either.

Fuck.

What was I doing? There I was in a public toilet, just about to open the only closed door in the whole place because I *thought* I saw someone loitering in the doorway, beckoning me closer, and then *thought* I heard them hiss my name.

What if some poor, unsuspecting person was inside having a pee and I shoved open the door to check if there was someone in there? How would I explain that one? "Sorry to intrude, but did you call me?" Nope. Didn't think that would fly.

I lifted my hand from the door and took a step back. This was not my bag. Not at all.

"Rebecca."

The blood in my veins seemed to stop to listen. That voice... God, I knew it! And not just because I had heard it coaxing me inside the loo. The owner of the voice seemed surprised that I was there, even though the reason I was there was because it had led me there, so the surprise bit was a non sequitur. My head was beginning to hurt, but I couldn't drag my eyes away from the closed door. It was shit or bust.

Excuse the reference to bodily functions, especially considering I was standing in the apex of a toilet cubicle.

I gave the door a hard shove and it pinged off the inside wall, exposing a stall that was quite empty, apart from the toilet paper strewn all over the urine spattered floor and the broken toilet seat dangling from the bowl.

What the fu—

"Rebecca?"

I stepped inside, pulled the door back from the wall, and looked behind it. Nothing. Of course. The woman would've had to be thinner than a slice of bread to fit in the space between the door and the wall.

Then I felt a hand, or should I say fingers, touch my arm and pull at me. A scream exploded from my mouth as I made a rush towards the doorway, only to slam straight into a warm body. This scream was muffled by what felt like a jumper. A zip scratched the side my face. A hand gripped me firmly, probably the same hand that had touched me moments before, and I struggled as if my life depended on it. At that instant, I believed it did. I raised a fist to smack my assailant anywhere I could, hoping it would land hard.

But no. My hand was captured easily and held fast. "Whoa, whoa, whoa." The voice sounded surprised. Join the club.

The person holding my arm and my hand had probably gotten a good look at me before tackling me, but I didn't have that luxury. I struggled like a cat in a pillowcase—a strange image, but one that was definitely apt at that moment. I'd just gotten my hand free and was going to thwack my assailant about the head, but stopped when she announced herself.

"Rebecca, stop. It's me—Clare."

"Clare?" I drew back, and she released her grasp on me. My back slapped against the toilet door, and that was the only thing that stopped me slumping to the floor, something I would be forever grateful for after all the pee I had seen swimming around on it.

Her expression was concerned, her hands extended as if to balance me if I should fall. Her hair was soaked and sticking to her face, but the brown eyes were dark and engaging. "What's... what's going on?"

She took a step towards me, but apparently decided better of it. I didn't blame her. I must've looked a sight, and not just because I was rain-soaked. Instead of answering her, I took her hand. Remembering how I had been drawn into the situation in the first place, I wanted to make sure she was real. Feeling her chilled skin against mine made me feel better, more in control, though I couldn't have said why.

Clare gently brushed my wayward hair away from my face, and even that slight touch sent sparks through me. The frantic beating of my heart slowed, as did my panicked breathing. Her hand cupped my cheek and my eyelids fluttered closed, absorbing the sensation. A soft kiss landed on my forehead, and sensation shuddered down my spine. I took a deep breath, inhaling her scent. The smell of her was the final element in the calming process, and I felt as if I could speak without stuttering.

I opened my eyes and luxuriated in looking at her. Clare Davies was so beautiful, so goddamn beautiful that my heart seemed to swell. I licked my lips and then moistened them into action. "Were you in here a moment ago?"

Clare cocked her head, a thing I'd noticed she did quite a lot when she was assessing a person or a situation.

"Before me, I mean."

Clare frowned. "Before you?"

I nodded.

"Nooo." The word was drawn out, as if she was thinking before she continued. "I saw you come in, and I waited outside for a little while. Then," Clare looked over her shoulder as if she thought she might be overheard, "I heard you call my name."

"Me? I called you? No I didn't."

She snorted and released my hand, stepping back to create a gap between us. "I know what I heard." Her usual light tone had an edge to it.

I couldn't understand why she was getting so arsey. "But—"

Clare waved off any explanation. Considering I had barely said anything, that was rather presumptuous.

"I don't know what you're up to, Rebecca, but I don't think this is funny." She spun on her heel and made for the door.

I seemed rooted to the spot, but I knew I had to stop her before she got away. I had a fleeting thought that she was being a little overly dramatic when that behaviour should have been mine. After all, I'd been the one who'd had the crap scared out of her, and in a public toilet of all places.

"Wait!" I called. Seeing that she kept moving, I finally got my backside into gear and went after her.

Thankfully the rain had stopped, but that was the only thing in my favour. Clare was striding across the car park like an athlete from Team GB, and I knew if I didn't run, I would lose her. Yes, I had her mobile number, and everything else to contact her, but if I didn't explain what had happened, I doubted she would pick up her phone or return an email.

"Clare! Please!"

No response, not even a backwards glance. I knew I had screamed in her face, nearly twatted her, and then all but called her a liar, but I still couldn't fathom why she was pissed off. No wonder I was single.

Clare was passing the Ark Royal pub by the time I caught up with her. To say my reception was frosty would be an understatement.

I'd thought I was cold before, but my previous chill was positively scorching compared to the rime she was creating.

"Please believe me, I didn't call you."

Maybe persisting in my denial was not the best way to calm her down, but I was struggling to think of something more persuasive. I grabbed her arm and she flicked it away from her like an irritating bug, her lips tight and her expression inviting an argument.

"It's complicated." That was unfortunately something a person also says to someone just before he or she dumps the other.

"You're telling me." Her voice was low and unexpectedly menacing. "You hover outside the toilets, then slither inside them like you're on a ninja mission."

Ninja?

"Then after *you* call me inside," I let that slide for the moment, "I find you investigating the inside of a toilet cubicle."

That last bit was true, but I hadn't called her in. I didn't know how to respond to her torrent of anger.

"And when I tried to be sure you were okay, you screamed and tried to hit me." She snorted again. "To top it all, you call me a liar. A fucking liar!"

The last bit was loud, loud enough to make people stare in our direction. I cringed and mouthed, "I'm sorry" to them, but that incensed her even more.

"Yeah. Apologise to people you don't even know. What about me? Where's my fucking apology?"

Funny thing was, at that moment I was thinking about how when I had first met her, I thought she had apologised for saying the word "shit." It seemed like we were well suited after all.

"Why are you smiling, Rebecca? Am I funny to you?"

I shook my head vigorously, my mouth opening and closing like an out-of-water goldfish. She turned to leave, and the single word I could manage was, "Clare."

She swung around, her finger jabbing in my direction. "Like that. When you called me, you said it *just* like that." A sarcastic laugh slipped out. "It may be 'complicated' to you, but for me it is quite simple." Clare leaned closer, her face inches from mine. "Goodbye, Rebecca." Clare straightened and turned to go.

I felt as if I had been slapped. Why had Annabel and Ellen worked so hard to get us to meet and then let this happen? In hindsight, it was obvious to me that the woman in the loos had been Annabel. It was probably her who had called for Clare to come inside, although I didn't think Annabel sounded anything like me. Even so, why had she called Clare into the loo? That had fucked everything up between us. I had already been struggling with how to tell Clare about all the weird things that had been happening, but if Annabel was trying to help me out, she was even worse at sorting out problems than I was.

Clare was still walking away, and I was beginning to panic. There was no point racing after her again. That hadn't turned out the last time.

"Annabel sends her love!" She didn't, but I couldn't think of anything else to say. "And Ellen, too!"

Clare halted momentarily, but kept moving away. She'd nearly made it to the corner before I came out with the golden one. "Annabel and Ellen were lovers!"

Clare's head turned and her eyes met mine. If looks could kill, I'd have been six feet under.

I grinned, a very cocky grin. "Your great aunt was a lezza just...like...us!"

Shit. Shit, shit, and shit. Her back went stiff, and she began walking towards me. Scratch that. She was marching back, as if on parade. She was back in Team GB mode. Maybe I'd pushed too far. Maybe outing her was a mistake. She lived in this town, after all, and she might not want people to know she was of the Sapphic persuasion.

"What did you say?"

She must have heard me gulp, but she just stared and waited until I bottled it and had the balls to explain myself. I stood straighter, shoulders back, my attitude returning. "You heard me." The cocky grin was back. I didn't want it to be, but it was. "*This* time, of course." I honestly thought she would go nuts and march off again, but she didn't. She just waited for me to get over myself. My smugness started to slip. "Erm."

"You mentioned Annabel and Ellen being lovers." Clare's eyes were intense. They glowed and sparked enough for me to wonder what was going on in her mind. "How did you know that? No one knows that." The words were whispered in wonderment.

"It's complicated."

Her tongue planted itself firmly inside her cheek, making it bulge, and her eyes narrowed. I waited for her to tilt her head in assessment, but she didn't. She just continued to stare.

"Can we go somewhere else?" I nodded at the smattering of people who were watching us to indicate to Clare we were the centre of attention. It was probably the highlight of their day, as they probably only rarely got to watch two sopping wet lesbians having a spat in broad daylight. Judging by the way Clare purposefully strode back to me, they probably thought there were going to be fisticuffs, lezza style. "Let's find somewhere a little more private."

Thankfully, she didn't leave me hanging. She nodded, and then walked away. Without me. Again. She'd made it to the corner before she turned back to me. "Are you coming, or what?"

With a grin, I followed like a lamb, hoping I wasn't a lamb going to the slaughter.

Chapter Seven

We bought fish and chips and then went to Clare's house, which was a short walk from the car park. The conversation was essentially limited to "Cod or haddock?" and "You want salt and vinegar?" with a bit of a spat about who was going to pay. The friction between us was palpable, and I was definite that if I'd had a knife, I would have been able to gouge huge chunks out of it. It was probably because we were both on edge about what we were going to discuss. We had tacitly agreed to wait until we got back to her house to talk about it. At least that was how I took the silence between us. Given my track record, I was probably wrong. It seemed that I could be in Clare's bad books by speaking or not speaking; it didn't matter which.

She lived about five minutes away from the quay, and I was pleasantly surprised when I saw her home. I don't know why, as I hadn't ever given it a moment's thought. The outside of the house belied the size of it. It looked quite small before I stepped inside, then it seemed to expand to Tardis proportions.

What was it about her family and rustic? I could smell the wood as I stepped in the front door. Dark timbered floors creaked beneath each footfall, only to be silenced by the smattering of haphazardly placed throw rugs. It wasn't like Annabel's, it was more like a fisherman's cottage, but I had to admit it was traditionally set up and eerily like her great aunt's house.

Clare plonked our lunch on the side table in the hallway and took off her coat. "You can hang your coat there," she said, hanging hers up. "It'll dry near the heater."

Before I had the time to say anything, she walked away, carrying our lunch with her.

I don't consider myself childish, not at all. Actually, I consider myself to be very mature. Considering I was thirty-four, I should be. So, I don't really know why I pulled a face, stuck two fingers up in the air, and yammered stupidly in a singy songy voice, "It'll dry off near the heater. My name's Clare, and I'm a twat."

"Did you say something?"

Fuck.

"No. Sorry. I was just shivering myself into warmness." I was quite impressed with my response, although I was still wondering about my behaviour. Clearly it must have been because I'd gotten wet and then had a fright.

By the time I'd joined her in what turned out to be the dining room, Clare had unwrapped our lunches and placed them onto plates. She had left them in the paper, just how I liked them. One should eat fish and chips out of the wrappings; it would be sacrilege to plonk them straight onto the plate.

Clare picked up her plate and went to sit in the armchair near the fire, leaving me to decide whether I should sit in the chair opposite her or at the dining room table. It might not seem like a huge decision, but I was wary about pissing her off even more. I'd been on the receiving end of her wrath for the last forty minutes, and I was hoping that during lunch we could both be a little more civilised.

I grasped the side of the plate and deliberated a moment longer before biting the bullet and moving to sit in the other armchair. I noted that Clare was watching my progress with interest. Seemed an odd thing to note. Maybe it was because I was on red alert for another temper tantrum.

Another funny but not so funny thing was the change in Clare's temperament that I'd witnessed since we met that afternoon in the loo. When I'd met her at her great aunt's house, she had seemed so different, so calm and understanding. I would've never expected her to go off on me just because I said I hadn't called her name. Didn't she realise it could've been anyone that she'd heard? Could've been a friend shouting to her from the car park. It could've even been the weather making noises that appeared to sound very like her name.

That was what I was thinking, but I kept my mouth shut, at least I didn't open it to talk. I did keep opening and closing it to eat my lunch.

I could ramble on about how wonderful the fish and chips were, but they could have tasted like fried shit and I would've eaten them, since eating precluded conversation. The silence also gave me some time to think, as if a week hadn't been enough. It always seemed to happen that way. All that time I'd had to figure out what the dreams and experiences had meant, and how I was going to explain everything to Clare, and there I was scrambling to formulate an opening sentence.

I imagined her expression if I were to say, "I had a dream I had fantastic sex with your great aunt and then your granddad tried to strangle me, or your great aunt tried to strangle me. Or I tried to strangle..." Nope. Not really working. I probably wouldn't even get to the "your granddad" part before I was turfed out on my arse in the centre of Wells.

I had barely scrunched up the chips paper when Clare spoke.

"How do you know about Annabel and Ellen?"

There's nothing like getting straight to the point. I should try it someday.

"I only found out for definite when...when I read Annabel's journal."

Clare stood as she repeated, "When?"

She came over to me, and I looked up at her with an expression of apprehension. A soft smile curved her lips, and I felt that spark ignite inside me. Bloody hormones. Couldn't they understand that this was not the time to get all mushy and romantic?

Clare held out her hand and I stared at it, and then up at her. Was she inviting me to stand? Why? Were we going somewhere? Was I being turfed out after all?

"Paper."

Shit. She was asking for the rubbish, although very rudely, if you asked me. The spark that had ignited seemed to fizzle. Mushy and romantic time, over and out.

I was beginning to wonder why I found her so attractive, even given her soft smile. Attraction is not just about looks; it is so much more than that. When I first saw Clare, I was mesmerised. Was it because she had reminded me of her great aunt, or was it because Clare was so bloody beautiful, so kind, so compassionate? It was different from how I'd felt about Annabel when I'd first met her. With her, I'd focused on the sense of safety she had given me, especially since, at the time, I'd believed I was being hunted like an animal. Her arms around me had almost convinced me that nothing or nobody could hurt me.

I could not honestly say I felt any sense of safety at this moment. Clare was too mercurial. Her moods changed like they were being manipulated by an out of control Swingometer. I didn't like that. Call me old fashioned. I much preferred knowing where I stood and what the triggers to psychotic behaviour were.

I handed her my trash, trying to keep my hand from shaking. This was getting ludicrous. Why on earth was I worried about what Clare would or wouldn't do? She was pissed off, that was all. I had almost hit her, insulted her, and then I called her great aunt, her grandmother, and her all lesbians in the street in front of people who were her neighbours. In retrospect, I would've been pissed off too.

Clare disappeared into the kitchen, and the rattling of cups drifted back through the open doorway. At least I was going to get a warming brew before she unceremoniously kicked me out. That was likely to happen when I started to tell her about the things that had happened to me over the previous week.

A ticking attracted my attention, and I looked for the source. Annabel's clock stood centre stage on the mantelpiece, and I couldn't help but grin. It seemed appropriate for it to be sitting smack bang and pride of place in Clare's house and in full working order. I was surprised I hadn't heard it whilst we were eating our lunch.

"Here you go. Tea. It'll warm you up." The tray Clare balanced in her hands was laden with teacups, sugar, a teapot, and a milk jug.

I stood to help her, but she laughed and nodded for me to sit back down. At least she'd laughed instead of throwing the tray at me. A couple of minutes passed as she was finalising the tea. After she'd poured and I had accepted milk but no sugar, she settled into the seat opposite mine. Déjà vu, only not.

"So, Rebecca." Clare settled back in her armchair, and again I was struck by the similarities between her and her great aunt. Even starting the conversation the same way. "Once again, how do you know about Annabel and Ellen?"

Pity she hadn't stuck to the script that I had playing in my head of when I had been with her aunt, as up to that point it had almost been word perfect to the conversation I'd had with Annabel. At least I would have sounded a little saner. I opened my mouth to answer, but she interrupted. "And no saying 'it's complicated,' either."

I took a sip of tea, winced at the heat of it, swore in my head about the possibility that Clare couldn't be any more like her great aunt if she tried, and placed my cup on the saucer on the small side table.

How the hell should I start? I certainly wasn't going to tell her I found out about them in a dream. That would be stupid, even for me.

"I had a dream about it." Jesus Christ. Please, no! "About your great aunt." Why couldn't I have started with something else, something that didn't sound as if I was a paid extra on a ghost hunting show, or even just a fucking weirdo?

Clare leaned forward and I cringed, expecting her to either laugh or go ape. But she did neither. She just looked interested.

"Well, that's not quite right," I editorialised. Too damned right it wasn't, but I don't know why I said that, either.

Clare's head cocked and she half closed her eyes, as per usual. Why didn't she say something? Anything. She could call me psychotic or delusional. At least it would be a start.

I sighed. "It happened two nights before I met you."

"Thursday?"

At last! A response from her! "Erm...yes." Her question about a bloody day of the week threw me right off what I was saying, as if I even knew what I was going to say next.

She nodded knowingly. "Thursday, 30 October?"

What was her fascination with the date? "Erm... I don't know. I..."

Clare stood up and left the room, and I felt like a knob as I sat there on my own. How could my not knowing the date suddenly make her bugger off? That thought had no sooner whipped through my head than she was back, carrying a calendar.

The sound of frantic flicking of pages filled the silence, and I wondered what the hell she was doing. If she was looking up last week's date, all she had to do was turn back one page, didn't she? It wasn't as if it was that difficult to work it out. All she had to do was take away nine days, though I supposed that the change in the month might be a bugger to—

"The thirtieth." Clare nodded her satisfaction.

Slam. The calendar was closed and tossed to the side. We both stood and watched the trajectory of the calendar, saw it land, skid, and fall off the dining room table to splat skew whiff on the floor.

"I... Why... What..." I drew a deep breath and tried to present an entire thought. "I don't understand. Why are you so interested in the date?"

When Clare returned her attention to me, her eyes seemed to spark. Once again, worry spurted through me.

A grin flashed over her face. "It's complicated."

I supposed I deserved that. She sighed, but it wasn't a sigh that denoted she was pissed off. For a change. It was a wistful sigh, a sigh that said Clare felt quite contented and a little bit smug. It was fascinating to watch her grinning to herself, her eyes never leaving mine. I knew she was waiting for me to challenge her, and if I hadn't been so interested in hearing what was special about the 30th, I would have left her grinning to herself all afternoon.

"Okay, I'll bite. What do you mean by 'it's compl—'"

"That was the day before Ellen disappeared."

I scrunched my face. "But she ran off, didn't she? That's what..."

I didn't believe Ellen had run off, but I wasn't going to say so at that particular moment. All I wanted to admit to was what Clare had originally told me.

"Nope." Clare leaned forward and placed her hand on my knee, her voice excited. "That's what I was told. However..." She froze, as if she had suddenly realised that what she was going to say might sound implausible. "Well, erm...I read it in the journal."

It was my turn to cock my head and assess her. She was a little nervous under my perusal and I didn't blame her, as I was studying her intensely. This was the second time she had hesitated whilst talking about what she knew and its relation to Annabel's journal.

"What?" Her eyebrows lifted as if they were trying to hide in her fringe.

I pursed my lips and made a low whistling noise as I continued to examine her. Clare's face was getting redder and redder, and she was beginning to squirm.

"What? Why are you looking at me as if I'm lying?"

Fuck. Not the "calling me a liar" scenario all over again. It was about time one of us had the balls to say something instead of skirting around the edges. I decided it would be me.

"You've seen her, haven't you?" Brown eyes opened wide, and I knew I was right. "Which one—Annabel or Ellen?"

"Ellen? Why would I see Ellen?"

Annabel it was then. I stood up and pulled my chair closer to Clare's. Even though I could see she was on edge, she didn't shift away.

"Today, when you said you heard me calling you, it wasn't me."

Clare rolled her eyes and opened her mouth to retort.

"Please listen to me. I know it sounds really fucked up." She closed her mouth and made a zipping motion. "It wasn't me that called you, it was Ellen."

I was convinced that it had to have been Ellen, although I wasn't convinced Ellen was my voice double. Annabel sounded way too different from me for it to have been her.

This was the moment of truth, the moment when I thought she would lose the biscuit and maybe punch my lights out. She didn't do either. She just sat there staring with that wide-eyed expression and her mouth slightly open.

"I met your great aunt a week last Thursday." There, it was. Out. Sitting in the air like a dare. Clare said nothing. "I was lost. Saw the lights on at the house and stopped to ask for help." Still no reaction. "Annabel invited me inside, gave me a cuppa. Let me stay the night."

A sigh hissed from Clare's mouth. "My great aunt is dead, Rebecca."

Funnily enough, Clare didn't make the assertion with much conviction. What she had said were mere words—empty, flat, unbelieved words.

I slipped my hand into hers. She didn't pull hers away, so I squeezed it reassuringly. "At the time, I didn't know that she was...not living. I didn't find that out until I met you on Saturday morning."

The clock sounded loud now. Each tick was challenged by each tock, as if they were vying for importance. If it hadn't been for that, the room would have been screaming silence, and I would have been back to counting elephants—especially the huge elephant in the room that we were both too scared to address.

"I did wonder how you knew her." Her voice seemed to reverberate around the room, though she had spoken quietly. "My great aunt didn't socialise, didn't make friends easily. She lived the remainder of her life nearly a recluse."

I nodded in agreement, although I had no idea why.

Her hand shifted in mine, and I squeezed her fingers gently. Her eyes filled with tears, but only one little daring chap decided to make a break for it down her face. She clumsily swiped at it. "I thought I was going mad."

She seemed so young, so unsure of herself that my heart lurched. "If you're going mad, then we both are." I wasn't sure that was the right thing to say, but what else was there? I continued cautiously, "Why did you think you were going mad?"

Clare shook her head, swiped at another escaping tear.

Just seeing her like that nearly broke my heart. "Hey, come on. You can tell me." I trailed my fingertips down her face. More tears spilled, and I brushed them aside with my thumb.

"I'm...I'm sorry about...today." She grabbed me and pulled me close. Sobs wracked her body, and she shook violently in my arms.

Stroking her back, I shushed soft words into her ears. "None of what happened at the car park matters. It's okay, Clare. Really."

"I thought you were making fun of me. I know, I know..." She sniffed back the tears. "You didn't even know what'd been happening, but part of me thought it all had something to do with you."

That explained her earlier behaviour at any rate.

Clare lifted her face away from the haven of my shoulder and looked at me. Her eyes shone brilliantly, the tears creating a depth that drew me in. I knew it wasn't the time, definitely wasn't the time, but I leaned in until our mouths were so close it was impossible that they were not touching. Having her so near, feeling her hot breath on my face, I couldn't help myself. My lips met hers and waited, almost as if they were in shock. Then I felt the pressure of her lips in response, felt them part and a warm tongue timidly beg permission of me. I opened my mouth to her.

The feeling of her tongue making contact and the increased pressure of her mouth on mine made me surge forward to explore her lips more thoroughly. Her hands settled in my hair and pulled me in, pressing me closer still. A soft moan filtered into the air, but I couldn't say which one of us had made it. I think I could have kissed her all day, but there was something else plaguing me. Not the connection I was feeling, definitely not that. It was what was happening to the two of us.

At that thought, I gentled the kiss. I didn't want to. God, I didn't want to, but one of us had to, and judging by the noises Clare was making, I doubted it would be her.

As I pulled back, Clare moved forward, her lips finding mine over and over again. The ache I felt would have been sublime, if not for the fact that I had to put a stop to it.

Sitting back on my haunches, I maintained our connection by holding both of her hands. "Do you want to start, or should I?"

Chapter Eight

It was so strange to hear my story hit the light of day and be acknowledged by another person. At times I felt stupid relating the events that had transpired over the last nine days, but I had to keep going. Describing how I'd gotten lost, how I believed someone was watching me, how Annabel had greeted me at the door—all took on new meaning. These things had actually occurred. The woman I had spent the night with had been dead a month, but from the sounds of it, for the last sixty years, she had just existed.

After I had laid the foundation, I related the dreams—the feeling of being someone else, and the belief that that somebody else had been Ellen Howell. Embarrassment coloured my face as I recounted the events of the dream I'd had the night I'd stayed at the hotel, but I couldn't tell Clare everything I needed to tell her without including the great love between Ellen and Annabel as I'd experienced it.

At last I came to the final dream, the one with the hands around my neck, the choking.

All the while I was talking, Clare didn't say a word. Her facial expression didn't alter one iota, and I cringed internally with each additional word. When I'd finished, I waited for her to speak. And then waited some more. I watched avidly as she bit her lip, then pursed them; as her eyes squinted in contemplation. Did she believe me, or was she working out how to get out of the house without me cottoning on?

"Interesting."

It most certainly was, but the response I'd been hoping for was, "Believable." I made a move to stand, but she gripped my fingers tightly and pulled me back.

"Where are you going?"

"I...um..."

"Don't you want to hear my side?"

"Of course I do, I just thought..."

Clare smiled at me, a genuine smile. "Given what you've told me, I think you'll understand what I have to tell you a lot better than I did when it was happening to me."

I very much doubted that, but I settled myself back into my position at her feet, the rug underneath me thick and warm.

Clare's tale started simply. "After Great Aunt Annabel died, I went to Kirk Langley to sort out the funeral arrangements. Granddad tried to dissuade me from staying in Annabel's house, but considering he was living in a care facility, it was either Annabel's or a hotel. It seemed stupid to waste money on a hotel when there was a perfectly good house to stay in. Besides, it would give me the chance to sort out Annabel's papers and belongings. I can't say that I noticed anything specific to begin with, but still something was amiss from the first time I stayed there."

She paused to take a sip of tea, and I stayed silent, as she had when I was describing my own experiences.

"Ah, I guess you wouldn't know anything about Annabel's death," she continued. "Apparently a neighbour dropped by to visit Annabel and found her seated next to the kitchen window, her face turned as if she was looking out. There wasn't anything sinister about her death. It was just old age that claimed her. The doctors said it was a quick passing."

I frowned. I couldn't understand why Clare looked so troubled. "But that's a good thing, isn't it? It sounds as if there is a 'but' coming in your story."

"I hadn't seen Aunt Annabel for quite a while, even though she'd called me a number of times and invited me to visit. So when I heard she had died, I felt kind of guilty. Guilty that I hadn't made an effort to go up to Kirk Langley more often, guilty that I had acceded to my grandfather's wishes that I have little to do with her. My entire life, he insisted that I not become overly familiar with his own sister, a woman he considered the black sheep of the family. So, when weird things started to happen, I thought it was just my imagination punishing me."

So, it was the guilt that Clare blamed when the fucked up shit started to happen.

"Actually, between seeing to Granddad's needs and making the arrangements for the funeral, I didn't have much time to sort through Annabel's belongings at first. It was difficult to even find anyone who knew Annabel well enough to attend the funeral. Everyone in Kirk Langley knew *of* her, but they really didn't know her. Even the bloke who had found her body only knew her because he would run errands for her now and again, as any good neighbour would. Still, people being as they are, about a dozen villagers turned up to the funeral. That wasn't many, considering Annabel had lived over eighty-five years in the same house.

"The first instance I experienced something odd happening was at the funeral. Everyone was huddled around the grave, and the vicar was going through the motions of delivering a memorial that seemed more impersonal than anything. Freddie felt unwell that day, and didn't go to the funeral. That left me and the handful of villagers.

"As the coffin was being lowered into the ground," Clare glanced at me, as if she wanted to watch my reaction to what she was about to relate, "I felt a strange sensation, as if I was being observed. I was watching the casket being lowered, but I lifted my head to look at the faces of the townspeople. All eyes were on the oblong wooden box that held the body of my great aunt, but I could still feel someone watching me.

"I looked over the heads of the other mourners and spotted a figure standing alongside a stone angel. It appeared that the person had been looking at me, but they were too far away for me to tell for sure. Even though it was difficult to make out any features, the figure seemed familiar."

Clare took a deep breath and exhaled it slowly, then in a rush, as if she wanted to get it over with, she said, "It seemed almost as if it was me, standing there in the distance."

She waited for any comment I might make, but I gave her the same courtesy she had given me. I just listened.

"The person was about the same height, and had the same hair and build." Clare shrugged and looked at her hands. "It was like a fucked up out of body experience."

"Doppelganger."

Brown eyes met mine. "Huh?"

I repeated, "Doppelganger" then clarified. "Your double."

I didn't add that seeing one's Doppelganger was supposed to be the harbinger of bad luck or a portent of death. I figured she was upset enough already without me making matters worse with my limited knowledge about paranormal lookalikes.

"I suppose it could've been." Her voice lacked conviction.

"What about your mother? Was she at the funeral?" And why was I trying to find an alternative explanation for what was so clearly the ghost of Annabel?

Clare shook her head. "My mother doesn't associate with her father, and she had no way of knowing that he wouldn't be there. But she got on well with Annabel. Boy, that used to really piss Granddad off." She paused in thought. "Why do you ask?"

Fucked if I knew. "Erm...well, it could've been your mother... erm...coming to pay her last respects but not wanting to come closer." That was a shit idea even for me, but thankfully Clare didn't look at me like the idiot I knew I was.

"My mother lives in France with my stepfather, George. I called her to see if she wanted to make the journey over, but she said she couldn't. I think it was more like 'wouldn't.'"

An expression of hurt flitted across Clare's face, and I decided to save the subject of her relationship with her mother for another time. I'd also wait to ask why it was her stepdad rather than her father. I wasn't the perfect daughter by any stretch of the imagination, and that was something I made a resolution to work on.

"I called right after the funeral, and she was still in Vannes. She fell out with Freddie years ago."

"So *you* thought maybe it could've been her?"

Clare shook her head. "No. My mother looks more like Ellen than like Granddad."

There went my theory, if I'd actually had a theory to start off with. I guess it was more like a blurted comment.

"As I was saying..."

I took that to mean, "Shut up and listen to my story. I listened to yours." So I did.

"Apparently I appeared so distracted that the vicar stopped his inane farewell to Aunt Annabel to ask me if there was anything wrong. Instead of saying no, as I probably should have, I asked him if he knew the woman standing over by the stone angel. Obviously, when everyone turned to look in the direction I was pointing," she winced, as if the memory was still embarrassing, "they said they couldn't see anyone. But I still could."

It wasn't what Clare said, it was the way she said it that made the blood feel like ice water in my veins.

"The woman beckoned me over—"

"Did you—"

"Did I fuck!"

"What did—"

"Give me a chance to get it out." Instead of being angry at my example of someone with Interrupting Goat's Disease, she laughed. "I just said 'my mistake' and told him to continue with the service."

My brow furrowed.

"What are you thinking?" Clare asked immediately.

I couldn't tell her, because I didn't know. Even though my brow had furrowed in thought, no thought had yet materialised. The inside of my head appeared to be as blank as a cleaned white board.

"What happened then?" I did well getting those three words out.

"Not much." Clare sighed and leaned back in her chair, and the sudden space between us was filled with emptiness. "I remember looking toward the angel at the end of the service, and the woman was gone."

She was quiet for a minute or two, and I thought her tale was over. I was startled to hear about the woman at the churchyard, but I couldn't understand what that had to do with how upset Clare had been earlier in the loo. It could've easily been her mind playing tricks on her, or the sunlight making shadows shape into human form. Still, the fact that Clare thought the woman could've been herself was a sticking point.

"That was the start of it."

My head swung around quickly, my eyes capturing and holding hers.

"Before I begin, do you fancy another cuppa?"

It took Clare quite a while to relate all the events that had befallen her—dreams, apparitions, voices, and all of them seemingly from the late Annabel Howell. It was small things at first, the misplacing of keys and the like, mainly when she was at Annabel's house, not long after the funeral. Things also appeared, things Clare had never seen before—a battered copy of *Madeline's Rescue*, a thick jumper when the evening was nippy, photographs of her mother when she was a young girl.

But the crux of it all came on October 30, the night I had arrived at Kirk Langley. Clare had travelled up from Norfolk late that evening and arrived at gone one in the morning at the care centre where her granddad lived. Instead of going on over to Annabel's house, Clare had decided to stay in a hotel near the home, which was not the one I'd stayed in.

"I was feeling a little unsettled about staying at the hotel when I should have gone right over to check Annabel's house. I had a feeling that something was up, but I couldn't put my finger on what that might be.

"That night, sleep was fitful at best. But even though I was half asleep, I know for certain that I heard a voice saying my name."

I placed my hand on top of Clare's and was surprised by the chill of her skin.

"I clicked on the bedside lamp and saw only an empty room. But even though the room appeared empty, I *knew* there was someone there, watching me."

That was exactly how I felt the night I stayed in the Marriott for the convention.

"I called out and asked if there was anybody there. Stupid, I know."

Clare laughed nervously, and I grinned supportively. "Classic scary movie moment."

She put a fearful expression on her face and vocalised dramatically, "Is there anybody there?"

I giggled and she blessed me with one of her mesmerising smiles, and for a moment everything seemed normal. That didn't last.

Clare sighed and took my hand in hers, her eyes fixed on the back of it. "To be honest, I didn't really expect an answer." Brown eyes met mine. "So you can imagine how I felt when I heard one."

My back went rigid, and when I opened my mouth nothing came out.

"I knew."

What did she know, and how did she know it?

"She didn't say her name, but I knew it was Annabel. I just knew it."

"What did she say?" Did I really want to know?

"She's here."

"Who's here?" I looked over my shoulder, expecting the ghostly presence of Annabel Howell to be looming over me.

"Not here, silly. That's what Annabel said that night in the hotel—'She's here.'"

"Who's here?" Clare rolled her eyes, and I hastened to add, "Not now, then. Who did she mean?"

Clare shifted nervously in the chair, then sighed. She leaned forward to make sure I was looking straight at her. "Remind me what date you got to Kirk Langley."

"The thirtieth, but you know that." Even as I said it, I could feel my own eyes widening in disbelief as I got her inference. Even after all the unexplainable things that had happened, that would be a little too freaky.

"I think she meant you." No shit, Sherlock. "Who else could she have meant?"

"Ellen, maybe?" A big part of me was hoping that was exactly what the disembodied voice had meant.

When Clare shook her head, a wave of nausea washed over me. I had to get some fresh air, regroup. As I struggled to my feet, Clare gripped my elbow and steadied me. "I need to..." I couldn't even finish the sentence.

Thankfully my sense of direction took me to the back door, and I rushed into the garden and started gulping down lungfuls of air. The moment Clare dismissed the possibility of the voice in the hotel room being Ellen's, it seemed as if I couldn't breathe properly. It felt like I was stuck in a small space that had all the air sucked out of it. The rain had stopped, but it was still cold. Or was that just me?

Then it hit me. How on earth could Annabel have been visiting Clare in the hotel, when she was in her own house with me? None of it made any sense, even without the addition of a ghostly wanderer who visited people in their hotel rooms when she was supposed to be looking after me. It was not as if the hotel was right next door to the house, and, to be honest, I think I would've noticed Annabel sneaking out of the house in the early hours of the morning. After all, I was sleeping on the couch at the time.

I shook my head at my own stupidity. I was trying to make sense of the movements, and motivations, of ghosts. It wasn't as if Annabel's spirit would have physically walked down the stairs, popped her head around the door, and informed me she was "just popping out to frighten the crap out of my great niece," before climbing into her ghostly car and disappearing into the night.

But for Annabel to have said, "She's here" on the night I was actually there... *That* I couldn't wrap my mind around.

"Are you okay?"

I turned and saw Clare standing behind me, her expression concerned. I gave her a small smile and a shrug. "I'm not too sure. The thought that Annabel was announcing my arrival to you seems too fucking weird."

Clare frowned and stepped closer. "Considering everything you've gone through, I'm surprised that *this* is what you feel weird about."

I took her hand in mine and gave her fingers a gentle squeeze. "I know. I should be hardened to almost anything by now." I laughed nervously.

"Maybe we should wait a while before I tell you the rest," Clare suggested.

"No. We need to get everything out in the open." I gave her a gentle tug so she came closer to me. Claire's eyes caught mine, enchanted me and held me safe. I was surprised I could even think straight. I swallowed the lump of emotion in my throat. "And I think we should start writing stuff down, to see if we can make any more connections between the past and the present."

A slight nod of her head accompanied the noise of agreement she made.

So, if our plan of action was to continue Clare's tale and write things down, why were we standing in her back garden like stone statues?

"The happenings at the hotel seemed to be a one off, as I didn't experience any new events until after you returned to Norfolk. I had almost dismissed the voice in the hotel in town, until the evening I was in the hotel near the hospital where Granddad was being kept for observation."

She glanced at me to see if I was keeping up with the note taking, and I nodded for her to continue.

"The next meeting with Annabel came when I was wide awake. I was sitting on the bed, flicking through the hotel handbook, when something caught my attention. Out of the corner of my eye, I could see a figure seated at the desk in another part of the room. Although the spot was less than ten feet away from me, the figure was indistinct, as if it was out of focus.

"I just sat there, too frightened to turn my head and look at whomever was there. It was almost as if a panic attack was settling in my chest, because my heart was racing and my breath was coming in short pants. To make matters worse, the figure got up and came over to where I was sitting."

Clare was shaking now, just at the thought of whatever it was that had happened, and I wanted to take her in my arms and make her feel safe. But it might be better for her to talk about it and thereby diminish her fears. That's what I went with.

"I wanted to run as far and as fast as I could, but, for one, my legs wouldn't move, and two, the figure was between me and the door. I could feel the presence next to me, knew the person was staring down at me. I was so conscious of the figure not being just an ordinary human, it scared me even more.

"And then it spoke. 'I won't hurt you, Clare. I would never hurt you.'" She looked at me. "I recognised the voice, even though it sounded so much younger than I had ever heard it."

When she paused, I prompted, "What came next?"

"The voice said, 'Find her for me. Let us rest.'" Clare looked at me pointedly. "Us," she repeated.

"And then?"

"As I tipped my head back to look into her face, she began to fade. I think her eyes will haunt me for the rest of my life."

I sat up, pad and pen propped on my knee. "Why?"

Clare looked straight at me, her sadness obvious in her expression. "The eyes looked so lost, so...so..."

"So?"

"I don't know. Empty?"

An ache spread through me. I understood what Clare meant. I was very familiar with emptiness; I had experienced it throughout my life. Weirdly enough, I had felt less alone since

I had visited Kirk Langley, since I had met Annabel Howell. It wasn't the same kind of fulfilment that I felt with Clare. That seemed to transcend all.

"Your grandmother was murdered." Fuck. Where had that come from? Talk about easing a girl into hearing bad news. No wonder I didn't do volunteer work for the Samaritans.

I held my breath, expecting Clare to dispute what I'd said, call me an idiot and a fuckster before turfing me out after all.

Strangely, Clare didn't bat an eyelid when she answered, "I know."

What? That certainly wasn't the response I had expected. Now I was the one who was surprised. I wanted to continue with "Your grandfather murdered her and hid the body," but I felt that would be pushing it.

"So, given what we have discovered so far, something happened on October 30." I should give up my job selling stationery and work for CSI. "And Annabel wants us to do something about it." *See? Chief Inspector, at least.*

I looked down at the almost blank paper I had on my knee. I had been so enthralled with Clare's tale, I hadn't written anything down since the first few notes. As I slipped the paper to the side and laid the pen on top of it, I wondered whether Chief Inspectors got their own secretary.

"But who would hurt Ellen?"

I bit my lip.

"I mean, she never hurt anyone," Clare continued.

My teeth almost drew blood.

"From what I can make out, she was a lovely wo—"

"She committed adultery," I blurted. Shit. I shot a glance at Clare. She'd gone rigid, brown eyes cold as they bored through me.

"No she didn't." The words squeezed through gritted teeth.

I snorted. "I hate to be the one to break it to you, Clare, but I'm pretty sure that sleeping with your husband's sister has always been classed as adultery."

Clare stood, and for a moment I thought she was going to smack me in the face. Instead of making me see little birdies dancing about my head, she stormed out of the room.

Before I had a chance to make a break for it, she was back. In her hand was a very familiar notebook. Clare stopped in front of me, agitatedly scanning through pages. Slam. Her hand slapped the book, and her face sported a triumphant look when she held the notebook towards me. I felt my lip curl into a smile in response as I reached out to snatch it from her, just as she moved to stand beside me.

"Read this bit." Her finger slipped over the lines of the page before stopping on a particular passage and tapping insistently.

I glared at her before focusing my attention on the neatly written lines.

> "... It's about time she did something. But telling him she wanted a divorce was the last thing I expected."

I raised my eyes and looked at Clare.
"Carry on reading." Her voice was thick, expectant.

> "It's not because I love her so much that I want her to leave him. I mean, she doesn't think of me that way. To her, I'm just her husband's sister."

I repressed a snarky grin as I looked at Clare. "Doesn't mean Ellen ever did leave him though, does it?"

Clare gritted her teeth, then deliberately unclenched her jaw. "It means that Ellen told Freddie the marriage was over."

"And? I could tell you I'm leaving my job and joining the circus. It doesn't mean anything until I actually do it."

Clare snatched the diary back.

"Look, I'm not trying to put a spoke in the cog here. I'm just trying to help." So why did my voice sound so pious?

Clare slumped down onto the chair and set the notebook on her lap with a sigh. Leaning forward, she pinned me with a look that seemed to read me. Her gaze softened. "I know it doesn't say she divorced him, but the intent was there." A sad smile flittered over her lips. "Annabel loved Ellen."

I nodded. I could've told her that without resorting to the notebook.

"And when you read the rest of it, you'll know what I mean about it not being adultery."

"Did she divorce him?" I cocked my head, encouraging her to explain.

"Not exactly."

I harrumphed. "Well, then she—"

"She told him the marriage was over, that she couldn't be with him as his wife anymore."

"But she was still married to him," I couldn't help pointing out.

Clare swallowed hard. I think she was trying to swallow the growing anger she was feeling for me. "There is more to a marriage than a stupid piece of paper."

"True. But it's still a lawful contract."

"After she told him she wanted a divorce, she moved out of their bedroom and shared her daughter's room."

That did surprise me. "Bella's?"

Clare's eye widened. "My mother, yes."

Despite all we had experienced and discussed to that point, it was surreal to realise that I had been in the house with Clare's mother when she was three years old, even though I hadn't seen her.

"And what was Freddie's reaction?"

Clare shook her head. "He wouldn't give her the divorce. Ellen wanted to leave him, but her own family wouldn't take her in. They said she had made her bed, and it was time to lie in it."

"What about Annabel? She'd have taken Ellen in, Bella too."

"Of course she would've, but Freddie only lived a couple of miles away. Do you think he would've let his wife settle in with his sister, letting everyone in the village know he couldn't keep his woman?" She made a pffting noise and shook her head. "Annabel offered, and that's pretty much what Ellen told her."

Before I could ask how she knew, Clare was flicking through the pages of the notebook again. "Here." She tapped the page, then held out the notebook. "Read this whilst I make us both a cuppa."

I'd barely taken the book from her hands before she was gone.

Looking down at the page she had indicated, I couldn't resist running my fingers over the words. Annabel had put all her hopes, dreams, and fears into this book, and I felt privileged to be reading it. A clanking sound coming from the kitchen snapped me from my flight of fancy.

The page was toward the mid-section of the book, so I flicked over to see the date before returning to where Clare had directed me. *May 17, 1951.* Before I started to read, I rechecked the date at the beginning of the book. *December, 1949.* It had been seventeen months since Ellen had given her the notebook. Annabel had said *"To her, I'm just her husband's sister."* I would beg to differ. Not many people would sign the front of a book *"To you, from me. x E x"* if all they felt for their sister-in-law was affection.

"Do you want a biscuit?"

Already losing myself in Annabel's world, I grunted. "I'll take that as a yes."

"Every day I try to think of an excuse to see her. Every damn day. Just one of her smiles is enough to keep me going for a while, but then I always have to go back for more. I just can't seem to get enough of her. Knowing she is with him makes it harder. I know she doesn't love him, but I also know she doesn't love me. Why would she? I'm a woman. She isn't like that, isn't like me.

I offered for her to stay here, but she won't. She's probably worried about what the villagers will say about two women living under the same roof when one of them is married to someone living a stone's throw away. I don't care what they say. They can go hang for all I care.

Would these idiots around here support a man who hits a woman? Can't they see her bruises? The black eyes she's had on more than one occasion? Why don't they get together and beat the hell out of him?

I know Freddie and I have never been close, even more so when I got dad's house instead of him. There is no way he would let Ellen move in here. That would make him second best once again. He hasn't forgiven me for Dad saying he'd rather torch the place than leave it to him.

What I can't understand is why she won't let me say something to him. Why won't she let me tell him I will inform the authorities outside of the village? Surely they would do something about his abuse.

Fear, most likely. Freddie Howell may be my brother, but he is, and always has been, an out and out cruel bastard."

Something was behind me; something slick, insistent, pressing against my back. It was moving slowly, making almost a dragging motion across my shirt. I could feel the chill of the air as the material was lifted from my skin, and then the heat emanating from the presence. Too frightened to move, my fingers clutched the notebook. A dark shape flickered at my side, but it was just a bit too far out of view for me to make out what it was.

How does a person defend herself against something that might not even be there? Certainly not with wishful thinking or what ifs.

Closing my eyes, I tried to muster the strength to confront whatever was behind me. I briefly considered calling for Clare, but what could she do? Maybe she wouldn't even see what I would.

"So, that's what you're up to, is it? I thought you'd done a runner?"

Clare's voice was in the room with me. Well, it was either Clare or Annabel. They did sound the same, after all. And what did she mean by "that's what you're up to?" I didn't know that my being scared shitless could be phrased as if I was up to no good.

"What's the matter, Rebecca? Do you want me to get rid of her?"

Fuck yeah. And quickly. Too scared to speak, I nodded.

"Sorry. I didn't know you were afraid of cats."

Cats? A cat! A bloody, arse licking, meowing, razor clawed, scar making cat?

"Come on, Maggie. Out."

"Meow." It looked like Maggie had plans other than going back outside into the cold.

I turned and smiled up at Clare. "She's fine." I shifted my attention to the tabby cat seated behind me. "I like cats." Holding my hand above Maggie's head, I let her rub herself against my palm. My heartrate was returning to normal, but I could still feel a modicum of fear pocketed away, ready to spring again.

Maggie was purring softly, and I looked up into Clare's eyes. "Honestly. She's fine."

Clare's eyes narrowed as she tilted her head to the side. "That's not the impression I got when I came in. It looked as if you were readying yourself for battle."

The heat of the blush spread along my neck, and I imagined my embarrassment blossomed on my cheeks like spilt wine.

"You're not allergic to cats, are you?"

Clare sounded so concerned, I felt even more self-conscious.

"No...no. I'm fine, honestly." So why did I sound as if I was going into anaphylactic shock? I had the redness, the burning, the difficulty breathing, and a definite hoarseness, but they had nothing to do with the cat who, at the moment, was trying to climb onto my lap as her concerned owner tried to pull her off me.

It ended up with a tussle over the cat—Clare trying to remove Maggie, and me trying to get the cat to stay. It was making the situation ten times worse than it should have been. I had been shitted up by a cat rubbing on my back, eager to believe it was something otherworldly instead of considering it might be something that was relatively common in a single lesbian's house.

I'd had enough. "Stop!" It must've been the volume of the shouted command that even made the cat freeze on my lap. "The cat is okay. Okay?"

The cat dug her claws into my thigh. Maybe Maggie had her own ideas about what okay meant.

Clare withdrew her hands and stepped back. Her lips were pursed, and I knew she wanted to say something, but I was hoping that she would just leave it alone.

"I'll just bring the tea in."

She turned and left the room, leaving me looking down at the pile of fur purring on my lap, vainly holding back the smug grin. "I win," I whispered to the cat.

Weirdly, the cat didn't move, but a voice from the kitchen called, "What was that?"

"What was what?" I winked at the cat, who gave me an interested-yet-bored cat stare.

Silence resounded from the kitchen. It seemed a little too quiet.

My eyes flicked to the clock on the mantelpiece. The second hand was moving, but it wasn't making its usual loud tick tocking. Now that I thought about it, I hadn't heard it for a while.

A quick check of my watch showed the same time as that displayed on the clock, but I was still confused.

Clare appeared holding a tray of cups and biscuits. "Sorry. Do you have to be somewhere else?" Her expression was unreadable.

I didn't know whether I should say, "Actually, yes." I thought that might be the answer she was waiting for. It wasn't as if we were really hitting it off, apart from the mind blowing kisses we'd shared. All we had done since meeting was argue and become defensive. Well, to be fair to myself, the last bit was mainly Clare.

Then, just before she turned her head and busied herself by placing the tray on the table and fiddling with the tea things, I saw tears sparkling in her eyes. That and the slight slump of her shoulders told me that she didn't want me to go. To be honest, I didn't want to go. Sure, we had argued. Yes, we had picked up on piddly things to nark the other, but to be honest, I loved being with her. It felt as if that was where I should be— bantering, arguing, kissing Clare Davies.

"Me-oow." Maggie was sitting up and staring at me, her green eyes knowing.

"I'm all yours." The words slipped from my lips like a confession. On the surface, they meant I didn't have to go; I could stay longer. However, somewhere deep inside, I knew they meant something completely different. They were a promise from me to her, although I doubted she would interpret them that way.

Clare's head turned, and her eyes captured mine. A smile crept up from the depths of her, and the room felt brighter for it. "Are you, now?"

I nodded. "Yes." The word croaked from my lips, so I cleared my throat and repeated, "Yes."

Clare raised an eyebrow, then turned back to the tea things. I stared at her back, enjoying her graceful movements. It seemed so right to be sitting in her house, a cat in my lap, waiting for a cuppa before discussing the writings of a dead woman who was haunting the both us.

Maggie jumped to the floor and ran into the kitchen. I opened my mouth to ask Clare what had spooked her, then I heard the ticking of the clock. Instead of speaking, I pointed at it. A stupid thing to do, considering Clare's back was towards me.

Again I opened my mouth to speak, but I stopped. It wasn't because I didn't know what to say, but because my attention had shifted from the clock to the armchair, the armchair Clare had been sitting in. There, bold as brass, sat Annabel. A soft smile graced her face, and she tilted her head toward Clare. I tentatively pointed in the direction of her great niece, and Annabel nodded.

"Clare."

"Nearly done."

"Clare!"

She looked over her shoulder at me, her expression showing puzzlement.

I said straight out, "Can't you see her?"

"See who?"

I tipped my head towards the armchair, and Clare's focus shifted.

The clank of the spoon hitting the tray echoed through the room. "Fuck!"

I couldn't have put it any better myself. I was surprised that Clare came closer to where I was seated.

"Can you see her?" she whispered.

I was surprised Clare asked me if I could see Annabel, considering I was the one that had given her the heads up.

"Ahum."

"Annabel? Is that really you?"

Maybe the question was rather lame, but Clare was doing a damned sight better than I was at stringing a sentence together. "What is it you want us to do?"

Annabel didn't speak. She nodded at the notebook that was beside me on the arm of the chair.

Clare looked at the notebook, and then back at her aunt. "Do you want it back?"

The figure's gaze shot straight to Clare's, flicked to mine, then back to Clare's.

The ticking of the clock was almost deafening, and the temperature in the room had dropped significantly. A shiver raced down my spine, and I wasn't sure whether it was because of the actual cold or the fact I was sitting in a room with a ghost.

Clare reached down and picked up the notebook. She held it out towards Annabel, but the woman just gave it a dismissive glance before looking directly at her great niece. A slender hand slowly moved forward, the spirit's eyes never leaving Clare's. I thought Annabel was going to take the notebook, but she didn't. She leaned forward and placed her hand on top of Clare's.

Clare gasped, and her entire body shivered. I craned my neck to see if there was anything else that could have made her react the way she did, but it didn't even look as if they were touching. Until Annabel's hand went straight through Clare's.

"Oh God, no!"

Clare's cry snapped me out of observer mode, and I staggered to my feet to help her. I barely managed to catch her before she fell. I gently lowered her to the floor, my attention solely on her. Tears were flowing freely down her face, so I knelt beside her and wrapped my arms around her shaking shoulders. Words of comfort spilled from my lips, though I couldn't tell you what I said. Likely they were absurdities intended to calm and reassure, nothing concrete.

As she grew calmer, I began to get angry at Annabel. How dare she come back from death and try to ruin the lives of the living. What had happened all those years ago had nothing to do with me or Clare, though we had both been willing to try to help. And now Annabel had hurt Clare in some way, made her cry uncontrollably. Why?

"Fuck you, Annabel." The words growled up from my innermost depths. Unadulterated anger radiated from me as I turned to the now empty seat. "What the... Where?" I shook my head at myself for questioning the disappearance of a ghost.

"The pain...of it! *The pain.*"

Clare hiccoughed the words, and my anger dissipated. I slipped my fingers around her wrist and drew her hand to me. There were no marks on it, nothing I could see anyway. I kissed her knuckles, hoping the childhood palliative would ease her discomfort.

I ducked my head to look down at her on the floor, comfort her with the knowledge that I was there, and nothing and no one, alive or dead, was going to hurt her. Her expression was a mix of understanding and bewilderment. Tears fell silently down her face and she pulled her hand towards her chest, taking mine with it.

"The pain of it, Rebecca. Here. The pain. Here."

Initially I was confused, until I realised it wasn't her hand that was hurting; it was her chest. Panic shot through me. Had the events with Annabel frightened Clare so much she was having a coronary? I needed to call an ambulance, but as I tried to pull away, Clare held me fast.

"It was awful. Seeing that. Awful."

To be honest, I was a little surprised at the way Clare had reacted to Annabel. She had seen the presence before, and had seemed perfectly all right with it until Annabel's hand had appeared to go straight through her own.

"Do you want me to call an ambulance?"

Clare shook her head and held me tightly. I couldn't help myself; I inhaled the scent of her hair. I also couldn't help placing a soft kiss on her the top of her head. That was probably more for my benefit than hers.

The room became quiet again, so quiet that I realised the clock had stopped making the tick tock sound I had noted earlier. The room seemed warmer, too. Instead of commenting on those two snippets of observation, I continued to hold Clare close to me, waiting for her to explain further.

We must've sat like that for ten minutes, but I didn't mind a bit. I also didn't mind that my legs were becoming numb. As long as I could feel Clare, that was all that mattered. As long as I could give her some semblance of comfort, the world was right in my book.

"I saw things." Her voice seemed to reverberate off the walls, even though she spoke softly. "When Annabel touched my hand, I saw things."

I felt the hairs at the back of my neck rise. "Things?" But did I really want to know?

"Images. Reruns. Events."

"Of?" I was pretty sure that I really didn't want to know, but I couldn't leave her alone in her misery.

Clare's eyes lifted to meet mine. "I could feel her pain, Annabel's, I mean."

A sense of sadness swept over me like a tidal wave. I stared at her, hoping she would go on without me having to speak.

"The images, they were of her—Annabel—trying to find Ellen. I could feel her desperation, her agony." Clare rubbed her chest again, as if the pain was still throbbing. "I felt as if it was me living it."

I had experienced the same feelings with Ellen, and I could empathise. What scared the hell out of me was the possibility that I might sometime experience Ellen's death in my dreams. As Ellen, I'd experienced many emotions—love, confusion, fear, and near death, but I didn't recall having suffered the final moment. I hoped beyond hope I never would.

Clare curled against me and rested her head on my chest whilst I held her. I knew she was thinking about what she had envisioned, but I allowed her the silence and the time to get it sorted in her head before she tried to share it with me.

Chapter Nine

I couldn't believe I fell asleep, that after everything that had transpired, I had fallen asleep with Clare hugged tightly to me. When I woke, the room was dark and I could feel the heat of her pressed against me. Thankfully, I had settled back in the chair, thereby giving us a bit of support while we slept. It felt wonderful to have Clare so close, but it was far from comfortable having a numb backside and the base of a chair jamming into my back. Even the bloody cat had more sense. Purring peacefully, Maggie was curled up on the cushion of the chair where I had been sitting.

"Clare?" I whispered. The warm body harrumphed. "Clare?" I felt her stir as sleep seeped from her and reality slipped in.

"Becky?"

Her voice was soft, vulnerable, and I wanted to keep holding her as if I was a protective shield.

The memory of what had happened must have galvanised her, and she shot forward, almost stumbling as she got to her feet with a groan. She must've been as stiff as I was.

"Hey, love," I cringed at my inadvertent use of the endearment. It was too soon to be getting all doe eyed.

Clare's head appeared to turn in my direction. I couldn't tell for sure, as the room was too dark to make out the finer details.

"It is you, isn't it, Becky? Actually you?"

I nodded, a little confused by her wanting confirmation of my identity, then I realised she couldn't see me clearly, either.

"Yes. It's me."

A warm hand settled on the side of my face, a single finger tracing the outline of my mouth. I resisted the urge to kiss it, but my self-restraint was rapidly diminishing. I opened my mouth, but was silenced by warm lips. Before I could return the kiss, cool air replaced the softness. Clare pulled back, and her figure moved across the room almost eerily.

The flash of the ceiling light made me squint and, for a few seconds, the brightness of the room seemed surreal. By the time my eyes had acclimatised to the change, I realised it was just Maggie and me in the room. The cat mewled lazily, stretched her legs, then curled into a ball and fell asleep.

I gripped the arm of the chair, hoisted myself into a Neanderthal posture, and staggered across the room to look for Clare. A toilet flushed in the recesses of the house, and I realised I needed to go too. Considering all the cups of tea I had polished off since arriving, I was a bit surprised I hadn't wet myself in my sleep.

I followed the sound of the flush and waited outside the closed door of what I surmised was the bathroom. I heard the sound of running water, and I knew it wouldn't be long before Clare emerged. Leaning back against the wall, I tried to make some sense of everything I had heard and seen that afternoon. A cynical laugh escaped as I realised how truly fucked up everything was. Why me? Why involve someone who just had the misfortune to get lost whilst attending a convention? It didn't make any sense. Clare, yes. She was a direct descendent of both Annabel and Ellen. I was a nobody, a nothing, a not very interesting person at all. My mood slid into something darker, more introverted.

Did I want this, to get embroiled in something I knew nothing about and was no party to? Was it wise to get into a relationship so quickly? Ever since Clare and I met, it seemed as if I had a connection with her, an attraction to her. But was that real? Or was it a result of what I had experienced with Annabel Howell in my dreams?

The door clicked open, light cascaded over me, and Clare Davies stepped out of the brightness. Her hair was slightly damp around the edges, as if she had washed her face.

"Oh, sorry." She laughed. "Didn't know you were waiting."

I pulled a smile up from the depths and tilted my head toward the open doorway.

"Sorry again."

Clare stepped aside to let me to pass. As I stepped over the threshold and into the bathroom, she touched my arm. I don't know why I stiffened, but I did.

"Are you okay with staying for a little while longer?"

I couldn't look at her as the lie slipped out, too easily. "Erm... Sorry. I have to make tracks." I honestly didn't know why I said it, when all I really wanted was to stay. Confusing, but the truth. "Maybe another time, eh?" I turned and looked at Clare.

She tried to hide her disappointment, but it was a little slow in leaving her face. "Sure. Yep. Great."

A moment went by, a very long moment that seemed uncomfortably not like a moment, but more like a lifetime in its silence and expectation. "I..." I nodded my head towards the bathroom.

"Oh God! Sorry!"

Clare's face displayed her embarrassment, something I would usually have found cute and endearing, but at the moment I was too occupied with feeling like a twat. Without another word, she was gone, and I was left wondering why I'd told Clare I had to leave. Worse still was knowing that I was scuppering my chances with her by saying I had to leave, and still I was set on leaving.

Less than ten minutes later, I was putting on my coat. Clare busied herself with washing teacups whilst I got myself together. I was waiting for her to dry her hands, the scene blaringly real and surreal at the same time. Her smile was forced; so was mine. The good-bye seemed clumsy and self-conscious, as neither of us could decide whether it was appropriate to hug or kiss. In the end, I gave her a brief hug whilst silently hoping I wouldn't allow my body to relax into her.

As I walked away, I could feel her watching me from her doorway, and my heart begged me to at least turn and wave. Thankfully, my heart won out. I turned around to face her, and then started walking backwards, waving like the Queen. Clare's facial expression shifted from disappointment to laughter, and happiness bubbled up inside me. I wanted to go back, to apologise for being such a jerk, but that would have made me feel even more of a fool than I already did. Then she blew me a kiss, and I was lost.

Stuff feeling like a fool. I would have been a fool to leave her without a goodbye kiss. I raced towards her. There was no hesitation, no trying to read her expression to see whether my intended action was welcome. I grabbed her head, pulled her to me, and kissed her. My lips told her more than words could ever say.

Her fingers wrapped in my hair and pulled me closer. The heat from our mouths juxtaposed with the cold night air felt glorious.

I pulled away, only to press another quick kiss on her lips before leaning forward and resting my forehead against hers. Our breathing was ragged, and the air between us turned to mist.

"Glad you came to your senses."

Her voice was warm, like honeyed wine, and I knew she was smiling without even looking at her. "Can I see you tomorrow?" It felt as if the question held my future in each syllable.

Clare pulled back slightly and looked into my eyes. I knew it was going to be a refusal even before she said it.

"I have to work."

Weirdly enough, I had never thought about Clare working. I had no idea what she did for a living. "I know this sounds a strange thing to ask, but, what's work to you?"

Clare's head fell back, and she laughed. I laughed too, even though I didn't have a clue what I was laughing about. Eventually I asked, "What's funny about that?" Part of me was hoping she wasn't a stripper, but then again...

"I own a craft shop."

What was so funny about owning a craft shop? "A craft shop?" I was hoping she would explain why a shop housing craft accessories would be funny. She didn't. She just laughed again, and I was a little irked. "What's so funny about that?"

"Nothing."

Her eyes met mine, and she apparently realised that I was staring at her like I was trying to figure something out. Probably because I *was* staring at her and trying to figure something out.

She wiped the smile off of her face. "It's just because I can't believe you haven't asked before."

I felt like a shit, a self-absorbed shit. "Erm..." I could feel myself going red, the heat racing to my cheeks and exposing me for the fool that I was.

Clare leaned forward and captured my lips again, then pulled back and gently rubbed her nose against mine. "It's not important. We've had other, more important things to talk about."

True. It was not every day one got haunted.

"I have to go in tomorrow to do a stock take." Her fingers trailed down the side of my face, sending tingling sensations to the deepest regions of my body. "I've been away for over a week, and I like to keep on top of things."

My mind wandered to what I would like to get on top of, and it wasn't stock.

"Sally and Dale have been covering for me. I trust them both, but..." Clare shrugged. "You know." She delivered a breath-taking smile, then became serious. "They're both coming in to help, so I can't get out of it."

"That's okay. I understand." And I did. Work was work, whether one owned the business or not.

"But I'm free next weekend, if..."

The question dangled in the air, and I was just about to accept when I realised I would be in Wales the following weekend and wouldn't be back until the Tuesday. I gritted my teeth and scrunched my nose.

"Not good for you, huh?"

I shook my head.

"The following week?"

I noted thankfully that her voice sounded hopeful. I mentally worked through my appointment schedule before nodding enthusiastically.

"I finish at lunchtime on Saturdays. Perks of being the boss."

Instead of responding, I kissed her again. In my book, that was the same thing as saying "yes." If I'd been a dog, I'd have wagged my tail and licked her face.

Chapter Ten

The week dragged on and on, followed by more of the same on the weekend. Fuck. The descriptor "interminable" sprang to mind. The highlight of each day was talking to Clare in the evening or reading the emails she sent, telling me about her day or sharing things she had worked out from the notebook. I'd never felt such a connection with another person. I admit I'd had my reservations in the earlier days, even considered not allowing Clare to become too special to me, but that was a thing of the past. All I could think about was her—her smile, the taste of her lips, the way she tilted her head to the side and squinted her eyes when she was reading me. Even if I had wanted to stay a Billy-No-Mates, it was too late for that. I was smitten, and I was hoping that she felt the same.

By the second week, I was wondering why we had only arranged to see each other at the weekend. I wanted to see her more often than that, wanted to see her all of the time. I got to the stage where I was fixating on my phone. No longer just a device to make business calls and set up appointments, it had become a channel of hope and expectation. I found myself constantly checking for emails and new text messages. More pitifully, I kept rereading Clare's emails and previous text messages. I realised I was obsessed with the prospect of hearing from her, but I couldn't help myself. Each time I received a new communication, I felt a jolt of joy, completely absorbed every word, and then felt emptier once I had read it and replied.

It was Wednesday of the second week. I had been home from Wales for a day, and I was distracted. Too damned right I was.

I didn't have to go in to the main office until the next day, and I was feeling antsy. I knew Clare would be at work, and I didn't exactly know where that was, but I did know about a thing called the Yellow Pages, or, better still, Yell.com.

I couldn't believe how many craft shops were in Wells: Little Prezzies, The Old Station Pottery and Bookshop, Ashley Studios. Then it hit me. Maybe her shop wasn't even in Wells. She'd said she had a craft shop, and she finished at lunchtime on a Saturday. She was going to meet me at one, so maybe that was her usual lunchtime. It seemed reasonable that she would finish work just beforehand and then walk to meet me just a few minutes away. Or maybe she finished at twelve, and would get in her car and drive countless miles.

Bollocks.

As I looked out the window, I rubbed my hands together as if I was rubbing two sticks together to start a fire. The sky was blue; the day was clear and dry. I knew it would be cold, but I could always wear a jacket. A drive to Wells seemed like a marvellous idea. If I couldn't find Clare's shop, I would take a nice walk down to the sea. Fresh. Enriching. Exhilarating.

Who was I kidding? If I couldn't find Clare, I would feel too gutted to go dancing up to the sea for a paddle.

I scooped up my phone and looked down at my new best friend. Its smooth black case beckoned me to open it and send a text message. I shook my head. If I was going to do this, I wanted it to be a surprise. I didn't want to be all needy, even if I was.

Decision made, I put the phone in my pocket, grabbed my jacket, bag, and car keys, and followed my heart. First time in my life I had ever done anything so rash. I felt like I'd conquered the world.

Fucking Wells. Fucking wind. Fucking rain. Why hadn't I checked the weather before I left, instead of depending on the blueness of the sky in Norwich? Maybe because I was a knob. A knob that was soaked through and wandering around Wells-next-the-Sea looking like a vagrant. I'd checked out all of the addresses that I'd found on Yell and came up empty, at least as far as finding Clare was concerned. I hated walking into shops and having sales assistants hover around, pestering me with a "May I help you?" even though my own job was for me to be the one doing the pestering. I'd hung around outside each shop for way too long, until it looked as if I was about to rob the place, then I had to walk in and be intercepted by overzealous Alan Sugar wannabes. Reason? Easy. Clare didn't work alone. She had Sally and Dale. I didn't know what Sally or Dale looked like, so I had to take my chances. Thankfully, I'd only bought one thing from each shop, so it wasn't too expensive. Unfortunately, the things I did buy were heavy enough for me to have to go back to my car and put them in the boot.

As I slammed the lid, I felt a sensation running through me. It wasn't like I was being watched, just that I should turn around and look about me. Predictably my focus landed on the public toilets I had been lured into the previous time I had visited Wells, but there was no figure lurking in the doorway, beckoning me inside with the potential to scare the shit out of me. There was only a woman with two young children and a third in a buggy blocking the doorway. The woman was deflecting questions of "Why can't we have an ice cream?" by systematically giving each child a spit wash. It would've been easier to take them inside the loos and use the sinks in there, but who was I to put in my ha'penny's worth? Maybe she felt it was more hygienic to use her own spit rather than deal with the smell of urine and myriad of germs collecting in the small necessary.

Next I spotted two elderly couples chatting. One couple had a dog with them who looked like he must've rolled in as much mud as he could. There was a sense of pride in the voices of the owners, as if somehow the condition of their dog was something to boast about. Even though these life scenes were gripping, the persistent feeling inside me indicated I was looking in the wrong direction. My gaze drifted to the right, and my heart seemed to pause before kicking hard inside my chest.

A figure moved just out of my view before I had the opportunity to fully digest who it was. Long dark hair drifted backwards, leaving an echo of her in its wake. I was sure it was Clare, absolutely sure. But then again, could it have been Annabel?

In the time between leaving Clare in her home and that moment, I hadn't seen Annabel or Ellen. Hadn't dreamt of them, felt them near me, had thoughts about what had happened, nothing. So why now? Why in Wells?

I had to follow the figure and see who it was, but my legs seemed to be rooted to the spot. Frustration clawed up my throat, and I growled. That seemed to break the statue spell, and I raced down the car park to the spot where I thought I had seen Clare.

The figure disappeared around the corner, just a glimpse of a wisp of long hair drawing me forward. I shouted Clare's name, but the elusive person didn't stop or turn back.

I was more annoyed than intrigued now. This was turning into a wild goose chase, and I was the pillock doing the chasing. I grabbed my phone from my bag and scrolled to Clare's mobile number. Stuff surprising her; it would be more of a case of surprising myself if I ever found her.

My thumb had nearly made contact with the "call mobile" button when I heard my name. Lifting my head, I saw Clare walking towards me from the direction I had been heading.

"Becky?"

I flipped the cover shut and stuffed the phone in my pocket, summoning what I hoped was a charming smile. Considering I had just about dried off from the full wash and spin the Wells weather had given me, I hoped I still looked presentable.

"You look like a drowned rat." Maybe not. "Come on. I was just nipping home for lunch." She held out her hand and waited for me to slip my fingers into it. "Let's get you out of those clothes."

My head shot up, and I stared at her.

"No. NO! That's not what I meant at all. You're we..."

I could've given her one of those cheap, flirty retorts, but I just grinned and lifted an eyebrow suggestively. Her blush was instant.

"I meant wet, as in rain."

By now I was feeling sorry for her, as I doubted her face could get any redder.

"I'll get you warm in no time." As soon as the words left her mouth, her lips peeled back as if she wanted to drag them back in again.

"I bet you will." I grinned and winked at her. Then a thought struck me that turned the grin into a frown. "Did you just walk past the car park?" Considering we were in the process of having a bit of sexual banter, my question must have seemed off topic to Clare.

"Yes. Erm... Why?"

So it *had* been her. I didn't know whether or not to be relieved to know it was a mere mortal that had lured me to this spot. Weird to think that the urge to follow the figure had felt so right, almost as if that was my path, my way forward.

"Just thought I saw you, that's all."

Clare pulled me against her, tilted her head down, and pinned me with those fabulous brown eyes. "I've missed you so much, Becky." Her voice was a whisper, but the words reverberated around inside my head and chest.

I cupped her cheek and rubbed my thumb along the smooth skin. I fairly ached to kiss her, to taste the lips I had been yearning to taste again for ten days. Reason prevailed. Kissing her in the middle of the street in broad daylight didn't seem the proper thing to do. Not because I felt it was wrong to kiss Clare, but because the people passing by might have other ideas about two women kissing in public.

"For God's sake! Kiss her and get it over with!"

I turned and located the speaker, an elderly gentleman on the other side of the street.

"If I was younger, I'd do it for you. Bah! Kids today."

Clare's laugh bubbled up and burst into the air. Soon mine joined hers.

"Can't disappoint him, now can we?"

Her voice was thick, enticing, but I didn't get the chance to kiss her. She kissed me first, and everything in my world was right once again.

"About time," came the comment from behind us.

We broke apart with a laugh. Seeing her like that, so open and vulnerable and beautiful, well, I was worried that my smitten heart wouldn't be able to take the joy of it. It was at that very moment that I realised it was more than just attraction I was feeling for Clare Davies. Much more.

Did it bother me? Did I want to run away screaming into the hills? Yes and no. Yes, because I had never allowed anyone to get that close to me before. I had never let my guard down long enough for anyone to see the real me, quivering in fear. I was scared that when Clare could see who I actually was, she wouldn't be interested in someone like me.

Happily, the "no" part of my thought process was so much stronger. I couldn't help myself now. It was immaterial whether or not Clare loved me in return. I was lost, lost in her, lost and falling in love with her.

And yes. I thought the L word. And after only seeing her four times. God, what would I be like after seeing her five times?

Clare had been going home for lunch. What I hadn't said was that she usually didn't go home for lunch.

"You're lucky to have caught me. I just had the urge to go home and grab a bite." She leaned forward and picked up an egg and cress sandwich from the plate on the table. She paused as she lifted it to her mouth, and the bread flopped slightly, as if it was trying to avoid being consumed.

"Weirdly, I'd just gotten home and something made me feel as if I should go back to work." Clare laughed, a single shake of her head making my heart skip a beat. "Then I saw you." Her eyes glanced my way before turning back to her sandwich. "You being here seemed right."

Clare took a bite of her sandwich and chewed slowly. I just stared at her, my own sandwich forgotten in my hand. "What do you mean by me being there seeming right?"

Clare swallowed, blinked. A shake of her head accompanied the "I don't know. Just...just like I was expecting you to be there." She half-closed her eyes and tilted her head, her focus solely on me. "Do you know what I mean? It was like you should be there walking towards me."

I nodded. I agreed that it was weird. But it seemed that so much weird shit had been happening around us of late, one more thing didn't really register very high on the weird-o-meter. It was almost becoming run of the mill.

Clare was still looking at me. Under her scrutiny I felt a little exposed, almost as if she could read my mind, not that I had anything particularly embarrassing floating around in there. Maybe my unease stemmed from the knowledge that my head was devoid of anything; the vacuous space was huge and echoey.

I cleared my throat and tried a normal conversational gambit. "So, what've you been up to?"

Clare continued to stare at me and I stared back, unsure what I should do next. Even though it was probably only a moment before she sat backwards, her posture straightening significantly, it felt longer.

"Work!"

I started with surprise at the volume of her voice, and my eyes widened. Clare leaned forward and placed her hand on my arm. For a moment I honestly believed she would be able to feel the drum of my pulse thud against her fingertips.

"Sorry." She laughed softly. "Work. I've been working most of the time." She patted my arm, and when her hand moved away, it left a definite coolness behind. "You? What've you been up to?"

"Work. Well...erm. No, work it is." I laughed, and she joined me.

"Talking of which, I need to get back." Clare pulled an apologetic face for cutting our lunch short.

"Oh, right. I..." Flustered, I stood. "I should let you get back. Sorry. God! I didn't mean to hog your time." The heat of embarrassment started at my neck, and I fanned my face to keep it from appearing there.

"I was hoping you'd want to come and see my shop. You know, so you'll know where to find me if you have the urge to visit again."

I stopped fanning and met her eyes. "I'd love to see it. If you have time, that is."

The smile she gave me indicated she wanted me there as much as I wanted to be with her. The blush won out, colouring my cheeks.

The shop Clare owned was magical. Local artists had works for sale, and the pieces were breathtakingly beautiful. Watercolours, pencilled sketches, charcoal drawings of views and sea birds adorned the walls. There were also some sculpted pieces, and art made from drift wood. It was the perfect coastal craft shop. Funnily enough, I hadn't seen the name of this shop when I'd googled earlier. I would've been drawn to this name more than the others. It was called *Howell's*. Even I might have made the connection.

"My mother, Bella, opened this shop with money given to her by Annabel." Clare reached out and lovingly touched a framed picture of a pencil drawing of a shipwreck. "Art was kind of her thing. A bit like me I suppose."

"Who do you mean, Annabel or your mum?"

Clare's finger lifted away from the picture, a slight hesitation in the movement. "All of us, I suppose. Annabel was more into art work, and my mother more into the supplying of it."

It seemed that Clare had more in common with her aunt than just physical appearance. I wanted to ask her why Bella would start a business so far from Kirk Langley and her father, when she could have worked with Annabel in a local art shop close to home, but I felt uncomfortable about it.

Annabel's source of income could have surprised me, but it didn't. As with Clare, I hadn't really thought about how Annabel made her money. The house she had lived in was quite large, and even though her father had left her the house itself, she would still have had to keep up with maintenance, such as paying the bills. But I had only ever thought about her in connection with Ellen and the events surrounding her disappearance. Well, that and the fact that Annabel was haunting Clare and me.

One of the displays in *Howell's* was an array of stationery, and I felt drawn to it. Fine drawing equipment was stored neatly in compartments, and I felt like a kid in a sweet shop. Different leaded pencils, kneadable rubbers, blending stumps, pastel crayons, and a wide range of artist sketch pads were on sale, and I had to stop myself buying things that I most certainly didn't need. I was in the business, after all.

Dale and Sally were nice enough. Young, eager, and creative, they were perfect for the store. Sally was dressed like I imagined an art student would dress. Her blonde hair hung loosely across her face, intermittently hiding her pretty blue eyes, which were overly accentuated by the dark make up around them. Dale was as camp as a row of tents, if I may use that expression, although, weirdly, he gazed adoringly at Sally. Ah, the complexity of young love.

"Do you want to see my office?"

Clare's voice seeped into my thoughts, and I couldn't help the grin that appeared on my lips. "Sure. I'd like that."

Her office was at the back of the store, and the corridors leading to it seemed endless, narrowing and expanding erratically. At one point it struck me that I should have brought a piece of chalk to mark the walls so I could find my way out. I could feel a shift in the atmosphere as I moved along, like the air was getting mustier, colder.

As soon as Clare closed the door behind us, she pinned me against the wood, her lips finding mine. Her hand was on my breast and kneading hungrily. A gasp left my mouth and sank inside hers. That spurred her on, and her kiss became harder, more insistent. Although we had kissed many times, neither of us had ventured to second base, although I had wanted to right from the very first kiss. I thought fleetingly, "Why now?"

But with arousal escalating, rational thought was pushed out. My nipple rose eagerly to her palm, and I pushed myself against her hand. It was not a time for questions. Clare's mouth dipped to where my shoulder met my neck, her lips sucking, teeth nipping, tongue trailing. The real world was fading, and I didn't care. All that mattered was this moment.

Her hand abandoned my breast, and it ached for her return. However, in mere moments I felt her tugging my shirt from my jeans, then her fingers moving on my skin. There was no preamble, no foreplay to what was about to happen. She didn't trail her fingers lightly over my skin. No. Her hand cupped the whole of my breast and squeezed. My legs buckled slightly, and my breathing came in rasping gulps. Clare pushed her thigh between my legs and pressed against my apex. Need sizzled through me, and I couldn't help grinding against her insistent leg.

A lift and a push, and my bra moved away to expose my breast to her. I heard her sigh as she held it, ran her thumb over my nipple. Sensation formed at the peak and spread like spilt water throughout my body.

Clare moved her head downwards, her face pushing past the material gathered around my chest. Hot lips captured my nipple and an avid tongue flicked it, making it stand up and beg for more. Her hips were building a rhythm as they pressed against my need. As the wetness collected, I matched her thrusts, the pulsations complementing her sucking, licking, flicking, and pressing. My hands grabbed her hair and pulled her closer to me, and her thrusts became harder. The door banged behind me each time she pushed into me, and the sound kept time with our frenzied connection.

Her other hand moved to the button of my jeans, and she fumbled at it. Her teeth moved aside the cloth covering my other breast, then her lips began to nibble.

Pop. Button open. Zip ripped downwards. Fingers grabbed the side of my jeans to push them down. God, I wanted her. Wanted her to slip her fingers inside me, wanted her to feel how wet she had made me in such a short time.

I heard her growl of frustration as the jeans, still slightly damp from being out in the rain, barely moved. Instead of trying again, she lifted her mouth from my breast and claimed my mouth again. Her kiss was hard, demanding. Fuck. I was so fucking turned on.

Fingers pushed inside my panties and along slick folds. I was wet, more than ready for her to take me, to make me cum. Clare pulled back and down, back and down, and I found myself riding her hand.

"God, baby." Her voice was thick with arousal. "I've missed this so much." Her fingers were at my opening, although my jeans were delaying her entry. "I love you so much, Ellen."

Ellen! What the fuck?

Initially I was too shocked to say a word, but I could act. I grabbed her hand and pulled it out of my jeans, the wetness trailing onto my stomach. I shoved her away from me, noting her confused expression as I did so. She stepped closer, her hands held out to me, but I sidestepped her and slipped along the wall of the room, using it for support as my legs were still unsteady.

"Becky, I—"

"What the fuck do you think you're doing?" I was thankful that my voice box had started working again.

"I don't know what... God! What happened?"

My laugh was shrill, manic. "Don't give me that shit. You were fucking me up against the door, and then you fucking called me Ellen!" And I hadn't tried to stop her, until she called me by her dead grandmother's name. I'm not an innocent when it comes to having sex, but I'm not a slut either.

Clare took a single step towards me, but I backed away. She held her hands up in the air as if she was giving herself up to be arrested. "Honestly, Becky, I...I...I don't know what happened."

I narrowed my eyes and took her in. She did look confused; so was I. She was flushed; definitely like I was. Her eyes were shifting from my face to my chest, and then to my open jeans. Her face scrunched and her mouth moved as if she was working something out. I pulled my top down, zipped up my jeans, and fastened the button, all the while watching her.

"No!" Her disbelief was loud. Her eyes widened in realisation, and, if it hadn't been such a tense moment, her facial expression could have been described as comical. She started to move towards me, then realised she shouldn't and pulled back. "Please, please tell me I...I didn't...do that."

It was the sob when her voice broke that got to me. What had happened between us after we entered the room was not reality. Clare hadn't been herself when she came into the room. She looked the same, tasted the same, smelled the same, but the actions of the woman who had pinned me against the door were those of someone else.

I released a long, shaky breath, my shoulders slumping with my mood. "Sit down, Clare. We need to talk."

Her hands dropped to her sides in resignation. She gave a small nod as she pulled out her office chair and slumped down onto the leather. She rested her elbows on her knees and dropped her head into her hands. Clare's shoulders were quivering. The room was quiet for a moment, and then I heard a muffled sob, another sob, a sniff, muffled words.

The pain cracking through my chest took my breath away. Seeing Clare crying was agonising. I hesitantly moved forward, my hand outstretched, but she flinched when I touched her shoulder. I moved my palm in slow, soothing circles, the heat of me travelling into her. Then, and only then, did she seem to relax.

"I can smell you on me."

Not exactly what I was expecting her to say, but it was a start.

Clare lifted her head, squared her shoulders, then looked into my eyes. There was such confusion in her eyes, such sorrow, that I knew I would forgive her anything. If there was anything to forgive.

She looked away. "All I remember is opening the door to my office. The next thing, you pushed me away." She shrugged, adding a slight shake of her head. "I have no clue as to what happened in between. None."

Kneeling beside her, I let my hand rest on her shoulder whilst the other guided her face to meet mine. "It wasn't you, Clare. Whatever, or whomever it was, it wasn't you."

Clare released another sob. "Who...who was it?"

At that precise moment, her office phone rang. Clare looked at it but made no move to answer, just stared at it until it fell silent.

I tried to connect the dots inside my head. The obvious culprit making love to me so roughly was Annabel. She loved Ellen, ached for her. I opened my mouth to share my observation, but the phone rang again.

Clare didn't even look in its direction this time.

"Maybe it was Annabel." That had sounded so much better inside my head.

Clare pulled back, her face exhibiting how angry she was.

I took a deep breath to try again. "Look, we were supposed to get together to find Ellen. I don't know about you, but I haven't seen Annabel since a week last Saturday." I waited to see if that was sinking in before I continued. "Maybe it was Annabel's way of reminding us that she is about."

That was a stretch of the imagination, but at least I was trying to come up with something.

"But why do that?" Claire asked. "Why not just appear like she has before?"

I shrugged. "Could be to give us a graphic demonstration of how much she loved Ellen."

Another stretch. I vaguely wondered to what lengths the imagination could be stretched.

I sat back on the floor, and my hand slipped from her shoulder to rest on her knee. I thought back over what had happened and decided that my deduction could fit. Yes, the passion was there. Yes again to the desperation. The behaviour would be consistent with that of someone who hadn't seen the person she loved in a long while. But something didn't ring true. Clare, or Annabel, or whoever it had been, was a little aggressive in their need for sex. The kiss was harder than it needed to be, considering it was completely unexpected. There was no lead up at all. Not that I hadn't enjoyed it; I had. And the forcefulness of the attention to my breast, the lack of preliminaries when it came to feeling it naked, just seemed out of place. Also, there had been obvious frustration at being unable to shove my jeans down and push inside my underwear to take what is there.

The phone rang for a third time.

"I think you'd better…"

Clare nodded and leaned over to take the call. I stood up and moved away to give her some privacy, but there was really no place to go in the small room. I could hear her side of the conversation, and it made me feel like vomiting.

"So, he's awake now?" Clare's face was ashen. "What did the doctor say?"

I figured she must be talking about Freddie. Clare hadn't really mentioned any other males in her life, at least no male that would warrant a phone call to her if anything was to happen to him.

A few minutes later, she clicked off her phone. Clare stared at the plastic object, seemingly transfixed.

"Everything okay?" Of course I knew that it wasn't, but it's the thing a person says at times like that—state the obvious.

Clare's eyes widened, and her mouth moved as if she was working the jaw muscles. She looked at me. "Granddad had a turn about fifteen minutes ago. Seems like he...like he...died for a few moments."

"Died? For a while?" Personally, I didn't care if he died for good, but I knew that Clare loved him. "How is he now?"

"Stable. That's what they said. They've moved him to the hospital to monitor him." The air around her seemed thick, almost as if a cloud had enveloped her and was now settling.

I quickly rounded the desk and took Clare in my arms. She was trembling, almost vibrating. I pulled her close, stroked her back, kissed the side of her head.

Her arms gripped me. When she spoke, her words were muffled against my hair. "I have to go and see him."

I leaned back and looked into her eyes. Worry filled them. It was obvious that she believed her granddad was not long for this plane. I couldn't let her go like this, couldn't leave her to deal with all of this alone.

"When are we leaving?"

"We?"

I cupped her cheek. "You didn't think I would let you drive up there all on your own, did you?"

Clare pulled me against her, sobs wracking her body, words of thanks spilling onto my shoulder.

No. I definitely wasn't going to let her drive all the way to Kirk Langley whilst she was upset. That would have been an accident looking for a place to happen.

As I held her, my mind was racing. It was not good thoughts that came through, not good thoughts at all. It seemed more than a bit of a coincidence that Freddie had a brush with death at just about the time Clare tried to fuck me against the door in her office.

It was obvious to me now that it wasn't Annabel who had possessed Clare; it was the mean spirited Freddie Howell. I couldn't let Clare walk straight into his trap. If he wanted to play dirty, I was his woman. Too damned right.

Part 3

"Kiss me again, but don't let me see your eyes! I forgive what you have done to me. I love my murderer—but yours! How can I?"

Emily Bronte

Chapter Eleven

After the phone call, Clare asked Dale and Sally if they could pop in and feed Maggie, then she went home to pack, and so did I. I phoned work and told them I wouldn't be in, feigning sickness. My supervisor was more than a little surprised, as I never took time off for ill health. It was difficult enough for the company to get me to take the holidays I was entitled to, because all I'd ever had before was my job. Past tense. Now I had something else, someone who would be part and parcel of my future.

We'd been driving for over four and a half hours, but this time we took turns, and also made sure we stopped to eat and use the restroom. Clare called the hospital several times to be sure that Freddie was okay. Unfortunately, he was. I know that sounds callous, but that man did not deserve to live to a riper old age after what he had done. Too many good people die in this world, leaving the bad ones to continue living, something I thought was totally unfair. He also had his granddaughter travelling over a hundred and forty miles, in the dark, just to make sure he was still breathing. I was only going because of Clare. End of.

Although we had been in the car for a fair amount of time, I hadn't yet mentioned to Clare what I'd worked out about our encounter earlier that day. It's not the kind of thing one tells the woman she is falling for. Imagine me saying, "By the way, you know when I thought you were trying to have sex with me earlier? It was your granddad. No, listen, love, it's not what you think. He was dead at the time. Why are you so angry? After all, he's alive again." That probably wouldn't go down too well. Exactly. Mouth well and truly shut.

When I realised that Clare was taking us to Annabel's house, I felt a little unnerved. I had assumed we would be staying in a hotel, but Clare apparently had other ideas. I hadn't noticed the black bag stuffed down behind her seat that contained fresh bedding, or the box of food on the floor in the back. All I had done was throw my travel bag in the boot of her car and grin stupidly at the thought of going away with Clare Davies for a few days.

When I stepped outside the car into the dark November evening, I felt as if someone was watching me. I furtively looked over my shoulder. There was no one there, just blackness.

Clare carried some things to the porch, unlocked the door and switched on the porchlight. The artificial yellow beams spread like cheap margarine over the driveway, and instead of making me feel more at ease, it unnerved me even further. I scurried around to the boot, grabbed a bag, and scuttled to the porch.

Slam. Boot shut. Slam and slam. Doors shut. Thunk. Car locked. That was Clare. I thought I did well waiting outside until Clare had finished off, but the truth was, I was a little apprehensive about going inside the house alone.

"You okay?"

Clare was next to me, the black bag in her arms. I nodded, looked stealthily into the darkness beyond the lit driveway, and then picked up another bag from the porch.

It still amazes me that some people don't have the light switch close to the front door. Why would someone purposely put it halfway down the hallway? And why was I such a bundle of nerves?

Entering the living room, I was bombarded with memories of the last two times I had been there. The fireplace was empty, the ashes gone, but there was wood stacked to the side, ready for a blaze to burst into life again. Instead of hurrying over to claim my chair next to the non-existent fire, I stood and just stared at it, bags in hand. My breath appeared in visible puffs, as the room was freezing.

"Do you know how to start a fire?"

Clare's voice came from outside the room, and I could hear her rustling through the bags in the hallway.

"Not really." How could an answer be "Not really?" It was either yes or no, wasn't it?

Clare's voice seemed muffled, as if her head was inside a blanket. The words "emersion" and "on" floated to me from the vicinity of the stairs.

Setting my bags on the floor, I moved closer to the fireplace, knelt down, picked up a piece of wood and stared at it.

A laugh came from behind me, and I dropped the wood. The loud clatter it made on the floor made my nerves scream, and my teeth clamped together.

"You're not going to get it lighted like that. Here, let me."

Clare knelt beside me, her hand reaching out and taking the wood. "Go and find some newspaper or something, will you?"

I nodded and stood, scanning the room. Everything was as I expected it to be—the leather sofa, the chair, the coffee table. Unlike the last time I had been, there were magazines on the table. My teeth worried the inside of my cheek. Nerves, I think. Would they be dated 1953, like the first time I had been there? Or would I, with relief, find copies of *Bella* and *Woman's Own*?

"I think I left some newspapers in the kitchen that I can use to help start the fire." Clare looked at me briefly before continuing to stack the wood in the grate. "I was wrapping up Annabel's things in it."

I didn't relish the thought of going into the kitchen on my own, but I wasn't about to tell Clare that. My ego wouldn't allow it.

The kitchen was exactly how I remembered it. The Aga was still there, looking even more dated than I remembered. The wooden table was pushed to the side, the chairs stacked on the top. The only major difference was the fridge. It was a newer model than the one I had seen on my first visit. I don't know why, but that made me feel a little better.

I spotted a stack of newspapers to the side and went over to grab them. Just as I picked up the heap, I heard a noise from behind me and automatically looked towards the window. But I knew the noise hadn't come from there; it had come from the corner of the room.

Most people probably would have thought it was rats, that the scraping sound had been caused by tiny feet. Not me. I'd had experiences in this kitchen before, and none of those happenings had been due to rats.

Closing my eyes, I swallowed down the fear. It refused to go anywhere. I tried to swallow it again. Tentative, I opened one eye, then the other. I had to look.

Hugging the newspapers to my chest as if they would protect me, I turned so my back was against the kitchen counter. The wooden table was in the centre of the room, the chairs tucked neatly underneath. I couldn't make a sound. But even if I could've, I was too busy trying to keep my heart from launching out of my mouth.

Click.

The noise came from the side, and I shifted my attention from the table. The back ring on the Aga had lit on its own. Lit. On. Its. Own.

I shuffled towards the door, the newspapers clutched against me. I didn't want to turn my back on whatever was in there, but I also didn't want to stay in the kitchen alone.

When I reached the doorway, I turned and ran back into the living room. Clare was just standing as I got there, her expression alive with pride because of her ability to stack wood for the fire.

"Piece of... What's the matter? Becky?" Clare strode over to me, reached out and grabbed my shoulders, her face full of concern. "What's happened?" Without even waiting for an answer, she was off towards the kitchen. "What? Oh."

It was then I realised I was in the living room on my own, and I hastened after her.

"You've put the kettle on." She beamed. "I never could work out how to use that thing." She opened the cupboards and lifted out the teapot and cups, the same teapot and cups Annabel had used when I had been there the first time.

"It wasn't me."

Clare turned towards me, her face displaying her lack of understanding.

"I didn't..." I pointed to the kettle, then to the table. "It wasn't me."

Her brow furrowed, and she shook her head. "If it..."

"Not rats." Why had I said that?

"Rats? Are you feeling okay?" Clare came and slipped her arm around my waist. "You're shivering. Come, I'll light the fire and get you warmed up."

I allowed her to lead me back into the living room. Anything to get out of the kitchen. We were welcomed by the crackle of the fire.

"What the fuck?"

Clare's exclamation summed up what I was feeling.

"But you were with me in the kitchen."

Considering I didn't know how to make a fire in the first place, the fact that I had been with her didn't really matter.

Clare looked at the newspapers still in my grasp, then back to my face. I could almost read the thoughts and emotions skimming through her in the myriad expressions crossing her face. When a smile blossomed, I was a little confused. Why would she be smiling when someone, or something, was fucking us about?

"Kettle on, fire started. Looks like Annabel is welcoming us to her home."

Apparently Clare thought that would make me feel better—a ghost popping the kettle on, arranging the furniture, and then lighting a fire. Not so much. I was too much of a coward to feel a sense of ease in that scenario.

Clare led me to the leather sofa and eased me down, then stepped back into the hall and returned momentarily with a duvet. "Here. Get warm." Her fingers brushed against my face, brushing my hair back behind my ear. "Annabel isn't out to hurt us, Becky." A soft smile graced her lips, accompanied by a slight nod of her head that was meant to reassure me. Clare placed the duvet over me, tucking it around my body so cold air couldn't seep inside. "I'll just see to the tea, and I'll be back." She kissed me, and I felt a little calmer.

I could hear the banging of cups onto saucers and the muffled whistle of the kettle coming to boil. I hoped that it was Clare and not the bogey man that was making my cuppa. My attention returned to the fire. The flames danced and curled around the logs that Clare had expertly stacked. As I stared, my thoughts were invaded by the memory of the last time I had seen the fire lit. It had been a perfect moment. I was sitting on the sofa, soft music playing, Bella asleep in bed upstairs—

Bella asleep? Jesus! That had been in my dream, not when I had met Annabel Howell for the first time.

I shifted in my seat. Something hard was jamming into my side, and I felt around with my hand to find it. Even before I lifted the object from underneath the duvet, I knew what it would be—Annabel's notebook.

I held it up and examined it. It was old and worn, as if it had lived a lifetime in the hands of another. I could see the tip of the bookmark where Clare must've left it, and I opened the notebook to that page. I set the bookmark aside and started to read.

"She's gone. Gone. I don't believe it. She wouldn't leave Bella, wouldn't leave me. I know this. With all that I am, I know it. I saw her just this morning as she was gathering her things together to go home. She didn't say that was the end of us, that she didn't want to be with me anymore. She was all smiles, all love, all kisses. I keep closing my eyes and trying to visualise that scene again. I was just off the porch, and Bella was holding Ellen's hand as they stood in the doorway of my house. Her smile was for me. I know it! If only I hadn't left her there and gone into town. At least I would know what happened."

I looked at the date at the top of the page: October 31, 1953. If I wasn't mistaken, that was the night after I'd had my ghostly dream encounter, but I couldn't swear to it, as I was trying to project my reason into a totally unreasonable place.

My eyes flicked back to the entry I'd been reading.

"God, I hurt. Inside me. Deep inside me. There is something wrong, I know it. I've looked everywhere. No one in town has seen Ellen. Freddie claimed that he was late getting home from work because he'd hit his head on some machinery and had to get the cut cleaned up. He said that he thought Ellen had lost the plot, as she had left Bella on her own. She wouldn't do that, wouldn't lose the plot like that. She wouldn't leave her young daughter on her own. Not Ellen. Not her. She loves Bella, loves me..."

"Hey, whatcha reading?" Clare was carrying a tray of tea things balanced in her hands. She turned her back to me as she placed the tray down onto the coffee table, her hands busy making us each a cup of tea.

"Annabel's notebook."

Her back stiffened, her hands went still on the milk jug. She slowly turned to face me.

"What?" Maybe my one word query sounded a bit harsh.

Her eyes noted the duvet, her head tilting to the side as it always did. "How did you get it, when it looks as if you haven't moved?"

"Because you left it on the sofa?" The statement turned into a question without my intention.

"No I didn't. It's at the bottom of my travelling bag."

I waved the notebook at her, physical evidence that she was mistaken.

"I should say, it *was* at the bottom of my travelling bag." She lifted her face to the ceiling and said, "Thank you, Annabel!" Her face broke into one of her mesmerising grins, and then she turned and finished off the tea.

I just stared at the back of her head in wonder. She was so bloody beautiful. I felt the need to pinch myself at being alone with her. Amazing to think I hadn't thought of pinching myself when all the supernatural happenings had been going on. It seemed like I found the existence of ghosts easier to believe than that a gorgeous woman would be interested in me.

Clare turned and stood in front of me, cup and saucer extended, and I took it carefully and balanced it on the duvet over my knee.

"What part have you read to?"

"Where you left off."

"But I've finished it. I thought I told you that."

I gestured for her to take my cup and, after she had, I felt beside me for the bookmark. Lifting it, I waved it in her face. "Where you left this, then." Clare leaned forward, her body bending her face closer to mine. I didn't wait for a response. I closed the gap between us and stole a quick kiss.

Clare laughed and leaned down to my lips. Softness met softness, and everything else faded away. I wanted to pull her against me and deepen the kiss, but Clare was holding two teas and I was still hanging on to the notebook and bookmark.

She sighed when I pulled away, and our eyes met and held. So much passed between us in that single, simple moment that my heart seemed to swell. I felt the words form in my brain, those three words that I knew I should not let pass my lips. It was too soon, for her *and* for me.

"That's not my bookmark. I haven't got a bookmark from the Peaks."

I looked at the strip of leather. *Peak District National Park* was emblazoned at the top, and below that was a stone circle that was emblematic of the area. I lifted it to my nose and sniffed, had a think, then sniffed again—leather, and a hint of perfume that was not Clare's or mine. There was just a hint of scent, but it was still discernible. Sherlock Holmes I definitely wasn't, but there was something unfamiliarly familiar about the scent.

I offered the bookmark to Clare, who sniffed it twice and then looked puzzled. "Is it aftershave?"

That prompted me to sniff again. I couldn't be sure; the smell of the leather was masking it. I shrugged. I didn't know. That was a shit answer, but the only one I had.

"Never mind. Here." Clare held out my cup, and I took it. "Remind me. Where are you up to?" She lifted the edge of the duvet and settled beside me, pulling the cover over us both.

After describing to her where I'd stopped reading, we both began to read. It was heart breaking to read about Annabel's bewilderment over Ellen's disappearance. It was like witnessing the five stages of grief without a dead body to mourn over. Initially she tried to deny that Ellen was gone. She tried to believe Ellen would be back, that Freddie was lying and Ellen's clothes hadn't disappeared with her. She didn't believe that Ellen could just leave her, leave her own daughter's welfare in the hands of a brute such as her brother was.

Annabel's anger flared, anger at Freddie, and at herself for falling for Ellen in the first place. Anger at the situation. Finally, her anger was turned on Ellen. The cruelty of the words on the page was such that if I hadn't known better, I would have thought Annabel might have killed Ellen herself. Strangely, her emotions went backwards. Annabel once again denied the loss of the love of her life. The words were smudged, the ink exhibiting signs of having been wet. Some sentences didn't even make sense, just words jumbled together.

Annabel moved from denial into bargaining so swiftly, I had to reread the link numerous times. The words she had written were full despair and the agony of loss. The love Annabel had shared with Clare's grandmother was nothing short of earth-shattering, and it had been suddenly ripped from her. She wrote that she would give up her love, just be friends, if only she could see Ellen again. There were countless references to sin, her sin, the sin of being a lesbian, and she swore she would never go against God again. If only Ellen was there with her, she'd be happy just being able to see her, even if it was just to say goodbye.

At that point, my tears were coming thick and fast, but I kept reading. I had to know it all, to feel what Annabel had felt to understand what it had been like for her. The ache in my chest was growing with each word, each syllable, each moment of Annabel Howell's broken existence. How would I feel if Clare left me?

I glanced at her sitting beside me, sniffling. Her attention was totally on the notebook, her eyes moving quickly over the words. Dark strands of hair had fallen forward, encircling her face in an embrace of sorts. And even though I barely knew her, had only seen her a handful of times, my heart knew that I was in love with her. So utterly and completely in love with her, I believed I couldn't survive without her in my life. It was as if my heart had been closed until I met her, and then it opened wide to allow her inside and make me whole.

My eyes went back to the notebook, but it took me a while to pick up the thread of Annabel's story. The epiphany of one's love for another could not easily be brushed aside as if it were insignificant.

To read of Annabel's depression stage was awful, especially now I realised it could so easily be me who could lose the euphoria that came with finding true love. Annabel was willing to give it all up to see Ellen one more time. I knew I would feel like that, too, and the thought scared me. Annabel had spent weeks looking for Ellen, asking the locals, confronting Freddie. But no one knew what had become of her, or if they did, they weren't telling Annabel. Their apparent apathy mixed with Annabel's anger, and the combination was almost deadly. She wrote of an encounter she'd had with Freddie that had resulted in Annabel being arrested.

"She was arrested?" Clare's voice squeaked in surprise.

The family must've kept that a secret, too. I was surprised they had room for clothes with all the skeletons in their closets.

The diary was very explicit about the events leading up to Annabel's arrest. The entry also confirmed that Freddie had been in the local pub when Annabel had eventually hunted him down.

"My brother is a liar. A liar! A bad husband and a bad father. When I said that to his face outside the pub, he laughed that superior laugh of his and told me to go home where I belonged. Told me that what went on with him, his wife, and his daughter had nothing to do with me. It has everything to do with me. Everything! My instincts were telling me there was something wrong, and that Freddie knew exactly what that wrong thing was.

He thought that would be that. Didn't expect me to follow him into the pub and his nest of cronies, and tell him to his face that no real man would treat a woman the way he had treated his wife. He tried to laugh it off, tried to act cocky. I knew he was showing off in front of his mates, but the look he gave me, the same look I remembered from when we were kids, that look was warning me off.

When he turned to his mates and said, "To be honest, lads, I'm glad the old slut has gone. I was gonna kick her out anyroads," I saw red. The anger I'd been trying to tamp down seemed to burst out from me.

"Slut?" I could barely get the word out.

He leaned forward, his leer firmly in place. "A fucking slut."

I stepped back. If I hadn't, I'd have punched him straight in his lying face, but I didn't want to lower myself to his level.

That didn't stop me announcing, "Freddie Howell is a wife beater and a coward, and can only be a man when he has the upper hand or by hitting a woman."

I didn't expect him to lunge at me. But then I don't think he expected me to give him the pasting I did. In front of all his so-called friends, too.

The next thing I knew, the police were there. Seems as if Freddie had at least one friend, after all, especially since the doctor was called, too. It was only later that I found out I'd broken his cheek, his nose, three ribs, and two of his fingers. The only things hurt on me were my knuckles and my heart, and perhaps my reputation when it got about the town that I'd been arrested.

Freddie didn't to want to press charges, probably thought the incident would be forgotten sooner if he didn't play it up, but they arrested me anyway. I was taken to the cells to cool down a little. For that I am grateful, as there is no guessing what more I could've been capable of at that moment.

It was when I was sitting in my cell that I knew for sure that I'd never see Ellen again. The pain that ripped through my chest had nothing to do with the fight I'd had with my brother. This pain, this agony, came from the realisation that the love of my life was lost to me, had evaporated into thin air without a word of goodbye. I also know that if she had left, it was for a very good reason. Ellen didn't leave me because she didn't love me, any more than I could have left her. All I have to do is picture her eyes as she looked at me, and I know. Ellen loved me just as much as I loved her. I will love her for the rest of my life. My love for her is the best part of me."

I felt numb. No, not numb, drained. Annabel had written that she had accepted that she would never see Ellen again, but I didn't believe it. When I first met her, she was waiting for Ellen, thought I was Ellen. She had held me close and said, "I knew you would come. Knew it. God! I've looked everywhere for you. Everywhere." Her voice had been full of pain, her agony stark and cutting. The way she held me, pulled my head to her chest, kissed my hair. I had felt safe in her arms, so protected. I remembered looking into the woods and realising the person chasing me couldn't hurt me now.

The person chasing me couldn't hurt me now.

I sat up quickly, and the notebook toppled from my knee whilst the cup and saucer hit the floor with a crack. "Fuck me!"

Clare jumped up and looked around the room. "What? What did you see?"

My jaw slackened, then I smiled widely. Looking into startled brown eyes, I said, "Everything."

Chapter Twelve

It felt weird telling Clare about what I had realised, but wonderful, too. Not the events, as she already knew them, but rather what they indicated: Ellen had been trying to get back to Annabel. She had been running through the woods, and someone was chasing her. I'd seen it, lived it, or maybe only dreamt it, but I was certain it had happened. When I'd stopped at the side of the road to answer the call of nature, I felt someone watching me. Later, I dreamed I was watching myself. Fucked up? Yes. But it happened. When I arrived at Annabel's house, someone was still watching me, although it felt darker somehow. As if it wasn't Ellen anymore. Obviously, that watcher was the one who attacked Ellen, and my money was still on the bastard Freddie Howell. Had to be him.

Seeing the figure at the kitchen window, that was real. I remembered I was awake at the time, and although I was in the middle of some paranormal time shifting shit, it felt totally tangible. That episode was followed by me dreaming of being outside the kitchen window, tapping on the glass, then feeling that I had to leave before I scared the living shit out of the other "me" who was carrying a tray into the kitchen. I remembered how I had wanted to get Annabel's attention, to tell her that someone was after me. But before I could do that, he got me. He grabbed me from behind and growled in my ear, "*Ya thought she'd 'elp ya, eh?*" That hateful voice of his was dark and cruel and just as wickedly spiteful as it had always been. I recalled thinking, "*This time it wouldn't just be a beating,*" and that had to mean Freddie. Ellen's husband was a wife beater. I'd seen the bruises on myself in my dream, and also when I'd awakened.

Lastly I shared my final realisation, that *"This time he would take everything, including my life"* had, tragically, come true.

Clare was utterly quiet and still. Her face was white, and her lips were drawn into a thin line. I hadn't even considered that maybe she wouldn't believe me when I told her that her granddad had killed her grandmother, that she might be angry at me for suggesting it. I had already shared most of those things on previous occasions, but this time I actually knew what they inferred. I hoped beyond hope that Clare would not just reject the possibility that Freddie was a murderer.

The silence in the room was deafening, and I wanted to break it, but I waited for Clare's response.

"You think Granddad killed Ellen?" Her voice seemed louder than it actually was, and the strident tone stung my ears. "You want me to believe that he killed her and hid the body?"

I nodded, grimacing in anticipation of what I feared would be her disbelief. It was.

"If what you say is true, then how could Granddad have been at home on the day she disappeared?" Clare held her hand up to stop me from interrupting. "You said that he chased her through the woods, yes?" I nodded. "It was dark. Ellen had just made it to Annabel's house when he caught up with her. Is that what you are saying?" Another nod from me. "But didn't you also say that Annabel had been looking for Ellen all day?"

"What do you mean?"

"If Ellen wasn't at home, if she had disappeared, then how could she supposedly be running through the woods to Annabel's house that same evening? Do you think she had been hiding somewhere until Freddie was out of the way?"

Shit. Clare was right. I'd assumed that Ellen was already dead by the time Annabel had gone around to Freddie's, but she couldn't have been. It didn't add up.

My stomach turned over as I remembered my final dream. It took no effort at all to conjure the images of hands around my throat. I could even feel the pressure of those strong, capable hands, and how weak I'd felt, as if I was losing consciousness. But then, I also had seen the mark a noose had left, indicating that it wasn't hands that had tried to throttle the life out of me, it had been rope.

"Ellen. Look at me, Ellen!" Annabel's voice in my memory was unmistakable, although it did sound as if she'd lost the plot.

Other thoughts vied for attention. Annabel asking Ellen, *"I'm not like him, am I? You know—with my anger?"* The words seemed to echo again. I'd thought about them before, but now...

No. Annabel wasn't like her brother. She wasn't a wife beating, murdering bastard. Her notebook was a testament to how much she loved Ellen, and how she nearly lost her mind when Ellen disappeared.

"Maybe he knocked Ellen out, or hid her away for a while." Even to my ears that sounded lame. But before Clare could respond, I asked, "Did Ellen ever try to kill herself?"

Clare's mouth opened, but she snapped it shut again without answering. Her head tilted to the side as she thought. As if a light bulb went off over in head, she lunged forward and grabbed the notebook, then frantically flipped backwards to a previous section.

I sat and waited. There wasn't much else I could do to fuck things up. I mean, I accused her grandfather of murder and wife beating, thought about her great aunt strangling her grandmother, and then went for the suicide route.

"Jesus!" Clare's voice brought me out of my internal review. "I don't know how I could've forgotten this."

She held out the notebook, and I reached out and took it. The date was June 2, 1951. I hadn't gotten to that portion yet. I'd skipped to the bookmark, and so had missed out on a huge chunk of the text. The last thing I had read in sequence was Annabel saying how she wished Ellen would leave Freddie, how she knew he beat her, how Ellen had told him the marriage was over. I looked down at the page Clare had selected.

"She nearly left us all today. I stopped her. I couldn't believe what she was planning to do. Couldn't believe it when I walked into the barn and saw her there. I want to write more, but I promised her I wouldn't tell a soul. Truth is, I'm worried sick. What if I'm not around next time?"

I looked up at Clare, and she nodded. "Looks to me as if Ellen tried to kill herself, don't you think?"

What I was thinking was that this passage would definitely explain the marks around my neck from a rope and my recollection that Annabel was present during a strangling episode.

"Maybe she did run away, and died as a result?" Clare suggested

"No," I said.

"No?"

I shrugged and pursed my lips. "At the time we are assuming Ellen tried to kill herself, as described in that passage, she wasn't yet *with* Annabel, not as a lover anyway."

"And?"

"And...once they were together, Ellen wouldn't have put Annabel through that. If Ellen loved her so much, she wouldn't willingly break Annabel's heart."

There was no need to discuss with Clare whether Annabel and Ellen eventually became lovers. It was obvious we both knew that had eventually happened, especially since I had 'dreamed' about them together and Clare had read Annabel's notebook.

Clare sighed and ran her fingers through her hair. "I can't think straight. It's all too overwhelming." Tired brown eyes looked at me. "I'm beat."

I felt the energy seeping from me, too. It had been a long day.

Clare stood and held out a hand. "Shall we go to bed?"

Fuck. Bed. One bed. Me and her in one bed. Alone together. In a bed. At night. My expression must have given away my surprise. I would never have been any good at poker.

At first Clare looked baffled, then a lopsided, interested smile appeared. "What's the matter? Scared you'll get molested in the dark by things that go bump in the night?"

I hadn't thought of that. But now that she had mentioned it... "Where are we, erm, I mean I, sleeping?"

Clare leaned back and looked at me, really looked at me. I felt as if I was being analysed by her eyes, the eyes half squinting in contemplation.

"You have two options," she said, her voice silky.

"Two?" I was quite proud that my voice didn't squeak.

"You can sleep down here on your own..." She paused and gauged my reaction. I tried to assume the non-existent poker face. "Or, you can share the bed upstairs. With me."

Why had she added "with me?" It wasn't as if I would be sharing it with Annab—

Even if I hadn't thought of being downstairs, on my own, with ghosts of Christmases past, I believed the option of snuggling up with Clare, who was alive, was definitely my best option. "With you." My only concern was that I would become fresh with her in the night. Get a little bit too "up close and personal" when all she was suggesting was that we sleep in the same bed.

A smile flickered across her lips. "Of course, there is my mother's old room, but it is full of boxes."

Was she trying to get out of sharing a bed with me? Had she spotted the lascivious look in my eyes? Should I back out, tell her I didn't mind sleeping in a room full of boxes?

"And the bed in there is dismantled," she added with a smirk.

What was Clare trying to do? I'd already said yes.

"But if you prefer, I could try to put it together."

I stared at her and waited for her to think up more excuses. She didn't disappoint.

"Or I could sleep down here." She smiled graciously.

I'd had enough. "Look, it's not like I'm going to molest you in your sleep."

Clare looked startled, then she laughed. "Shame."

The blush that infused my face burned in its intensity.

Clare stretched, and her shirt rose up, exposing delicious skin. "The water should be hot now. I'm going to grab a shower."

She leaned down, and her breath skimmed over my overheated face. Clare was so close that I had to flick my eyes from one to the other of hers to try and focus.

"And..." her fingers trailed over my top lip, "if you're interested..."

I was certain that she must've been able to hear me swallow, or try to swallow.

"...there's..." the brush of her lips made my spine tingle, "plenty of hot water."

Then she was gone and I was left panting on the sofa, believing that I didn't need hot water; I needed a cold shower.

I think that was the quickest shower I ever took. It wasn't just the sound of the old pipes clanking that made me a bag of nerves. When I was in the bathroom, it seemed as if there was a presence that shouldn't be there. Washing my hair with my eyes open was a challenge, but with lots of stinging, cursing, and rinsing, I managed it. The bathroom was cold, too. I couldn't believe that people could live without central heating. My whole body seemed to buzz as its heat encountered the coolness of the air, and even the vigorous towel drying did nothing to alleviate the chill inside me.

I gratefully slipped into my flannelette pyjamas. I would not be voted *Sexiest Dressed Woman of 2013*, but at least I was warming up. I slipped into my slippers, and then a dressing gown. All I needed was a hat, gloves, and a scarf to complete the outfit, and I'd be set. And warmer.

As I entered what had been Annabel's room, Clare was sitting in bed, the lamp alight on the table next to her as she read Annabel's journal. The room was warm, and I turned to see a roaring fire in the fireplace on the wall in front of the bed. The room was quaint, old fashioned but very comfortable. The brass framed bed looked huge, definitely big enough for two. In the corner, there was a padded chair that was covered in a dusky pink, crushed velvet cloth. Not exactly my cup of tea, but then again, the last time this room had seen a lick of paint, I hadn't even been born. The rest of the furniture was dark wood, very rustic, just like the rest of the house.

"Feel better?" Clare's voice was gentle, appealing, and the smile on her face was welcoming.

I closed the door behind me and slowly went over to the bed.

"Are you okay sleeping on the right?" She nodded at that side of the bed.

I'd never thought about it. I generally sprawled in the bed like da Vinci's *Vitruvian Man*, as I typically slept alone. I nodded, grinned sheepishly, and pulled the duvet back to climb in beside the woman I was head over heels for, but couldn't touch. When I turned onto my side, I could feel Clare's eyes on my back. I snuggled down under the cover.

A minute went by in silence, then, "Becky?"

I grunted. Brilliant.

"Can I ask you something?"

I pulled a face before answering with a shaky, "Sure."

"Are you going to sleep all night with your slippers on?"

Shit. I'd forgotten to take them off.

"And won't you be a bit warm wearing your dressing gown?"

I pushed the covers back and slung my legs out of bed. Just as I reached down to take a slipper off, a loud crashing sound came from the next room. Clare jumped out of bed and ran to the door, but her hand froze on the handle. By that time I was behind her, and I could see her flexing her fingers as if she was willing them to turn the knob.

I grabbed her arm and eased her to the side. "Allow me."

To any lay person, I might have appeared to be in control. To this same lay person, it would seem I was the leader type, the "not scared of anything" kind of woman. In actuality, I was crapping my pants, but considering I had just turfed Clare out of the way, I had to follow through.

Taking into account that I'd not heard a squeak from the door as I had entered the room not five minutes before, it had suddenly gotten the joints of a ninety-year-old. The sharp creaking made my ears thrum, and I believed the only way to stop them hurting was to grit my teeth until my jaws ached.

"What's happening? Who is it?"

Clare's panicked questioning made me jump, and I shushed her. Moving out of the room and then along the corridor, I felt as if it was getting more and more difficult to put one foot in front of the other. A weight came over me, holding me back, then I realised that Clare was hanging onto the back of my dressing gown. "What the fuck are you doing?" I hissed over my shoulder.

"Staying close."

I wanted to laugh at the stupidity of the situation, but now wasn't the time. I had to check out the spare room, and I wasn't too chuffed about what I might find in there. The door handle to what had once been Bella's room was ice cold. I knew metal was usually cold, but this was beyond that, beyond even the chill of the house. Part of me wondered if the knob had been drenched in liquid nitrogen, and I considered whether I would be able to remove my hand in order to let go of it.

Just like the door to Annabel's bedroom, this one's hinges squealed their disapproval as I pushed it open. My hand felt along the wall until I found the light switch. Click. Nothing. Still dark. Click click click click. Maybe I was hoping it was powered like a dynamo battery, and the more I clicked, the better the chance that I would be able to get the bulb to light up.

"Wait here."

Clare's hand left my dressing gown and she disappeared down the stairs, leaving me halfway in and halfway out a room from which we had both heard a loud crashing sound. Fear choked my throat and threatened to spill over into the air in either a guttural scream or vomit. I could hear Clare banging about downstairs, and I wanted her to come back so I could show her what an absolute coward I really was.

Suddenly something caught my eye. A small circular light seemed to hover in front of what looked like a chest of drawers. At any other time, that might be of little significance, but not now. It hovered for a moment and then flitted to the corner of the room. Was it the beam of a torch? A firefly? We didn't have fireflies in this country. And we didn't have fairies, either, at least not the kind that turned themselves into balls of phosphorescence and danced about deserted spare rooms.

The orb was back to the dresser, bouncing about as if it was supercharged.

I took a tentative step into the room, my fear replaced by curiosity. Another step, and I was fully inside the spooky room. The light orb stopped, quivered, as if it was waiting for me to make a move.

"Here."

I jumped about a foot! Fuck. I hadn't even heard Clare coming up the stairs. Turning, I could just make out her outline. Her hand was outstretched, as if she was handing me something. "Jesus, Clare. You could've warned me." I reached out to accept whatever it was she was offering, and... Nothing. My hand seemed to pass straight through hers, and I felt the chill of it, the emptiness of something that should've been there but wasn't. My insides churning, I took a step back, which took me further into the room.

The figure advanced, closing the door before it came forward. It was just me and it. Just me and the thing I couldn't see now, because the room was in pitch blackness. I moved further back, my heart racing inside my chest. Nausea gripped me, frantically alerting me to my own mortality. This wasn't Clare. Obviously. I didn't know who it was I was sharing this confined, dark space with. Even the orb had buggered off.

Cold fingers touched the side of my face, and I jerked my head away. They moved to my hair, making the strands flutter slowly, as if they were being sifted through, and then the disembodied fingers ran along my shoulder. Although I knew I wouldn't make physical contact, I batted at them frantically, as if they were a swarm of aggravating flies.

"It's me."

Me? Who the fuck was "me?"

I croaked out a response, but it didn't make any sense, which made it fit perfectly with what was happening at that moment.

I tried to step to the side, but there was something blocking my path. I stumbled and fell to the ground, and something sharp jammed my calf. The pain was excruciating, and I was definite I could feel blood leaving my body.

"Here." The voice was right next to my ear.

I couldn't help the scream I let loose as I scrabbled on my hands and knees in the direction I thought the door was.

Slam.

The door opened with such force that I was surprised it was still on its hinges. A figure stood in the entrance, the face masked in darkness whilst the light pooled around her outline. This time I knew it was Clare. A sob ripped from my throat, and became airborne, then another, and another.

Warm, living arms wrapped around me, and Clare's scent overwhelmed me with the comfort of her presence. She was shushing and reassuring, holding and protecting me. My fingers grasped her arms and dug in, but she didn't flinch, didn't grumble.

"Come on, baby, come on. Let's get you out of here."

She half lifted me to my feet, then wrapped an arm around my waist to support me. The back of my leg hurt, and I could feel blood trickling down into my slipper. Any amount of pressure on my foot made me wince, and I slid along on my tiptoe as we moved along the hallway, back into Annabel's room. Tears streamed down my face, and I brushed them away.

It wasn't until I was sitting on the bed and she was examining my cut that she spoke. "What happened?" Brown eyes flicked up to meet mine before settling back on my leg. She pressed one of her t-shirts against the wound, lifted it away to check the damage, then pressed it harder to stem the bleeding.

I delayed answering by removing my robe. I was hoping the extra bit of time would enable me to recall what had happened with a little more clarity. To no avail.

"I freaked myself out."

That wasn't exactly the truth, but I was too drained to go into detail. All I wanted to do was get away from that house, and everything in it. I'd worked out that it had been Annabel in the room with me. Judging by the size and shape of her, it had to be. The voice seemed a little different, but then again, I wasn't rational at the time. It occurred to me that if Annabel would allow me to become so terrified, keep touching me, following me, shutting the door to obscure the light, then perhaps she was not as kind hearted as I'd thought she was.

That was a not a comforting realisation. Not a comforting realisation at all. What if the notebook was a fake? What if Annabel killed Ellen and wrote the notebook afterwards to make people believe she had loved her too much to do such a thing? I tried to recall everything I knew about her, but my head hurt too badly.

"I think it'll be okay. The bleeding has stopped."

Clare's voice drifted up to me, and I gave her a watery smile.

"I'm just popping downstairs to get the first aid kit. We need to clean that." She stood, then leaned towards me and cupped my jaw. "Will you be all right for a minute?"

I wanted to say "no" but my head nodded.

"Sure?"

I nodded again. Soft lips landed on my head, remained a moment, and then withdrew. After she left the room, I kicked my slippers off and repositioned myself on the edge of the bed with my left pyjama leg hiked up. It seemed as if all of my energy had left me; I felt so tired of it all. Did I really want to know what had happened to Ellen? Did I really care if Freddie had killed her, or if Annabel had done the deed?

At that precise moment, I didn't care at all. I just wanted my life to go back to how it had been—easy. Empty, but easy. No ghosts, no having the shit scared out of me.

I looked at Clare as she re-entered the room. She seemed paler than she had been earlier. A first aid kit in her hands, without looking at me, she knelt down to clean my wound. Her hands shook as she applied the antiseptic, and I felt my heart kick start. When she struggled with opening the casing of the plaster, I reached out and covered her hand with mine.

"Let me do it." My voice was gentle, coaxing, but she didn't look at me.

I tore off the covering and passed the plaster back to her. She covered the cut. I watched every move she made, mesmerised. She seemed to fumble whilst putting everything back into the first aid kit, organising and reorganising the contents. It took me a moment or two to realise she was crying.

Ignoring the twinging that I knew movement would cause in my leg, I slipped from the bed and sat on the floor in front of her. When I lifted Clare's chin, I gasped at the absolute misery I found in her eyes. They were the darkest I had ever seen them, and also the most sorrowful. An ache spread through my chest, and I felt my heart break a little. I wiped the tears away, then kissed her cheeks, her eyelids, her nose. Clare's arms wrapped around me, and she buried her face against my shoulder, muffling her sobs. I stroked her back, wondering why she was crying in the first place. Was it from fear? Had she finally had the crap scared out of her enough to make her go to pieces in my arms?

I kissed the side of her head and then drew away in order to look at her. I fully expected her to snuggle against me again, but she didn't. Her attention was not on me, her eyes downcast.

"What's up, love?"

Clare's lip trembled, and she gave a slight shake of her head.

"There must be something, else you wouldn't be crying." I made sure my voice was gentle and accompanied it with an encouraging smile.

"You must hate me."

Hate was not what I was feeling for her, far from it. Stuff the single life, the "easy" way out. If being with Clare meant that I would continually get the shit scared out of me, then so be it.

"Why would you say that?" My voice was still gentle, but I let her hear my surprise.

"Because of what just happened. Because of what *always* seems to happen." She shifted away from me and stood.

I quickly followed, and grabbed her hand to keep her from leaving the room. "I'm a big girl, Clare. I wouldn't be here if I didn't want to be. I'm the one who invited myself along, remember?"

She still had her back to me, so I tugged her hand and made her stumble backwards and into me. "We are in this together, okay?" I turned her towards me and wrapped my arms around her. I needed to see her eyes, to see she had understood. I didn't want her to act like a martyr, to say she couldn't do "us" because she didn't want me to have to suffer through everything we were experiencing. I think that would have killed me.

"I...I ..." I was willing myself not to say I loved her. It was still too soon, too damned soon. Yes, I believed that some people, somewhere, had probably fallen in love at first sight, but I would never have classified myself as the kind of woman that would do so. I was too rational for that. Too rational for ghosts, too, as it happened. Instead of finishing what I was going to say, I grinned at my own internal observation.

Clare pinned me with one of her looks, sniffing loudly. "Why are you grinning?"

My grin just grew wider, and she moved towards me, a small smile breaking through the tears. "What were you going to say?" she prodded.

Was she hoping I was going to confess my undying devotion for her, admit how much my heart ached for her? Or was she just genuinely interested in my unfinished sentences?

I slipped my hand onto her cheek and made sure her eyes were looking into mine. "I was going to say I like you very much."

Her lips captured mine and made me forget everything but that perfect moment. It seemed as though every moment shared with Clare was perfect. Her hands caressed my back, and then slipped up to rest in my hair. I wanted to be closer to her, so much closer, but Clare pulled her mouth away from mine and began nibbling my ear.

"You are so beautiful, so very very beautiful."

It seemed like déjà vu, as if she had spoken those words before in a setting that was very different. The words seeped into me, warming my body.

"I...like you, like you so much, Becky."

At that moment I knew that Clare was aware it was me she was with, and I dropped all my defences. Back to kissing. Soft kisses. Gentle, teasing kisses. Kisses that told me she was the woman I'd waited for my whole life, kisses that wanted me to tell her I loved her.

Her lips left mine and travelled to my throat. Nips, followed by flicks of an inquisitive tongue fanned the warmth I was experiencing into a growing heat within me. I didn't think; I just acted.

Not breaking contact, I walked the two of us backwards until I felt the base of the bed frame hit the back of my calves. Pain shot up my injured leg, but I didn't care about that. It paled in comparison with the other sensations rippling through my body. I lay back, pulling Clare with me. She came willingly, her body covering mine. The thickness of my pyjamas was now frustrating me. I wanted to feel her skin next to mine.

It was Clare who sat up and pulled her pyjama top free in one gorgeously swift movement. The soft curve of her breasts enticed me, drew me to them like a moth to the flame. I tentatively traced my finger along the swell of one, then the other, luxuriating in the silkiness before trailing my hand down her taut stomach.

Clare began to open the buttons of my top, and my eyes drifted from her breasts to her fingers. Such long, feminine fingers, fingers efficient in their purpose. She pushed the flannelette aside and exposed my breasts. Hands cupped each, worshipping them. I had never experienced such adoration in my life. A thumb grazed across my nipples, and my breath caught as I shivered in anticipation.

Her hands still holding my breasts, Clare leaned forward. Her lips met mine, gently at first, then with a growing need. Her hands were squeezing, not hard, perfectly. I could feel the warmth of her body, and I ached for the sensation of breast against breast, skin on skin.

I slipped my hands up her back and pulled her into me. The kiss deepened, mouths opening, tongues searching. Her thigh moved my legs apart and swiftly slipped between them, until her lower body was pressing into mine.

"God!"

She pushed into me again and again, her hips moving, establishing a tempo. Wetness began to collect in the place where I needed her to be, and, with each push, my need for her became more insistent. Feeling her fully against me, full body contact, her skin coat mine like a promise, that was what I needed. Her kiss was divine, her hands on my breasts delicious, the rhythmic pressing of her pelvic bone against mine delectable, but I needed more.

I shifted forwards, making her shift away, and her lips momentarily lost contact with mine. Her hands moved from my breasts to my jaw, cradling it ever so gently, as if she was afraid I would break. For that I loved her even more.

I grasped the waistband of her pyjama bottoms and pushed them downwards over shapely hips. I wanted to look at her, absorb everything about her, but I was taken over by soft lips.

Clare broke the kiss and left me gasping. Her brown eyes seemed darker, hungrier, almost sparking with overflowing energy. Her skin was flushed, and sweat collected at the base of her throat. I leaned forward and licked at it, the saltiness adding to the tastes that I was beginning to associate with purely Clare.

Her moan spurred me to lick her throat again. Strong fingers twined into my hair and drew me closer, encouraging me to taste more of the silken skin. She slipped out of her pyjamas. A swift kick, and they were gone.

"I want to see you, feel you," she whispered in my ear. Once again, the feeling of déjà vu struck me, but I pushed it away. It was not the time to overanalyse everything. Definitely not the time.

I shifted further onto the bed and I raised my hips, indicating that she could do whatever she wished. The smile she gave me was almost blinding, making me tingle all over as if it was dancing over my skin. In a moment, I was naked. So was Clare.

She knelt beside me on the bed, her eyes taking me in, closely followed by her trailing one lone fingertip from my forehead, down my nose, lips, and chin. It paused, then continued down my throat and along my collarbone from right to left, before delving lower. It passed my breasts and journeyed down my stomach to reach the triangle of hair between my thighs.

Deliberately teasing me, she bypassed the spot where I most wanted her, continuing her examination down my leg, past the knee and onto my foot. She intermittently looked up into my eyes, as if looking for my reaction. I was transfixed by the contrasts in the movement of her fingers, her touch pure yet carnal.

Her finger started upwards, this time on the inside of my leg. She hesitated at the plaster, her brow furrowing before she continued with her teasing. Anticipation welled within me, and I wanted to urge her to touch me more intimately. Once again, she purposefully avoided the vee between my legs and started to touch my other leg.

I groaned in disappointment, and when she laughed, I reached out and grabbed her hand, and pulled it towards me. Her body slipped on top of me, and I instinctively closed my eyes and recorded the moment—the first time I was feeling the total connection of our naked bodies.

Clare's lips grazed my throat as her hands slid down my sides until they rested on my hips. My fingers were pressing along her back and inching down to her round, firm butt. Her thigh separated my legs, and the sensation of her pressing herself against me was electrifying. I could feel her heat and mine, my moisture slicking her thigh. She pushed against my centre, and jolts of pure pleasure spread through me. Her hands were steadying me, holding me in place, but it wasn't imprisoning or dominating; it was perfect.

Grabbing her butt, I pulled her closer against me. A guttural groan escaped her, which elicited one from me. I pulled again, matching the rhythm of her hips with my own. Our skin was slick with sweat, whether from desire or the heat from the fireplace, and our bodies moved freely, each against the other.

Clare moved one hand from my hip and placed it beside my head so she could lift her upper torso away from me, her face a few inches from mine. Watching her expression as she thrust against me nearly made me cum. Her hair hung forward, stray strands sticking to her face, her eyes intense and focused on mine. Rasping pants came from deep within her, her lips slightly parted, her tongue slipping out to moisten them.

I opened my legs wider. I was desperate to have her closer.

She moved her hand from my hip to grab my leg and position it at her waist. And she kept pressing, claiming me with her pelvic movements.

I wrapped my hand around her neck and pulled her down. My lips pressed hers, while my fingers gripped the hair at the nape of her neck. This inflamed her, and her movements became more primitive. Each deliberate thrust was more agonisingly beautiful than the previous. I knew I wouldn't last long under her attentions, and I contemplated stopping her, but I couldn't. I was lost in her, lost to her.

Clare pulled her mouth away from mine and stared deeply into my eyes. That was it—the catalyst, the last piece of the jigsaw puzzle. I broke into a million pieces. Lights blinded me as I came, and "I love you" was right there in my throat, waiting to be declared, but I pushed it down.

Clare nuzzled my neck, and I could hear her voice but not the words she was saying. I stroked her arm and delighted in her shiver. She pulled her face from its nook and kissed me hard. I couldn't believe the spark of arousal that shot through me with just one kiss.

Even if I was too scared to tell Clare that I loved her, it was definitely time to show her how I felt.

One quick flip and I had her on her back. With another swift movement, I was straddling her. The look of surprise on her face was priceless, but I didn't have time to be smug. I needed to taste her, to love her, to make her mine. I needed to make sure she knew how I felt, and that I would always feel that way.

My hand grazed her breast, and I luxuriated in the smoothness of it. Her nipples strained to meet my hand, so I brushed over them lightly, then caressed each hardened peak. Clare's hands were on my hips, trying to pull me down and against her. I had other plans.

Scooting sideways, I straddled her right thigh, then leaned over her and breathed onto the sensitive skin of her breasts. The soft breaths were to cool her down whilst hopefully heating her at the same time. My tongue slipped from my mouth and glided around the swell of her breast. Clare tried to move closer, tried to position her nipple closer to the path of my tongue, but my mouth slipped away to the other curve.

My thigh was pressed against her mound, and I could feel how slick it was, how hot in her special place. When my fingers skimmed along the inside of her thigh, she gasped a breath and held it expectantly. Unlike her, I didn't tease or torment. I positioned one finger to swirl in her slickness. Another circle, and her hips bucked. As I drew my finger upwards and along her folds, I also flicked my tongue against her nipple. A guttural gasp shot from above me, and I grinned into my task. My lips covered the hard nub and cocooned it within the warmth of my mouth, and sucked.

"Fuck!"

I sucked again, whilst gliding my finger through her folds, coating them fully along the way. Tasting her, having her beneath and waiting for me to love her, I was overwhelmed by sensation, by emotion, by her.

I lifted my head to look at her, and wasn't at all surprised to see her watching me. It was so intense, meeting the eyes of the woman I was making love to. I'd never purposely done that. Before Clare, I had never really wanted to.

My fingers pushed down, and Clare's eyelids fluttered. Her tongue moistened her lips, and then white teeth nipped at the bottom lip. My hips were moving rhythmically on her thigh, slick and sleek and wet. My fingers stopped at her opening, circled it, then pressed gently. Clare's hips bucked as she tried to take me inside, but I pulled away and slipped along the line of her labia.

"Please, baby."

"Please what?" My voice was husky with arousal. I added a second finger near the opening between the lips of her sex and nipped the moist edges together, before slipping my fingers along the length of her wetness.

Clare gasped and thrust her hips forward. "*Please...*"

Instead of going inside her, I brushed my fingers over her folds again, making her cry out. A memory of another time skittered into my head, a time when I'd mouthed, "I love you." I shook my head against the idea.

"Tell me. Tell me what you want, Clare." My fingers circled her opening.

Her breathing was ragged, her chest rising and falling rapidly, and she struggled to speak. "You. That's all...all I..."

I didn't give her a chance to finish. My fingers slipped inside her easily, her walls clasping at them, drawing them deeper inside. Her back arched and she groaned with pleasure, and the world seemed to freeze time. It was as if a camera had clicked inside my head, and I was capturing the divine instant when I experienced truly belonging.

The thrust of her hips alerted me that Clare was waiting. I couldn't believe I had stopped mid stroke to capture the scene to memory. I withdrew my finger and circled her opening. When she groaned, I didn't wait any longer. I entered her, and her cry was nearly my undoing. I could feel another orgasm building in me just from watching her, feeling her, hearing her. But I needed to focus on Clare. She was most important, would always be most important.

My fingers moved rhythmically, her slickness easing them along. The tempo increased with each thrust, each stroke. Delving, dipping, demanding more from both of us. Her hips were moving more quickly and I kept the pace, the muscles in my arms hardening, tensing, delivering the pressure I knew she needed.

I shifted forward, allowing my fingers to enter her even more fully, my knuckles pressing against the outside of her opening. Faster, harder, deeper, faster, harder, deeper. Her moans were coming thick and fast, and each one made me clench against her thigh. She was so wet, and hot and ready to burst open like a blossoming rose.

Dipping my head, I captured her nipple in my mouth and sucked, then flicked the hardened nub with my tongue. I felt her tense, felt her walls clasp at me, felt her stiffen. I didn't stop, couldn't stop. I had to make her tip over into all that was good and right.

Curling my fingers, I dragged along her tightening walls, pressing hard against the spot that would deliver her to the place where lights dance and illuminate the world with pure joy and sensation.

It was as if her body went into slow motion, mine along with it. Her hips dipped before they lifted and lifted and lifted, taking me higher with her. I glanced up at her, and she was looking straight at me. Her lips moved but I couldn't make out the words. It seemed as if they were important, but I didn't want to stop her at that moment to ask what she had said.

At this instant, her head flew backwards sharply and slammed into the pillow. Her cry sent jolts throughout my body and I ground down on her thigh as the shock of my orgasm registered. We moved as one, the movement of our bodies seamless as we crested together.

Strong arms grabbed me and pulled me forward to land on sweat soaked skin. Breasts pillowed on breasts, legs were entwined, and breaths mingled and married each other. Her heart hammered loudly against the side of my face, its cadence frantic. Gentle fingers drifted through my hair, sifting the locks onto my shoulders. I kissed her collarbone and smiled into her skin, my eyes drifting closed. A feeling of contentment flooded through me. This was what I wanted for the rest of my life—to be with her, be held by her, feel safe, loved.

My eyes darted open as the memory of my dream surfaced—Annabel and Ellen. Or should I say Annabel and me. When I had dreamed of making love with Annabel, I had experienced the same sense of contentment, the feeling of wanting to be only with her, held by her, safe and loved. Why I was thinking about that now?

Now that my mind had turned in that direction, it worried the similarities like a dog worries a bone. When Clare had said, "I want to see you, feel you," the words had given me pause. I'd had the feeling that I had heard those words before. Still, they were an expression of a fairly basic element of making love. It wasn't as if the words were extraordinary. But then later she had used the exact same words as her great aunt again. "You are so very beautiful." I couldn't help wondering whether it was another coincidence.

I scolded myself for being overly sensitive, laying the blame on the house, the setting, the reason we were back there. All of those elements were playing on my mind, trying to get me to make connections that were not real. But I couldn't entirely rationalise away the feeling of déjà vu of some of the actions we had shared as we made love.

Clare murmured something above me, trailing her fingers down the side of my cheek. A chill passed through me. Was all of this, me and Clare, just an echo of the past? Was what I was feeling actually *my* emotions, or the emotions of another? Falling for Clare had happened so suddenly. Who really falls in love with someone after only meeting them three times? I had never fallen in love before, not even after knowing the woman for a much longer time.

Then another thought struck me. Never mind my feelings, what was Clare feeling? Was she believing I was Ellen and reliving the love of her dead great aunt? She hadn't said my name whilst we made love. She'd said it just before, but not during.

My chest constricted, and a surge of anxiety overwhelmed me. My heart was pounding so loudly, the thumping ricocheted inside my head. I struggled forward, throwing Clare's hands from me. I couldn't breathe. Panic coursed through me, and I started to wheeze.

Clare was beside me, her face showing concern. "What's up? What's— Are you asthmatic?"

Unable to speak, I shook my head.

She was in front of me now, her hands on my shoulders, cupping my face, shaking me slightly. "Baby, what..."

My eyes were watering. I didn't know if it was tears or because I couldn't catch my breath. Clare started to rub my back, adding sharp smacks as if I was choking. Her voice was cajoling. I think that she was hoping to calm me enough so I could tell her what was wrong, but I could hear the alarm in her voice.

"Say...say..." I wheezed.

"What? Say what?"

Her fright was apparent. I didn't want her to be frightened. She began rubbing circles on my back with both hands. I could feel her anxiety seeping through my skin and adding to my own.

If this *was* a panic attack, it wasn't because I was afraid of dying, wasn't the possibility of me losing control and doing something stupid. It was more because I believed that I was going crazy. How else could I explain why I was questioning the wonderful thing that was happening in my life and comparing it to the relationship of a dead couple?

What I needed was for Clare to say my name. That was all. Just to say my name and reassure me that she knew who I was, and hopefully that I wasn't Ellen Howell.

I cupped my hands over my nose and mouth. If I was hyperventilating, I needed to inhale the carbon dioxide I was exhaling. I didn't have a paper bag handy, so my hands would have to do.

Clare apparently realised what was happening, and what I was attempting to do. "Hold your breath," she instructed.

What the hell? I was trying to catch it, not hold it.

"Hold your breath for as long as you can. It prevents the dissipation of carbon dioxide."

I clamped my lips shut and held the breath inside until my lungs were burning. I held on for about ten seconds.

"Do it again."

I looked over the tops of my fingers at Clare's face. She was so bloody beautiful that I held my breath again without question. After about four or five repetitions, my breathing began to come easier and my chest lost some of its constriction, and for all of this time, Clare had been stroking my back.

"Better?" Her voice was comforting.

I nodded, coughing to clear my throat.

Clare wrapped her arms around me and pulled me against her, then held me close, the heat of her naked chest soothing me. It felt so right being there. I must've interpreted things incorrectly. Clare definitely knew it was me she was with, and I was definite the feelings I had were for her and only her.

"Becky?"

Happiness flooded through me, and I nestled into her. Her arms tightened as she hugged me to her. "Becky?"

"Ahuh?"

"What happened?" I wondered at the note of sadness in her tone. "Was it because, well, because we made love?"

I swiftly turned and was met by brown eyes filled with pain. "Good God, no!" She blinked, and a single tear trickled down her cheek. More quietly, I added, "Being with you is the most wonderful feeling in the world."

Clare shook her head, and another tear fell.

I had to pull out of her embrace in order to brush the tear away, but I did, my fingers gliding over her flushed cheek. My hand was shaking, and I knew it was not the aftermath of my panic attack but because I had upset Clare.

I had to tell her I loved her. It was the only thing I could think of that could calm her fears. Even if it was too soon, even if she laughed or brushed me off, I had to tell her how I felt. I could always leave first thing in the morning.

"I am in love with you, Rebecca."

What?

I leaned back and looked into her captivating eyes. "I think I've been in love with you from the first moment I met you."

Her bottom lip tucked up behind her top teeth for a moment before she sighed. "I'm not expec—"

"*Iloveyou.*" Unlike the crooning of my first declaration of love, those three words shot from my mouth as if they had been fired from a gun. Clare's eyes widened, making her expression almost comical. I inhaled deeply before trying again. "I am in love with you, too, Clare."

She pulled me closer, until her face was inches from mine. It was as if she was trying to read me, trying to work out whether I was telling her the truth or just parroting her.

My eyes pleaded with her to believe me. Leaning close, I brushed my lips over hers almost as if I was sealing my profession of love with the kiss. I did it again, and would have done it for the third time if she hadn't pulled me against her and held me, her body trembling. She sobbed softly into my hair, and it wasn't long before she had me crying too. It wasn't because I was hurt or angry, disappointed or sad. It was obviously because I was so ecstatically happy and, I believed, so was she.

Chapter Thirteen

Morning came around quickly, and the fogginess of reality supplanted my dreams. My back was curled against Clare's front, her body spooning mine and sealing warmth between us. The night had been full of the tender connection of heart, body, mind, and soul. That is not to say our love making was always tender; there were times when it became frenetic, all-consuming, and fierce. But it was always perfect, just like Clare. Just like the taste of her, the smell of her, and the absolute essence of her both in body and soul.

Being in her arms was the most magical feeling I had ever experienced, and just thinking about being with her sent a shiver through me.

A soft kiss landed on the side of my head, pleasantly surprising me. "Morning, beautiful."

Her voice was thick with sleep, and its timbre rumbled through me. My smile was instantaneous, and I nestled back into her.

"How did you sleep?" she asked, landing another kiss on my head as I turned my face so I could see her.

I had always thought Clare was beautiful, but seeing her first thing in the morning made that assessment pale. She was, in fact, the most stunningly beautiful woman I had ever seen in my life. Dark hair was mussed up, but that just added to her beauty.

"Perfectly." The word came out with a bit of a squeak, and I coughed to clear my throat. "At least for the time we actually spent sleeping."

Her laugh was like music, and I could feel it vibrating in her chest. We shared a kiss, a delicious kiss that promised to escalate into something more. Breaking away, I gazed at her, her smile instant.

"You are so very beautiful, Clare." Apparently embarrassed, she looked away from me. "Hey, you are," I insisted. "You should be told every day how beautiful you are."

Clare dipped her head, then raised her eyes to meet mine. This time she looked more collected. "You are the beautiful one, Becky."

My heart skipped a beat. The scene was so romantic, so utterly wonderful. The sound of my stomach growling like a puma on the hunt broke the spell.

"I see your belly is awake." There was note of amusement in her words.

I nodded, patting the rumbling offender, which, embarrassingly, growled again.

A full bodied laugh came from Clare. "I think I should tame it before it attacks." She delivered a swift kiss to my forehead, and then climbed out of bed.

Watching her stretching was like viewing a finely sculpted piece of art come to life. She lifted her arms above her head, and I could see the definition of the muscles on her shoulders and arms. I probably should say Clare was toned rather than muscled, as she wasn't like a body builder; she was just, as always, perfect. Apart from a couple of marks on her back that I believed I had put there the previous night, her skin was flawless. She bent down next to the bed and retrieved her pyjamas, slipping the top on first and buttoning the last two buttons. I could see her cleavage, and the memory of what lay underneath the cloth made my mouth water.

As she was pulling up her bottoms, her eyes met mine. "Can't have my woman hungry," she teased.

I loved the sound of her voice. The way it rippled through me made me hungry for something other than breakfast.

Clare leaned across the bed to kiss me again. "Water should still be hot. I forgot to turn off the immersion heater last night."

With that, she was gone, and I was left grinning stupidly.

After I'd showered, and both of us had eaten breakfast, Clare called the hospital to check on Freddie.

"Granddad had a very comfortable night." As she spoke, Clare seated herself at the table and pulled her coffee cup towards her. "His heart rate is good, and so are his oxygen levels."

The comment, "Pity," sprang to mind, but I kept my mouth shut.

"To be on the safe side, they are going to keep him under observation in hospital for a couple of days."

"Seems fair." I really didn't know what else to say, at least not anything that would not offend Clare.

"Fair?"

"I mean it seems about right, keeping him to check on him."

Clare tilted her head and looked at me intently for a moment, then lifted her cup and took a sip, her face scrunching with distaste. "This is cold. You want a fresh one?"

"I'm good, thanks."

As Clare prepared another cup, I watched how her body moved, totally enthralled by each nuance.

"I told the nurse at Reception I will be visiting him at lunch time."

"Today?" Even to my ears, my voice was a tad shrill.

Clare looked over her shoulder, the tinking of the spoon against the cup seeming painfully loud. "That is why we're here, isn't it—to see if my granddad is okay?" Her voice seemed softer than usual, and the sparkle was absent.

My laugh was intended to help ease the tension between us, not piss her off. "Sorry." I pulled a face, more for me than her. "Of course it is. Ignore me. I was having an idiot moment."

Clare turned to face me fully, her back resting on the kitchen counter, the cup of coffee in her hand and stopped on its journey to her mouth.

"You don't have to come with me. You can stay here if you'd prefer." She took a sip from the cup.

That was the most awful thing about her having to visit Freddie. I knew I would have to go with her, even if it was only for moral support. I could've stayed at the house on my own, but, to be honest, I wasn't up for it. I would rather take my chances drinking a cuppa from the hospital cafeteria than stay in Annabel's house and risk a visitation.

"Of course I'm coming with you." I stood and went over to her. "I'm here for you, okay? I was having a dippy moment. Again."

Brown eyes met mine, and I saw a glint of something that I hoped was amusement.

"If that's the case, I'd better get ready." She leaned forward and brushed her lips against mine. "I'll take my cuppa with me."

With that, she was off, and I was left wondering if she had got one over on me somehow. Maybe she knew I would prefer to be at the hospital, even waiting outside the ward, than be left alone in a haunted house. Instead of feeling miffed, I grinned and shook my head.

Whilst Clare was showering, I thought I would investigate the spare room. It was broad daylight and I was feeling a little braver, but only because Clare was on the same floor I was. Yvette Fielding from the show *Most Haunted,* I was not.

The door to Bella's room wasn't quite closed, so I pushed lightly against the wood. As it opened, not a sound came from the hinges, unlike the previous night when they had seemed to be screaming. The first thing that struck me was the window, the window that didn't have any curtains on it. "Why was it so fucking dark, then?" I wondered aloud. I frowned at it, as if expecting it to answer my question. The next thing I noticed were the boxes in neat stacks all around the room, all but one. That little chap lay on its side, its contents spilling from it like guts at a murder scene.

I stepped inside and grabbed the nearest box to prop open the door. I didn't want a recap of the previous night's events, especially as now I would be able to see the thing that was in the room with me.

It was then that I remembered what I had been thinking about Annabel the night before. Was she really an evil spirit? Could she have murdered the woman she professed to love and then written the journal to help provide her with an alibi in the event that she needed one?

I closed my eyes and thought of what I knew about Annabel Howell and the times I had seen her. She didn't strike me as the type who would kill, even though her writings did admit to her having a bit of a temper. If Annabel had killed Ellen, even if she had done it out of jealousy or anger, I knew she would have come clean about it. Why? Because when all was said and done, anyone could write lies, anyone could try to cover his or her tracks by acting desperate and beside him or herself with grief. But I'd had the opportunity to look into Annabel's eyes. I'd felt her shake as she held me on her porch when she thought Ellen had come back to her. Even Clare had felt it when her hand had passed through the apparition of her deceased great aunt. She had described the feelings of devastation and the agony of loss.

I opened my eyes and looked around the room. In the light of day, it looked innocent. The next thought that came was why

Annabel would purposely frighten me, keep on trying to touch me even when I had fallen to the ground.

My calf ached, a reminder of the injury I had sustained. I didn't even know what I had banged into. All I knew was that whatever it was had been close to the ground. Scanning the floor where I believed I had fallen, I could see something sticking out from underneath a child-sized desk.

I knelt down to look at the object. It was a poker, the kind used to jostle coals or wood in a fireplace. Why on earth would a poker be stuffed under a child's desk? I peered over the top of the desk and noticed a small protrusion that I thought might have been a mantelpiece. It wasn't rocket science to put two and two together.

Straightening, I noted that the distance from the door to where I was standing seemed a lot further than I would have thought.

A sharp clang came from my right, and my head swivelled around to locate the source. My heart leapt forward and slammed against my ribcage, as I spotted something sticking out in the vicinity of where the noise seemed to have come from. I tentatively moved closer. Some sharp wires were poking through the space between the boxes. I touched the end of one and winced. It was like a razor blade. Sure enough, when I looked at the tip of my finger, it was bleeding. It was a good job I had only run into the poker when I was in the room in the dark.

My eyes widened in realisation. Annabel hadn't been trying to hurt me; she was trying to keep me from walking straight into the wires. Her cold fingers touching my face, touching my hair, running along my shoulder... She knew I would move away from her, move away from something that could have been lethal.

One thing still bothered me. If Annabel was out to save me, why did she say "Here" twice? Why did she slam the door with us inside, leaving me in the dark?

"Find anything?"

The sudden sound of another voice in the room made me jump backwards and nearly into the wires.

"Hey, careful." Her hands clutched me and pulled me forwards. "You okay?"

My mouth was clamped tightly closed, holding back a scream, so I only nodded.

Clare moved past me and examined the wires. "Jesus. It's a good job you didn't meet this last night." She moved the box that was at the side of the sharp protrusions and whistled. "It's also a good job you didn't want to sleep in Bella's bed. These are the springs from it."

I moved to stand next to her and saw the array of sharp metal wires sticking from the metal frame. Fuck. I would have been sliced to buggery if I had run into those.

"What's this?" Clare moved away from me and knelt on the floor next to the spilt box and started to pick up the contents and put them back inside the container.

I went over to stand beside her. "Wait. Don't put them away."

Clare looked up at me, her hand full of papers. She cocked her head and her eyes narrowed in question.

"I think there is a reason why that stuff is everywhere," I said. Clare chewed at her lip in contemplation, so I gave her a hint. "Why did we come in here last night in the first place?"

"The loud crashing noise?"

I dipped my head towards the box. "Could that have made a loud crashing noise?"

A grin appeared on her face, and her head bobbed in agreement. "Shall we?"

"Too right."

"Here?" she asked.

For a split second, I felt a chill at hearing the word. That was what Annabel had said to me the previous night. The thing was,

I had thought it didn't quite sound like Annabel. Now I knew why. It had sounded like Clare.

"Are you all right? You've gone white."

I *felt* white, too, ghostly white. I kept telling myself that the voice I'd heard couldn't have been Clare's—she had been downstairs, she had come after I had screamed.

"Becky? What is it?" She was in front of me now, the box forgotten. Her hands gripped my arms and gave me a shake.

"N...nothing. I'm fine." We both knew I was lying, but I just didn't want to have to go through it all again.

I'd had enough of the spare room, enough of fucking second guessing and jumping to conclusions. If I had the chance to find a single clue about what had happened to Ellen Howell, I was going to grab it with both hands. And part of me believed the box held something that could shed some light on things. "Let's take the box downstairs and go through the contents after breakfast."

As I helped Clare gather everything up and put it into the box, her eyes occasionally flicked to me. I knew she wanted me to tell her what had happened, why I had freaked out, but I didn't want to. I was feeling completely drained of it all.

After breakfast, I washed up the dishes whilst Clare showered and got dressed. I waited until she was with me in the living room before opening the box.

The top layer was papers, leaflets, and old receipts, and I initially thought we were sorting through a box that should have been sent out with the rubbish. Then a paper wallet was uncovered, oddly enough, about in the area where the spilling of the contents had ended. Inside were a handful of photographs, all of them containing one or more of three people—Annabel, Ellen, and Bella. Seeing them together, love and joy on their faces, was heart-warming. They looked the epitome of a happy family. One of the pictures showed Annabel looking adoringly at Bella whilst Ellen was favouring Annabel with a similar look. There was no doubt about the way Clare's grandmother was looking at her granddad's sister. The love shining from her eyes was clear for all to see. I flicked the photograph over and saw the same neat handwriting that was in the notebook: *Ellen, Bella, and Me. The Roaches. June 1953.*

Clare's voice broke through my reverie. "I wonder who took the picture."

I shrugged. 'Freddie?' I looked at Clare, who scrunched her face and shook her head. "Why not?"

She released a sigh, leaned over, and took the picture from my hand. "Because if Freddie took this picture, there is no way he could not have known they were lovers." She passed the photo back. "And then Ellen would have disappeared a lot sooner than October." I opened my mouth to speak, but she cut me off. "They probably put the camera on a timer."

I didn't even get the chance to argue about whether cameras even had a timer in 1953, as Clare was pulling a box from inside the cardboard box.

She peered inside. "Fuck me!"

I could've been crude and offered to comply, but I was too interested in why she had cursed, so I just looked interested.

"A Leica IIIf!"

Surprise skimmed over my face before I reassembled my facial expression to try to appear knowledgeable.

Clare's hands shook as she opened the box. "This must've cost a fortune. Do you have any idea how expensive these were in the 1950s?"

I didn't, mainly because I didn't know what she going on about. I watched as she stroked whatever was inside the box as if she was touching something precious.

Finally she turned from the box and looked at me. "In today's money, this would set you back a couple of grand."

That did it. I reached over and grabbed the box to see what was so special. Inside it was a camera, a fucking camera.

Clare looked at it with adoring eyes. "Isn't it beautiful?"

I failed to see the attraction. "It's a camera."

"It's not *just* a camera."

What was it then, a Rolex watch, too? That would explain the price. Apparently my face showed my disbelief.

"It is a Leica IIIf, one of the most popular cameras of its day. There was a two *year* backorder when this first came out about 1950 or 51, and you had to be pretty well off to afford it." When I just stared at her blankly, she said, "What?" A grin spread across my face, and she repeated, "What?" as she gave me an uncertain smile.

"You seem exceptionally knowledgeable about this antique camera."

Clare tilted her head. "You calling me a nerd?"

I tried to look unjustly accused, but her expression became more threatening, so I laughed and shook my head. "No. *I'm* not calling *you* anything."

Instead of laughing with me or responding to what I said, Clare jumped to her feet and yelled, "Jesus Christ!"

I immediately looked towards the spot I thought she was looking at, but there was no one there, alive or dead.

"The picture of Ellen!" She jabbed a finger in the general direction of the paper wallet.

My eyes cast downwards to the pile of photos, then shifted back to Clare. "What about it?" The photo was beautiful, yes, intimate, yes, captured the love of the moment, most certainly. But I couldn't see why she had suddenly gotten her knickers in a twist.

"Granddad has a picture of Ellen that he always keeps with him." Clare stumbled backwards, almost tripping over the coffee table. "He told me it was taken when they were courting, but... but..." Her hand gestured at the other pictures we had looked at. "It was taken on the same day as these. It had to be."

"Why would he lie about it?" As if I didn't know. Freddie Howell had lied about many things, so this newly discovered lie didn't come as a shock. However, I could tell just by looking at Clare's expression that she had still held out some hope that her grandfather was not a lying, murdering old fucker.

Clare knelt in front of me. "He knew about them. He'd seen the photographs, had even taken that one." Her hands grabbed mine, and she squeezed my fingers so hard I thought my knuckles were going to pop. "What I can't understand is why he kept that photo he has with him in the home."

Realisation dawned on me as if the light had become brighter in the room, or more accurately, in the grey area inside my head. It had been in front of us from the very first time I met Clare. Freddie kept the photograph of his wife with him for one reason only, to gloat. He knew the look on his wife's face was not for him, that the love shining in Ellen's eyes was for his sister. That had undoubtedly made him seethe inside. It could only be the setting that had made him keep that snapshot close. The Roaches had to be the place where he had buried his wife!

"Fucking hell!" I jumped to my feet, knocking Clare backwards in the process. "Fucking hell!" I could hear the panic in Clare's voice as she asked me what was wrong, but I erupted in another, "Fucking hell!" before I leaned down and searched her eyes, wanting to see her reaction when I shared my epiphany. "I know where Ellen is." Clare opened her mouth to speak, but I cut her off. "She's buried somewhere near the Roaches."

Clare's face drained of colour, and her eyes grew big. "Wh...at?"

I felt like Poirot at the point in a novel where he reveals the murderer and their motive. The part where there usually is an audience and he points his finger at the murderer, who then crumbles and admits all. But there were only the two of us, and the murderer was tucked up in bed at the Royal Derby Hospital, probably being spoon-fed and treated like a dear old gentleman.

"We need to go to the home." I held my hand down to her, and her hand that took it was trembling. With one pull, she was upright and standing in front of me. I looked into her eyes. "We need to get that picture and go find the spot it was taken."

I didn't have to tell her why. Her expression clearly showed that she had finally made the connection.

"And then we will have a chat with Freddie," I added.

Even though the thought of seeing him made me queasy, it was past time to lay this all to rest—time that Freddie paid for his crime, and time that Annabel and Ellen Howell received eternal peace.

Chapter Fourteen

Arriving at the hospital, I honestly thought I would be a bag of nerves, but I wasn't. I was on a mission, and no one and nothing was going to stand in my way. Clare was wan, but as resolute as I. I wanted to just kick the door in and demand that he tell us what he had done and where Ellen's body was buried, but Clare had her own approach in mind as we stopped outside his door.

"Becky, could you please wait outside for ten minutes before you come in?" I opened my mouth, but she held up a hand and cut off my objection. "Please don't get angry. If you are accusatory, we'll get nothing from Granddad."

True. All he had to do was pull the "sick old man routine" and we would both be turfed out. We could have gone straight to the police, but what would we have told them? That we had solved a sixty-year-old missing person's case because we could talk to the dead and we had an old picture? The station door wouldn't have had the time to hit us in the arse as we were invited to leave. We needed evidence, solid, bullet proof evidence.

Clare kissed me, and her lips were so soft, so tender, that I would have agreed to anything. "Okay," I allowed grudgingly. "I'll wait ten minutes and not a second longer. I know he's your granddad, but even so, I don't like you being alone with him."

She smiled and kissed me, and I felt a piece of me go with her as she turned and entered Freddie's room whilst I stood and watched the door ease back into place. There were chairs in the hall for people who were waiting to go in to see loved ones, but I decided leaning conspicuously against the wall was more convenient. If Clare needed me, I would be there in a hurry.

Ten minutes usually seems like a short span of time, but those ten minutes seemed to drag and drag and drag some more. I lost count of the number of times I checked my watch, and I also stopped counting "one elephant, two elephants" when I noticed the strange looks I was getting from the people going to and fro. This was not the time to act as if I was auditioning for *One Flew Over the Cuckoo's Nest*.

I had no idea what Clare was saying, as the drive to the hospital had been completed in silence. Clare had either stared out of the window or at the picture, and her expression was unreadable. Was she going to tell Freddie what we knew, or was she going to try to get him to admit what had happened? Maybe she would ask about Ellen's picture and watch for his reaction.

Finally I couldn't wait any longer. I grabbed hold of the handle, my hand steady, firm, and in control. It was a shame my stomach didn't feel the same. Easing the door open, I saw Freddie sitting up in bed, reaching for the photograph that was perched on his bedside table, perfectly set in a beautiful silver frame. Even from my place in the doorway, Ellen's face smiled out at me, her eyes so full of love that even an idiot would have had to be blind not to see that her emotion was aimed at the photographer. There was no doubt that the framed photograph was part of the batch we had found at Annabel's house. They were all taken in the same spot. The problem facing Clare and me was that the Roaches was not a small stretch of land, and she would have to try and elicit the exact location from Freddie before the search could go any further.

As he held the framed photograph in his hands, there was a sad smile on his face. If I hadn't known better, I would have thought he was still pining for the woman he had loved and tragically lost.

"After all'a these years, I still can't believe she just up and left, Clare. I wouldn't 'ave believed she would just leave me and yer mother."

I shook my head. Neither could we. That was the reason we were there in the room with him.

He sniffed as if he was fighting back tears. "I mean, one minute we were fine, and then..."

At that point *I* wanted to strangle *him*, but a glance from Clare and a warning shake of her head pinned me near the door. It didn't stop me from talking. "But did she leave you willingly, Freddie?"

His head shot up at the sound of my voice, and cold brown eyes glared into mine. I mustered a smile and took a step forward. "Rebecca Gibson, Mr Howell. Good to see you again."

He didn't look away from me as he snarled, "Clare, git 'er outta 'ere."

My smile became broader. "Why is that, Freddie?" I moved closer to his bed. "Is it because I look like her?" My eyes flicked to the photograph and noted that his fingers were gripping it as if it would spring to life. "Or is it because I know?"

He cocked his head, and his face closed up. "Ya know what, exactly?"

I shook my head. "I don't have to spell it out for you, do I?"

"Git 'er outta 'ere, Clare. Told ya before, I din't like 'er."

Clare didn't move. She stood to beside his bed, her attention on me.

"Your wife loved your sister, didn't she?"

Even if I hadn't seen the anger bubbling up inside him, I would have felt the air shift. He didn't answer.

"They were lovers, weren't they?"

The framed photograph came at me so fast, I was surprised it didn't hit me in the face. I heard the glass shatter against the wall behind me, heard the frame crash to the floor. My hands balled into fists.

"Becky, don't!"

I couldn't believe Clare was telling me to stop, and I shot a look at her. One look into her eyes confirmed that she wasn't arguing with me, she was working up to something.

"If I were you, Becky," Clare continued, "I would think really hard about what you are saying."

Her slight nod indicated that I was supposed to fall in with her plan. God, I wished at that moment that we had talked about it during that wasted time in the car.

Clare leaned closer to her grandfather. "Ignore her, Granddad. I told her she was loopy. You wouldn't hurt Nanny, would you?"

His eyes flickered to Clare's, then came back to rest on mine. The hatred in them would have been enough to floor a man. But I wasn't a man, I was a woman. A woman who wanted to put this entire situation to rest.

"A' course I wouldn't 'ave 'urt Ellen. I loved 'er."

Clare took his hand in hers and rubbed it. "I know you loved Nanny. That is so obvious." She looked straight at me and said, "Would you please pick up the pieces of the picture, before you leave, Becky?"

I opened my mouth to argue, but she raised an eyebrow and nodded at the broken frame. I was at a loss. I knew she was plotting something, but I couldn't figure out what it was. Gritting my teeth, I nodded and started to clean up the broken glass. I could hear Clare talking to Freddie in soothing tones between his angry exclamations about stupid women knowing nothing. I looked over at them. Was this a case of good cop, bad cop? Was that what Clare was doing?

I gingerly gathered all of the shards of glass I could and piled them on top of the pieces of the frame. The picture was hanging out, but Ellen's smiling face seemed to be undamaged. I brushed a finger across her mouth. "Shit!" hissed from between my lips as a small piece of glass embedded itself in my index finger.

A drop of my blood dripped from my finger and onto Ellen's face. I tried to rub it off, but that just smeared it. I needed a tissue, and to get out the bloody glass splinter from my finger.

I went into the small en suite bathroom and tentatively pulled the cord to illuminate the room whilst juggling glass, frame, photograph, and a bloody finger. I laid the debris to the side of the sink and turned on the tap. Cold water gushed over the cut, easing the ache by numbing it. I pressed the sides together, and eventually the offending shard poked out far enough for me to pluck it out with my fingers. I snatched a few tissues, wrapped them around the wound, and applied pressure.

My eyes flicked to the picture. The red streak seemed eerily real, as if the blood was oozing from the photo. I cautiously eased the picture from the remnants of its broken home and touched the red splotch. It was dried. I dampened a tissue and wiped the smear from the youthful face of Ellen Howell. Without really thinking, I turned the photograph over and saw Annabel's handwriting. It said "Ellen May 1953." Near the bottom of the picture, quite faint, something else had been written. The handwriting was different from Annabel's, and what was written there wasn't words, it was a series of numbers.

53.171762, -1.999212

I had no idea what the numbers meant, but I knew that Annabel hadn't written them, and neither had Ellen. To my mind, that left only one possible person—the old fucker in the bed. I could make out Clare's voice as she spoke calmly to him. I doubted very much that he would suddenly grow a conscience, or a pair of testicles, and tell the truth, even if I confronted him with the picture as evidence. I had to get Clare out of the room and ask her what she thought about this new information.

I gathered the broken frame and dropped it into the bin in the bathroom, then placed the picture to the side and washed my hands. The cut had closed, but it still stung when the soap made contact with it. I sucked air in between my teeth and kept washing.

I was rinsing my hands when I realised I was not on my own. My face turned to the open doorway and I fully expected to see Clare standing there, but the doorway was empty. It wasn't until I turned back to the sink that I noticed my reflection in the mirror. It was me, but I was not alone. Ellen Howell was standing to my left. The number of times I had seen ghosts of late should have prepared me, but this time it was different, so fucking different. I had seen Annabel more than once, I had seen Ellen seated next to me in my car, but they looked like living, breathing persons. The woman standing next to me looked dead, in the extreme. The left side of her face looked sunken, as if it had been caved in, and the blood seemed fresh, as if the wound had been recent. I couldn't move, couldn't speak, couldn't even blink at the horror of it. Ellen opened her mouth, and I could see teeth missing from the broken side of her face. Blood oozed over her swollen lips, and she gargled something unintelligible before the redness turned brown and flaky, and insects scurried from her mouth.

I screamed. Scrambling back, I caught my foot on something that I hadn't seen on the floor as I'd entered the room. It seemed to drag me downwards, to catch, hold, and pull at me with the strength of ten men. I felt the coldness of the tiles as I hit the floor, and the pain of its solidness crashed into my skull.

When I came to, I was surprised to see a man standing over me. Brown eyes searched mine, as fingers poked and prodded the side of my face. Pain flooded through me, and I wanted to vomit. I tried to sit up, but lights danced in front of my eyes.

"Don't move."

His voice was stern, but I knew he wasn't trying to hurt me. A light flashed into my eyes, making me squint.

"Just checking for concussion, Miss."

My tension eased as I realised I was being examined by a doctor or a nurse.

"Did you faint?" Flick. Click. Flick.

I was finding it hard to concentrate with the distraction of the light moving from one eye to the other. It was only when he stopped and looked at me that I shook my head, which made me wince.

"Fall?"

"Yes. I think." Either that or I was pulled down to the ground by an invisible spectre who wanted me dead or out of the picture.

"Ah. You must've tripped over the towels."

I hadn't seen any towels on the floor when I'd entered the room, but then again, I was otherwise engaged, carrying loads of shit and nursing a bloodied splintered finger.

"Looks worse than it is. Just a couple of butterfly stitches over your eye should do the trick."

He leaned back and I noted he was a doctor, if the white coat was any indication. It was either that, or the people in the white coats and vans with square wheels had come to take me to the loony bin.

"Clare?" My voice sounded needy, reflecting how I was feeling.

"I'm here, love."

Her voice drifted over from the doorway, and my heart eased.

"Can you sit up for me?"

I scooted backwards and leaned against the bathroom wall. From that angle I could see Clare standing nervously in the doorway, her hands clasped in front of her, her face ashen. I forced a weak smile. "I'm okay, just a little shaken." And not from the fall, either.

I could hear another voice coming from behind Clare and initially thought it was the murdering bastard in the bed. But when Clare moved out of the way, a porter entered the room pushing a wheelchair. What the fuck? I wasn't paralysed.

The doctor smiled at me. "Hospital policy, I'm afraid. We need to get you to A & E to stitch you up, and you can't walk there."

Yes I could. I had a bump to the head; I wasn't mowed over by a truck.

He shrugged at the refusal on my face. "As I said, hospital policy."

To say I wasn't happy as two men lifted me into the chair would have been an understatement.

As they turned the wheelchair and pushed me towards the door, I slammed my foot on the floor. "Just a mo." I stood up, leaned over and grabbed the photo of Ellen, then sat down again. "Ready when you are." I didn't want them to see that the effort of getting up had nearly made me pass out again. And I certainly didn't want the glowering Freddie Howell to see how delicate I was as I passed by his bed and out of the door. I had to repress the urge to wave the picture at him as I went by. I didn't want that bastard to know anything until I had proof.

Looking down at the numbers written on the back of the snapshot, I grinned, winced, and tried not to grin again because it hurt. I knew that the numbers held the key. If I, or should I say Clare and I, could crack them, then I thought we might have proof enough to go to the police with what had happened to Ellen. I don't know how I knew it; I just did.

It was a shame that I couldn't get the macabre vision of Ellen Howell out of my head. That was the only thing stopping me from thoroughly enjoying the moment. That, and the fact that I had smashed up the side of my face enough to need stitches. My wound would heal. Without Clare's and my help, Ellen's couldn't.

A sobering thought, considering that even with our help, Ellen Howell would still be dead.

It took six butterfly stitches and way too many torches flashed into my eyes before I was deemed good to go. Clare waited for me outside of the cubicle where I had been sitting for the last hour and a quarter, and knowing that she was there was all that kept me focused. It wasn't until we were seated in the car in the parking lot that I pulled out the photograph.

Clare said exactly what I was thinking. "I can't believe I didn't make the connection sooner. He always kept that picture close to him. Though I was a bit surprised to see that he had thought to bring it with him when he was brought to hospital."

My attention was fixed on the smiling, living woman in the snapshot. Ellen had been a beautiful woman, but her image blurred into the vision I had witnessed in Freddie's bathroom. Seeing Ellen's attractive face covered in blood, her teeth missing, her inability to voice how she was feeling made my stomach roil.

Silence filled the space between us, and I tore my eyes from the picture to look at Clare. She was staring at me with such sadness, I felt my heart constrict.

"What happened, love?" Her voice was gentle, soothing, quintessentially Clare.

I pointed to the picture. "See Ellen on here?" Clare nodded. "I saw her in the bathroom."

Her eyes narrowed, then she lifted her chin, indicating I should continue.

"It wasn't like when I saw her before." I tapped the photograph with my index finger, the one I had stabbed with a splinter of glass. "She didn't look like this." Swallowing rapidly, I tried to form the words to describe what I had seen. Instead I started to cry.

Strong arms wrapped around me and pulled me close. Just Clare's scent helped to calm the horrors exploding inside my brain. Shushing words cascaded over me, coating me in safety, and long languid strokes of her hands on my arms and back alternated with her running her fingers through my hair. I don't know how long I cried, but Clare held me the entire time.

Eventually my tears started to dry up, followed by hiccoughs of frustration. A tissue appeared as if by magic in front of me, and I accepted it gratefully.

More time elapsed, but Clare sat in silence and held my hand. Initially I couldn't look at her. I felt so vulnerable, probably because I had been crying.

"Her face had...was... Fuck!" I cleared my throat and started again. "Ellen's face was battered." Clare momentarily stopped rubbing the nape of my neck. "On the left side of her mouth, her teeth were either missing or broken. Blood...there was so much blood..." I started crying again, words falling from my lips as if they needed saving, just like me.

Clare didn't say anything, so I turned to look at her. Her complexion was white, either from shock or anger.

"Here." I shoved the photograph towards Clare, who stared at it as if she was unsure what she was supposed to do. "Look at the back."

Long slender fingers accepted the picture and trailed over the glossy image. She seemed reticent about turning it over, lest the image I had described be etched on the reverse of it. Eventually, she did, and I watched as her eyes scanned the words, noting her frown when she came to the numbers.

"Numbers?"

I nodded.

Her face crinkled with concentration as she tried to work out the significance of 53.171762, -1.999212 in relation to the green-eyed, smiling woman. I immediately saw the small curve at the side of her mouth as her lips moved upwards. Her eyes sparkled as her smile grew. By the time she turned to face me, she was grinning.

"Got it."

I shook my head and looked at her idiotically. "And?"

"Wait."

Wait? I wanted to know what the fuck she had gotten.

Clare leaned past me and tugged open the glove compartment. Empty wrappers, CD cases, pens, and myriad other bits and bobs spewed from the small space. Eventually she pulled out something flat, something very recognisable, and waved it in my face.

I could see the orange colouring mixed with a waterfall image, and also her grinning face. I grabbed the leaflet from her and studied the front. It was an Ordnance Survey map. And not just any Ordnance Survey map. This one was titled *OL24 The Peak District: The White Peaks*.

"Coordinates," she said triumphantly.

Such a simple word, and such an astute deduction. It was obvious to me now. Freddie had written the coordinates on the back of the picture so he would always know that was where he buried his wife. I had thought he had kept the photo close to him so he could gloat, but it turned out it was also because it held the evidence of his crime. He was too shit feared of anyone else getting hold of it to leave it lying about.

"No wonder he wanted me to go into the bathroom and get the picture back from you." Clare's voice seemed lighter. "When he chucked it at you, I don't think he thought it all the way through."

At that point, I laughed, the force of it hurting my throat with a delightful throb. Clare joined in, and it wasn't long before tears were running down our faces.

"I bet he wanted to kick himself," Clare spluttered.

Wiping the tears from my face, I answered, "He should have asked. I'd have kicked him."

Eventually we collected ourselves enough to put our plan together. Either we were going to the police, or we'd go investigate 53.171762, -1.999212 for ourselves. Naturally we opted for the latter. All we needed was a compass, a camera, solid walking boots, and the inclination. We had all of them, although we would have to go back to Annabel's to collect everything apart from the inclination.

It was time to put things to rest.

Chapter Fifteen

Kirk Langley, Ashbourne, Leek, Upper Hulme, then we were on to the Roaches. On the way there, we were full of anticipation, of streaming adrenaline, but for the first part of the journey, we were both quiet—probably both thinking about what we would find once we arrived.

Clare eventually broke the silence. "I hope you know why I asked you to leave the hospital room."

I answered with a grunt, my attention on the vast openness.

"Becky?" I turned to face her. "You do know I didn't ask you to leave the hospital room to get rid of you, don't you?"

I shook my head. "You were pulling a 'good cop' routine on Freddie."

Her laugh vibrated through the car. "Nothing gets past you, does it?"

She flicked her eyes my way, and I grinned at her. "To be honest, you did confuse me for a moment. At first I didn't understand why you were asking me to stop talking."

Clare patted my leg, her hand resting for a split second before moving back to the steering wheel. "Given the shift in his behaviour, I knew that he was clamming up because you were in the room."

"Did you get anything more out of him?"

Clare shook her head. "As soon as he realised that you had the photograph, and with it the coordinates, he wasn't the willing witness I had hoped he would be." She sighed.

"So all the 'you wouldn't hurt Nanny' and 'I told her she was dreaming' were for nothing, eh?" I wanted to add that maybe we'd underestimated the old fart, and that he wasn't as addled as we had hoped he would be, but decided that was something that didn't need saying.

Clare sighed again. "I've no idea what was going on inside his mind, but I'm hoping he thinks I'm on his side."

"And I'm not." I turned and grinned at Clare, who smiled back.

"We're here."

We parked in one of the parking bays, Clare's door snug against bushes and overgrown weeds, which made her exit from the vehicle a little difficult. As soon as we were both out of the car, we changed into our walking boots, slipped on thick jackets and gloves, and tutted at the lack of light. Even though Clare seemed a lot better at reading a map than I was, even she would find it difficult to navigate in the dark. We had brought torches, just in case, but the Roaches was not the kind of place one would want to be walking about in after the sun went down. There were no other people in the vicinity, and not surprising either, considering it was November. The iciness of the air was enough to freeze a witch's tit. Thank God for thermals and long, fleece lined jackets.

Whilst Clare was fiddling around in the car, I looked at the view. To my left, I could see the vastness of the fields dipping downwards, the outline of Tittesworth Reservoir like a huge shadow on the land. Streaks of red, orange, and yellow blended with the grey clouds, and rays of sharp winter sun sparked through the gaps. Darkness seemed to be overwhelming the light and drowning out the colour. I inhaled the sharp, crisp air, filling my lungs with freshness. Everything seemed so open, so wild and free, and the sheer size of it was almost too much for me to take in.

Turning back, I was greeted by the magnificence of the Roaches. Hen Cloud's outline loomed ominously, almost like a guardian. The gritstone escarpment joined by Ramshaw Rocks seemed to be watching Clare and me, frowning down on us, sneering at our insignificance and threatening us with their size and silence.

A shiver passed through me, and I shifted my attention away from the Titans and back to Clare. "I think we are going to have a problem with the lack of light." Stating the obvious was part of my charm.

Clare pulled the map from the pocket in the side of the door and started to unfold it. "Good job I brought my extendable lantern torch then." She looked up at me, a teasing grin on her face. "We can leave this until the morning if you want."

"No. I was just concerned we might..."

"Get lost?"

I made a pffting noise and shuffled my feet. "No. I just think it will be hard to keep reading the map *and* the compass by torchlight whilst looking for the proverbial needle in the haystack."

Clare perched on the bonnet of the car, the passenger car door open and leaking the light onto the grass verge. An image of a time when I had stepped out into the dark to perform my ablutions—well, not exactly ablutions, but to have a pee at the side of the road—came to mind. Then ding, the interior light pinged off. I did jump just a little bit, even though it wasn't even real dark yet.

Weirdly enough, as soon as the car light went off, my mind saw the light, as if a bulb had clicked on in my brain. Susan. Little bitty Susan. Susan who couldn't find her way out of a paper bag. Susan, who had stopped talking to me when I was lost that fateful night, but thought it was perfectly acceptable to suddenly announce "Turn left" when I was teetering on the emotional edge.

If we had been in my car, I would have pulled out my old mate Susan and smugly placed it in front of Clare, waiting a moment to gloat before telling her to put in the coordinates. Instead, I said, "Have you got a Sat Nav?"

"No."

I slumped against the car. Well, that was my brainwave up shit creek.

"But..." I looked at her, and she continued, "I do have OS Locate and Google Maps on my phone."

I could barely make out her features now, as darkness was slithering over us. "And a phone has a light, too, yes?"

Click. Clare turned on the torch and put it under her chin. Shadows danced over her skin, and a tingling surged through me. As if I wasn't shitted up enough.

Clare dipped into her jacket pocket and pulled out her phone. She placed the torch on top of the car and began to swipe through her phone menus. "Can you read the coordinates to me?"

I grinned widely. Teamwork. That's what it was all about.

Fucking teamwork? More like Abbott and Costello or two of the three Stooges. Because Clare looked all knowledgeable at the side of the car reading a map like she had been weaned on them, I believed that she actually had a fucking clue. *And* she had OS Locate *and* fucking Google Maps on her phone. In retrospect, that should have popped me a clue. Why would a person need two maps on her phone? Because she couldn't find her way out of a brightly lit, single lane tunnel that had huge fucking arrows directing her, that's why. And I wasn't Bear Grylls, either. If it was left up to me, we would have still been walking in circles around the car.

It was pitch black. The Roaches did not have any mercy for idiots with thermals and fleece lined jackets, however big their extendable torch was. If I fell down once, I fell down fifteen times. The ground was uneven, as it should be considering it was in the arse end of nowhere, and my language was getting a little sparky, to say the least.

Clare's phone was as useful as cat shit on roses, and I was losing the will to live. If Ellen's body was up there somewhere, I was definite mine was going to join her soon. And if Clare made me bugger over onto gorse again, hers would be there with us.

Slam. All my muttering and moaning and not paying attention caused me to walk straight into Clare's back. At least this time, I stayed upright.

Clare glanced back at me. "I don't think we'll be able to find anything tonight." No shit, Sherlock. "We should get back to the car before we get lost."

"You mean you *actually* know where we are?" I couldn't help the sarcasm. I was cold, pissed off, and lost. My knees were creaking like a broken rocking chair, and I was sure I had uninvited guests riding along in my hair. I was not best pleased, to say the least.

Clare turned and held the torch at the side of her face and focused it on me. "I know exactly where we are."

I thought it wise to hold back my initial retort and think of something kinder. *"Really?"* was the best alternate I came up with. She nodded and gave me one of her crooked smiles, and I felt a sliver of anger slip away as I stepped closer to her.

"We are here." She lifted the phone to show me, and all I could see were lines, green blobs, and 53° 10 18.3"N 1° 59'57.2"W, wherever the hell that was.

I bit my lip. The nastier retort was back and wanted a showdown. I counted to five in my head before commenting. "But, dear Sherpa, do you know where the car is?" I heard a mumble that didn't sound like a yes, so I rephrased the question. "Can we get back to the car?"

A piercing cry came from near us, closely followed by my scream. Clare grabbed hold of me and pulled me closer, and my hands gripped her jacket.

"What the..."

The scream came again, but seemed further away this time. My heart was beating so hard inside my chest that I believed Clare couldn't help but feel it, even through the layers of clothing.

Her breath floated over my hair, and I am sure I heard her lips smack. "I think...I think it was just a bird."

I didn't think birds flew around at night, except maybe owls, but I wasn't going to argue. If my brain could process and accept the shriek as having come from a bird, who was I—in my cowardice—to deny it?

Her heat seeped into me, and just being held close steadied my nerves. Slightly. A soft kiss landed on the side of my head, and I closed my eyes and allowed the safety of her to wash over me. So what if she couldn't read a map? Who cared if she knew where the car was? Maybe the cold and dark were getting to me after all.

"I love you, Becky."

My eyes closed in contentment, and my lips moved into a smile and pressed against the shoulder of her jacket. "Love you too." Her arms squeezed me more tightly and I snuggled deeper into her, taking comfort in the warmth.

When I opened my eyes, I thought I saw a light about twenty feet away from us. Was someone else out walking in the dark? And if they were, were they idiots too? Was it Mountain Rescue? Had someone seen our deserted car and guessed that we were lost? Nah. We hadn't been out that long. At least not long enough for someone to become concerned and call it in.

A flitter. A flick. A definite light. I pulled away from Clare and tried to analyse the moving glow. It didn't seem like a torch, or a lamp, or anything I had seen before.

I was wrong about the last one. I had seen it before. A couple of times to be exact. Standing a little closer to us than when I'd first noticed the light was Ellen Howell. This time she was what a person would fully expect to see when encountering a ghost, not the horrific image I had seen when standing in a brightly lit bathroom. It was almost like she was a hologram—light and bright and staring right at me, and I was staring back at her.

"Clare? Don't freak out, yeah?"

"What—" She started to turn and look behind her, but I stopped her. "You're just shitting me up, right. What is it?" she demanded.

"I think we really do have a Sherpa now."

Clare moved out of my arms and spun around. Ellen shifted her attention from me to Clare, but didn't say a word, then she nodded, turned, and began to move away.

I couldn't move. Or maybe it was a case of me not wanting to budge from the spot, in case she was leading us to our deaths.

The air around us was silent, so still, it was as if we were suspended amid reality. Cold was beginning to seep through my jacket, and the wet grass beneath my feet was not just slippery, but the chill of it was seeping inside my boots. We couldn't just stand there and freeze to death. We basically had two choices. We could follow Clare's phone to God knew where, or we could follow the luminous presence that had stopped and was surveying us. Either of them was taking a huge chance.

I grabbed hold of Clare's hand and pulled her to me, then cupped her chin and tilted her face toward mine. "I don't know about you, but I vote we follow her." Of the two options, following Ellen seemed like the better choice, even though it was like a fucked up version of *Wuthering Heights,* with Clare and me playing the part of Heathcliff. And look what happened to him. He ended up dead, arm stretched out of his bedroom window, seemingly reaching out to the dead. Still, there was one real point in favour of this choice—Ellen Howell had been buried on the moor for sixty years, so she shouldn't need a map to find her way about, not to mention the added advantage of her being luminous. Two huge ticks for going with the ghost lady, obviously the more reasonable option.

A tremor rippled throughout Clare, followed by a clacking sound. I reached out and guided her other hand to her face so the torch would illuminate her features. I expected to see a look of terror, but I realised her teeth were chattering with cold.

"Come on." I tugged on her hand to indicate we were leaving, but she stood stoically on the spot. "Look, love, if we stay here, we could freeze to death." I lifted her hand and kissed it right through her glove. "What have we got to lose?"

Actually, I knew we could lose quite a lot, but there might also be much for us to gain.

Clare closed her eyes briefly, but when she opened them, there seemed to be an added determination in them. She nodded decisively. "Let's go."

I kissed her. It was a short kiss of agreement, an affirmation that we were in this together. What we were doing was complete madness, utter stupidity. We were going to follow a dead woman across uneven land and areas with sharp drops, drops that could lead to serious injury or even death. That was a scenario a person would watch in some lame B movie whilst shouting, "Get the fuck away!" or "Use your phone and call for help." Maybe even "Let Mountain Rescue track you, you fuckwits!"

But this wasn't a B movie. However fucked up it might be, this was reality. It included two dipshits stumbling around in the arse end of nowhere, even encompassed the ghost of a murdered relative in its dramatis personae, but it was life as we were beginning to know it. We didn't want Mountain Rescue; we wanted to end this, to lay Ellen Howell's spirit to rest. The woman had suffered enough.

As we moved forward, Clare dipped the torch downwards once again whilst my brain began to stew everything over. What if we did find the spot where Ellen was buried? It wasn't as if we could dig her up. We had no shovel, and even if we did, we might damage vital evidence. And how would we know Ellen was actually buried wherever she led us? Would we be able to tell the land was hiding a grave? It had been sixty years since Ellen disappeared, so the ground would certainly not show the telltale signs that would be visible if it had been newly dug.

Ellen's form disappeared from view, dragging me out from my mental meanderings. Clare was following close behind me, her ragged breath on the back of my head.

"Where's she gone?"

Clare's tone told me that she was unnerved. We were keeping tabs on the compass in her phone, and it was obvious, even to us, that we were moving away from the car park. We knew this because we had clambered down and then up two inclines since we had begun following Ellen. When we had believed ourselves to be totally lost, we had climbed only one incline and partway down the other side.

Suddenly I was filled with dread. Dread and fear and everything else that would evoke the feeling of being totally screwed over by a ghost, a ghost that we assumed was trying to help us. Showed how much we knew.

"There. Did you see it?"

The tone of Clare's voice had shifted to one of excitement, and I tried to see what she was trying to show me. Even though I moved my head frenetically from side to side, the thing she had spotted eluded me.

"There! To your right," she directed.

A sharp turn of my head allowed me to catch the glow of the figure stopped near what appeared to be some kind of bush. "Why doesn't she come closer? If she wanted us to follow her, why the mystery?" I was frustrated, and getting a little bit annoyed with the situation. "Ellen! For fuck's sake!"

"Becky! You can't swear at my grandm—"

"Jesus, Ellen!"

At first I thought it was my imagination when the shape seemed to come closer. So I shouted again, then again. Finally the figure of Ellen Howell was standing a scant ten feet away from us. It was only then that I realised why Ellen had moved from us so quickly before. Her expression indicated she wanted us to move faster, to stop hanging about and tripping over heather, stones, and plants. She wanted us to find whatever she wanted to show us, and she wanted it done now. I knew she had waited a fair while for this moment, but she needed to understand that unlike her, we were only human.

Ellen started to move away again, and I had to shout out to her to stop. "We will find you, Ellen, but you have to stay with us."

She seemed to rise from the ground, although I couldn't see her feet, as her legs seemed to stop halfway down her calves. She slowly lifted her arms so they were out to the sides of her body, forming a crucifix. Her head tilted back, her mouth opening in a silent cry. The effect was intimidating and terrifying.

I know I didn't blink. I didn't even close my eyes for a millisecond, but one moment she was standing ten feet away, and the next her face was right up close to mine. The air in front of me was a column of ice. Her hair drifted around her face as if being softly blown, and the tendrils passed through me like icicles. Eyes that I knew to be green, seemed grey, and were full of desperation. Her hand came closer and hovered next to my cheek. I flinched in anticipation of her touch, but when the contact happened, it was nothing like I imagined it would be.

I saw images of a darkened landscape, of a man half dragging, half carrying a body. A spade was strapped to his back, and as he struggled onwards, it kept swinging forward only to be angrily shoved away. The words that tumbled from his mouth were full of hatred and wickedness, words that identified him as Freddie Howell, words that identified the body as that of his wife.

The image faded and left a feeling of profound sadness, Ellen's and mine. A sob tore from my throat, and Clare's arms wrapped around me and pulled me against her. The sensation of my body touching both the living and the dead was surreal, and I tried to struggle away. Neither woman relinquished her hold, and I had to endure the agony of being in limbo. Time seemed to race, yet stand still. I felt suspended, yet grounded. Hot, yet cold.

"I will not hurt you."

Ellen's voice was clear, light, bright, and calming. She withdrew her hand from my face and took a step back, her head tipping to the side, her eyes half closing in thought. The mannerism was so like Clare's that I felt a sense of tranquillity settle over me.

"Let me show you." She tilted her head as if asking if I understood her request. I nodded back, unable to voice my response. She slowly moved backwards before turning away.

Clare was still hugged up behind me, her torch and phone on the ground at my feet. A warm cheek rested on mine, and her voice drifted over my skin. "Are you okay, love?"

I nodded and breathed out, "Yes."

"Then shall we?"

I nodded again. Feeling Clare move away from me sparked me into action. Bending, I retrieved the dropped items and handed them back to Clare. Instead of just taking them, she touched my hands and gave them a reassuring squeeze.

"Come on, let's go." The words seemed unfamiliar in my mouth, as if I hadn't spoken in years.

Following Ellen was difficult, but I imagined it would have been worse if she had kept her distance. The light she emitted helped us to see the uneven terrain, especially small bushes or rogue plants that jutted out. We could also see more ominous dangers, like sheer drops. Ellen completely avoided such hazards, which helped to reassure us as to her intent. In less than ten minutes, she stopped near a small rock outcropping half hidden by bushes.

The blood in my veins seemed to freeze. There was only one reason she would be stopping there. Fuck. Fuck. And fuck. But wasn't that the exact reason both Clare and I were on the fucking Roaches in the first place?

It was different now that we were finally a few feet away. It had a finality to it, provided some structure to the weird shit that had been happening for nearly a month.

I didn't know what to do besides just stare at the spot Ellen was indicating. We had found her final resting place, but there was nothing we could do. Even if we'd had the forethought to bring a shovel, and even if we could have started to dig without doing damage to a crime scene, I didn't think I would have the balls to actually do it.

"We need to mark the spot."

Clare's voice seemed muffled, even though she was right next to me.

"Huh?"

"We need to mark the spot so we can find it again tomorrow when we bring..." she drew a deep breath, "when we bring the police."

Clare's voice still seemed different. Hesitant, I turned to look, all but convinced that I would find myself standing next to Annabel. But no, it was Clare. And I understood why her voice sounded different. I couldn't make out the finer features of her face, but I could tell by the movement of her shoulders that she was crying. Also, her hand angrily swiped at the tears on her cheeks.

Shit. I had always known I was insensitive, but I hadn't quite understood how much so until that moment. Of course Clare would be upset. She'd found out from the ghost of her grandmother that her grandfather was a murderer who had buried his victim in a cold, unmarked grave on the Peaks. That would have been enough to make anyone cry. I had been so absorbed with nailing the old bastard for Ellen's murder that I hadn't considered the bigger picture: Clare loved her granddad. I couldn't understand it, but she did.

Without saying a word, I slipped my arms around her and pulled her to me. Her body quaked against mine. Stifled sobs disrupted the stillness of the night, and I wanted to smack myself for being totally oblivious to what she had been going through. It had been less than a month ago that her world was perfectly normal and her grandfather played a huge role in her life. She had told me more about him than about her own mother; that should've shot me a clue.

Digging in my pocket, I located some scrunched tissues and handed them to her. By the light of the torch, I could see her watery, grateful smile as she took them, and then proceeded to blow her nose. I took off my glove to stroke her cheek. I had to feel her skin next to mine, just to know that she was okay. Stupid, but that's how I felt. I needed the contact, and so did she. A few minutes passed as she reined in her emotions.

Ellen had been waiting patiently near the spot where she had stopped, as if she was aware of what was transpiring with Clare. Even a ghost had understood before I did. Didn't say much for me and my intuition.

"We need to mark the spot so that we can find it again." Clare's voice sounded stronger, more controlled.

I shrugged. I had no idea what we could use to mark the spot. It wasn't as if we could mark it with a rock and hope we would find the exact same rock again when it was daylight.

The ground was teeming with rocks. "Roaches" actually fucking meant "rocks" in French, for God's sake.

Clare pulled back from me, and the cool air that drifted between us seemed even more chilling after being so close to her. She dug about in her pockets and eventually pulled out a cylindrical object. "Spray paint."

"Spray paint? Why on earth did you bring spray paint?"

Clare's laugh was musical. "So I could vandalise walls by spraying graffiti everywhere, obviously." When I just stared at her, she added, "To mark the spot, Becky. To mark the spot."

I still didn't get why she would carry a spray can of paint. I understood what she had said about marking the spot, but how on earth had she thought of it in the first place?

Clare came up alongside me, and her mouth found my ear. "It's not rocket science, Becks. Find a rock and spray it. Get the coordinates logged into my phone. Done." Her quick kiss landed partly on my nose and partly on my cheek before she moved away.

It was official—I was an idiot.

Chapter Sixteen

I am not going to go into detail about lugging a rock to the spot Ellen indicated and Clare spraying it canary yellow. I don't think I should rattle on about saving the coordinates into the phone, either. The trek back to the car took us about thirty minutes, but it would have taken a lot longer if Ellen hadn't guided us. I figured that as soon as we marked the spot, she would fade into nothingness and we would be left to find our own way back to the where the car was parked. But no. Ellen waited patiently whilst we did what we had to do, and then beckoned for us to follow her. To be honest, I had an awful feeling that she might be leading us to another unmarked grave, and another of Freddie's victims. For Clare's sake, I was happy that didn't happen.

When I saw the outline of Clare's car, I felt almost giddy. It had been utterly rash to attempt to find Ellen's burial site under the circumstances. It hadn't just been dark; it had been freezing, too. This hadn't been just a stroll down a country lane; it had the potential of ending fatally, and we were very fortunate to have survived the ordeal.

As soon as the car was in view, Ellen turned to face us, and her expression was serene. A smile appeared on her beautiful features, and for a moment I sensed how Annabel must have felt every time Ellen had graced her with one of those.

Then she was gone. Bam. Disappeared into the night like a will-o'-the-wisp, leaving my eyes reeling at the lack of light.

A disappointed "oh" came from Clare, and I reached out and took her hand. "Just you and me now, love," I said, but my tone held promise.

When we got into the car, we were amazed to realise that it was almost midnight. We had been traipsing over the hills for nearly six hours. No wonder we were knackered and frozen to the bone. Clare started the engine and ratcheted up the heat, whilst I got out the flask that we had forgotten to take with us on our hike. Failing to have carried such vital equipment with us was just another disqualification against our trying to be professional orienteers, as if crap map-reading skills wouldn't have been enough to ban us from the club in the first place.

The coffee was still hot, and as the aroma filled the car we began to be revitalised even before we took our first sips. The cup trembled in my hands, and it took me a few tries to lift it to my lips without spilling it all over myself.

It was too late to go to the police. It wasn't as if Ellen or Freddie was going anywhere. Ellen had been in the same spot for sixty years; one more night wasn't going to make any difference. Freddie could have another night of freedom, as free as being stuck in a hospital bed could offer him.

As I sipped my coffee, I thought about what might happen to him. Would they arrest Freddie and put him in prison, even at his age? It wasn't as if he would serve his time and then return to the community and kill another hapless victim, was it? But, he had killed someone. He also had had sixty years of freedom, whilst Ellen had been buried in the Roaches.

Another thought occurred to me. Would the evidence we found be enough to convict Freddie? In reality, all we had was a photograph with a number in handwriting other than Annabel's on it. Yes, the photo had been in his possession, but it could have been a gift from the person who *had* killed Ellen Howell, someone trying to implicate Freddie to cover up his or her own tracks. Considering the photograph was definitely from the stack we had found at Annabel's house, the police could even point the finger at her, now that she wasn't around to defend herself. Ellen could have been killed in a lover's spat, or even because of love spurned, especially as the notebook would clearly substantiate the longing Annabel had for Ellen. Sure it mentioned that Freddie hit Ellen, even that Annabel suspected Freddie had killed his wife, but even I'd had doubts at one time about the veracity of the notebook.

Fuck. And times that expletive by a thousand.

"Are you okay?"

Clare's voice broke through my mental investigations, and I couldn't help sighing.

"What's up? We're dry and on our way home, aren't we?"

I shrugged. "I don't think the police will think it was Freddie."

Clare frowned. "What do you mean? We have proof."

"No we don't."

She snorted. "If they dig up a body, isn't that proof?"

"But what's to stop them thinking it was Annabel who killed Ellen? Or someone else we haven't even thought of?"

The air inside the car seemed to freeze, even though the heater was on full. Clare raised her cup to her mouth and tapped it rhythmically against her lips. She squinted through the windscreen, into the light cast by the headlights.

Slam. The cup hitting the dashboard made me jump.

"Fuck!" She smacked the steering wheel with her open palm. "FUCK!" It seemed as if Clare had worked it out without my prompting. She turned and looked at me. "He can't get away with it. He can't!"

Too damned right, but it was beginning to look as if he might. We couldn't very well tell the police that we had been visited by the ghosts of the deceased women. They would tell us to take a hike, and we had literally done just that to find where the body was buried. We were not about to take another one. It also wasn't an option to try to trick Freddie into spilling his guts; he was on the defensive now. He knew we had the photo and the coordinates; he was probably just waiting for us to accuse him of murder so that he could trot out an alibi he'd had ready for years.

I rubbed my face to get the blood circulating through the numbness, catching the stitches over my eye in the process. I was so very tired. It had been a long and exhausting day, even before we went hiking up the sides of hills in the dark. What had happened at the hospital with Freddie had been draining enough, and then seeing Ellen so badly beaten, the sheer gamut of emotions I had run through would have been enough to stun an elephant.

"Let's go back to the house and get some rest. You look done in," Clare said. I felt it, too. "We'll talk this over in the morning, try to get at angle on how to put this across to the police, okay?"

Before I could respond, she put the car into gear and moved off. I was still staring at the hulking shapes of the hills standing watch in the darkness.

After a hot shower, I climbed into bed. The events of the day took their toll, and in mere moments I was asleep. I stirred when Clare climbed in beside me and pulled me to her. The security of her body close to mine helped me to drift off into the black void. I truly expected to dream, but I didn't, at least not that I could remember when I woke.

It was light. The starkness of the November day crept past the half open curtains. I was still in Clare's arms, her gentle snoring coming from behind me. Shifting on to my back, I studied her face in slumber. Long, dark eyelashes rested on faintly flushed cheeks, and her lips were slightly parted, allowing air to easily pass in and out. Dark strands of hair wisped over her cheek, and I felt the urge to brush them back. Instead I tentatively slipped my thumb over her eyebrow, then down her nose and across her cheek. Her lashes fluttered, and I was treated to the full gaze of her beautiful brown eyes. At that moment, I fell in love with her all over again.

Clare leaned closer, until her breath was touching my face. Our eyes met, and nothing else mattered. Soft lips brushed mine, and yearning raced through me. Another kiss, a little firmer this time. My arm wrapped around her and pulled her closer, and her body shifted into perfect alignment over mine. Even through our sleepwear, I could feel the definition of her body, the soft firmness of her breasts. The kiss became deeper, more desperate, and my hands slipped inside her top to touch the soft, silken skin.

Clare broke the kiss, and her mouth moved to nuzzle my neck. Sensation rippled through me, and the jerk of my hips told Clare that I needed more, needed her. I slid my hands around to her front and struggled with the buttons on her pyjama top. We were too close for me to get a proper hold on them.

Clare leaned back and grabbed the hem of her shirt. With one swift motion, her enticing breasts were on display. For a moment, I was surprised into inaction, but that didn't last. My hand traced her collar bone, and then my fingers roamed freely over her skin. They travelled to the hollow of her throat and paused. Clare leaned slightly forward, as if inviting me to move lower. I trailed two fingers down to the valley between her breasts, biting back the impulse to capture the pliant flesh. Instead, I moved slowly over one breast and then the other, then back to the middle again. My exploration continued along the line of her abdomen, then reversed direction and moved upwards. Countless times I followed the same route, and each time I was enthralled by the feel of her skin, watching in fascination as her muscles rippled beneath my touch. I bit back a groan at seeing her nipples standing expectantly.

Finally I allowed myself the pleasure of cupping both breasts and holding them for a moment. My thumbs slipped along the curvature, flitting across the peaks to tease and excite. Clare leaned back and pushed her breasts into my hands. A low moan slipped from her throat. Her hips ground into my stomach, and wetness began to gather between my legs. Again, and again, and again, and more moisture, more delicious sparks at the spot that ached for her touch. I pressed my palms against the soft, supple skin of her breasts, my thumbs insistent against erect nipples.

"God!"

Her voice was throaty, sultry. Her hips moved faster, but the heat of her body could not contact my skin because of my pyjamas. I wanted her naked body to settle on mine, or mine on hers.

As if she was reading my mind, her hands, shaking slightly, came forward and undid my buttons. One swift tug and I was fully exposed to her, and not just physically. It was obvious how much I wanted her. My love for her was visible in the crisp light of morning.

Clare leaned forward and captured my nipple in her mouth, sucking gently then flicking it with her tongue. As the sensation ricocheted inside me, hitting every nerve and emotion, it was my turn to groan. In one fluid movement, Clare slipped her body up mine, the feel of her skin creating an ever deepening longing for her. My hands caught the band of her pyjama bottoms and pushed downwards, my fingertips deliberately sliding along her backside in the process. Clare lifted one leg, twisted, lifted the other and kicked the bottoms away, leaving her naked on top of me. Her left knee pushed between my thighs, opening me to her, her right leg soon followed by. Instead of settling between my legs, she leaned back and pulled my bottoms from me, lifting each leg to remove the sleep trousers. Her legs between mine, her hips pushed upwards to press her pelvic bone against the spot that was yearning for her touch. Clare's mouth met mine, and her kiss was hungry, needy. One of her hands cupped my ass, the other curved around my shoulder, securing me in place for her thrusts. A tendril of hair fell over her face, and I pushed it away. I wanted to watch as she made me feel so wholly loved. I gripped her backside, making each push, each thrust, each delicious forward motion a little more insistent than the previous.

Our breathing was ragged with exertion, but that didn't slow us down. I wanted her to love me, to take me to heights that only she could. And then I wanted to do the same for her. Nothing else mattered but that moment, that feeling, that love we were sharing.

"Becky." Her voice was breathless, urgent. "Becky...I..."

Her lips crushed against mine and our tongues danced together as if they were waltzing. Bodies moulded together as the fire between us leapt and burned. I knew I was close.

Clare ripped her lips from mine and stared straight into my eyes, her face flushed, her movement never stopping. "I love you, Becky."

My orgasm erupted with a force that was white, bright, all consuming. I heard Clare cry out, and her head tilted back whilst her hips bucked into me, bonding us. Then she buried her face against my neck. I couldn't say whose heart it was that was thundering. At that moment, our two hearts beat as one.

It should have been enough, but it wasn't. I wanted to taste her, to be deep inside her. And I wanted her to do the same to me.

Before I could make a move, her hand slipped between my thighs and two fingers entered me. Clare shifted back slightly, withdrawing her fingers, only to position her hand more securely. She curved her body so her hand had room to manipulate, but also so she could press herself as close against me as she could.

The loving was primal, instinctual. Hot breath on my throat was followed by hungry lips. My world was ablaze with sensation, and felt myself being swept away in the power of it. Each kiss, each affirmation of love led me further down the path of no return. My hands gripped her back, my fingers digging into her skin. And then something deep within me sparked, igniting a conflagration of sensation, a connection of two people finding their home, their love, their future.

Chapter Seventeen

We finally struggled out of bed at gone ten o'clock the next morning. After we had both showered, and I had tended to my eye and the wound on my calf, we ate a late breakfast. Over the food, I was frequently caught staring at her, mesmerised all over again to know that someone as beautiful as Clare Davies was interested in me. It warmed my heart to know that most of the times I looked at her, she was looking at me. I blushed when that happened, and I realised that inside I was still a teenager after all.

After breakfast, we sat down on the sofa in the living room to discuss our options.

"Shouldn't we go to the police and tell them what we know?" I thought it was a logical place to start, they were the authorities after all, but Clare nailed it when she pointed out the obvious.

"We have a photograph with numbers on the back that we think are coordinates, a diary that could have been written by anyone for any reason, and the two of us who keep on seeing ghosts."

"One of those ghosts guided us to the place where she was likely buried." That probably wouldn't sound any more convincing to the police. "And we marked the spot with a yellow rock." That sounded far-fetched.

Clare tilted her head, her lips pursed slightly as if she was actually giving my suggestion serious thought. "I think, and please don't take offence at this, the police would tell us to fuck off."

The way Clare said it made me laugh. "I guess they would. To be honest, I would too, if someone came to me with what we have. So what are we going to do? Our options are limited if we can't involve the police."

"We could confront Granddad again and get him to spill the beans some way or another."

"And try to get him to admit what he did to the police?"

Clare nodded. "It's worth a shot, don't you think?"

"Knowing Freddie, he would more than likely stitch us up to the police to such an extent that we would end up doing time for a crime he committed, despite the fact that neither of us was even born when it happened." I wanted to add "Sly old bastard that he is," but given the expression on Clare's face, I decided I'd best keep my thoughts about Freddie to myself.

"I think you may be exaggerating, Becky."

Clare was right. Not having been born when the murder happened likely would keep me from being incarcerated for a crime I didn't commit. But Freddie had escaped justice for nearly sixty years. It was frustrating to know for sure it was him and not be able to sell our conclusions to anyone else. It was definite that no mention of dreams or ghosts or misplaced keys would be spluttering from either of our mouths to the authorities.

Clare sighed and rubbed her hands over her face in exasperation, whilst I sat there and stared at how beautiful her fingers were.

"Fuck it!" Clare stood abruptly, breaking me away from my daydream. "What have we got to lose?"

"Erm..."

"I'm going to the police. If they believe us, bonus. If they don't, they don't."

The last bit was less enthusiastic, which was understandable. If we went in there cock handed, we would bugger everything up and they would never believe us, even if we turned up film footage of Freddie killing his wife.

She was part way to the door, her determination clear in even the way she walked, when she stopped, turned, and looked back me. "Are you coming, or what?"

Too damned right. I wouldn't miss it for the world.

It wasn't easy convincing the police to take notice, at least not at first. When Clare stepped forward and announced to the man behind the desk, "I have information about a woman who's disappeared," the officer nearly fell over himself grabbing a pen and a pad.

"Name of missing person?"

Clare looked at me and gave a slight nod, as if to suggest that maybe it wouldn't be as difficult to convince the law after all. "Ellen Howell. My grandmother."

The pen scratched the words onto the sheet of paper.

"And when was the last time you saw your grandmother."

"Oh, I've never met her."

The silence in the station deafened my ears with its resounding scream, and the time it took the officer to look up at us from his pad was a tad longer than was comfortable.

"You've never met her?"

Clare shook her head.

The officer bit his lip, sighed, then set the pen on the counter next to the pad. "So, if you don't mind me asking, how do you know she is missing? Another relative? Your grandfather, for example?"

Part of me didn't want Clare to have to say the thing that had to come next, and I wanted to pull my jumper over my head and hide.

"To be honest, there is reason to believe my grandfather has murdered her."

The officer's mouth dropped open.

"And buried her on the Roaches."

The policeman stared into Clare's face and then turned to me as if he wanted me to either support or deny what she was saying. I, like a perfect witness, shrugged and grinned stupidly.

"So, you're saying your grandmother has disappeared and you think your grandfather is responsible, and that he buried her on the Roaches?" He nodded at Clare, and she nodded back. "But you have never met her? Is that your statement?"

"Yes. In point of fact, she disappeared sixty years ago."

That that was the moment I wanted to ground to open up and swallow me whole. The noise the policeman made in his throat was something I don't think I would ever be able to replicate.

"And we have a feeling we know the spot where she is buried," Clare added helpfully.

I was inwardly praying that Clare was not about to divulge any more than that we found the coordinates on the back of a photo, an entirely concrete piece of information. Otherwise, I had the distinct feeling we were both about to be turfed out of the station.

"I know it sounds far-fetched, that you are probably thinking I'm a sandwich short of a picnic, but can you just check the files? There will definitely be something there about Ellen Howell. I promise you."

The officer stood stock still, the air between him and Clare thick with expectation.

"Just hold on a minute." He squinted at Clare. "Wait a moment, Madam." He moved to the rear of the counter area and place a call, presumably to the officer in charge of lunatics who was situated elsewhere in the building.

Turning to Clare, I forced a grin. "At least he didn't tell us to sling our hooks."

Clare released a tense laugh. "Not yet, at any rate." She nodded in the direction of the officer on the phone. "He's probably telling the other boy in blue that he's got a couple of weirdoes in Reception and wants a psych report done ASAP."

The officer looked in our direction, his demeanour reflecting more alertness than previously. When he moved his hand to half cover his face, a feeling of unease travelled through me.

"I'm not too sure that..." I didn't finish, as the officer hung up the phone and was on his way back to the counter.

"It seems as if there was an Ellen Howell after all."

I bit back the "No shit, Sherlock."

"Seems as if Mrs Howell's case file was used for training purposes for a number of years. Fortunately Bill Edwards, the officer I called, has a vague recollection of that missing person case study when he joined the force nearly thirty years ago."

Clare leaned closer to him, her hands gripping the edge of the counter. "What does he remember about it?"

"Not much. Just that a woman went missing in the early nineteen fifties, there was an intensive manhunt for her, but she was never found."

"I'm sorry for sounding stupid," I said, speaking for the first time. The officer looked at me, his expression blank. "Why on earth would they use Ellen Howell's case for training purposes? They never found her, right?"

"I'm sorry, Miss. I'm not sure what point you're making."

"Wouldn't they usually use a case study where there was an outcome? You know, so the officers studying the case could come to the correct conclusion."

He shrugged, his eyes flicking to Clare before coming back to rest on me. "No idea. Maybe it is because Kirk Langley is not a very big place, and we don't get many missing person reports.

From what Bill told me, we've only ever had the one—Mrs Ellen Howell. Her disappearance caused an uproar, especially as they never found her."

The door at the back of the office opened, and another officer entered the small reception area. He nodded at his colleague and then came to the counter, lifted the hatch, and joined us on the outside. "Good morning, ladies. I'm Sergeant Edwards. Seems as if you think you know something about what might have happened to Mrs. Ellen Howell over sixty years ago. Is that about it?"

"Maybe." Why was I playing hard to get? I wanted them to believe what we had to say, not piss them off.

Clare turned to me, her expression confused, then she turned back to the sergeant. "What Rebecca is trying to say is, what do you already know? We don't want to waste your time if our information is repetitious."

I think the sergeant knew that was not what I had meant, but he played along.

"We still have the case files from the investigation into Ellen Howell's disappearance. We have statements from her husband, her sister-in-law, and character witnesses, all saying that she basically vanished into thin air."

Clare almost vibrated with suppressed excitement. "Can we read the files?"

The sergeant shook his head. "If what you say is true, then the statements could potentially be used as evidence at trial."

I couldn't help myself. "Evidence?"

The policeman turned to face me. "Evidence to either convict or absolve any suspect that might be taken into custody as a result of a new investigation."

I knew which way I wanted that to pan out, but I didn't say anything.

"The file also shows that Ms Annabel Howell was arrested at the time of the disappearance."

When nothing more seemed forthcoming, Clare said, "But not for murdering her sister- in-law, right?"

The sergeant shook his head. "Far from it. According to the arrest report, Ms Howell was taken into custody for giving her brother a beating in the local pub and calling him, and I quote, 'a murdering bastard' in front of everyone there." Sergeant Edwards rubbed his hand over his face. "This case has been cold for so many decades, it is unlikely that you will be able to provide information sufficient for us to reopen it. It really wasn't even a case, more of an investigation, since it never developed into anything more sinister."

"Was Freddie Howell, her husband, ever a suspect?" Clare asked.

"Yes, but his story was unshakeable. He said he came home from work a little late that evening and found his daughter Bella on her own, with no sign of his wife."

"So the investigation was dropped? But Ellen wouldn't have just upped and left, she couldn't. She had no money, nowhere to go. Couldn't the police see that something was wrong with Freddie's story?"

Clare's voice had been escalating in pitch, and I rested my hand on her arm to calm her.

The sergeant shook his head. "The investigation wasn't dropped right away." He grimaced. "Ms Howell was a suspect, but we found witnesses who said she was in town purchasing supplies at about the time Mr. Howell had said he'd arrived home. Unfortunately, the witnesses saw Ms Howell buying things that indicated she was going on a trip, so that didn't help matters."

"What do you mean it didn't help matters?"

"The deputy inspector's report includes the information that it was common knowledge that Ms Howell had a thing for Mrs.

Howell. The whole town said it was obvious just by the way Annabel looked at Ellen."

"But how did it not help matters?" I asked again.

It was Clare who answered. "They thought Annabel killed Ellen because she couldn't have her."

"What the fu..."

"Becky." Just by the way Clare said my name made me stop.

Sergeant Edwards cleared his throat, and we both looked at him again. "As with Mr. Howell, the police had no actual evidence of her guilt."

I looked at Clare. If they had prior evidence that pointed to Annabel as the killer, what on earth would ours do? We had a notebook that could have been falsely written and a photograph with coordinates written on the back of it, a photograph that came from Annabel's collection and taken by Annabel's camera.

Clare looked at me, then at the sergeant, then back to me. I had no idea what she was thinking, but I could tell by the glint in her eyes that something was afoot.

"Do you see this woman here?" Clare pointed at me. "This woman, although no relation, is the spitting image of Ellen Howell."

Bill, the officer behind the counter, came out at this point and looked at me from top to toe. I felt a little exposed at having his professional scrutiny focused on me.

"Here." Clare pulled the photograph of Ellen from her bag.

The officers huddled around the snapshot, looking from it to me, and back again, and murmuring about the uncanny likeness.

"And what has this got to do with anything?" Sergeant Edwards finally asked.

Clare smiled her most captivating smile, then continued. "This similarity has everything to do with a part of our evidence."

Even I had lost the thread, so God only knew what the officers were thinking.

"When my granddad, Freddie Howell, first saw Rebecca," Clare gestured to me, and I had the urge to curtsey, "he immediately lurched towards her, his hands balled into fists and ready to strike her."

"Was she a surprise to him?" Bill asked.

"Probably."

Bill shook his head. "Well that is hardly—"

"He shouted Ellen's name as he went on the attack. Not really the actions of a man who had lost the love of his life, are they?"

"He could have reacted that way for any number of reasons." Sergeant Edwards appeared to dismiss the inferences, but still he waited for what Clare was going to say next. So did I.

"Turn the picture over." They did. "We are certain that those are the coordinates for where the body is buried."

Both officers looked at her, but it was Bill Edwards who spoke. "And how on earth do you know that?"

"Because Freddie Howell kept this picture with him at all times." Clare held the picture up and gave it a slight shake. "Because these coordinates are written in his handwriting. And because these coordinates lead to the Roaches, where this photo was taken." Clare paused for effect. "And if you follow these coordinates, like Rebecca and I did last night, you will be led to a place marked by a yellow rock, and the ground seems slightly different from the surrounding area."

In the darkness, I hadn't noticed whether the spot was any different from its surroundings, but I was just thankful Clare had not mentioned being led there by the ghost of Ellen Howell. The atmosphere in the station thickened, as if it had been coated with maple syrup.

"Jesus Christ." Sergeant Edwards turned to Bill, who was open mouthed.

Clare slipped her hand through the loop of my arm, and I turned to look up at her. A silent message passed between us. We had intrigued the officers. We could only hope that it was enough to get them to follow up on possible evidence that could help solve a case that was decades old.

The station became a blur of activity. It was like watching the Keystone Cops on fast forward and in colour. Calls were made to the Forensics team to send them out to the Roaches. Following the coordinates in Clare's phone, they could find the bright yellow rock Clare had painted and try to uncover its secrets. Other officers were assigned to interview Freddie. Clare and I stood around like a couple of spare parts.

As the officers going to interview Freddie moved toward the door, Clare stopped them. "I'd like to be there when you talk to him."

"Sorry, Miss Davies, this is a criminal investigation," the team sergeant said in his best "I'm in charge, so don't fuck with me" voice.

Clare's spine stiffened, and she stepped closer to him. "Sorry, Officer, but I'm not letting you speak to my grandfather if I am not present. I know him better than anyone, and I can learn things just by watching his behaviour when you are questioning him." She paused before adding. "And I will just go to the hospital anyway. As a family member, I'm allowed in his room."

The man's face seemed to harden into concrete, his bottom lip protruded and the muscle in his jaw flexed. He nodded sharply, although it was obvious he wasn't happy about letting a civilian into his investigation in any capacity.

Tough titties, really. We had come so far, there was no way Clare and I were going to let the police march in there and fuck it all up, not that we had done much better the day before. They were professionals; I hoped they could handle things a damned sight better than us.

Clare and I drove in her car, and thirty minutes later, we all met up at the hospital. The butterflies in my stomach must have been wearing steel toe capped boots, if the sensation in my gut was any indication. I felt sick and excited, and maybe on the verge of passing out, but I wanted to be there to see the smugness ripped from Freddie's face. Sixty years, he had gotten away with it. Sixty fucking years. It was time to nail the bastard.

Clare went into the room first, followed by the two police officers. I was chomping at the bit to see how things would unfold, and I nearly smacked into the younger of the two men when I followed them inside.

"Sorry, Miss. Family only."

Family only? Family? Only? After all I had been through, I should certainly be classed as fucking family. It was on the tip of my tongue to say I *was* family, but I doubted he would pick up on the innuendo.

He forestalled any potential protest. "If we all go storming in there, he will get defensive and we'll get nothing."

Now *that* I could understand, as I'd had previous experience of it, but it didn't stop me feeling gutted.

His voice softened. "I promise you, you'll know everything that happens, okay?"

A sigh of resignation left my lips. I looked up into his face, and soft hazel eyes peered down at me.

"You have my word."

I nodded, the butterflies in my stomach sinking as if the steel in their boots had become too heavy. He held his hand out, and I clasped it.

"Officer Marsden, Stephen Marsden."

I shook his hand. It was warm, sturdy. And when I looked into his eyes again, they reflected confidence. For the first time since this bizarre adventure had begun, I felt some flicker of hope, hope that this would all be resolved after all.

I scuttled off and commandeered a chair so I could sit right outside the door in hopes I would be able to hear what was going on. But I heard nothing. Zip. Nada. No raised voices, no screaming match, no doctors rushing in dragging a trolley with a defibrillator. Disappointment ripped through me as I decided Freddie must be talking his way out of a prison sentence yet again.

At one point Officer Marsden stepped out and spoke into his portable police radio. I couldn't make out what he was saying, though I nearly fell off the chair trying. Just before he re-entered the room, he smiled at me and nodded. Did that mean they had cracked the old fucker, or was the officer just being polite? Then he was back inside, and I was left to wait.

To add insult to injury, the tea trolley came around and entered the room. Considering the amount of time the orderly was in there, they must've all had a cuppa and a bloody biscuit.

It felt as if hours had passed since they'd first gone into the room, though it had been less than forty minutes. I slumped back into the chair. Being shut out was harder than I had imagined it would be. I should have kicked off, told them I was a relative, lied through my grinding teeth. That way, I would have been in the thick of things, sipping hot tea and chomping on a Hobnob instead of sitting outside and adding two and two to come up with forty-seven. Another twenty minutes passed, and I could add "thirst" to my list of complaints.

The door opened, and I shot to my feet like an overeager concierge. Clare appeared, tears streaming down her face, and my heart sank. Shit, shite, and bollocks.

Her hands clutched at me and pulled me to her, and her head slumped on my shoulder. Sobs wracked her body, and I slipped my arms around her, then my hands stroked her back in calming circles. Weirdly, I wasn't angry; I didn't want to race into the room and beat the truth out of Freddie. All I wanted was to comfort Clare, reassure her that whatever would be, would be. At that moment, nothing mattered but her. Whether Freddie Howell got away with murder or not paled in light of Clare's distress.

"It's okay, baby. Let it out."

She did. And I was there to catch her as she crumbled. Holding her was the most natural thing in the world; and being with her was the only thing that counted for anything. I barely registered the arrival of two more police officers, didn't blink when they entered Freddie's room. They could deal with whatever was going on in there; I had something more important to attend to—the woman I loved was in my arms, and I was comforting her.

After a bit, I sensed there was something amiss. The officers hadn't closed the door behind them, so I could hear them talking, their voices getting closer to the doorway. I will feel the sensation of that next moment forever. The memory will always be lurking about, ready to resurface. It wasn't the exit of the two police officers that framed the moment; it was the exit of the second two. They were pushing a wheelchair that held the subdued figure of Freddie Howell.

My head shot up, and my body assumed meerkat alert stance. Clare lifted her head from my shoulder and a solitary sob escaped her and followed the figures down the sterile corridors of the hospital. Puffy, bloodshot brown eyes watched as they wheeled him away. One officer loitered nearby, as if he wanted to speak to Clare.

I was dumbfounded. They had arrested him? Actually arrested him? And more importantly, why would he spill his guts to them after all this time? If I believed for one moment that he wanted to make amends before he met his Maker... No. Gut instinct told me he wasn't the type to fear otherworldly retribution, however old he was.

As they disappeared around the corner, I turned my attention back to Clare. No wonder she was distraught. They had arrested a member of her family for murder.

"It's for the best, baby." Her brow furrowed and her lips parted, and I brushed tears from her cheeks. "You knew this was going to happen."

Clare shook her head.

Why was she sticking up for him? Or was that a moral debate titled "Would you grass up a member of your family if you found out they had done something wrong? Discuss."

"Yes, it is. You know it."

"But—"

"I know you love him, Clare. But—"

"He didn't kill her."

What the fuck? It was a little late to have doubts about it now.

"Clare—"

"Seriously, he didn't kill her." She drew out of my embrace. "He told us."

What the hell was going on? We had spent God knew how long trying to put his crime to rest, and now Clare wanted to switch sides? I tried to pull her back against me, but she pushed my hand away.

"I know you're upset, but—"

Clare screamed, "You don't know fuck all! He didn't kill Ellen!"

Anger jolted through me, and I gritted my teeth to keep from yelling back at her. I drew a deep breath, released it slowly. "Okay then, he didn't fucking kill her. So, enlighten me. Who did?"

She closed her eyes and opened her mouth wide, as if the words would harm her on the way out.

"Who, Clare? The bogeyman?"

Her face full of anger, she spat, "My mother!"

A nervous laugh replaced my anger. Her mother? Her fucking mother! A three or four-year-old girl had killed Ellen Howell and fucking buried her on the Roaches? On her own? And then she drove her car home and sat and waited for Daddy to come home from work? Why on earth would Clare believe such an out and out lie? Why would the police believe it? That story was totally fucking stupid. Why couldn't anyone else see that?

Clare raked her fingers through her hair and part way through, her hands curled into fists. I just stared at her, too confused to know what to do.

"Grandad told us everything. Everything. It all makes sense now." Her voice was soft, resigned.

I stepped forward tentatively. I needed to make contact with her, to make sure that I was in fact awake and hadn't nodded off in the chair outside the room. I gingerly touched her arm and felt her tension ease. The fight left her, and she fell into my arms and began to sob.

As I stood there and let her cry, I accepted that this was what was meant to be. Freddie had had his alibi ready after all, and he apparently thought nothing of blaming his own little girl to get himself off the hook. What an out and out cunt.

The policeman, who had lingered, stepped over to us. "Excuse me, Miss, but could you please give me your mother's phone number? I'm afraid that we'll have to ask her to come back to England for questioning."

Shortly after Clare gave him the number, we left the hospital. The ride home was made in silence. I wanted to ask Clare exactly what Freddie had said, but I knew I had to bide my time until we were home and settled.

When we were back at Annabel's, Clare went straight into the living room and lay on the sofa, her back towards me. I wanted to give her time to come to terms with whatever had happened, whatever had been said. I knew she would eventually tell me what had transpired in the hospital room, and I didn't want to push, so I settled myself on the chair opposite and waited. It was over an hour later that she turned to face me, her ashen skin making her lips appear redder than usual.

"Are you thirsty?"

She nodded, and I scurried off to the kitchen to make tea.

By the time I got back, she was perched on the edge of the sofa, her hands dangling between her legs, her head hanging. It wasn't until I offered her a cup of tea that she made eye contact. I felt a crack inside my chest, and the heartache spread through me like spilt liquid.

She sipped at her drink and winced at the heat of it, then placed it on the floor near her feet. It was so quiet in the room, I could hear my breathing, but I waited for her to speak.

"I know it seems fucked up." Not the words I was expecting, but I did not respond. "But it all makes sense." I doubted that it did, but I didn't say so. "Freddie told us everything. He didn't even need prompting. As soon as he saw the police, he told them what had happened."

I knelt at her feet and looked up into sad brown eyes.

"He knew about Ellen and Annabel, had known for months they were lovers." I slipped my hand over hers and squeezed.

"It wasn't a case of Annabel taking away what he loved. He just didn't want her to win again."

"Win?"

She shrugged and nodded. "He was always jealous of her. She always got whatever he wanted—the family home, the great business, the woman he had married." A tremor shivered through her. "But he didn't love Ellen. He only married her because he could."

"Married her because he could?" I didn't understand what Clare was saying, or why I was parroting.

"He did the one thing that he knew his sister couldn't. He knew Annabel was gay, another reason why he hated her."

I still didn't understand what the hell was going on. To me, that sounded like the perfect reason to kill his wife.

"Come and sit by me."

Clare pulled at my hand and I joined her on the sofa, her body slumping against mine. The elephant was back in the room, but instead of it being between her and me and our relationship status, it had to do with what had happened to Ellen.

I didn't want to make her go over everything before she was ready, so we sat in silence. I missed the sound of Annabel's clock.

Clare leaned against me and curled her arm over my stomach. "I always knew there was something up." I waited her out. "Between my mum and Granddad, I mean."

"Something, like what?"

She sighed and shook her head. "Don't know, really. There always seemed to be an atmosphere every time they were together, like an undercurrent."

I had to bite my lip from exclaiming that Clare's mother had only been three years old when Ellen was killed. How the fuck could there have been an undercurrent between her and her father?

"He came here to this house on the day Ellen died."

"Freddie?" I felt her nod against my chest.

"Ellen was packing stuff in a bag in Bella's room. He just walked up the stairs and confronted her."

A perfect time, and motive, for him to kill her. I stifled the thought and let Clare talk.

"By his account, she admitted it straight away. Told him she was in love with his sister and that they were leaving, together."

Ellen must've have had some balls to do that. From what I had learned, Ellen was very aware of her husband's temper. I'd seen the bruises. It made me wonder why she would admit to her plans when she was alone with Freddie. Why not just leave a note and slope off into the night, or at least wait until Annabel was there to support her?

"He tried to have sex with her, although I think it was more like rape. Tried to show her what a real man he was." She began to tremble. "She grabbed the fireplace poker and hit him with it."

The image of the poker I had seen in Bella's old room sprang to mind, and my calf twinged. It was the poker Annabel had steered me to. Had Annabel known it had been used as a weapon, or had that been coincidence?

"Granddad showed us the scar on the left side of his head. She must've cracked him really hard."

For a fleeting moment I felt a sense of pride for Clare's grandmother, then I remembered that Ellen had died not long after striking her husband.

"Bella came into the room and saw the blood pouring from Freddie's head, and she started crying. She'd been downstairs when he arrived at Annabel's, but must've gone upstairs when she heard them arguing."

Fuck. Fuck. I hoped it wasn't true, that he wasn't going to get away with his part in it.

"Ellen chased after Bella to calm her and Freddie followed, although he says he was staggering. His vision wasn't clear, but he certainly remembered what happened next." She swallowed hard. "Seems like there was another scuffle at the top of the stairs."

Clare's voice broke, and I could see the difficulty she was having in formulating the words to continue. "Bella...Bella grabbed Ellen to pull her away from Freddie, but...but she ... she was off balance...he was off balance...and Ellen didn't want to accidentally knock her daughter down the stairs." The tears came thick and fast. "She staggered into Bella."

What a bastard. Bella hadn't killed her mother, hadn't purposely pushed her. If they were having a scuffle, it had been Freddie that had caused it, not his daughter.

"Bella pushed her mother back. Freddie said she shouted. 'No, Mama!' and just pushed."

I couldn't speak, couldn't articulate any of the comments that had been racing through my mind.

"Ellen fell down the stairs and broke her neck." Clare's voice sounded distant, clinical, like she was describing the climax of a film. "Bella started crying again and telling Ellen off for lying at the bottom of the stairs."

"So why didn't he just report it to the police if was an accident?" If what he had told Clare was true, it had been an accident. It didn't matter that Bella had pushed Ellen, or shouted "no." She was a child. She wouldn't have understood what was going on.

Clare sighed. "He said he panicked, that he wasn't thinking straight after being hit in the head. He was afraid that because everyone knew he had hit his wife in the past, no one would believe him."

I certainly didn't.

"He thought if he could get rid of the body, clean up the scene, and act ignorant, it would all blow over."

Clare picked up her cup of tea, took two sips, and then the cup rested against her lip. Eventually she turned and looked at me. "He went into the room, cleaned the blood off the poker and hid it under a chest of drawers, then finished packing Ellen's bag. It was then that he found the stash of photographs."

I had wondered how he had gotten the picture, but never in a million years would I have conjured this scenario.

"He took the one of Ellen on the Roaches, and that's when he had the idea."

Silence hovered in the air as I processed everything. I supposed it could have happened that way, but I was far from convinced. To me, it was more than a little farfetched. I got the idea of the scuffle at the top of the stairs, but then to go and bury his wife on the moors and not tell a fucking soul? And what about Bella? Had she never mentioned it? How would you keep a child quiet about seeing something like that? She had been three, for fuck's sake. If a policeman had asked her when she had last seen her mummy, that would have been it.

"I know what you're thinking."

I narrowed my eyes and looked at her, my head cocking to the side, inviting her to go on.

"It was his final victory over Annabel. If he buried Ellen and stayed mute, he knew his sister would always think Ellen had not loved her after all." She sucked air between her teeth, as if she trying to calm herself. "I never knew he was so evil."

There was nothing I could say to that. I didn't disagree.

"To ruin his own sister's life with a lie. To let his daughter grow up believing she'd killed her mother."

"But...." I drew a breath and modified my response. "That's what I don't get. Bella probably wouldn't remember it. She was so young, Clare. And if she did remember, what was to stop her telling someone?"

Clare shook her head and laughed derisively. "He made sure she remembered. Why do you think Bella never said anything to the police? Why do you think she hated her father?" She stood up quickly, sloshing tea over the floor. "He told her she had killed her mother, that the police would take her away and lock her up."

I gaped at her. "Did he tell you that?"

She turned and looked at me, her eyes flashing with anger. "No. I worked that out for myself."

Chapter Eighteen

Clare tried to call her mother, but it appeared Bella's mobile was switched off. So, after eating and showering, we had an early night. Although we both were exhausted, sleep eluded us. I couldn't speak for Clare, but every time I closed my eyes, I saw the scenario Freddie had described. It was as if my brain was trying to find fault with his story. Unfortunately, as Clare had said, it actually did make sense.

A couple of times during the night, Clare started to cry, and I held her close. I felt gutted, so God only knew how she felt.

Dawn made its way into the room tentatively, as if the arrival of morning would upset us even more. Both of us were awake, my body curled around Clare's like a protective shield, though it was a little too late for that. The warmth of our entwined bodies created a cocoon of safety underneath the duvet.

THUMP! THUMP THUMP THUMP!

Someone was at the door. We shot up into a sitting position. Who on earth would knock on the door at just turned six in the morning?

THUMP THUMP THUMP!

And knock on it with such force?

"I'll go and..."

I grabbed Clare's wrist and held her back. "We'll both go." Relief flashed across her face, and her smile confirmed that I had made the right decision.

The knocking continued, but we didn't hurry downstairs. It didn't seem as if the knocker was going anywhere.

Despite all we had found out yesterday, it took walking down the stairs in the light of the next morning to make me imagine Ellen Howell's crumpled body lying at the bottom. Jesus. Just the thought that I was walking over the exact spot where Ellen had met her Maker sent shivers down my spine, and the hairs on my arms stood to attention. At the foot of the staircase, the bannister was supported by a thick pillar with a wooden base that had sharp, solid corners, and I wondered whether Ellen had smashed her head on it, or if she had died as soon as her neck was broken.

Nausea swept through me and I instinctively reached out and grabbed the top of the post for support. Instant images of events long past blasted into my mind, and my stomach roiled. It didn't stop. Voices invaded my brain, voices that seemed as if they were coming from right behind me, screaming hatred and ownership and threatening terror. My body seemed to fold into itself as I fully expected to feel the weight of a person slam into it, fully expected the events of sixty years ago to play out to their deadly conclusion.

Then, nothing. No images, no voices, no contact, and I was standing stupidly at the foot of the staircase, horror at what I had seen and heard sweeping through me. My hands shook, my knees felt as if they would give way, and my stomach threatened to expel its contents.

Clare was opening the door, her attention on pulling back the stiff bolts rather than on me. I wanted to stop her, tell her what had happened. I was afraid that perhaps, in addition to me grabbing the post, whoever was waiting on the doorstep had triggered the scene I'd just experienced.

A voice drifted through the open doorway, a voice I thought I recognised but didn't. It was a woman's voice with a rich timbre. It wasn't Annabel's... Fuck! What was I thinking? Of course it wasn't Annabel. Dead or alive, she wouldn't have knocked on the door of her own house.

Then it struck me. Didn't dead people haunt the place they died? If that was the case, why had I only ever seen Annabel in this house and never Ellen? Ellen had always appeared outside—in my car when it was parked on the driveway, outside the kitchen window like fucking Catherine Earnshaw, again at the hospital and on the Roaches, but never inside Annabel's house. Never in the place Freddie said she had died.

I wanted to tell Clare that something was terribly wrong with Freddie's story, but she was talking to the person who was accompanying her into the house. My breath caught. For one solitary moment I thought I would have to rethink my previous conclusion. The woman was toting a small suitcase. Blonde hair shone like sunlight, and I actually believed Clare was having a discussion with Ellen Howell or, more likely, her ghost.

"Why are you here?" Clare's voice was cold, unwelcoming.

I stepped forward to see the woman up close, see whether she had any physical indications of ever having fallen down a staircase. I didn't even consider why Ellen would be carrying a suitcase. In my mind, everything seemed to make sense. She *must've* died here. This was the very evidence I needed to put Ellen inside Annabel's house when she passed over.

"And hello to you, too." There was that rich timbre again. But was it as I remembered it? "Is that a proper way to greet your mother?"

Mother? Mother! My brain was having a hard time distinguishing the real from the paranormal. Apart from appearing a lot older than when I had previously seen her, this woman looked like a living, breathing Ellen Howell.

I should have known this was Bella, should have sensed it with my new-found, fucked up psychic abilities, but all I sensed was the hostility between mother and daughter, and a deeply rooted sadness at the dashing of my belief that Ellen Howell had walked into the house and was having a tete a tete with her granddaughter. I don't know why I should feel sad that it wasn't her, I just did. I took another step forward.

Clare stepped to the side, granting her mother unimpeded access to the house. Bella passed her daughter without so much as a kiss on the cheek. Man, I thought my relationship with my parents was a bit off, but this took the biscuit. It made me feel as if I should be up for "Daughter of the Year." Suddenly I wanted to disappear, maybe call my mother and see how she was. If I was able to make my escape, maybe I could think through what had just transpired between mother and daughter, and maybe think about my epiphany about never having seen Ellen *in* this house. A little quiet time might help me reason my way through the sudden uncertainty that was trickling through me.

"Mum, this is Rebecca Gibson."

Clare's words broke through my mental gymnastics, and I looked over in time to see her gesture in my direction. Bella looked me over, gazing through me as if I was made of glass. Green eyes met mine.

"Rebecca is my...erm..."

What would Clare say I was? Lover? Partner? Friend?

"My girlfriend?"

Was she questioning what we meant to each other? After what we had been through? After we had declared our adoration and enduring love? My heart ached as if it was about to burst.

The expression on Clare's face made me realise that she wasn't questioning her relationship with me; she was asking my permission to introduce me as being hers. A smile surfaced on my face as a spurt of unadulterated joy drowned out my insecurities. They had likely been brought on by me experiencing the demise of Ellen, closely followed by the appearance of a visitor I believed was the woman herself. Granted, I was wrong, but it does take a moment to adjust to the shift between the unreal and the real.

A smile brightened Bella's previously stoic face, making her seem younger "Nice to meet you, Rebecca." She turned to Clare. "Why does it take a murder investigation for me to know you have a girlfriend?"

I thought she was serious, that she was having a go at her daughter, but then Clare laughed and clasped her mother in a bear hug.

Bella enjoyed the embrace, whilst noises of greeting were murmured and kisses were exchanged. I stood there trying to figure out what the fuck was going on. Did they like each other or not?

Clare drew back a step and looked squarely at her mum. "You don't deserve to get the gossip, not after what you did."

Shit. Was she going to accuse her mother of murder even before the front door was closed? I was sure my face reflected my disbelief.

Bella laughed and turned to me. "Do you see how she talks to me?"

Yes. So why was she laughing? I totally didn't get what was going on. Maybe I was still in shock over what had happened a few minutes earlier, or maybe I just couldn't grasp the reality of this situation. I grafted a smile onto my face, knowing I must look like a dimshit. I could always conjure one of those when I was at a loss as to what was going on or what I was going to say.

"I just couldn't make it back."

For what—Death Match, round two? I felt like an observer who was only privy to part of the conversation.

"More like you wouldn't," Clare retorted. "Aunty Annabel would have loved for you to be there."

Ping. The penny dropped. It sounded like Clare was pissed off at her mother for not travelling back to Kirk Langley for Annabel's funeral.

Bella sighed dramatically and gestured to the open door. "Shut that." She then pointed at Clare's mouth. "And shut that, then make your mother a cuppa. I've not had a decent brew in hours."

"I'll make it," I quickly volunteered. It was my chance to escape. Thank God.

By the time I made a pot of tea and took it into the living room, Clare and Bella were nestled together on the sofa. The visitor had discarded her coat and was leaning back into the leather. She didn't look as if she was worried about what the police were going to say; actually, she seemed to be emanating a sense of relief. I busied myself with preparing the tea, asked the customary questions concerning milk and sugar whilst trying to ear wig the conversation between mother and daughter. It was mostly small talk, mainly about the trip from Vannes, the drive from the airport, nothing of note.

I handed Bella her cup, and she looked straight at me. "You know, young lady, you look like my mother."

I wanted to say that she looked like Ellen, too, an older version, the version that Ellen would have grown into if life had permitted. This was not really the thought I wanted to be having, considering Clare was related to both of them, and now had a girlfriend that looked like them. I held on to the saucer, and Bella smiled and gently pulled it from my grasp. "I suppose you are both anxious to know what happened, yes?"

Clare sat up straighter, her interest in planes and taxis disappearing.

Bella sighed, then took a sip of her tea. "That hits the spot." She slapped Clare's knee and let out a short laugh. "You should keep hold of this one, love. Good tea makers are hard to come by. George can't make tea for toffee." The cup settled back on the saucer, and Bella stared at it for a moment.

By the expression on her face, I could tell she was trying to sort things out in her head before she started to speak. It didn't stop me wanting to hurry her up.

"To be honest, I can't really remember details, just flashes." Clare placed her hand on her mum's knee and squeezed gently, and Bella smiled at the gesture of comfort. "I was only three at the time, not really old enough to recollect the finer details of the day my mother died, but I had plenty of time afterwards to build on my memories. Sixty years to be exact."

Her tone had become harsher, and I had already worked out why. Her next words confirmed my supposition.

"Your grandfather never let me forget what happened. Never."

She picked up her cup, and I saw her hand was shaking. I knew it wasn't fear that made it shake; it was anger. After a small sip, she replaced the cup on the saucer and then set them on the floor near her feet.

"I think I do actually remember them arguing." She gestured towards the upstairs. "I think I remember her falling, but I'm not sure. Are these my memories, or the memories my father put here?" She tapped the side of her head. "Evil old bastard."

I wanted to laugh, or agree, or both, but I did neither.

"I have a vague recollection that my father and I went for a drive, but I couldn't swear to that. I couldn't say where we went, I just remember feeling lost, you know? Lonely, as if something important to me was gone."

Clare took her mother's hand, and Bella smiled gratefully. She waggled their joined hands and gripped Clare's tightly. I just sat there trying to process what she was saying. There was something niggling at the back of my mind, but I couldn't put my finger on it, and the thought stayed just out of reach, far enough away to make my head hurt if I focused on it. I shifted my focus back to Bella.

"I do remember Annabel coming to our house later that day, though, and how she looked, if not what she said. In retrospect, I know she was frantic with worry, and yet she was still so kind to me that day. I remember crying when Dad told her to leave and never come back."

Her tears flowed so suddenly, they startled me. Bella seemed as if she had everything under control, as if she was taking what had happened in her life in stride. Her tears showed that we all have our weaknesses, however hard we try to hide them.

Clare held Bella, shushing her when the hiccupping started, and I just stood there like a prick. I sat on the floor, as if that would improve the situation, or my ability to comprehend anything. Like an illusionist, Clare produced a wad of tissue from somewhere and passed it to her mother, who tried to pull herself together.

"He...he told me that I...I had killed my mum. That she...that she had been bad, and I...I had killed her."

I would write the C word here, but I've already said it with regards to Freddie Howell. "I remember he made me sleep in the cellar sometimes. He'd say that the police were looking for me, and I had to hide."

Bella blew her nose and reached down to get her tea. Amazing how the British believe tea will make everything better. What was more amazing was that it usually did. After a couple of sips, Bella seemed stronger, more in control.

"He put the fear of God into me. Said to me if I ever told anyone anything about what had happened that day, I would be taken away and locked in a room and I'd never see anyone ever again."

I reverted back to my initial diagnosis. Freddie was a Class A cunt.

"Every day he reminded me, every bloody day. He told me he had helped me because he loved me and didn't want me to go to the place where the bad people were kept."

"But surely you know by now that he was making you believe you did something bad when whatever happened was just an accident." I couldn't believe I had spoken the question aloud.

Green eyes seemed darker as they looked at me, a sign of her distress.

"Of course I knew." She sighed and dabbed at her eyes. "But not for years. I didn't even know for sure until I had Clare."

I looked at Clare who looked at Bella, then turned in my direction with a puzzled expression. She shrugged, then murmured, "Why then?"

"Simple. When I had you, I knew for definite that I could never do anything bad to you and you could never do anything bad to me, either. If I had done anything to my mother, it would have had to be an accident. I knew from that moment that my father had been lying to me all along."

Clare's eyes filled with tears, and I could hear her gulping back her emotions.

"I imagine you're wondering why I didn't go to the police."

That probably would have been my next thought, but I had been too concerned about Clare to formulate it.

"It had been nearly thirty years. Thirty years. I couldn't walk into a police station and tell them I had kept the secret of my mother's death for all of that time. I didn't know where she was buried or any of the details."

That hadn't stopped me and Clare, although we did have specific information about where they could find Ellen Howell's remains.

"No. That's not entirely it." Bella sighed again and turned to face her daughter. "I suppose I was scared of what the police would find. What if I had done it after all? And if I had done, what would happen to you?" Clare shrugged, a weak smile on her face. "That's when I first thought about moving away. I thought if I went far enough away, he wouldn't have a hold on me."

"I don't get it." Both mother and daughter turned to look at me. "Sorry, but I don't."

Bella leaned forward, her eyes penetrating. "What don't you get?"

"First, I don't understand why it took thirty years for you to realise you hadn't done anything wrong and that Freddie had been lying to you. Second, you haven't mentioned seeing Annabel in the thirty years you lived in Kirk Langley—"

"Becky!" Clare said my name in an almost threatening tone.

"Also," I continued, ignoring Clare's warning, "didn't your aunt ever ask you if you knew anything? What about the police? What about the villagers?"

"Becky, what are you trying to do?" Clare asked.

I shrugged. "Why did you only think about moving away? Why not just go?"

Bella's lips tightened, and I shrank from her anticipated retort. If she had one on the tip of her tongue, she swallowed it down before answering.

"Because, Becky, I didn't want the same thing to happen to me as had happened to my mother. I was married to someone who was very handy with his fists, just like my father."

Clare had been looking at Bella appraisingly, but now she gasped. Her face was ashen, her expression one of total shock. "Dad hit you?" Bella shrugged, as if to say it didn't matter, it was over. Clare persisted. "Dad hit you?"

"That part of my life is over. Gone. Annabel gave me the money to leave, to set up a business."

The shame of my accusations washed over me. I had been too quick to judge the actions of a woman I didn't know, and now I felt dreadful. However much I might think I was a fair detective, I knew beyond the shadow of a doubt that I was crap at it. Bella had gone through the exact same battering as her mother, and I had been too ready to find any faults in her story. I opened my mouth to apologise, but Bella raised a hand and forestalled me.

"Please, don't. My marriage to Will wasn't all bad."

"But he hit you like Granddad hit Ellen." Clare's voice seemed so small, so young, that I wanted to pull her to me and wrap her in my arms.

"And unlike Ellen, I got away. I divorced your father and began a new life. That is another reason I never went to the police. My past, like my mother, was dead to me."

"How could you remember Freddie hitting Ellen, but not remember anything about the day she died?" I don't know what made me say it, but I did.

Instead of being offended, Bella laughed. "My, Clare, you'll never get anything past this one," she teased.

Clare glared at me, and I smiled back, but I kept waiting for an answer.

"Because, dear Rebecca, do you think my mother was the only person he ever hit?"

Fuck. I turned to look at Clare and saw that this last piece of information was her undoing. Her face crumpled, and she dropped her head into her hands. Her shoulders heaved as she began to sob. I felt awful, bloody awful. Why hadn't I just let it rest?

"Honey?" Bella's hands stroked Clare's arms in an attempt to soothe her. "It is all over now, all in the past. He only ever hit me once."

Once was one time too many. Men should not hit women. That was a given. I also didn't condone a woman hitting a man, believing that he wouldn't hit her back. Physical violence is never an acceptable course of action, but even more especially so from a person who supposedly loves their victim. Never!

Watching the interplay of mother and daughter, I wanted to comfort Clare, but I let Bella do it. Sadness filled me, choking my breathing, and I tried to swallow it down. I couldn't stop the tear that trickled down my cheek, but I quickly brushed it away.

Moments passed, and Clare's tears eased enough for her to lift her head and accept the tissues her mother hadn't used. "Why? That one time he hit you, why did he do it?"

Bella stroked Clare's cheek, her attention fixed solely on comforting her. "Because I went to see Annabel, and he found out." She shifted away, giving her daughter some space. "He slapped me a few times and told me he used to do the same to my mum for exactly the same reason."

"Because Ellen saw Annabel? He hit her because she went to see Annabel?" I was incredulous.

"I think we both know he didn't hit my mother just because she went to see Annabel. It was because they were in a relationship that he used to hit Ellen."

Clare beat me to the question. "Did he tell you that?"

"And admit that he wasn't man enough to satisfy his wife?" A sad smile flittered over Bella's face. "Pity he didn't think hitting his wife was unmanly."

A moment passed as we digested what she had said.

"When Freddie hit you, did that put a stop to you seeing Annabel?" The question popped out and broke the silence.

This time Bella laughed loudly, shocking Clare and me. We stared at her in amazement. This woman was something else. She had survived years of mental abuse from her father, physical abuse from her husband, had been led to believe that she had killed her mother, and she was laughing out loud about it all.

"Not a bloody chance." She patted Clare's leg. "Actually, it made me more determined to see Annabel. That's what a teenager would do after all, isn't it? Rebel against her father?"

Yes, but...

"I told him if he ever laid another finger on me, I would tell the police everything. That I'd rather go to prison than let him hit me again. Seemed to work, too." She bent down and retrieved her tea, and finished it off in a couple of gulps. "Any chance of another, love?" She held the cup out to me, favouring me with a brilliant smile.

A sense of relief washed through me. At least she didn't seem to be holding a grudge against me questioning her. She must've have known it was because I wanted the truth, not just because I was being nosy.

"Sure. Clare?"

Clare gave me a watery grin and nodded. "I didn't get one in the first place, so yes, please."

I feigned a grimace.

"You were too busy giving me the third degree, weren't you, sweetheart?" Bella turned to her daughter. "I think that should be my prerogative, grilling the future daughter-in-law."

A blush raced up my throat and spread like wildfire over my face. I am not too sure why I blushed. I didn't know whether it was because she had pulled up on my detective finesse, or that the thought of being Bella's future daughter-in-law thrilled and excited me. I just felt a little exposed.

I turned hastily, tripped over my own feet, and stumbled towards the table. As I slammed the cup and saucer onto the tray, I heard giggles coming from behind me.

"I hope she doesn't do that when she's walking up the aisle on your wedding day," Bella said.

"Mum!"

More giggling and whispering.

At that precise moment, I knew three things: one, I could not go any redder; two, I really liked Clare's mum; three, I hoped I didn't trip walking up the aisle either. To be honest, the third item on the list wasn't as much something I *knew*, but more like what I hoped would be. And I didn't mean about the tripping, either.

Chapter Nineteen

I made breakfast to go along with the tea, and we chatted for a while longer, but Bella seemed exhausted, her yawns coming more frequently. She had not slept in over twenty-four hours. There had been too much to do, too much to sort out to for her to make time to rest. All she had really worried about was how Clare had handled the revelation from Freddie that Bella had killed Ellen. I wanted to ask why she hadn't just called Clare and asked her, but I didn't have to.

"I would have called you, honey," Bella said, "but just exchanging words over the phone wouldn't have made me feel much better. I wanted to wait until I could see you, touch you, reassure you that everything you heard was not as it seemed. It's not every day that a person's mother gets accused of killing a relative, is it?" She searched Clare's eyes for a reaction and was rewarded with a half-smile. "A text would have been okay, to let you know I was on the way, but I decided to just come and explain in person, so the sooner I could come, the better.

"When the police contacted me, they told me that you were staying in Kirk Langley. I figured that it had to be at Annabel's house, and that was that. The police don't yet know that I have arrived. I came straight here. I couldn't wait to see you. You will always be my priority. Still, I suppose I should give them a call."

"You need to get some sleep before we go to the police station, Mum," Clare urged after the hundredth time Bella had yawned whilst at the table. "I don't think a few more hours will make much of a difference, do you?"

Bella didn't even try to argue. She stood, kissed her daughter, and turned to go upstairs, then she turned back to the table and kissed my cheek. "Lovely to meet you, Rebecca."

I mumbled a reply and blushed. I seemed to be doing that a lot.

Bella went to bed in Annabel's old room, and Clare and I curled up together on the sofa. I held her in my arms, and she rested her head against my chest. The contact was comforting, and it wasn't long before we both nodded off.

The ringing of Clare's mobile woke us. Thankfully, it wasn't too far away, so Clare managed to stay snuggled up close to me whilst she answered it. I was half asleep but started to wake when I heard her side of the conversation. It seemed that the excavation team had discovered the remains of a female in the location we had specified.

It seemed different now that everything we had shared with the police had proven to be true. Part of me had hoped we were right, but there was also a part of me that wanted to believe that I'd gotten it so badly wrong, it could be classed as funny. When it came to death, when it came to a senseless taking of a life, I guess no one really wants to be right.

Clare's voice filtered through my mental ramblings, and I heard her tell the officer on the other end of the line that her mother had arrived from France. Shortly afterwards, the call ended, and she turned to me.

"The police are going to be calling in the next couple of hours so they can talk to Mum."

I pulled her to me. There were no tears, no aggrieved ranting, just a pervasive sense of sadness. Even without asking, I knew she was thinking about Ellen, about the wasted life and the situation her grandmother had been stuck in because of circumstances and the times in which she'd lived. Sadly, it still happened.

Even today, things might not turn out different if a married woman fell in love with her sister-in-law. One could only hope that the people around her would be more supportive, would give her an option for her life other than just sticking it out with an abusive husband. "You know what I think?"

Clare's response was muffled against my chest, her face half turning.

"Considering so many people seem to accept, understand, and hold out a helping hand to those who don't quite fit into society, I can't understand why there is still so much violence in the world."

Clare lifted her head and looked at me. "Do you mean because no one helped Ellen, or in general?"

"Both. Just because someone is gay, he or she is treated differently because some people refuse to accept that others can love differently from them."

Clare nodded in agreement. She leaned forward and brushed her lips against mine, then lowered her head back onto my chest.

"And another thing." Clare lifted her head again, her face turned to mine. "Sixty years may seem like a long time, but in the broad scope of the history of the world, it would not even be a blip on the time line."

"I have no idea what you mean by that." She tilted her head and half closed her eyes. "Or are you saying sixty years since Ellen died?"

To be truthful, I didn't exactly know for certain if the number alluded to Ellen or not, it just had.

"In a way, yes."

Clare moved back even further, her expression inquisitive. "What do you mean 'in a way?'"

"Well, just thinking about what we have achieved in the last sixty years blows my mind. Who would have thought back then that in some countries a man could legally marry another man, or a woman marry another woman?"

"Some people are not so lucky, Becky. Today, I mean, not sixty years ago." Clare stroked my face. "There are still countries, whole countries, who would say what we have is wrong, that me loving you is a sin." She gave me a sad smile.

It was true. There were countries that considered themselves modern, forward thinking, progressive. And those countries still dictated how people should act, think and feel, and declared war and created dictatorships, even if they were not as glaringly obvious as Iraq's rule of torture and oppression. How could these countries be considered progressive when they were going backwards? How could *not* following the path laid down by society's will, be wrong? Could denying love ever be considered the right thing to do?

"We need to wake Mum."

I blinked a couple of times to return my focus to the here-and-now. There I was, sitting and holding the woman I loved with her mother's blessing. I was one of the fortunate ones, especially considering it was on the same couch where, sixty years ago, two women had to hide their love, and probably not just from Freddie Howell. I wondered how they would have fared out in the world if they had gotten away to start a life together. Would they have pretended to be relatives, best friends? Would they have been shunned with knowing looks? Or would they have had to keep moving on each time they were treated in the same manner as they had been treated in Kirk Langley? No one had stepped up for Ellen, not her family or neighbours. Only Annabel.

"Becky, I need to go and wake Mum."

Clare's voice was little louder this time, probably because I kept on slipping off into my own thoughts. "Erm...yeah...right."

"You okay?"

I nodded and released my grasp on her, which had been getting progressively tighter as I had dwelled on the topic. "I'll go and wake her." I shot up off the sofa and up the stairs to Annabel's room, where Bella was sleeping.

As I neared the half open door, I heard Bella talking. Initially I thought she was talking to me, and I opened my mouth to answer her but stopped when I realised she had no idea I was there. She laughed again, and then continued to speak.

I grasped the door handle and just stood there, thinking about what I was hearing. Bella laughed, true, but the voice that came after, I was definite it wasn't Bella's. The tone was different; it didn't have the rich resonance I had noted earlier. But even if that was the case, I knew who the second speaker was. I had spoken to her myself on more than one occasion.

I tilted my head and peered through the small gap between the edge of the door and the frame. Bella was talking to Annabel as if the dead woman had just popped by and they were having a catch up natter. Bella was perched on the side of the bed and Annabel was standing at the foot of it, her back towards the door. A shiver sizzled down my spine as my overactive imagination kicked in and I wondered whether she had stood there whilst Clare and I had been asleep. Or, even more embarrassingly and spine tinglingly, whilst we were otherwise engaged.

"You may come in, Rebecca."

Bella's voice made me jump back a bit, pulling the door closed with my motion. I grimaced, trying to work out what I should do. I didn't want Bella to think I was peeping at her through keyholes or cracks of doors, that I was a pervert.

The door opened, and I saw Bella standing next to the bed. It would have been impossible for her to be there *and* open the door.

"Come on in, love," Bella said.

Her smile was warm, welcoming, not at all the expression of someone who had just been chatting with a dead woman, a dead woman who was still opening doors, or so it appeared.

"Clare...erm...Clare told me to tell you the police are coming soon." Her expression didn't change, but I did see her eyes flick sideways as if she was glancing at someone. "I'll let you get sorted."

I didn't wait for a response. I nearly broke my bleeding neck swerving around at speed and dashing down the stairs. Talk about irony. I heard laughter come from behind me, and it wasn't just Bella's.

I slammed headfirst into Clare who was coming down the hallway toward the stairs. Oomphs were knocked from our bodies, and I grabbed hold of her to keep us both from falling over.

Almost breathless, she whispered, "I was just coming to find you. You've been gone for ages." Her voice was close to my ear, and the tingle from her breath on my skin spread through me. "Thought my mother might have been telling you some embarrassing childhood stories about me." A small laugh riffled my hair.

I closed my eyes and enjoyed the thrill of it all before pulling back and looking up into brown eyes. A soft smile played around Clare's lips. "Nope. She was too busy chatting with Annabel." Her brow furrowed and the kissable mouth shaped itself into a small o. "Seems like they were catching up on old times."

A sharp laugh left Clare's mouth, but her expression held a trace of disbelief. "You are joking, right?" An eyebrow lifted.

I smiled sweetly and pulled out of her embrace.

"Becky? You're joking right?"

I smiled sweetly and made an attempt to dodge past her, but she blocked me. I had anticipated her feline moves and darted to the other side and raced past her. I heard her laugh as her footsteps chased me down the hallway.

The police arrived just over an hour later. We asked Bella if she wanted us to stay for moral support, but she shook her head and waved us off, and Clare and I left them to talk with Bella alone. We knew what she was going to tell them, but I felt uneasy about the whole thing. I mean, what was the case law on something like this? Ellen's death had apparently been an accident, even though Bella was a little unclear on the details. Would the brunt of responsibility for the crime fall on Freddie because he had purposely perverted the course of justice? That alone should earn him life imprisonment, although with him being well into his eighties, a life sentence would not be nearly long enough.

And where was Freddie, anyway? Was he in cells, back at the home, in hospital? If anyone should get charged with what had happened to Ellen, it was definitely Freddie. Bella had only been a child. Bollocks to him "protecting her." Ellen's death was a direct result of him wanting revenge, pure and simple. If Ellen hadn't fallen down the stairs, would she have survived his anger in the longer run? He'd actually admitted to trying to rape her, even though he phrased it as wanting to have sex with his wife. Surely they could get him just on that.

That left Bella, her knowledge about what had happened, and her failure to step forward before now. Would they throw the book at her to make an example of her? What about Clare? How would she react to whatever happened to her mother? To be honest, I was a little surprised when the police left after just over an hour and didn't take Bella with them. Surprised but pleased.

When Clare and I went back into the living room, Bella seemed quieter. Reliving the events of that terrible evening over and over again obviously was taking its toll on her too. Her face was pale, and the smile she tried to muster was lost in her sadness. After all this time, maybe leaving things as they had been for sixty years would have been for the best after all.

Clare perched on the sofa next to Bella and took her mother's hand, her total attention on her. Her voice gentle, she said, "What did they say?"

Bella sighed. "They want me to visit the burial site sometime in the next couple of days to see if it triggers any memories." She tapped the side of her head. "I doubt it will. I've not been to the Roaches in years."

Considering the sheer extent of the Roaches, I also thought it unlikely that Bella would be able to pinpoint any specifics that could be of help.

"They also have to..." she sucked her top lip inside her mouth and nibbled on it before continuing, "...perform a post mortem."

A post mortem? On a body that had been buried for over sixty years? It surprised me, but for once I kept my comment to myself.

"Just to make sure Freddie's story about what happened is consistent with any physical evidence they can still get from..." Bella's voice was calm and steady. "To see if my mother's neck was broken, and whether her injury would have resulted in her death."

I hoped against hope that I would never have to say anything like that about my own mother. "Excuse me." I hurriedly left the room, emotion welling up inside me and threatening to spill out and flood everything with my guilt over not keeping in closer touch with my own parents. I scrabbled around inside my handbag and pulled out my mobile phone, then went out onto the porch.

I scrolled through the numbers, and cringed at the picture I had to indicate my mum and dad's phone number. I should rephrase that. I cringed at the blank space where people upload pictures of people they love, and I wanted to cry at the outline of the blue undistinguished human form that had come standard on the device. I hadn't even taken the time to put a picture of my parents into the space provided.

I didn't realise when I pressed "call," or that I was holding my breath, until I heard my mother answer the phone with a confused "Hello?"

Just hearing her voice squeezed my heart. Imagining her confusion at me calling out of the blue was too much for me to bear. The tears that rose from my guilt flowed in such an outpouring of regret and release, that I couldn't even answer her. Words of apology and shame and love jammed in my throat and threatened to choke me each time I tried to utter "Mum."

"Becky? Is that you honey? Becky?" Still nothing but sobbing from me. "Becky? What's the matter, love? Where are you?"

I needed to tell her, to tell them both—they had never done anything wrong, it was me. Classic cliché excuse.

"Brian, come here! Something's wrong with Becky!"

I could hear my dad's voice in the background. It sounded panicked too. I had made a bollocks of everything all over again. I hadn't meant to scare them; I just *had* to tell them how sorry I was for having been such a tiny part of their lives for so long. The two or three visits a year that I always treated as a chore loomed large in my mind and fed my guilt.

"Mum...I'm...I'm sorry." It wasn't much, wasn't nearly enough, but it was a start.

"What for? Becky, you haven't done anything stupid, have you?"

Of course I had. I had been ungrateful and thoughtless and self-centred. I had disregarded the love of my parents whilst focusing on a career and establishing my independence. I had never even given a thought to how they must've felt when I didn't return their calls, or if I did, it was only because of a dire emergency. Apparently they decided my calling constituted an emergency for them.

"Where are you?"

My mum was crying now, because of me.

"Do you need an ambulance?"

I frowned, and then suddenly realised my mother thought I might be dying. Had our relationship come to the point where they thought I would only call if I was at death's door?

"Mum, stop. I'm fine. I just needed to hear your voice." The line went quiet, and for a moment I thought she'd hung up. I wouldn't have blamed her if she had. I would have hung up on me, too. "And I wanted to tell you I love you, I love you and Dad."

The crying started again, and I heard the phone clang against something. The next moment, I heard my dad's voice.

"Becky love, do you need me to come and get you? Just tell me where."

I shook my head and then realised he couldn't see me. I could hear my mum mumbling something in the background, and my dad making a noise in his throat.

"We…we love you too, honey." Then that noise again, which seemed to be my dad swallowing down his emotion. "We'd love you to come and see us, or…or we could come and visit you?" I heard my mum's voice again and my dad grunting in response, then he said, "How about today? You free today?"

I wiped my eyes on the sleeve of my jumper and took a deep breath to calm myself. "I'm at the Peaks at the moment, but I'll come for a visit as soon as I get back, okay?"

My dad relayed the message to my mum, but instead of hearing his voice come back on the line, it was my mum who said, "We can come and see you there, if you need us to."

My smile surprised me. It had been many a year since hearing my mum's voice had brought on a smile. "Don't worry, Mum. I'm fine, honestly. I have just had some things happen that made me realise what a total shi...erm...fool I've been all these years."

The door creaked open behind me, and I turned and saw a worried Clare hovering in the doorway. She mouthed, "You okay?" and I nodded and smiled at her. I could tell she wasn't convinced, as her eyes narrowed and she did the tell-tale head tilting thing that she did whenever she was trying to work something out.

"You've been busy, love. We understand."

"No, Mum. Don't make excuses for me. I do enough of that for all of us."

Clare registered what was happening and motioned that she would be inside, though I could see her indecision as she deliberated about closing the door.

"But you have been busy."

I sighed. "You understand that I live less than a twenty minute drive away from you and you only see me a handful of times a year?" My mum began to respond, but she couldn't find any words of rebuttal that would have been true. "Exactly, Mum. But I will make up for lost time, I promise. I love you, you know. Always have."

She started to cry, and so did I.

Chapter Twenty

It was likely so obvious what had happened that had made me so emotional, as Clare didn't ask, and I didn't say anything apart from that I had just called my parents. Her surprise reminded me that she didn't really know anything about my background or my family, and I told myself that I would make sure she was privy to both as soon as all this mess was cleared up once and for all.

Apparently Bella was in the kitchen, because back inside the house I could smell lunch cooking, and I realised I was hungry. Relief can do that to you.

"Mum and I decided to go and see Granddad after lunch. Fancy coming?"

I opened my mouth to tell her "no fucking way," but then closed it again. "I'd love to." The thought of making Freddie Howell uncomfortable was just the boost my day needed. I should have felt a pang of guilt at that uncharitable thought, he was an old man after all, but I didn't. He deserved it. Then it struck me that I didn't even know where he was. "Are you allowed to visit him?"

Bella turned from the Aga with a confused look. "Why not? Visiting at the home is 24/7."

"I didn't think suspects were—" Shit.

Bella smiled widely. "But we're not *suspects*. The police *know* Freddie and I did it."

I felt the blush rising and wished I'd kept my mouth shut.

Bella came to me and gently rested her hand on my arm. "Stop worrying, Becky. I know what you meant."

I tried to smile. Bella smiled in return and turned back to the stove.

"So, how do you fancy pasta?"

After lunch, when we all bundled into the car, Bella insisted on sitting in the back, as she wanted to look at the area again. "It was quite dark during most of my taxi ride to Annabel's. It was only the last few miles to the house that it became light enough for me to see clearly."

Something about what she said triggered a fleeting thought in my mind, but I shook it off. I was too intent on the imminent meeting with Freddie to start racking my brain over a comment about when Bella had arrived.

All the way to the assisted living facility, Bella took great joy in pointing out the places she remembered, and it was hard to believe that her childhood, and early adulthood, had been marred by tragic unhappiness. Her life in Derbyshire was built on such grief, and not just because of the death of her mother. A mentally and physically abusive father was her primary caregiver, and then straight after, she'd traded that situation for a violent husband. No surprise that she had never visited the place again. Of course, this time she hadn't had a choice, but now I understood why she had been reluctant to attend Annabel's funeral.

Freddie was in the TV lounge when we arrived, and his face lit up when he saw Clare. When he spotted Bella his smile wavered, but it was when he spotted me that the shit really hit the fan.

"Git 'er outta 'ere. Told ya before I dun't like 'er."

Bella went over and sat down next to him. "Oh, come on, Dad. You wouldn't begrudge our Clare time with her girlfriend, would you?"

Her voice was treacly sweet, but I knew the words were not truly intended to cajole the old fart.

"What the 'ell! Git 'er out. Dun't want 'er 'ere."

His voice was loud enough to attract the attention of the male carer, who glanced over at us.

Bella waved reassuringly. "He's fine. Just being his grumpy self." She chuckled as if sharing a joke with the carer, and then tilted her face closer to her father's. "Unless you want everyone in here to know you are a bigoted, ignorant, lying, cruel, violent old fucker, you'd better shut your mouth right now."

My jaw dropped. I would never have expected Bella to say those things directly to her father's face.

"You may have been able to control me when I wasn't strong enough to fight back, but, *Daddy*, your little girl has grown up."

Freddie's face went purple. I knew he wanted to shout out his rage to anyone listening, but there was something else lurking behind his plum hue—fear. What he was afraid of, I could only speculate about, but fear was there all the same. I'd have thought I'd feel joyous at seeing him taken down a peg, but all I felt was a deep sadness.

Clare moved closer to me and took my hand in hers. Freddie's eyes darted to our intertwined fingers, and the purple went a shade darker.

"And now, it is way past time that we have a little chat, don't you think?" Bella's voice didn't rise above a gentle, modulated tone, and her expression was open, even welcoming. "I think it's about time you told me the truth about what happened to Mum."

Freddie opened his mouth, perhaps to refute Bella's implication that he had ever lied to her, but she held up a hand and stopped him. "I know what you want me to believe, what you want the police to believe, but," she exhaled loudly through her nostrils as if she was bored, "we both know that isn't exactly what happened, don't we?"

Freddie leaned forward until his face was just inches from his daughter's. "What I do know is yer mother was a slut.

Whatever 'appened to 'er was punishment for fuckin' ma sister," he spat.

Bella wiped Freddie's spittle from her face, all the while looking at him with the same bored expression. "That the best you can do, old man—accuse a dead woman of sleeping with your sister? What about you trying to rape your own wife? What about you beating her just because you could, eh?" Bella stood up and leaned over him, the threat clear, the words squeezing out through gritted teeth as she added, "Beating me, too."

Freddie sank back into the chair, his eyes wide.

"Now you know what it's like to feel helpless." She took a step back but still towered over him. "The last time I saw you, I told you that you wouldn't be seeing me again. Sadly, because of the current circumstance, I had to visit today just to see if you had any conscience at all. Seems like you haven't. Looks like you will be dying alone after all."

Then she was gone, and Clare and I were left standing there wondering what had just happened.

"Clare, luv, dun't believe a word she said." His voice was pleading, as if Clare was his last hope.

Clare stared at him for what felt like an eternity. Without uttering a word to him, she turned to me and took my hand. "Ready?"

Nodding, I cast a look at Freddie, who just sat there frozen in... Fear? Amazement? I was the only one that even looked back at him. Bella had already disappeared and Clare was lurching toward the door without a backwards glance, pulling me along by my hand. I recognised that I was witnessing the fall of a bully, a tyrant. He seemed to shrink inside himself, fold in half, lessening in both stature and arrogance. If I hadn't known what he had done, the misery he had caused, I would have felt sorry for him. I didn't think it was Bella that finally crushed him; it was Clare's indifference.

Bella was waiting for us just outside the door to the care facility. None of us said anything as we made our way to the car. The air was thick, expectant, and I wanted to ask them to talk about it, or even just acknowledge what had happened. It wasn't until we were sitting in the car that I realised they didn't have to do either. The decision to leave Freddie to drown in his own pool of hatred was silently unanimous. After all these years, he was finally reaping what he had sown.

We stopped in Derby to do some grocery shopping before going back to Annabel's house. I guess I should have been thinking of it as Clare's, as it actually belonged to her, but to me it still felt like Annabel's.

On the return drive, I sat in the back and let Bella sit beside her daughter, who was driving. I could hear the murmuring of their voices as we made our way down now-dark country lanes. I rested my head against the window and looked out at the flash of trees whizzing by whilst behind them the blackness seemed impenetrable.

Bella and Clare stopped talking, and quiet pervaded the car. For some reason, it seemed too quiet, and I felt the urge to strike up a conversation just to fill the silence. I could see the lights from the dashboard reflecting off Clare's face, the shadows casting weird shapes. I stared at their movement, my eyes aching in the dimly lit car and threatening me with a headache that could be a monster.

I felt as if someone was watching me, so I looked up into the rear view mirror, fully expecting Clare to be making eye contact. But her eyes were firmly on the winding road ahead. The feeling was still there, still strong, still penetrating. A noise to the side alerted me, to what, I didn't know. I reluctantly turned my head to the right, and there, sitting next to me, was Ellen Howell. Her eyes were fixed on me, and my eyes widened. I felt an urgent need to alert Clare and Bella to the presence of an additional passenger. A smile broke out on Ellen's face, and it was as if the back seat of the car was bathed in light. I wasn't frightened. Why would I be? Ellen had never hurt me. From what I'd uncovered about her, she had never hurt anyone.

"Thank you."

"What did you say?" Clare turned and casted a quick glance into the back seat before returning her attention to the road.

It wasn't me who had uttered thanks; it was Ellen. And for once I had actually seen the words leave her mouth. Then, as if speaking those two words had set her free after all these years, she was gone.

"Don't worry, love. I'll tell you later." I leaned into the gap between the two front seats so my head was between mother and daughter, a feeling of lightness bubbling inside me. "How long before we get to the house?"

Clare peeked at me and then looked toward the road again. "Do you want to know something weird? I'm not too sure where we are." She laughed, but the sound was short and sharp. "Despite all the years I've driven these roads, I think I'm lost."

That thought that had been bugging me on and off throughout the day finally made it to the front of my mind. It was shaping into something I could work with, something I could try to make sense of.

Darkness. Trees. Lost. Me lost. The feeling of driving around in circles and seeing no one and nothing. Stopping at the side of the road and feeling watched, pursued. Jumping into my car and having the back door slam itself shut. Seeing Annabel's house—the welcoming light, the greeting, the feeling of safety. The awkwardness of being Rebecca Gibson and not the person Annabel was expecting.

Then there were the dreams. The feeling I was Ellen Howell. Ellen...Howell...standing in the darkness, looking into the kitchen window. Ellen Howell, who was scared for her life as someone stalked her in the darkness. The desperation as I, she, I tapped on the glass...tapped and tapped, and knowing deep down I had to get away, had to leave.

Footsteps on gravel. He was here. Freddie was here. He had known I'd run as soon as I could. I shouldn't have come, shouldn't have come to Annabel's. I should have gone into town, told the police what he'd done. I raised my hand to wave. I had to get her to see me, get her to help me, but I was too late. He grabbed my hand and pulled me against his hard chest. His voice was just as wickedly spiteful as it always was. "Ya thought she'd 'elp ya, eh?" This time it wouldn't just be a beating, not just a fall. No. This time he would take everything, including my life.

A cry burst from my lungs, and Clare slammed on the brakes throwing us all forward.

"Jesus!"

Clare's exclamation indicated how much I had scared her. Bella didn't say a word, just hung onto the door handle as if that would save her from whatever was attacking me in the back.

The ping ping sounded as Clare leapt out of the car and came into the back to see what the hell was the matter. Her hands shook as they grabbed my shoulders and I fell into her, the sensation of being safe wrapping around me. I wasn't Ellen. I was Rebecca. Rebecca. Rebecca Gibson. I wasn't crying, but I felt it would be better if I did. Emotions vied for expression, and the strain made my heart race as if it would burst.

Clare just held me, rocked me, soothed me. She didn't yet know that I had just experienced the final revelation: Ellen Howell had survived falling down the stairs, and Bella had likely had nothing at all to do with her mother's death.

Bella. She'd spent her whole life blaming herself for the death of her mother, when it had been one hundred percent Freddie after all. Much of her life had been poisoned by guilt and shame, and for what? So one evil man could fulfil his thirst for vengeance, so he could feel like he had won out over his sister and his wife.

"Not now. Just get us home." Why I said home, I didn't know, but I needed for us to get there.

Bella took over the wheel and Clare stayed with me in the back, holding me tight, her words comforting, reassuring. My head was buzzing with my epiphany about what had happened to Ellen on the night she died, but I didn't want to share it with the others in the middle of nowhere, too close to where it had really happened. And I felt vulnerable out in the open, to what, or who, I had no concrete idea. It wasn't as if Freddie would be stalking us. He was still fuming at the home, not to mention he was an old man, and I doubted he could have chased the car for twenty miles.

Ten minutes later, the light outside Annabel's house came into view. The sense of comfort that washed over me was the same as what I'd felt the very first time I'd seen it. However, there was no bubble of excitement when I looked at the yellow glow that was gradually getting closer.

"Did you turn the light on, Mum?" Clare's voice rumbled through her chest, where I was resting my head.

"No. It was light when we left. I didn't even think about putting it on."

Clare ran her fingers through my hair, then kissed the top of my head. Even without seeing her face, I knew she was thinking. I could feel it rumbling through her, though that could have been her heartbeat.

The crunch of the tyres on the gravel seemed deafening to the point of making my ears hurt. It was probably because of the silence in the car, the only exception being Clare's question about the light.

The car's engine was shut down, and the sense of stillness Inside the car seemed to morph into a loudness that was more deafening than the crunching of gravel. With a sigh, Bella opened the door and climbed out. She stood at the side of the car, the light from the porch illuminating her outline but darkening her expression. I could just make out the hint of worry etched on her features, and initially I thought it was because the porch light had been left on. Then it dawned on me—she was worried about me. I had spent so many years trying not to get involved with anyone, trying not to need anyone else, I had almost forgotten how to act in front of others. Clare had easily broken through that barrier, and it appeared her mother was doing the same thing. It was amazing to me to realise that the dead had helped me learn to live again. If it hadn't been for Annabel, I would never have met Clare, never have started feeling something beyond indifference.

I pulled my attention away from Bella and looked up at Clare. She was already gazing at me, her expression calm, yet concerned.

"You okay, baby?"

Her voice was soft, soothing. I nodded and blinked, being overly dramatic about indicating I was getting there.

"Let's get inside then, yes?"

At my nod, she pulled away, and the night air immediately felt cooler without her warmth.

Clare climbed out of the car, then bent down and offered me her hand through the open door, a gesture I readily accepted. Tingles spread from her to me, their electric boost making up for the short time we'd been separated. Either that or we had somehow received an electric shock from the car. I preferred to think it was because of our connection.

Inside the house, Bella went to make a pot of tea and Clare turned off the porch light and locked the front door. She took my hand and led me into the lounge, sat me on the sofa and knelt down in front of me.

"Are you going to tell me what happened in the car?"

Instead of answering, I asked, "Have you told your mum about us seeing Annabel and Ellen?"

Clare shook her head. "I haven't had the opportunity. She only arrived this morning. Why?"

"I think we should."

"What does that have to do with you shrieking in the car?" She looked at me steadily. "Did you see them again?"

"See who again?"

Bella was standing in the doorway, her expression indicating she had heard more than the last bit. We had been so involved with our conversation that neither of us had heard her come in.

Clare stood and turned to face her mother. "I need to...erm... We need to tell you something, Mum."

Bella titled her head and squinted at Clare as if reading her, and it was like I was looking at Clare's twin. "I gathered that." Clare cleared her throat, but Bella held up her hand. "Not without a cuppa." She sighed and turned back toward the kitchen, her voice drifting back to us. "I think I'm going to need it."

Chapter Twenty-One

I just wanted to get it all out into the open, set the truth free by releasing into the air. We took turns telling Bella of the events that had led up to that moment, and she just listened with reserve and patience as we garbled our way through them. Occasionally she opened her mouth as if to ask a question, but didn't, almost as if she didn't want to interrupt our story and maybe divert us from the path. By the time we got to the end of our joint recitation, Bella seemed almost as exhausted as we were, as if she too had lived through it. I was about to tell them about my experience in the car, when Bella spoke.

"I've seen Annabel three times since she died."

I had known about the one episode I'd walked in on, but three times?

"Weirdly, in the sixty years since she died, I have never seen my mother." She rubbed her hand over her chin, as if she was thinking. "At first, the first time I saw Annabel, I mean, I was scared. It's not every day you see your dead aunt standing in your kitchen, after all." Her small laugh wasn't one of joy. "At the time, I actually didn't even know she was dead. I found out a couple of hours later." Bella looked down at her clasped hands, then raised her eyes and looked at Clare and me. "I thought I was going mad, that it was some kind of punishment for what I had done all those years ago."

"You did nothing wrong, Mum. What happened to Ellen was an accident."

I wanted to tell them what I now knew, but Bella started to speak, so I waited.

"After Annabel's funeral, I saw her again. Again I thought it was because she was angry with me. I wanted to come and say goodbye to her, but I just couldn't face seeing my dad. And given my luck, I was also afraid your father would turn up."

Clare shook her head. "He's living in Scotland with his new wife. He sent a postcard."

That answered my unasked question about why Clare didn't talk much about her father.

"Poor, poor woman." Bella chuckled. "Though if I know Grace Blakely, she'll beat the crap out of him if he lays one finger on her."

I couldn't help my smile. Karma. Gotta love it.

Bella leaned forward and took Clare's hand and then mine. "The third time I saw Annabel was in her bedroom this morning. She came to say hello. By this time I had resigned myself to being haunted by the woman I believed I should have helped all those years ago."

"How, Mum? You were a child. What could you have done?"

"Annabel spent the rest of her life searching for her. I knew my mother was dead, Clare. I could've at least told her that."

That was true, but what good could chastising herself do now? I doubted that was why Annabel had visited her.

"When I was talking to her in the bedroom, it seemed as if she already knew what had happened to my mum."

"She probably heard us talking about it," Clare suggested.

It seemed logical, even in this fucked up situation. We were talking about Annabel as if she were a living, breathing person, not a ghost.

"I can't believe I did what I did." She held up her hands, waving them to shush us before we could even speak. "I understand it was an accident, but remaining silent about it... What was I thinking?"

I couldn't put off my latest revelation any longer. "You were thinking like a frightened child, Bella, and that fear followed you all through your life. Can't you see? It was never you." Ignoring Bella shaking her head, I continued. "And I don't mean about Freddie frightening you into staying quiet by saying you had killed your mother. I mean *you* didn't kill her. She didn't trip over you. She was pushed."

"What?" Mother and daughter spoke at the same time.

"But I was there. I remember—"

"You *think* you remember. It was what Freddie wanted you to believe." Bella was shaking her head and muttering her disbelief. "I know this for a fact, Bella." Fuck. How was this going to sound on top of all the rest of the could-be-fiction? I shrugged off my concerns about her potential scepticism and ploughed ahead. "The fall didn't kill her, Freddie killed her afterwards."

The room was still. Nothing stirred; there wasn't even a hint of breathing. The three of us sat like statues in a triangle—Clare and Bella staring at me, me alternately looking at each of them. It was uncomfortable, damned right it was, but I'd had to tell them.

"Remember the part when I got lost whilst driving and that eventually I found my way here, and that's how I met Annabel?" They both nodded. "And remember me telling you I dreamt I was Ellen?" Again both women nodded. "It supposedly happened on the same date that Ellen died, sixty years previous though earlier in the day." They stared at me, and I realised they didn't have a clue. "Look, if Ellen had died in the morning by falling down the stairs, why did I envision her coming to Annabel's house later the same day? Why was someone chasing her? Why was she so frightened that Freddie would get her?"

"But...but..." Clare spluttered over her words, took a deep breath, and tried again. "How do you know that your vision of being chased at night was of things happening the day Ellen died?"

"Because I just saw Ellen in the back of your car on our way back here. Because straight after you said you thought we were lost, I started making connections, started thinking as if I was Ellen."

By this time, I didn't even feel ridiculous saying all that. I knew it was the truth, and sometimes, as they say, fact is stranger than fiction. "I felt her fear. Freddie was hunting her. He caught her just outside Annabel's kitchen window. It was so clear inside my head, so bloody clear. She said, 'This time it wouldn't be a beating, not just a fall.' Ellen was frightened for her life."

Bella and Clare just stared at me, and I waited for my words to sink in. I knew exactly when Bella registered the import. Her face crumpled and a sob ripped from her throat. Clare shot towards her, but stopped. Instead she turned to me, her eyes sparking with what I could only guess was anger. At first I thought the anger was directed at me, that I had somehow stepped over the line.

"That old fucker. That mean, old fucker!" Her voice escalated in volume, and the anger I saw first in her eyes spread like lightning through her. She was physically vibrating with emotion. "I can't believe he did this...to Ellen...to Mum!"

"Clare, honey, it's okay." Bella's quiet voice seemed to ooze through the anger in a bid to defuse it.

"It's not okay!" Clare's exclamation was still loud, but she was trying to control her emotions. With a sudden movement, she was on the floor in front of her mother, her hands grabbing Bella's. "Can't you see, Mum? He made you think you had killed your mother. For all of these years, he kept you tied to him by a web of lies."

Bella nodded, her face full of sadness but not anger. I just sat numbly and soaked it all in.

"He killed your mother *after* she had fallen down the stairs." Clare's voice was a mere whisper.

Bella sighed and gripped Clare's hands firmly, her eyes reading her daughter's face. "That's how it appears, doesn't it, love?"

"How can you be so calm about it, Mum? Why aren't you—"

Slam. The sound of a door banging back and hitting a wall somewhere in the house stopped all conversation. I yelped, and Clare tumbled backwards onto the floor, her legs outstretched. Amazingly, she was still holding her mother's hands.

"What the hell was that?" Clare sounded winded, as if the fall had taken her breath.

I knew it wasn't just the fall that had done that; it was the realisation that she already knew the answer to her question. It had been the front door banging open and hitting the wall, the same front door she had locked after we were all inside.

Cold air swept into the room, and the curtains fluttered in the gust. The lights flickered, but thankfully stayed on.

"I think we should go and take a look." Bella and Clare looked surprised, and I had surprised myself by suggesting such a thing. I didn't really want to go and take a look, but it was either that or we sit with the wind howling around our legs all night. Bella nodded and stood, pulling Clare to her feet in the process.

Fear churned in my gut, as if it wanted to stop me moving into the hallway, and I rubbed my hand over my stomach in a bid to ease it. It didn't work. I was still shitting my pants. And I was still moving forward. Clare did try to step in front of me, but I pushed her away. Talk about a heroic move. Actually, I just wanted to be able to see everything around me so that there wouldn't be any nasty surprises, as if the front door opening on its own after it had been locked and bolted wasn't surprise enough.

Considering the wind seemed to be whistling through the hallway, the door stayed firmly against the wall as if it was propped open. The porch light was on again, and I turned and looked at Clare, who whispered, "Don't look at me. I turned it off."

I knew she had. I had watched her do it—*and* lock and bolt the front door—but that didn't change the fact that the light was on and the door had miraculously opened itself.

We stepped through the doorway onto the porch, and looked out into the darkness. The wind didn't seem as strong out there as it had in the house, but there was a cold wind whipping around us. The sound of the rustling trees made the evening seem alive with activity. Even with the light from the porch, I couldn't see into the blackness. All I could see was the splay of light over a portion of Clare's car in the driveway.

It was getting colder, as if the night chill was seeping into my bones. Bella and Clare were shivering, so it wasn't just me who felt it.

Crunch. Crunch crunch crunch. Some fucker was walking on the driveway. The sound of footsteps on the gravel was distinctive in the quiet. Even if we couldn't see who it was, we could bloody well hear their approach.

"Who is it? Who's there?"

I was so glad that Clare shouted out, as I knew for definite my voice would have come out just above a squeak, if at all.

At the sound of her voice, the crunching momentarily stopped, then started again. It was getting closer, closer, and closer still, but there was no one there, no figure approaching, alive or dead. I had begun to trace the location of each sound, and, by my reckoning, the person should have been standing right in front of us. But no.

Clump. Clump.

The sound of booted feet on the wooden porch steps made me take a step back, and I bumped into Clare and Bella. Nothing was on the porch. Nothing, no one, just the noise. If it had been Annabel or Ellen, wouldn't they have shown themselves? Wouldn't we feel it was them? But it didn't feel like them, didn't have their quality of goodness. It felt as if the person, or whatever the fuck it was, wasn't there for niceties, wasn't there to ask us to help them in any way, shape, or form. The presence felt as if it had come to threaten, to frighten, to destroy.

"Get inside," ground out between my teeth. "Now!"

As we turned, I felt a sharp coldness slice into me, like something was attaching itself to me. I frantically pushed Clare and Bella inside and was just about to follow them when the door swung closed, hitting me squarely in the face.

Pain exploded inside my head, and my legs crumpled beneath me. Clare's screams were coming from inside, but I couldn't answer, couldn't make a sound. I saw the ground coming up to meet me, and I didn't have the wherewithal to stop myself from falling.

And then everything went black.

Chapter Twenty-Two

I think I had been subconsciously dreading this moment ever since I had first felt a connection with Ellen and Annabel. I say *I'd* been dreading it, but I didn't feel like me. I knew that this wasn't really happening, that I was just conjuring things up whilst I was blacked out, but that didn't keep an absolute terror from rippling through me.

When I woke, or didn't wake, I was sitting in a chair in what appeared to be a shed. My neck hurt badly, but the most acute pain was in my wrists, ankles, and shoulders. It seemed as if I was tied to the chair with corded thin rope. The cord had abraded the skin of my wrists and ankles, and the areas were raw and burning. It had to be Freddie who had done this to me. The rope was so tied so tightly, it was pulling my shoulders back with such pressure that I believed they would be dislocated. Something was stuffed into my mouth, and over that was a rag that smelled and tasted of linseed oil. I wished I could gag without choking myself.

I tried to take in my surroundings, but it was very dark in the shed. The only light was coming in through the gaps between the wooden slats. It mingled with the dark and made shadows dance across the floor as if they were spirits trapped in there alongside of me. A part of me wished that the light wasn't there. Without the light, the shadows would be absent and I would be able to think more clearly without watching every movement with fear. Still, the light did serve a purpose—it allowed me to catch glimpses of what was stored in the small space.

This was Freddie's tool shed, and I knew that I was about fifty feet from the house. I also knew that he would be back soon to finish what he'd started.

Shoving the chair backwards, I was happy to note that he hadn't secured it in place. If I could just get over to his workbench, I could likely find something to cut through the cords before the light disappeared completely.

I had moved scarcely half a foot when I heard fumbling at the door, then it clicked open with a creaking that indicated it was a lock that needed oiling. I froze, hoping that when Freddie came in, he wouldn't notice I had moved.

Bright light flooded the room and initially I couldn't see who had come in, but I knew it was him even before he spoke.

"Told ya ya wouldn't be goin' anywhere, din't I, sweetheart?"

The endearment wasn't born of love. The way he ground out "sweetheart" made me flinch.

"I see ya've been tryin' ta git away agin."

Freddie slammed the oil lamp onto the table near me and peered into my face. I had hated him before, but that paled in comparison to how I felt about him now.

"See this?" He reached around me and grabbed hold of my wrists. I expected him to carry on speaking, but instead he yanked my arms upwards and pulled back. The agonising pain made me scream, but the sound didn't get past the dirty rag in my mouth. He laughed and released them with a chuckle. "That's just for starters."

I thought he was going to embark on the monologue the baddies always do in the films I had seen, the one where they admit all their sins before they off their helpless victim. But no. He started to undo the buckle on his belt. My eyes followed each movement of his hands, and I gasped when he pulled the belt free. He chuckled again. "Don't worry, Ellen luv. I'm not goin' ta hit ya with me belt."

Slam. He struck me across the face with the back of his hand, snapping my head to the left, pain ricocheting across my cheek.

"Why hit ya with a belt when I can use me 'ands?"

The sneer on his face twisted into a grin that promised there was worse to come. He pulled the stinking cloth from around my mouth and yanked out the gag, motioning for me to keep quiet. I gasped in a lungful of air, and the taste of the linseed oil burned my throat. As for screaming out, I knew it would be useless. I could scream all day, every day, and no one would ever hear me out in the shed. There was no point in enraging him further by even trying.

"Nope, I'm not going ta hit ya with me belt." He leaned forward, his face mere inches from mine, and I flinched. "I'm goin' ta fuck ya."

Instead of crying out again, I gathered as much saliva I could and spat squarely into his face. His eyes flicked shut and he wipe it away with the back of his hand and part of his shirt sleeve. Slam. He hit me on the same side as before. This time it was harder, but I seemed to recover a lot more quickly than I had from the first blow. Freddie stood straight and looked me squarely in the face, as if assessing me, then dug his hand into his pocket and brought out a long, thin object I recognised as his penknife.

Shit. Shit. He was going to stab me, slice me, torture me there in the shed where nobody knew I was. Was this how I would meet my end? Would I bleed to death—raped, beaten, and stabbed?

Freddie bent down, and his eyes met mine and held. "I'm tellin' ya now, if ya do anythin' stupid, I will kill ya. Ya understand?" He was going to kill me anyway, wasn't he? "And then I'll kill Bella."

The blood in my veins turned to ice. He couldn't kill his own daughter, could he? Me, yes. He didn't love me. But he loved Bella. Bella was his world. Wasn't she?

"I said, do ya understand?"

I didn't trust my voice, so I nodded. He peered at me a while longer, then bent down so he was between my legs. I felt a tugging sensation and knew he was cutting the cord that tethered my legs together. A tear slipped down my cheek. After all these years, it had come down to this, and just when I was so close to getting away from him, so close to starting a new life with Annabel.

"There ya go." Freddie stood up and moved his hand toward my face.

I flinched, expecting a slap, but he laughed and trailed his fingers down my cheek. His face twisted as his looked at the dampness on his fingers. I couldn't understand how the man could possibly not know that his actions would make me cry. Was he as insensitive as that? Of course he was. I'd found that out the hard way.

Mercifully, he didn't say a word, just moved around behind me and cut through the cord that bound my hands. Shooting pains raced up my arms as the blood rushed to areas where it had been lacking. My joints screamed in pain as I drew my hands around to the front. The first thing I did was to rub my palms together in an effort to ease the ache.

"Remember, no funny business."

I didn't even have the time to answer before he grabbed hold of my shirt, lifted me from the chair, and slammed me against his workbench. His mouth was hard on mine, demanding, the stubble on his chin abrading my skin as if it was made of tiny blades. He grabbed my shirt and yanked on it, but my being pressed hard against the bench prevented him from tearing it off. He grunted and stepped back, his hands going to his fly. That was just like him, always jumping the gun. I wanted to laugh. Even if he got his trousers down, where was he going to put his dick? I was still fully dressed.

As if he had read my mind, his hands stopped and dark eyes looked into me. "Git undressed." It was not a request.

I wanted to tell him that if he wanted me naked, he would have to do it himself, but when he stepped closer and repeated his command, I decided that it would be less painful if I just complied.

My shaking hands fumbled with the button on my trousers. I was disgusted with myself for even contemplating doing what he wanted, but what other option did I have? There was no one coming to save me. And if I didn't do what he said, he would rape and kill me anyway, and then he would kill my daughter. What kind of mother would I be if I let him hurt my child?

It did occur to me to wonder what was to stop him hurting Bella after he had finished with me.

I frantically looked around for anything I could use to defend myself, but Freddie realised I wasn't doing as he wanted. I didn't even get the chance to pretend to open my trousers before his fist shot out and slammed into my jaw. I couldn't save myself, couldn't maintain my balance. I pivoted to the left and slammed face first onto the workbench, the pain of striking the counter hurting less than landing on whatever object my jaw had hit. He grabbed the hair at the back of my head and yanked me upwards and around.

Freddie's face was close to mine, spit and stinking breath hitting me with each word. "I said no fuckin' about. Git it?"

I nodded. I even tried to conjure a smile from somewhere inside me, but whilst he was focused on my face, my hand was desperately searching for the object on the bench. I felt the metal, the solidness of the head, the smooth wood of the handle. My fingers were reticent about curling around the tool, but eventually they complied. Schooling myself to patience, I held it until opportunity presented itself.

It seemed like forever before he apparently believed I was going to obey him and relaxed. He stepped back, a smug grin replacing his look of hatred. "Good. Now git undressed."

He looked at his zipper, and I made my move. Considering my shoulders were still aching from being in the same position for so long, I surprised myself by the speed and power of my swing. The hammer came at him sideways, but he spotted it just as it neared his head. He tried to block it with his arm, which partly deflected the blow, but the loud thunk on the side of his head confirmed that I had hit my target.

He froze, swayed, his dark eyes glazed as if he couldn't quite believe what had happened. Neither could I. I had never hit anyone in my life, and the shock of it was just as harrowing as if I had been the recipient of the blow. Even when I had tried to hit him with the poker at Annabel's, he had snatched it from me and struck himself with it.

Thud. Down to his knees, his eyes blinking rapidly, shock clearly written on his face.

Thud. Face down onto the floor, his body twisted, his legs sprawled as if they belonged to a rag doll.

Had I killed him? I hoped so. The hammer dropped from my hand and landed beside him with a clatter.

I had to go, had to get Bella and go to Annabel's. She would know what to do, what to say to the police.

I stepped over him tentatively, fully expecting his giant hand to grab my ankle as I passed, the anticipation of being recaptured welling up through my body. But he didn't move. He just laid there—immobile, twisted, deathlike.

It wasn't until I stepped out into the cold night air that I realised that even though a blow like that might actually have killed Freddie, I wasn't going to take any chances. I needed to barricade the door, lock it, bolt it, and make sure that if he did come to, he wouldn't be able to follow me. But the door didn't have a bolt on it, just a hasp and staple. Freddie must've taken the padlock with him when he entered the shed. I felt sick at the prospect of going back inside, but I had to.

Thankfully the oil lamp was still illuminating the space near the door, and I spotted the padlock almost immediately. It was open, the key still dangling from the lock. And it was lying near the limp body of Freddie Howell. If he regained consciousness whilst I was reaching for it, I didn't have a weapon to take him down with this time. But I had no other choice. If he woke, he would catch me and kill me and my daughter.

A flash of anger energised me. He would never, ever get the chance to hurt my little girl. I would die trying to protect her.

Decision made, I sidled back into the shed, my back flush against the counter top, my hand frantically groping for the padlock. I was reluctant to take my eyes off my husband's prone body just in case he did make a move, but eventually, I had to glance at the work surface to locate the padlock. Reaching out, I grabbed it and pulled it to me. I shot another look at Freddie and realised he still hadn't moved.

I padlocked the shed, then ran to the house. Lights were on downstairs, but there was no sign of Bella. I raced upstairs to her room, but that, too, was empty. So was Freddie's room. Every room was empty. Panic swept through me again. Had he already killed Bella and pretended he would hurt her if I didn't do as he said?

No. No. No. He wouldn't. He couldn't kill our little girl! He loved her. For all his faults, he had always shown more love to Bella than he had to anyone else. He wouldn't have killed her.

"Bella! Bella!" I hurried through the house again, checking all the rooms to make sure I hadn't missed her. Nothing, not a sound.

I stood in the silent kitchen and listened intently. Apart from the usual noises one might hear in an empty house, there was nothing amiss, though I might not have heard anything above the thudding of my heart. I looked around the area to see if there was anything that might give me a clue as to Bella's whereabouts. My eyes landed on the pots neatly stacked on the drainer, and a flicker of hope flared in me. Bella's plate was there, its daisy pattern distinctive against the white plate next to it. He wouldn't feed her and then kill her. That wouldn't make any sense. But then again, was it supposed to?

As I turned toward the living room, I noticed something off to one side on the counter. It was a rag similar to the one Freddie had used on me. I approached it as if it might suddenly spring to life and attack me. A sickly sweet smell was coming from the piece of cloth, so instead of picking it up, I leaned forward and cautiously sniffed it. My breath caught, and I coughed. I didn't recognise the smell, but a part of my mind connected it to the disappearance of my little girl.

I opened the back door and looked out into the darkness. Where would he have put Bella? Obviously not in his tool shed or I would've seen her. The garage? But why would he put her there? If he was going to kill us both anyway, why separate us?

Bella was not in the house and not in the shed, so she had to be in the garage. That was the only place I could think she might be. I pulled my jacket from the hook behind the back door and stepped out into the cold night air.

Thump. It was muffled, but it was definitely a noise coming from the direction of the tool shed, where I had left Freddie. Was it Bella? Had she been there all the time and I hadn't seen her because I hadn't looked for her? I started to run in the direction of the shed, the key to the padlock in my hand.

The thumping was getting louder, more insistent. I listened for Bella's voice, but I couldn't hear her. Grabbing the padlock, I fumbled with the key.

THUMP!

The door vibrated violently, and I knew right then that it wasn't Bella standing behind it. How could I have been so stupid? Why on earth did I even consider that she might have been in the shed with me? I would have seen her. Freddie would have pointed her out to me just to drive home his point.

"Ya fucker!" Freddie's slurred voice came through the wood. "Ya'll never see Bella agin. I swear ya won't." Another thump, even harder than the previous one. I stepped away from the shed, my feet crunching on the dead leaves and twigs. "I kin 'ear ya. Yer daughter won't even miss ya."

I was terrified, and yet I took comfort from his words. He was threatening my life, so be it. But he had just told me that Bella was alive. Where, I had no idea. But she was alive, and that was all that mattered.

Smash. The top part of the shed door caved outwards, splinters of wood cascading all over me. Slam. Another hit, and the glint of metal shining as the lamp inside reflected off of it. Freddie was breaking loose, so why was I still standing there and watching him make his escape?

Bordering on hysteria, I looked about me. The only lights were from the shed and the house. My closest neighbour was Freddie's drinking buddy, and I doubted he would believe a word that came from my mouth. My only option was to get to Annabel. I would run to her house, and she would know what to do. She would save me, and Bella.

Another smash broke through my thoughts as well as the door, and I could see Freddie's hand trying to grab the padlock. He was strong, but was he strong enough to pull the lock hasp from its screws? The hand disappeared, then reappeared a moment later holding a long metal rod.

I turned and ran. I knew, beyond the shadow of a doubt, that if Freddie caught me, I would be dead.

As I ran, I prayed. Not for myself. Never for myself. I prayed that Bella would survive this, and that Annabel would be home to stop Freddie from committing further violence. And if Annabel wasn't home, I prayed that she would know that I would never voluntarily leave her. I loved her too much.

The brightness of the light was almost painful. It reverberated inside my head as if trying to find a weakness and tear its way out. My legs and arms were stiff, and when I tried to move, a pain ripped through my shoulders.

"Hey, stay still, love." I wanted to cry with relief when I heard Clare's voice. "You took a good old whack with the door, honey." I scrunched my face against the brightness and felt my nose click into place.

"Jesus!" I sat up, my hands flying to my nose. Sticky stuff was smeared around my nostrils, and I knew without looking that it was blood. How many more injuries could I withstand? I had a gash on my calf, stitches in my eyebrow, and now something that felt like a fucking broken nose. An image of Ellen popped into my head, and all my injuries paled into insignificance.

"Here. Lie back on this." Clare gently guided me backwards until I was propped against a cushion. "How are you feeling?"

Not yet acclimatized to the light, I squinted at her. Clare was propped next to me on the sofa, her butt half on and half off the cushion, and I wondered how on earth she had gotten me inside after the door had walloped me in the face.

"How is she?" Bella's voice came from behind Clare, and the penny dropped. They had carried me in together.

"I'm fine. Sore, but fine." My voice was husky, so I cleared my throat. "Any chance of a glass of water?" I licked my dry lips and was surprised at the faint flavour of linseed oil. No sooner had I recognised it, than it disappeared.

A glass was held near my mouth, and I reached out a shaking hand to grasp it. Clare made it clear that she would hold it for me, and I let her. I didn't feel as if I was sufficiently recovered from my encounter with the front door to hold the glass steady myself.

The water was ice cold, but it seemed to burn down my throat. The more water I drank, the more aware I became to my surroundings.

"Have you had enough?" When I nodded, Clare added, "The paramedics are on their way."

"Why?" The word came out harshly, so I smiled. "Sorry. Didn't mean to bite your head off, but why are they coming?"

"Because you were knocked unconscious."

Bella leaned over Clare's shoulder, her face full of concern. "We couldn't just load you in the car and drive back to Derby."

"But I'm fine. Honestly." Both women tutted, so I held my hand out in front of them and announced, "See? Four fingers and a thumb."

Clare grabbed hold of my hand and squeezed it gently, a soft sigh escaping her. "We are just worried, baby. We can't have you leaving a concussion untreated." Brown eyes searched mine, and I fell into her all over again. This woman was so bloody beautiful, so amazingly beautiful that my heart swelled inside me.

A knock sounded on the front door and Bella announced she'd get it, leaving Clare and me alone. I leaned forward and brushed my lips over hers. I needed to feel her lips against mine to assure me that I was once again part of the present.

Voices travelled down the hallway and I fully expected to see the paramedics to come bustling into the room, but the first people to enter were not the medical professionals. Bella returned sandwiched between two police officers, the ambulance men following them.

"I'm not that ill, am I?" I tried to joke about it, but the presence of all those people unnerved me. And why were the police there? I had bashed my face on the door. Granted, the door had been slammed shut by an unseen hand, but it still added up to just me being whacked in the face by a slab of wood.

"Sorry to disturb you, ladies, but we were wondering if we could have a word."

Bella was pointing the paramedics in my direction, and I knew what was coming next. They were going to go into the kitchen and have their "word," and I was going to be lumped on the sofa being poked and prodded by Britain's finest.

Chapter Twenty-Three

The police didn't stay long. The paramedic had barely had the chance to half blind me with the brightest torch in existence when I heard Clare and Bella bid them adieu. As mother and daughter came back into the room, I tried to get their attention, but "torch man" had other ideas. I glared at him with a look that threatened to put his light sabre into the darkest space in his body if he pulled my head around to face front one more time.

Eventually, as I suspected would be the case, he pronounced me fit to go, although I wasn't actually going anywhere. No concussion, no broken nose, and as the paramedic told me at the conclusion of his examination, just very bad bruising to my face. That was enough for me to start panicking. I hadn't given a thought to what I looked like when I'd been sitting throwing doe eyes at Clare across the room.

As the paramedics were packing their instruments back into their bags, I thought of something they might be able to help me with. "Can I ask you something?" The man looked up from his kit and pointed at himself. "Yes, you." Though he seemed a little nonplussed, he nodded. "Would you know what substance someone might put on a rag that would make it smell sweet?"

"Huh?"

I realised that my question was vague at best, and cudgelled my brain to rephrase it. "If you had a rag," I held out my hand as if I was holding the aforementioned cloth, "and you put something really sickly sweet smelling on it," like the dipshit that I am, I pantomimed sprinkling something on the imaginary rag, "and the stuff you put on it smelled so bad that it would make you cough, what would the stuff be?"

He tilted his head in thought, then gave it a slight shake. "I'm not sure."

I wasn't surprised. My rephrasing had been shite, and my charades weren't any better.

"Chloroform, maybe." He laughed as if dismissing what he'd said, but I shot up straight.

Fuck. Freddie had used chloroform on Bella. No wonder Ellen couldn't find her. She was knocked out somewhere, probably right in the house.

The paramedic frowned at me. "I wouldn't advise you trying to use it, Miss. Chloroform can kill if the exposure is excessive."

"Don't worry, I'm not going to use it."

His expression said that he was wondering why I'd asked him about it, but I didn't think he would believe me if I told him, so I fabricated a reason. "Just saw it in a film once and wondered what the man had used, that's all."

At that point I really wished I'd kept my mouth shut. I let out a laugh that sounded a bit maniacal. "It's not as if I could pop into Boots the Chemist and buy it over the counter, is it?" I did the idiot laugh again.

The paramedic stared at me a while longer, probably wondering whether his initial diagnosis was correct, or if I had suffered some sort of brain damage after all. "Good job, too. It is only used on mice in laboratories now." He stood up, pulled out his torch from his pocket, and flicked it in my eyes one last time. "Call us if you feel any light-headedness or nausea."

Bella saw them out, and we were alone in the house again.

The door to the lounge had barely shut on them before I turned to Clare, who was seated in the chair opposite. I saw that she had been crying. Without conscious decision, I was up off the sofa and next to her before she had a chance to tell me off for moving when I was to stay still.

"What's happened? What did the police want?" I wondered whether Freddie had snuffed it, and they had come around to break the news of his sudden demise. And if they had, would Clare be crying about it? Of course she would. He was her grandfather, after all. To stop loving someone did not happen overnight. Just because I would be doing a happy dance on his grave didn't mean she would.

"They came to give us the news about the post mortem."

Bella's voice came from behind me, and I turned to face her. She, too, looked as if she'd been crying. "What...what did they find?" I didn't want to know. I did, and didn't want to know.

Bella slumped onto the sofa, as if her body had been totally drained of energy.

I turned my attention back to Clare. "What's happened?" I'd asked quietly, but the words seemed to reverberate off the walls.

Clare inhaled deeply. "Well, it's for sure that Ellen didn't die of a broken neck." That came as no surprise to me. "They told us that they did find a small isolated fracture to the atlas," she pointed vaguely to the back of her head, "but that alone didn't kill her. It would have caused pain and could've affected her breathing, but was definitely treatable if she'd received medical attention."

Quietness pervaded the room again.

I felt sick, restless. I needed to know everything, and stuff how I would feel about the truth.

"Clare, tell me. Please tell me." My voice was scarcely above a whisper, and the slight quaver revealed how nervous I was.

Brown eyes looked at the ceiling, and Clare swallowed rapidly as she struggled against her emotions, before she turned and looked straight into me. "In addition to broken teeth, fractured cheek bones, broken ribs, and a broken wrist, Ellen could've died from asphyxiation."

Staggered by the graphic detailing of the injuries that Freddie had inflicted, I grabbed the mantelpiece, my face mere inches from the mirror above the fireplace. I caught sight of my reflection—my eyes seemed greener and wilder than they'd ever been before. "He strangled her? He fucking strangled her after all that?"

"No, they don't believe he strangled her, although the body having been buried for sixty years makes the evidence a little sketchy. It's only because the minerals in the soil were neutral that her body was preserved so much better than they expected. Even though Ellen's body was decomposed, there would have been even less of her if she had been buried in more acidic soil."

I just stared at Clare.

"In other words, they got better than typical test results with such old remains because the soil kept a lot of the physical evidence from being totally destroyed."

A piece of my dream from when I had first arrived home after meeting Clare flashed into my mind—hands around my throat, strong hands, capable hands. The hands added pressure, took the pressure away, increased it again. In this dream I was getting weaker, losing my fight to live, moving from life into something dark and unwelcoming.

But Ellen hadn't died. Annabel had saved her. She'd even mentioned it in her notebook. So, when Clare said that Freddie hadn't strangled Ellen, she wasn't inferring that Annabel had done it.

Dragging my eyes away from my reflection, I turned back to face them.

"They believe she may have asphyxiated on earth," Bella said quite matter-of-factly.

I stared at her in disbelief. "Earth?"

"As in soil," Bella clarified.

"Soil? What the... *Soil?*"

Clare broke into my exchange with Bella. "It means they believe Ellen was buried alive."

Everything froze. Clare was sitting forward, her mouth partly closed after she had told me. A loud buzzing sounded in my ears, and I had the urge to puke. My hand raised in slow motion, the action interminable, sluggish, until that self-same hand settled over my mouth to stop my strangled response from escaping. Nothing had prepared me for that outcome. I knew Ellen was dead, and I knew she'd been killed, but to be buried alive? For Freddie to bury his wife alive in that cold, hard ground on top of the Roaches and just walk away? To bury her and pretend she'd left him and their daughter? No. He had buried his wife alive, and then told his daughter she had killed her mother.

"He couldn't have...couldn't have..."

Weird as it seemed, I felt a connection with Ellen that probably surpassed even that of her own daughter. I'd been her, seen life through her eyes, experienced her love, her pain, and her terror. It was as if part of me had been buried alive with her. I closed my eyes, and all I could see was the image that had appeared in the mirror in the hospital bathroom. Ellen's face had looked sunken, caved in, with fresh blood that turned into something brown and flaky. Something that was full of scurrying insects. Soil.

The realisation of what had happened gripped my gut and twisted. I was going to vomit. I bolted for the door, praying I'd make it to the bathroom.

There's no point going into detail about what happened after that. It is obvious that I would share what I had been through with the other two women, although I couldn't tell them at that moment. That would come later. But nothing was really proven by my learning through a dream what had happened. The injuries Ellen sustained could've been caused by the fall down the stairs, and the fact that Freddie buried his wife, something that he had admitted to, only proved he was the man who had put her into the ground. Whether the police could ever prove that he knew she was still alive when he did so was another matter. The only solid evidence we had consisted of the notebook, which wasn't worth the paper it was written on, and a photograph with coordinates on the back that had led to the discovery of Ellen's remains. All my dreams, visions, whatever the fuck you want to call them, wouldn't stand up in a court of law. If they did, then the world would be even more fucked up than it already was. Just imagine the courtrooms if we could give evidence based on what we dreamed.

It wasn't as if we could go around to Freddie's house and fingerprint everything for evidence, hunt for a bottle of chloroform and soiled rag, check the tool shed for clues, or have the hammer tested for blood. The evidence was long gone. We had the poker, but that'd been wiped clean by Freddie sixty years previously and probably countless times since then by Annabel.

That night I couldn't sleep. I lay in bed with my arm resting on Clare's stomach and stared at the wall. I knew she wasn't sleeping either, but I didn't want to go over it all again, rake it all up, give myself any hope of catching the man who had gotten away with murder. My mind drifted to Bella who was sleeping on the sofa, her choice. Sadness flooded through me. For all those years she'd lived with the guilt of a crime she'd no hand in. She'd moved from one abusive relationship to another, carrying all the baggage courtesy of her father with her. To think she'd blamed herself for it all for so long, and only doubted it when she had a daughter of her own.

I was thankful that she'd had the opportunity to start fresh, to make a new life for herself and her daughter. It was a chance that Ellen never had. She had been so close to attaining her dream, but ended up just a knock on a kitchen window away from freedom.

When I thought of how terrified that little girl must have been, my heart broke all over again. An unbearable ache flooded through me when I told Bella what I'd experienced when I'd been hit by the door. And she couldn't stop her tears when she found out that the reason she'd never seen the ghost of her mother was because Freddie had willed it so: "Ya will never see Bella agin. I swear ya won't."

Now, as we lay in bed, my tears fell. Clare held me, her chest heaving in time with my sobbing. She was crying too, and I was certain sure that downstairs, Bella was crying as well.

All those lives devastated because of one man's ego.

No one slept that night. Just seeing the haunted expressions in the cold light of day made that apparent. Breakfast was quiet, all actions mechanical. Clare went for a shower and Bella decided to grab some fresh air, leaving me to sit and stew over everything.

I was in the bedroom when Clare's mobile rang, and I glanced at it rattling around on the bedside table. Then it went quiet, and I continued to sort out clean clothes to wear after my shower.

The mobile started again, insinuating the caller was going to be persistent. I scrambled over the bed and grabbed the phone. The Caller I.D. said *Brentwood Home*. I would have ignored it, but I was sure Clare would want me to answer a call from her grandfather's assisted living facility. And if she didn't... I pressed "accept."

A female voice spoke as soon as I connected. "Miss Clare Davies? This is Marjory Samuels at Brentwood Home." The woman didn't even give me a chance to say I wasn't Clare, but I also didn't try to interrupt her. I just let her get on with it, a mumbled "yes" as my only response. "I have some bad news for you, I'm afraid."

My eyebrows lifted slightly. "Yes."

"I'm sorry to say, your grandfather passed away about an hour ago." She waited for me to speak, but I was too angry. That old bastard had gotten away with it after all. "Are you still there, Miss Davies? Have you got someone with you?" I grunted, a noise that must've sounded as if I was crying, as Marjory Samuels quickly added, "I am so sorry for your loss. If it's any consolation, his passing was quick."

Actually, it wasn't a consolation. I wanted the old bastard to suffer. A lot.

"The coroner is on the way to pick up the body, but you are more than welcome to come and talk to me about how it happened. I will be here until eight tonight."

"Thank you for letting me know. I'll be in this morning."

"That will be fine. Well, goodbye, Miss—"

"May I ask you something before you go, Marjory?"

"Of course you may, dear.

"I was... Well, did he say anything before he died?" I was hoping for an apology, maybe a confession, but what I got was so much better.

"Funny you should ask that. He insisted he was afraid for his life."

I tried not to allow my grin to be reflected in the tone of my voice. "Really? Did he know his end was near then?"

"No. That's why I thought it was strange. He kept saying *they* were with him." Marjory made a harrumphing noise, as if she was clearing her throat. "Often, at the end people say they see relatives coming through to guide them to the other side. But I doubt it was like that for Freddie."

"Why's that, do you think?"

"I don't know." There was pause as if Marjory was thinking it through. "Whoever 'they' were, he seemed more scared of them than of death."

"Really?" A grin split my face, the first genuine one I had smiled in what seemed like a long time. Maybe his death wasn't due to natural causes after all. "Did he mention any names at all?"

It went quiet for a moment and I thought maybe she'd hung up, so I was actually startled when she spoke again.

"I think he said something like 'Ellen,' but I'm unsure of the other name. Maybe Anna, but I couldn't swear on my life."

No. She couldn't. But Freddie certainly had.

Revenge is sometimes a really great feeling, especially if the revenge was wreaked on someone who truly deserved it. And if there was anyone who deserved to get his just desserts, it was the late Freddie Howell. I couldn't help wondering whether Ellen and Annabel had made sure he paid the price for his cruelty, for his life-long lies, for making Bella grow up without a mother and tormenting her with the accusation that she had been the one to kill Ellen Howell. Had the women finally gotten their chance to exact retribution on the man who had denied them so much?

The pain and despair Annabel and Ellen experienced was unimaginable. Although I'd witnessed bits of it in ways I couldn't explain, I hadn't suffered what these women had at the hands of this contemptible excuse for a human being. Hell was too good for him; no amount of torment his wife and his sister might inflict on Freddie Howell could ever make up for the atrocities he'd inflicted on them.

On this plane of existence, Freddie had escaped the punishment he so richly deserved. If there was any justice that balanced the Cosmic Scales after death, he would be subject to a terrible judgement befitting such a cruel and abhorrent man.

I hoped he would never rest.

Chapter Twenty-Four

What had started out with me being lost on a country road had culminated in the discovery of the remains of Ellen Howell and the death of a bitter, twisted man.

I waited for Bella and Clare to come back into the room so I could break the news about Freddie's death. Although they had recently discovered the extent to which his perfidy had gone, I knew his passing would still be upsetting, especially for Clare.

"I've just heard from Marjory at the home. I'm sorry to say that Freddie passed away this morning." I didn't elaborate on why I was sad he had passed away. Adding that I was sad that he hadn't had to serve his just punishment was not the correct thing to say at that moment.

Clare began to cry, and Bella, though intent on taking care of her daughter, her tears came too. I couldn't feel any sorrow at his death, and it wasn't just because I hated him, either. To me, he was a man who murdered his wife—raped and beat her, and then buried her alive. I would not shed tears for such a monster. I wasn't Clare, who had known the better side of him all her life and only found out what he'd done in the last few weeks. I had no connection to him other than that he was a relative of the woman I loved. Bella had suffered at his hands, but she cried because he was also her father. Aside from Annabel, Freddie had been the only adult she'd known whilst growing up. A relationship built on secrets, guilt, and shame was not much, but it was a relationship all the same.

Less than two hours later, we were all at Brentwood Home. I wanted to stay in the car and leave them to sort out Freddie's belongings, but I knew that Clare needed my support.

Marjory was near the Reception desk as we entered. Her demeanour was that of the consummate professional, sadness radiating from her in measured waves. I should imagine in her line of work this was part and parcel of the working day, something I was sure she never really got comfortable with.

Freddie's belongings were all still in their places about his room. Apparently the home believed the family might get some comfort from collecting things themselves rather than picking up a box filled with the deceased's detritus.

After Marjory had repeated her condolences, she left the three of us in the room. It was odd to be amongst Freddie's things now that he was no longer with us. Mother and daughter began to pack his life away whilst I waited in the wings, ready to lend a helping hand or a shoulder to cry on as needed.

It didn't take long to pack away the remainders of the old man's life. Less than thirty minutes, in fact. Before we realised it, we were putting his stuff in the back of the car, the atmosphere subdued.

We didn't go home; we had one more place to visit before we went back to Annabel's. This was the one I was not looking forward to, but this trip was really for Bella's benefit. I was just along for the ride, and for the closure.

The Roaches was so much more beautiful in the daylight. Plunging views from all around exposed miles of green acreage, and the outline of Tittesworth Reservoir glinting in the sharp winter sun was a sight to behold. The sky was a mishmash of grey and white, with no blue in sight, but the sun shot rays across the landscape, as if they came straight from the hand of God. It was sublime, enchanting, almost bewitching. I breathed deeply, the sharp cool air eliciting a cough as reached my lungs.

The smell of moss, dampness, heather, of all things fresh and alive filled my senses.

The rocks themselves seemed different in the light of day. They were still magnificent, still overpowering, but their fear-inducing aspect seemed to have faded. The first time I had seen them, I'd likened them to guardians and, in a sense, they were. Hen Cloud and Ramshaw Rocks had protected the victim buried in their land. It was likely that Ellen Howell was not the only secret they held close. They seemed smaller, but the sneer was gone. They almost welcomed our presence. The secret was out; the body unearthed.

Two police officers met us near the gate to the footpath, their yellow jackets gaudy against the scenery, seemingly mocking the solemnity of the occasion. We followed them along the path in silence. The ascent seemed exhausting, mainly due to our emotions. A sharp veer off the path led us downwards through gorse and heather, the plants and bushes clutching at our legs, as if to delay the inevitable. The next officer that came into view was standing watch. The stark reminder of what he was protecting made my stomach lurch.

Minutes later we were standing next to a hole. I thought it was surprisingly shallow, considering what it had held. It was about three feet in depth and about six feet in length, the appropriate shape and size to hold a small woman. I don't know what I was expecting when I looked into Ellen Howell's makeshift burial site, but the soil piled around the recently excavated cavity filled me with emptiness. How could a person be *full* of emptiness?

I turned to look at Bella, but her face was blank, emotionless, giving nothing away. It appeared she too was having difficulty linking what she was seeing to the death of someone she loved. This definitely wasn't the same as standing next to a grave mourning the loss of a loved one, shedding tears, praying over their remains. It was a grave, of sorts, and we were there to release our grief and mourn over a tragically lost life, but it seemed remote, distant, not at all the same as people bidding farewell to their love, their life, their all.

My thoughts skipped off on a tangent concerning having someone as my all. And my all was Clare.

A solitary tear dripped from her chin as she stood near the pit that had held a woman she'd never had the good fortune to meet.

Brown eyes lifted and met mine, and the watery smile that slipped onto Clare's lips made my heart ache with love for her. We'd only just found each other, but that didn't matter. Love was love, and we should hang on to it for dear life, because life was unpredictable.

I stepped forward and held out my hand. The solid warmth of it reminded me that she was living, breathing, and I would spend the rest of my life, however long or short that was, loving her.

In the last few weeks, I'd discovered so much. Not that I could speak with the dead. No. Not that I'm crap at directions, or that I should invest in a new Sat Nav. Far from it. I'd thought I was happy, but I discovered that work should never have been my life, my all. Work should never have taken centre stage in the drama that has an indeterminate number of acts to play out. Nobody knows when that curtain will fall and shut us off from the rest of the world, and the only thing left would be the sound of one hand clapping, as if from a distance, signifying my last performance. Through death—Ellen's death, Annabel's death, and through their enduring love, I had discovered life. However much I had isolated myself, love had found me and brought me back into the light. Love made me see my life for what it could be.

"Let's go." Bella's voice broke through my mental life review. "We need to discuss funeral arrangements."

Clare turned away from the erstwhile grave. "I think Ellen should be buried with Annabel." She looked first at me, then at her mother. "I think them waiting sixty years to be together is long enough, don't you?"

Bella nodded, her lips pursing as if she was about to add something. Instead, she shrugged and stepped back from the graveside.

"Mum? What is it?"

Bella shook her head.

"Come on. Tell me." Clare reached out and grasped her mum's arm, not in the least aggressively, just as a means of keeping her mother from walking away.

Bella released a sigh and lifted her gaze from the makeshift grave to Clare. "I can't believe we're making plans to bury my mother with my aunt."

My spine stiffened. Did she mean because they were a couple? She'd never given an inkling she had a problem with that. I actually had the impression that she liked the idea of her mother having had some happiness in her brief life.

I wanted to shut the hell up, but I couldn't. "Annabel loved your mother." Bella's attention moved from Clare to me. "She's waited sixty years to be with her again."

Bella tilted her head as if she was reading me.

"Becky?"

I ignored Clare's unspoken query. "Bella, your aunt never gave up hope of being with Ellen one day." And vice versa. Annabel made sure someone heard her voice, a voice that had been ignored by her community, and that someone had been me. I didn't think she made contact with me purely for herself, either. I believed that one of her motives for hijacking my life that night was to show me what love could be like, how wondrous it could be. After the way she had changed my life, I guess I felt the need to defend her. After all, if I hadn't met Annabel I would never have met Clare.

Instead of becoming defensive, Bella smiled at me, a smile that changed into a grin. And before I could continue fighting on behalf of Ellen and Annabel, I was wrapped up Bella's arms.

"Thank you, Rebecca. Thank you for finding my mother." She held me close, her mouth next to my ear. "Thank you for helping her to her final rest." A soft kiss landed on my cheek and then she stepped back, her arms slowly releasing me. Bella nodded, and I could tell that words would be difficult for a while.

Emotion making me mute, I nodded in return and turned to leave. I am still not sure what happened, but I must've caught my foot on something. My body lurched forward, and the hole where Ellen had been buried for the past sixty years seemed to move towards me. I felt the contact of the soil, the dampness of it, the smell of the earth totally filling my senses. And then it all went black.

My head pounded, blood filled my mouth. Nothing seemed real, nothing made sense. I tried to move but the pain raged through me. Waves of it, bubbling, throbbing, pulsating. What was happening? Where was I?

Outside. I was outside, I knew that much at least. Cold. The ground beneath me was so cold. Had I fallen? Was I at Annabel's? I was just there, wasn't I, tapping on the window, crying for her? The memory slipped and slid around in my mind, blurring into snapshots of scenes I couldn't decipher. The effort of trying to hold onto it all was just a whirl of confusion.

I tried to open my mouth to call out for Annabel but the agony of it gripped me. I knew I was going to die, but I didn't care about that. I would've died a thousand times if I'd just known Bella was safe, known that Annabel knew I would always love her. But there was no way of knowing.

I was getting colder, almost freezing. Something was landing on my stomach. I tried to touch whatever it was that was covering me, but my hands wouldn't move.

I wanted to open my eyes, wanted to take it all in, but it was too hard, the pain acute. Every part of me hurt, especially my face. I needed to wake from this nightmare!

I was scared, but plunged into unfathomable depths of fear when I heard the voice of the cruellest man I'd ever know, heard him muttering and grunting. Even without looking, I knew Freddie was staring down at me.

"Ah. Awake, are ya?"

Fear jammed my response in my throat, fear that turned to terror at his next words.

"All the better. For me, at any rate."

Annabel. Bella. Would they be next? Would he kill them too?

I tried to move, but couldn't. Invisible hands seemed to come from the ground below me and clamp me fast. Was that a shift in the air around me? Was he standing next to me?

I forced my eyes open, excruciating pain lancing through my face at even that slight movement. Despite the blackness, I could see that he was holding something in his hand, something with a long handle and glinting metal.

Desperation surged through me, and again I struggled to move. I knew with dreadful clarity what he was going to do.

I had to get up and away from there. I had to escape, to tell Annabel and Bella how much I loved them. It ran through my mind like a mantra, a plea, a prayer. And unattainable.

Paralysed with fear and pain, I could see it coming towards me but couldn't budge. As Freddie struck me with the shovel, searing pain ripped through my jaw, my nose, my cheek, the sickening thud blending into the crunching sound of my bones breaking. I couldn't scream, couldn't do anything but lie there in unbearable agony and pray for death to come swiftly.

He resumed covering me, dirt filling my nostrils and my mouth, separating me from the life-giving air that I struggled to breathe, separating me from everything that was precious to me, except my love for Bella, and for my Annabel.

That he could never take. And I hoped he would live the rest of his life, and someday die, knowing that.

My eyes shot open, a scream bubbling up from my throat, terror still real inside me.

"Hey, hey, hey! Becky. It's me. It's Clare. You're safe, you're safe, baby."

Clare was in the hole with me, her arms pulling me to her. The scent of her covered the smell of dirt, and even though I knew I was in the here-and-now, I couldn't shake the grasping panic.

"What is it? Are you claustrophobic?" Bella's voice came from just beyond Clare, and I realised I couldn't just blurt out that I'd experienced Ellen's last horror-filled moments. In a rare instant of complete clarity, I knew that her family should never know how profoundly she had suffered. I hated Freddie more than ever, and I wanted people to know what he had done, but Freddie was beyond punishment. Knowing the full extent of his cruelty would heap unnecessary anguish on top of the pain and loss Clare and Bella had suffered because of Ellen's death. I had to keep this last heart breaking revelation to myself.

I managed a weak smile. "I'm fine, honestly. Just gave me a turn, that's all."

Bella came closer to the edge and extended a hand, which I grasped. Clare put both of her hands under one of my forearms and, with Bella's tug, the two of them helped me out of the shallow grave. Bella touched the side of my face. "You seem flushed." She cupped my chin and turned my face toward her. "Are you sure you're okay, Rebecca. You had a nasty fall and seemed to be out of it for a few minutes."

I nodded. "Not to worry. I'll be fine." I gently touched her hand and smiled to reassure her.

Bella didn't seem convinced by my plea of well-being, but patted the side of my face before helping Clare clamber up out of the hole.

Clare smiled at her mother and then turned to look deeply into my eyes. Her expression said that she didn't believe that I was okay, but thankfully, she didn't press the issue. She nodded, then took my hand, slipped an arm around my waist, and pulled me into her embrace. Her scent was more intoxicating than any heather on the moor. Just being next to her made me aware of how much fuller my life was with her in it, especially in the current circumstance of standing next the grave of a woman who'd had her life cut short.

"Are you sure you're okay?" Her voice was soft, almost a whisper.

I nodded and hugged her close.

"You would tell me, wouldn't you? You know, if you weren't okay."

I nodded again, then lifted my face to hers and brushed my lips against her cheek.

Bella turned and started down the path, but I didn't follow. I turned in Clare's embrace and peered up into her eyes. Her mouth formed into a smile that lit up the day, and vied with the beauty of the nature around us. "I love you, Clare Davies."

Her lips met mine, and I knew my love for Clare was as deep as Ellen's love for Annabel, true and everlasting. I would spend the rest of my life making sure that she knew it. And after life, I would spend eternity loving her. Clare was my destiny, and by loving her I had found my reason for living after all.

Epilogue

"You must forgive me, for I struggled only for you."

Emily Bronte

Ellen's remains were buried with Annabel's, and even though their lives had been tragic, we took some solace from knowing that the two women had finally found their peace, together.

I couldn't force myself to attend Freddie's funeral, not even for Clare's sake. I could not stand beside his grave and show any sign of sorrow over his death. I would've been waiting for them to bury the coffin so I could dance on the mound of dirt over it, maybe spitting on it for good measure.

For a few months Clare and I travelled back to Annabel's house now and again, our intention being to get the house in order to put it on the market. It wasn't long before we decided that Kirk Langley might be the place we wanted to call home in the not-too-distant future.

Life was too short to delay the things that we both wanted, so I knew that it wouldn't be long before I popped the question, or maybe Clare would beat me to it. All it needed was for one of us to pluck up the courage to ask the other, and we would be set for life.

Six months had passed, and it was the end of May when it happened—not the marriage proposal, something even more amazing.

It came in the form of a phone call at just turned six-thirty on a Sunday morning. I didn't even answer the phone call, Clare did, whilst I snuggled up at the side of her and inhaled her familiar scent.

"Hello." Her voice was a little ragged because she had just woken up, but all remnants of sleep quickly dissipated. "What is it? What's happened?" Her body tensed, and she shifted into a sitting position.

I sat up and waved my hand in front for her attention, mouthing, "Who is it?"

Clare covered the mouthpiece. "Mum. Don't worry."

Her saying her mother was calling in the early hours of a Sunday morning warranted more information than a "Don't worry," especially since all I could hear were Clare's responses.

Listening to half a conversation was driving me mad, so I decided to go make a cuppa. That way I wouldn't be trying to jigsaw words together, and also I would have a brew ready for Clare when she had finished talking to her mum and was telling me everything that Bella had said.

Fifteen minutes later, I was pushing the bedroom door open with my ass, my hands full with the tray of tea things. Clare was propped against the headboard, a smile on her lips.

"About time, too. A woman could die of thirst waiting for you to bring room service."

My eyes shot daggers at her. "You could help, you know."

Her smile widened. "Oh, I know. But you're doing such a fantastic job, I'd hate to get in the way."

I set the tray on the bed near Clare, then clambered up beside it. "So?" I lifted the lid of the teapot, dipped the spoon inside, and gave the teabags a tickle. "Any particular reason why Bella called so early?"

Clare picked up the milk jug, cautiously sniffing the contents before deciding that everything was as it should be. I just stared at her.

"What? I was just making sure it hadn't gone off in that dilapidated fridge down there." She poured some milk into each cup and then placed the jug back on the tray. "And also, I'm helping."

I stared for a while longer, and then cocked my head. "Once again, Miss Davies, what did your mum have to say? Or do I have to drug the tea to get any information out of you?"

She giggled childishly, a sound I'd never heard her make.

I began to fill the cups with tea, intermittently glancing at her as I did so. "Given the sound you just made, I'm even more intrigued."

She carefully took the cup I offered her and leaned back against the headboard. After setting the tray on the floor and securing my own cuppa, I sidled up next to her. "Look, what's a girl have to do to get the scoop on whatever your mum called about?"

Clare brushed her lips over my forehead, and their heat made my skin tingle. "I'll think about that and let you know later. Okay, I'll share. Are you sure you're ready for this?"

I grunted, pouted, then grinned.

"Remember how you told us that Freddie told Ellen that she would never see Bella again?"

"How could I forget? Not only did I experience him saying it, I was the one who broke it to your mum."

"Well, he was wrong." Clare smiled.

"Wrong? What do you mean 'wrong?'"

Instead of answering me straight away, Clare sipped her tea, slowly, then took another sip, totally ignoring the fact that I was glaring at her.

"What?" she said innocently.

"Stop being a git and tell me." I sat up straight and leaned over her. "Why was Freddie wrong?"

Clare shrugged, but her smile told me that she was pleased by whatever it was she'd heard. "Mum told me that in the early hours this morning, she was woken by a noise in her room."

"Your stepdad?"

Clare shook her head. "Nope. George is away at the moment—business, or as Mum says, 'a golfing contract.'"

I opened my mouth to ask another question, but Clare placed a finger against my lips, her expression fixed in feigned annoyance. "I can't believe you. You keep going on and on and on for me to tell you what Mum said, then won't shut up long enough for me to get the words out."

I kissed her fingertip and her face softened, her eyes twinkling.

"Now, where was I?" She took her finger from my lips, tilting her head as if daring me to speak. I shook my head, then made a zipping motion across my lips. "Mum was woken by a noise, but when she clicked the light on, there was nothing there. But that didn't deter her. Can I have a touch more milk here?"

"What? A noise in her room, and you want a touch more milk?"

"Please?" Clare held out her cup. "Turn a girl's throat brown, this could."

I clambered off the bed, retrieved the jug, tipped more milk into her cup, awaited approval, put the jug back on the tray on the floor, then climbed back into my spot. "Didn't deter her from what?"

"Investigating."

I was impressed with Bella. Fiery one, she was. Wouldn't let a small thing like being on her own in a foreign country stop her from tackling a burglar.

"There was no one there."

"Clare, I love you, honestly I do. *So* much. But *for fuck's sake* can you get to the point? My tea's getting cold."

"Okay, love." Clare grinned widely, her laugh silent. "Mum saw Ellen in her house this morning." My mouth dropped open. "*My* mum saw *her* mum in *her* house this morning. First time ever. Actually spoke to her. Gave her a hug that she could feel and everything."

"Your mum saw her mum, and they chatted and hugged?" I tipped my head and stared into Clare's eyes. "Are you pulling my leg?"

Clare shook her head vehemently. "No! Why would I do that?"

"Just seems...oh—I don't know—a little farfetched."

"A little farfetched? A little farfetched! You kidding me? How can someone who's dreamed they were a dead woman ever say something as reasonable as 'this could be far-fucking-fetched?'"

I winked at her, and her expression changed immediately from disbelief to amusement.

"You git." Her voice was playful.

I leaned forward and kissed her, our lips barely touching but the connection so strong it crackled in the air. My lips moved to her throat.

"Becky?"

I mumbled something against her skin that could've been translated as a "yes."

"Is it okay if I tell you the rest later?"

Another mumble, as my lips were otherwise engaged.

"Becky?"

"Ahuh?"

"Can I put my cup down?"

I realised I was still holding my cup, too. A moment later we were both crockery-free.

"Becky?"

Gazing into her mesmerising eyes, I knew that I would be completely under the spell of this wonderful woman for as long as I lived. Clare was my all, and my heart overflowed with my love for her. I could barely choke out, "Yes?"

"I love you."

After everything we'd experienced, I knew that it was possible for love to survive beyond the grave. Not only would I love Clare for as long as I lived, I'd continue to love her long after I was dead and gone.

But for now, I would make the most of every minute I had with Clare Davies, because being with her for eternity wasn't going to be nearly long enough for me.

About L.T. Smith

L.T. is a late bloomer when it comes to writing and didn't begin until 2005 with her first novel *Hearts and Flowers Border* (first published in 2006).

She soon caught the bug and has written numerous tales, usually with a comical slant to reflect, as she calls it, 'My warped view of the dramatic.'

Although she loves to write, L.T. loves to read, too—being an English teacher seems to demand it. Most of her free time is spent with her furry little men—two fluffy balls of trouble who keep her active and her apologies flowing.

CONNECT WITH L.T. SMITH:

Blog: ltsmithfiction.wordpress.com

Facebook: www.facebook.com/pages/LT-Smith/535475523205666

E-Mail: fingersmith@hotmail.co.uk

Other Books from Ylva Publishing

www.ylva-publishing.com

Once

L.T. Smith

ISBN: 978-3-95533-399-7
Length: 295 pages (77,000 words)

Beth Chambers' life is no fairytale. After four years in a destructive relationship, Beth decides enough is enough and leaves her girlfriend, taking Dudley, her dog, with her. At her lowest point, she meets Amy Fletcher, a woman who appears to have it all—and whom she believes would never want more than friendship. Beth needs to believe in magic once more for her dreams to come true. But can she?

The Red Files

Lee Winter

ISBN: 978-3-95533-330-0
Length: 365 pages (103,000 words)

Ambitious journalist Lauren King is stuck reporting on the vapid LA social scene's gala events while sparring with her rival—icy ex-Washington correspondent Catherine Ayers. Then a curious story unfolds before their eyes, involving a business launch, thirty-four prostitutes, and a pallet of missing pink champagne. Can the warring pair join together to unravel an incredible story?

Deliberate Harm

J.R. Wolfe

ISBN: 978-3-95533-368-3
Length: 300 pages (70,000 words)

Ever since Portia Marks learned her fiancée Imma was executed in Zimbabwe, she's struggled with grief. Then a stranger tells her Imma is alive, but he's killed before she can ask questions. To learn the truth, Portia teams with two friends in the CIA. Her search takes her across continents and entangles her in a terrorist plot that will rock the globe. Portia's quest becomes a race against time.

Barring Complications

Blythe Rippon

ISBN: 978-3-95533-191-7
Length: 374 pages (77,000 words)

When a gay marriage case arrives at the US Supreme Court, two women find themselves at the center of the fight for marriage equality. Closeted Justice Victoria Willoughby must sway a conservative colleague and attorney Genevieve Fornier must craft compelling arguments to win five votes. Complicating matters, despite their shared history, the law forbids the two from talking to each other.

Coming from Ylva Publishing

www.ylva-publishing.com

Blurred Lines

KD Williamson

Wounded in a police shootout, Detective Kelli McCabe spends weeks in the hospital recovering. Her only entertainment is verbal sparring matches with Dr. Nora Whitmore, the talented and reclusive surgeon.

Two very different women living in two different worlds. When the lines between them begin to blur, will they run from the possibilities or embrace the changes they bring to each other's lives?

Collide-O-Scope

Andrea Bramhall

One unidentified dead body. One tiny fishing village. Forty residents and everyone's a suspect. Where do you start? Newly promoted Detective Sergeant Kate Brannon and Kings Lynn's CID have to answer that question and more as they untangle the web of lies wrapped around the tiny village of Brandale Stiathe Harbour to capture the killer of Connie Wells.

Credits
Edited by Day Petersen
Cover Design by Amanda Chron